"I have vast affection for this story. I love the language, I love the gusto . . . I love that it has a sense of the sort of weird that I always loved . . . it was the kind of validation that probab[l]y made me think I could actually do this a bit . . . If you ca[n] write a few hundred words every day, let alone a thousand o[r] two thousand, you will finish the book before all that long."

## CHINA MIÉVILLE

"Writers should get out and live in the real world, observe real people, learn the rhymes and rhythms of the way people speak and behave. Science fiction actually isn't about the future, or about technology, or about anything except human beings loving, hating, fearing, hoping."

## BEN BOVA

"My process is a lot less dependent on inspiration now . . . Writing is something I do every day, a thousand words whether I feel like it or not. That's a much more sane approach. I think writers who rely on inspiration aren't very happy . . . Write a set amount every day. Finish what you write. Eschew ceremony, and don't get into habits . . ."

## CORY DOCTOROW

"[This story] made me think of myself as a writer earlier than I might have otherwise, and to throw myself into all my efforts with that project in mind, and to enjoy everything that happened as part of the process of becoming a writer."

## KIM STANLEY ROBINSON

"New writers are sometimes stingy with their ideas, in the belief that they're a non-renewable resource. Not so. The more ideas you use, the more that rise up to fill the vacancy they leave behind . . . Seeing my first story in print was a greatly needed encouragement that I wasn't entirely mad to think I could be a writer . . . Write what you love to read rather than what you think you should write."

## MICHAEL SWANWICK

# THE PLANET STORIES LIBRARY

STRANGE ADVENTURES ON OTHER WORLDS
AVAILABLE EXCLUSIVELY FROM PLANET STORIES!

FOR AUTHOR BIOS AND SYNOPSES,
VISIT PAIZO.COM/PLANETSTORIES

Publisher's Cataloging-In-Publication Data
(Prepared by The Donohue Group, Inc.)


Before they were giants / edited by James L. Sutter.

   p. ; cm. -- (Planet stories ; #28)

   Introduction: where it all began / by James L. Sutter – The guy with the eyes / by Spider Robinson --
Fragments of a hologram rose / by William Gibson – A long way back / by Ben Bova -- Possible to rue / by
Piers Anthony -- Craphound / by Cory Doctorow -- Highway 61 revisited / by China Miéville -- In Pierson's
orchestra / by Kim Stanley Robinson -- Destroyers / by Greg Bear -- Out of phase / by Joe Haldeman – The
coldest place / by Larry Niven -- Mirrors and burnstone / by Nicola Griffith -- Just a hint / by David Brin – A
sparkle for Homer / by R. A. Salvatore – The boys / by Charles Stross -- Ginungagap / by Michael Swanwick.
   ISBN: 978-1-60125-266-1

1. Science fiction--History and criticism. 2. Fantasy fiction--History and criticism. 3. Science fiction. 4.
Fantasy fiction. 5. Short stories. I. Sutter, James L. II. Robinson,
 Spider. Guy with the eyes. III. Gibson,
 William, 1948- Fragments of a hologram rose. IV. Bova, Ben, 1932- Long way back. V. Anthony, Piers.
Possible to rue. VI. Doctorow, Cory. Craphound. VII. Miéville, China. Highway 61 revisited. VIII. Robinson,
Kim Stanley. In Pierson's orchestra. IX. Bear, Greg, 1951- Destroyers. X. Haldeman, Joe W. Out of phase.
XI. Niven, Larry. Coldest place. XII. Griffith, Nicola. Mirrors and burnstone. XIII. Brin, David. Just a
hint. XIV. Salvatore, R. A., 1959- Sparkle for Homer. XV. Stross, Charles. Boys. XVI. Swanwick, Michael.
Ginungagap.

PN6120.95.S33 S67 2010
808.83/876

# BEFORE THEY WERE GIANTS

**EDITED BY JAMES L. SUTTER ♦ COVER ILLUSTRATION BY KIERAN YANNER**

## TABLE OF CONTENTS

PLANET STORIES is published bimonthly by Paizo Publishing, LLC with offices at 7120 185th Ave NE, Ste 120, Redmond, Washington, 98052. Erik Mona, Publisher. Pierce Watters, Senior Editor. James L. Sutter and Christopher Paul Carey, Editors. *Before They Were Giants* © 2010 by James L. Sutter. "Where It All Began" © 2010 by James L. Sutter. Planet Stories and the Planet Stories planet logo are registered trademarks of Paizo Publishing, LLC. Planet Stories #28, *Before They Were Giants*, by James L. Sutter. September 2010. PRINTED IN THE UNITED STATES OF AMERICA.

# Where It All Began
## by James L. Sutter

A uthors are, by their nature, exhibitionists.

As has doubtlessly been observed before, the old aphorism about writing what you know is redundant. The act of writing itself draws pieces of you into your work, and there are no characters (at least, no believable ones) that don't have a little piece of you at their core, that snippet of your essence that allows you to understand their motivations and make them come to life. In order to see through their eyes, you need to make them partially your eyes, and it's not uncommon for a writer asked, "So which character is you?" to truthfully answer, "All of them." In letting you read his work, an author gives you a glimpse of his soul, his unique worldview and his secret shames.

But while that's all true, it's also a lot of metaphysical crap. That's not the exhibitionism I'm talking about.

I'm talking about the real thing: the trench-coat-flasher urge that leads a writer to take his work—work upon which he likely bases much of his self-esteem, and his ability to call himself an author with a straight face—and actually show it to people. To let it all hang out in a public forum, in which those viewing his pride and joy are equally as likely to point and laugh as to appreciate. It's a terrifying thrill, and one that takes a thick skin, a touch of arrogance, and enormous—well, let's call them "leaps of faith."

These conflicting desires to both show off a story and protect one's pride only get worse when you know that the story in question isn't your best work, or is old enough that it no longer reflects your ability as a writer. Do you try to sweep everything but your latest masterpiece under the rug? Or do you let the readers see the literary equivalent of embarrassing baby photos, hoping they'll appreciate how far you've come?

To their credit, all of the authors in this collection were brave enough to choose the latter. Within these pages you'll find the first published science fiction and fantasy stories by fifteen of the field's greatest living writers, along with interviews in which the authors themselves critique their debut stories, pass on some of what they've learned in the years since, and offer insight into how the stories came to be and how they assisted in establishing the authors' future careers.

All of the authors here have different relationships with their early work. Some of them see those first forays as perfectly adequate, and wouldn't change a thing. (And some of them are even correct to feel that way—it turns out Ben Bova was *always* that good.) Others have practically disowned their freshman efforts, and aren't keen to be reminded of them—petitioning Charles Stross to include "The Boys" in this anthology was like producing a dead cat and asking him to autograph it. Yet one way or another, as sterling example or dire warning, each of these stories is now back in the public eye, many after long years of obscurity. And we're lucky to have them.

*Before They Were Giants* was designed to serve several functions. First and foremost, it's intended as entertainment—as with all books in the Planet Stories line, these stories aren't included just because of their historical significance, but because they're *fun*. Second, it's intended as a teaching book, a chance for aspiring (or established) writers to receive words of wisdom from their literary heroes and, in watching the greats analyze strengths and flaws in their own work, to help us all identify these traits in our own. Third, of course, is the fanboy urge to collect all of our favorite authors' work. In dredging up stories that until now were often lost in obscure and expensive back issues of out-of-print magazines, this anthology helps us all to rest easy knowing we've fully honored our completist compulsions.

Yet there's one last function of this book, a more subtle goal that trumps all the others.

As children of the modern age, we have a strange relationship with celebrity. Thanks to mass communications, we're confronted every day by a thousand images and sound bites about entertainment's elite, the actors and artists—and, yes, writers—who've managed to make it big, and are now placed atop the neon pedestal. In ascending to the ranks of the noteworthy, these individuals often cease to seem real in the same way our friends and neighbors do. They are Names and Faces, the little gods of the information age, and though we may worship at their altars, it's hard to identify with them. For aspiring artists, striving for our own chance to be heard, there are two common reactions to this phenomenon.

One is resentment. When presented with works of beauty and genius, it's neither comfortable nor heartening for the neophyte artist to consider the lifetime of work it takes to perfect such skill and mastery of the craft. It's far easier to say, "Sure, they're good, but I bet I'd be that good if I didn't have to work/go to school/watch the kids and could focus on writing all day."

This, of course, is the rankest of fallacies—of all the authors in this collection, not one started out with writing fiction as his or her primary vocation. Somehow, each of these authors made writing a priority, and in reviewing where (and who) they were when they published their first stories, we can catch a glimpse of how they made the initial jump from amateur to professional.

The second reaction is intimidation. It's easy to be cowed when reading any of these authors' current works, to throw up our hands in despair at the amount of artifice, talent, and creativity therein. Since all we ever see is the latest masterpiece, it's easy to presume that the authors must have always had the gift, springing forth fully formed like Athena from the head of Zeus. Yet this is a lie as well, for all of them, regardless of how far they've come, were once no different than anyone else—just fans with dreams and typewriters.

This book is about breaking those assumptions, and showing the giants in their formative years. Sometimes these beginning works are humble. Sometimes they're astonishing in their completeness. But all of them represent the first steps down the road to science fiction greatness. And in seeing the first steps of those who have gone before, this book is ultimately about taking your own.

Here's your trench coat.

James L. Sutter
December 2009
Seattle, WA

JAMES L. SUTTER *is the Fiction Editor for Paizo Publishing and author of numerous award-winning short stories and roleplaying products. His science fiction and fantasy has been published in such magazines and anthologies as* Black Gate, Apex Magazine, *and* Catastrophia *(PS Publishing), and his recent roleplaying credits include* City of Strangers, Seekers of Secrets, *and the* Pathfinder RPG Bestiary.

# The Guy with the Eyes
## by Spider Robinson

Callahan's Place was pretty lively that night. Talk fought Budweiser for mouth space all over the joint, and the beer nuts supply was critical. But this guy managed to keep himself in a corner without being noticed for nearly an hour. I only spotted him myself a few minutes before all the action started, and I make a point of studying *everybody* at Callahan's Place.

First thing, I saw those eyes. You get used to some haunted eyes in Callahan's—the newcomers have 'em—but these reminded me of a guy I knew once in Topeka, who got four people with an antique revolver before they cut him down.

I hoped like hell he'd visit the fireplace before he left.

If you've never been to Callahan's Place, God's pity on you. Seek it in the wilds of Suffolk County, but look not for neon. A simple, hand-lettered sign illuminated by a single floodlight, and a heavy oaken door split in the center (by the head of one Big Beef McCaffrey in 1947) and poorly repaired.

Inside, several heresies.

First, the light is about as bright as you keep your living room. Callahan maintains that people who like to drink in caves are unstable.

Second, there's a flat rate. Every drink in the house is half a buck, with the option. The option operates as follows:

You place a one-dollar bill on the bar. If all you have on you is a fin, you trot across the street to the all-night deli, get change, come back and put a one-dollar bill on the bar. (Callahan maintains that nobody in his right mind would counterfeit one-dollar bills; most of us figure he just likes to rub fistfuls of them across his face after closing.)

You are served your poison-of-choice. You inhale this, and confront the option. You may, as you leave, pick up two quarters from the always-full cigarbox at the end of the bar and exit into the night. Or you may, upon finishing your drink, stride up to the chalk line in the middle of the room, announce a toast (this is mandatory) and hurl your glass into the huge, old-fashioned fireplace which takes up most of the back wall. You then depart without visiting the cigarbox. Or, pony up another buck and exercise your option again.

Callahan seldom has to replenish the cigarbox. He orders glasses in such quantities that they cost him next to nothing, and he sweeps out the fireplace himself every morning.

Another heresy: No one watches you with accusing eyes to make sure you take no more quarters than you have coming to you. If Callahan ever happens to catch someone cheating him, he personally ejects them forever. Sometimes he doesn't open the door first. The last time he had to eject someone was in 1947, a gentleman named Big Beef McCaffrey.

Not too surprisingly, it's a damned interesting place to be. It's the kind of place you hear about only if you need to—and if you are very lucky. Because if a patron, having proposed his toast and smithereened his glass, feels like talking about the nature of his troubles, he receives the instant, undivided attention of everyone in the room. (That's why the toast is obligatory. Many a man with a hurt locked inside finds in the act of naming his hurt for the toast that he wants very much to talk about it. Callahan is one smart hombre.) On the other hand, even the most tantalizingly cryptic toast will bring no prying inquiries if the guy displays no desire to uncork. Anyone attempting to flout this custom is promptly blackjacked by Fast Eddie the piano player and dumped in the alley.

But somehow many do feel like spilling it in a place like Callahan's; and you can get a deeper insight into human nature in a week there than in ten years anywhere else I know. You can also quite likely find solace for most any kind of trouble, from Callahan himself if no one else. It's a rare hurt that can stand under the advice, help and sympathy generated by upwards of thirty people that *care*. Callahan loses a lot of his regulars. After they've been coming around long enough, they find they don't need to drink any more.

It's that kind of a bar.

I don't want you to get a picture of Callahan's Place as an agonized, Alcoholics Anonymous type of group-encounter session, with Callahan as some sort of salty psychoanalyst-father-figure in the foreground. Hell, many's the toast provokes roars of laughter, or a shouted chorus of agreement, or a unanimous blitz of glasses from all over the room when the night is particularly spirited. Callahan is tolerant of rannygazoo; he maintains that a bar should be "merry," so long as no bones are broken unintentionally. I mind the time he helped Spud Flynn set fire to a seat cushion to settle a bet on which way the draft was coming. Callahan exudes, at all times, a kind of monolithic calm; and U.S. 40 is shorter than his temper.

This night I'm telling you about, for instance, was nothing if not merry. When I pulled in around ten o'clock, there was an unholy shambles of a square dance going on in the middle of the floor. I laid a dollar on the bar, collected a glass of Tullamore Dew and a hello-grin from Callahan, and settled back in a tall chair—Callahan abhors barstools—to observe the goings-on. That's what I mean about Callahan's Place: most bars, men only dance if there're ladies around. Of one sex or another.

I picked some familiar faces out of the maelstrom of madmen weaving and lurching over honest-to-God sawdust, and waved a few greetings. There was Tom Flannery, who at the time had eight months to live, and knew it; he laughed a lot at Callahan's Place. There was Slippery Joe Maser, who had two wives, and Marty Matthias, who didn't gamble any more, and Noah Gonzalez, who worked on Suffolk County's bomb squad. Calling for the square dance while performing a creditable Irish jig was Doc Webster, fat and jovial as the day he pumped the pills out of my stomach and ordered me to Callahan's. See, I used to have a wife and daughter before I decided to install my own brakes. I saved thirty dollars, easy . . .

The Doc left the square-dancers to their fate—their creative individuality making a caller superfluous—and drifted over like a pink zeppelin to say Hello. His stethoscope hung unnoticed from his ears, framing a smile like a sunlamp. The end of the 'scope was in his drink.

"Howdy, Doc. Always wondered how you kept that damned thing so cold," I greeted him.

He blinked like an owl with the staggers and looked down at the gently bubbling pickup beneath two fingers of scotch. Emitting a bellow of laughter at about force eight, he removed the gleaming thing and shook it experimentally.

"My secret's out, Jake. Keep it under your hat, will you?" he boomed.

"Maybe you better keep it under yours," I suggested. He appeared to consider this idea for a time, while I speculated on one of life's greatest paradoxes: Sam Webster, M.D. The Doc is good for a couple of quarts of Peter Dawson a night, three or four nights a week. But you won't find a better sawbones anywhere on Earth, and those sausage fingers of his can move like a tap-dancing centipede when they have to, with nary a tremor. Ask Shorty Steinitz to tell you about the time Doc Webster took out his appendix on top of Callahan's bar . . . while Callahan calmly kept the Scotch coming.

"At least then I could hear myself think," the Doc finally replied, and several people seated within earshot groaned theatrically.

"Have a heart, Doc," one called out.

"What a re-pulse-ive idea," the Doc returned the serve.

"Well, I know when I'm beat," said the challenger, and made as if to turn away.

"Why, you young whelp, aorta poke you one," roared the Doc, and the bar exploded with laughter and cheers. Callahan picked up a beer bottle in his huge hand and pegged it across the bar at the Doc's round skull. The beer bottle, being made of foam rubber, bounced gracefully into the air and landed in the piano, where Fast Eddie sat locked in mortal combat with the "C-Jam Blues."

Fast Eddie emitted a sound like an outraged transmission and kept right on playing, though his upper register was shot. "Little beer never hoit a piano," he sang out as he reached the bridge, and went over it like he figured to burn it behind him.

All in all it looked like a cheerful night; but then I saw the Janssen kid come in and I knew there was a trouble brewing.

This Janssen kid—look, I can't knock long hair, I wore mine long when it wasn't fashionable. And I can't knock pot for the same reason. But nobody I know ever had a good thing to say for heroin. Certainly not Joe Hennessy, who did two weeks in the hospital last year after he surprised the Janssen kid scooping junk-money out of his safe at four in the morning. Old Man Janssen paid Hennessy back every dime and disowned the kid, and he'd been in and out of sight ever since. Word was he was still using the stuff, but the cops never seemed to catch him holding. They sure did try, though. I wondered what the hell he was doing in Callahan's Place.

I should know better by now. He placed a tattered bill on the bar, took the shot of bourbon which Callahan handed him silently, and walked to the chalk line. He was quivering with repressed tension, and his boots squeaked on the sawdust. The place quieted down some, and his toast—"To smack!"—rang out clear and crisp. Then he downed the shot amid an expanding silence and flung his glass so hard you could hear his shoulder crack just before the glass shattered on unyielding brick.

Having created silence, he broke it. With a sob. Even as he let it out he glared around to see what our reactions were.

Callahan's was immediate, an "Amen!" that sounded like an echo of the smashing glass. The kid made a face like he was somehow satisfied in spite of himself, and looked at the rest of us. His gaze rested on Doc Webster, and the Doc drifted over and gently began rolling up the kid's sleeves. The boy made no effort to help or hinder him. When they were both rolled to the shoulder—phosphorescent purple I think they were—he silently held out his arms, palm-up.

They were absolutely unmarked. Skinny as hell and white as a piece of paper, but unmarked. The kid was clean.

Everyone waited in silence, giving the kid their respectful attention. It was a new feeling to him, and he didn't quite know how to handle it. Finally he said, "I heard about this place," just a little too truculently.

"Then you must of needed to," Callahan told him quietly, and the kid nodded slowly.

"I hear you get some answers in, from time to time," he half-asked.

"Now and again," Callahan admitted. "Some o' the damndest questions, too. What's it like, for instance?"

"You mean smack?"

"I don't mean bourbon."

The kid's eyes got a funny, far-away look, and he almost smiled. "It's . . ." He paused, considering. "It's like . . . being dead."

"Whooee!" came a voice from across the room. "That's a powerful good feeling indeed." I looked and saw it was Chuck Samms talking, and watched to see how the kid would take it.

He thought Chuck was being sarcastic and snapped back, "Well, what the hell do you know about it anyway?" Chuck smiled. A lot of people ask him that question, in a different tone of voice.

"Me?" he said, enjoying himself hugely. "Why, I've been dead is all."

"S'truth," Callahan confirmed as the kid's jaw dropped. "Chuck there was legally dead for five minutes before the Doc got his pacemaker going again. The crumb died owing me money, and I never had the heart to dun his widow."

"Sure was a nice feeling, too," Chuck said around a yawn. "More peaceful than nap-time in a monastery. If it wasn't so pleasant I wouldn't be near so damned scared of it." There was an edge to his voice as he finished, but it disappeared as he added softly, "What the hell would you want to be dead for?"

The Janssen kid couldn't meet his eyes, and when he spoke his voice cracked. "Like you said, pop, peace. A little peace of mind, a little quiet. Nobody yammering at you all the time. I mean, if you're dead there's always the chance somebody'll mourn, right? Make friends with the worms, dig *their* side of it, maybe a little poltergeist action, who knows? I mean, what's the sense of talking about it, anyway? Didn't any of you guys ever just want to run away?"

"Sure thing," said Callahan. "Sometimes I do it too. But I generally run someplace I can find my way back from." It was said so gently that the kid couldn't take offense, though he tried.

"Run away from what, son?" asked Slippery Joe.

The kid had been bottled up tight too long; he exploded. "From what?" he yelled. "Jesus, where do I start? There was this war they wanted me to go and fight, see? And there's this place called college, I mean they want you to care, dig it, care about this education trip, and they don't care enough themselves to make it as attractive as the crap game across the street. There's this air I hear is unfit to breathe, and water that ain't fit to drink, and food that wouldn't nourish a vulture and a grand outlook for the future. You can't get to a job without the car you couldn't afford to run even if you were working, and if you *found* a job it'd pay five dollars less than the rent. The T.V. advertises karate classes for four-year-olds and up, the President's New Clothes didn't wear very well, the next depression's around the corner and you ask me what in the name of God I'm running from?

"Man, I've been straight for seven months, what I mean, and in that seven god damned months I have been over this island like a fungus and there is *nothing* for me. No jobs, no friends, no place to live long enough to get the floor dirty, no money and nobody that doesn't point and say "Junkie" when I go by for seven *months* and you ask me what am I running from? Man, *everything* is all, just everything."

It was right then that I noticed that guy in the corner, the one with the eyes. Remember him? He was leaning forward in rapt attention, his mouth a black slash in a face pulled tight as a drumhead. Those ghastly eyes of his never left the Janssen kid, but somehow I was sure that his awareness included all of us, everyone in the room.

And no one had an answer for the Janssen boy. I could see, all around the room, men who had learned to *listen* at Callahan's Place, men who had learned to empathize, to want to understand and share the pain of another. And no one had a word to say. They were thinking past the blurted words of a haunted boy, wondering if this crazy world of confusion might not after all be one holy hell of a place to grow up. Most of them already had reason to know damn well that society never forgives the sinner, but they were realizing to their dismay how thin and uncomforting the straight and narrow has become these last few years.

Sure, they'd heard these things before, often enough to make them into clichés. But now I could see the boys reflecting that these were the clichés that made a young man say he liked to feel dead, and the same thought was mirrored on the face of each of them: *My God, when did we let these things become clichés?* The Problems of Today's Youth were no longer a Sunday supplement or a news broadcast or anything so remote and intangible, they were suddenly become a dirty, shivering boy who told us that in this world we had built for him with our sweat and our blood he was not only tired of living, but so *un*scared of dying that he did it daily, sometimes, for recreation.

And silence held court in Callahan's Place. No one had a single thing to say, and that guy with the eyes seemed to know it, and to derive some crazy kind of bitter inner satisfaction from the knowledge. He started to settle back in his chair, when Callahan broke the silence.

"So run," he said.

Just like that, flat, no expression, just, "So run." It hung there for about ten seconds, while he and the kid locked eyes.

The kid's forehead started to bead with sweat. Slowly, with shaking fingers, he reached under his leather vest to his shirt pocket. Knuckles white, he hauled out a flat, shiny black case about four inches by two. His eyes never left Callahan's as he opened it and held it up so that we could all see the gleaming hypodermic. It didn't look like it had ever been used; he must have just stolen it.

He held it up to the light for a moment, looking up his bare, unmarked arm at it, and then he whirled and flung it case and all into the giant fireplace. Almost as it shattered he sent a cellophane bag of white powder after it, and the powder burned green while the sudden stillness hung in the air. The guy with the eyes looked oddly stricken in some interior way, and he sat absolutely rigid in his seat.

And Callahan was around the bar in an instant, handing the Janssen kid a beer that grew out of his fist and roaring, "Welcome home, Tommy!" and no one in the place was very startled to realize that only Callahan of all of us knew the kid's first name.

We all sort of swarmed around then and swatted the kid on the arm some and he even cried a little until we poured some beer over his head and pretty soon it began to look like the night was going to get merry again after all.

And that's when the guy with the eyes stood up, and everybody in the joint shut up and turned to look at him. That sounds melodramatic, but it's the effect he had on us. When he moved, he was the center of attention. He was tall, unreasonably tall, near seven foot, and I'll never know why we hadn't all noticed him right off. He was dressed in a black suit that fit worse than a Joliet Special, and his shoes didn't look right either. After a moment you realized that he had the left shoe on the right foot, and vice-versa, but it didn't surprise you. He was thin and deeply tanned and his mouth was twisted up tight but mostly he was eyes, and I still dream of those eyes and wake up sweating now and again. They were like windows into hell, the very personal and private hell of a man faced with a dilemma he cannot resolve. They did not blink, not once.

He shambled to the bar, and something was wrong with his walk, too, like he was walking sideways on the wall with magnetic shoes and hadn't quite caught the knack yet. He took ten new singles out of his jacket pocket—which struck me as an odd place to keep cash—and laid them on the bar.

Callahan seemed to come back from a far place, and hustled around behind the bar again. He looked the stranger up and down and then placed ten shot glasses on the counter. He filled each with rye and stood back silently, running a big red hand through his thinning hair and regarding the stranger with clinical interest.

The dark giant tossed off the first shot, shuffled to the chalk line, and said in oddly accented English, "To my profession," and hurled the glass into the fireplace.

Then he walked back to the bar and repeated the entire procedure. Ten times.

By the last glass, brick was chipping in the fireplace.

When the last, "To my profession," echoed in empty air, he turned and faced us. He waited, tensely, for question or challenge. There was none. He half turned away, paused, then swung back and took a couple of deep breaths. When he spoke his voice made you hurt to hear it.

"My profession, gentlemen," he said with that funny accent I couldn't place, "is that of advance scout. For a race whose home is many light-years from here. Many, many light-years from here." He paused, looking for our reactions.

*Well*, I thought, *ten whiskeys and he's a Martian. Indeed. Pleased to meet you, I'm Popeye the Sailor.* I guess it was pretty obvious we were all thinking the same way, because he looked tired and said, "It would take far more ethanol than that to befuddle me, gentlemen." Nobody said a word to that, and he turned to Callahan. "You know I am not intoxicated," he stated.

Callahan considered him professionally and said finally, "Nope. You're not tight. I'll be a son of a bitch, but you're not tight."

The stranger nodded thanks, spoke thereafter directly to Callahan. "I am here now three days. In two hours I shall be finished. When I am finished I shall go home. After I have gone your planet will be vaporized. I have accumulated data which will ensure the annihilation of your species when they are assimilated by my Masters. To them, you will seem as cancerous cells, in danger of infecting all you touch. You will not be permitted to exist. You will be *cured*. And I repent me of my profession."

Maybe I wouldn't have believed it anywhere else. But at Callahan's Place *anything* can happen. Hell, we all believed him. Fast Eddie sang out, "Anyt'ing we can do about it?" and he was serious for sure. You can tell with Fast Eddie.

"I am helpless," the giant alien said dispassionately. "I contain . . . installations . . . which are beyond my influencing—or yours. They have recorded all the data I have perceived in these three days; in two hours a preset mechanism will be triggered and will transmit their contents to the Masters." I looked at my watch: It was eleven-fifteen. "The conclusions of the Masters are foregone. I cannot prevent the transmission; I cannot even attempt to. I am counterprogrammed."

"Why are you in this line of work if it bugs you so much?" Callahan wanted to know. No hostility, no panic. He was trying to understand.

"I am accustomed to take pride in my work," the alien said. "I make safe the paths of the Masters. They must not be threatened by warlike species. I go before, to identify danger, and see to its neutralization. It is a good profession, I think. I thought."

"What changed your mind?" asked Doc Webster sympathetically.

"This place, this . . . 'bar' place we are in—this is not like the rest I have seen. Outside are hatred, competition, morals elevated to the status of ethics, prejudices elevated to the status of morals, whims elevated to the status of prejudices, all things with which I am wearily familiar, the classic symptoms of disease.

"But here is difference. Here in this place I sense qualities, attributes I did not know your species possessed, attributes which everywhere else in the known universe are mutually exclusive of the things I have perceived here tonight. They are good things . . . they cause me great anguish for your passing. They fill me with hurt.

"Oh, that I might lay down my geas," he cried. "I did not know that you had love!"

In the echoing stillness, Callahan said simply, "Sure we do, son. It's mebbe spread a little thin these days, but we've got it all right. Sure would be a shame if it all went up in smoke." He looked down at the rye bottle he still held in his big hand, and absently drank off a couple ounces. "Any chance that your masters might feel the same way?"

"None. Even I can still see that you must be destroyed if the Masters are to be safe. But for the first time in some thousands of years, I regret my profession. I fear I can do no more."

"No way you can gum up the works?"

"None. So long as I am alive and conscious, the transmission will take place. I could not assemble the volition to stop it. I have said: I am counterprogrammed."

I saw Noah Gonzalez' expression soften, heard him say, "Geez, buddy, that's hard lines." A mumbled agreement rose, and Callahan nodded slowly.

"That's tough, brother, I wouldn't want to be in your shoes."

He looked at us with absolute astonishment, the hurt in those terrible eyes of his mixed now with bewilderment. Shorty handed him another drink and it was like he didn't know what to do with it.

"You tell us how much it will take, mister," Shortly said respectfully, "and we'll get you drunk."

The tall man with star-burned skin groaned from deep within himself and backed away until the fireplace contained him. He and the flames ignored each other, and no one found it surprising.

"What is your matter?" he cried. "Why are you not destroying me? You fools, you need only destroy me and you are saved. I am your judge. I am your jury. I will be your executioner."

"You didn't ask for the job," Shorty said gently. "It ain't your doing."

"But you do not understand! If my data are not transmitted, the Masters will assume my destruction and avoid the system forever. Only the equal or superior of a Master could overcome my defenses, but I *can* control *them*. I will not use them. Do you comprehend me? I will not activate my defenses—you can destroy me and save yourselves and your species, and I will not hinder you.

"Kill me!" he shrieked.

There was a long, long pause, maybe a second or two, and then Callahan pointed to the drink Shorty still held out and growled, "You better drink that, friend. You need it. Talkin' of killin' in my joint. Wash your mouth out with bourbon and get outta that fireplace, I want to use it."

"Yeah, me too!" came the cry on all sides, and the big guy looked like he was gonna cry. Conversations started up again and fast Eddie began playing "I Don't Want to Set the World On Fire," in very bad taste indeed.

Some of the boys wandered thoughtfully out, going home to tell their families, or settle their affairs. The rest of us, lacking either concern, drifted over to console the alien. I mean, where else would I want to be on Judgment Day?

He was sitting down, now, with booze of all kinds on the table before him. He looked up at us like a wounded giant. But none of us knew how to begin, and Callahan spoke first.

"You never did tell us your name, friend."

The alien looked startled, and he sat absolutely still, rigid as a fence post, for a long, long moment. His face twisted up awful, as though he was waging some titanic inner battle with himself, and cords of muscle stood up on his neck in what didn't seem to be the right places. Doc Webster began to talk to himself softly.

Then the alien went all blue and shivered like a steel cable under strain, and very suddenly relaxed all over with an audible gasp. He twitched his shoulders experimentally a few times, like he was making sure they were still there, and then he turned to Callahan and said, clear as a bell, "My name is Michael Finn."

It hung in the air for a very long time, while we all stood petrified, suspended.

Then Callahan's face split in a wide grin, and he bellowed, "Why of course! Why yes, yes of course, Mickey *Finn*. I didn't recognize you for a moment, Mr. Finn," as he trotted behind the bar. His big hands worked busily beneath the counter, and as he emerged with a tall glass of dark fluid the last of us got it. We made way eagerly as Callahan set the glass down before the alien, and stood back with the utmost deference and respect.

He regarded us for a moment, and to see his eyes now was to feel warm and proud. For all the despair and guilt and anguish and horror and most of all the hopelessness were gone from them now, and they were just eyes. Just like yours and mine.

Then he raised his glass and waited, and we all drank with him. Before the last glass was empty, his head hit the table like an anvil, and we had to pick him up and carry him to the back room where Callahan keeps a cot, and you know, he was *heavy*.

And he snored in three stages.

# Spider Robinson

In 1973, a previously unheard-of author named Spider Robinson published a short story titled "The Guy with the Eyes," a fanciful tale taking place in an eccentric bar known as Callahan's Place. More than a quarter of a century later, the aliens, time travelers, and other characters introduced in the fateful story have grown to fill nine novels and short story collections. Perhaps more significantly, they have also spawned a cultural movement centered on Callahan's Law: the belief that shared pain is lessened, and shared joy is increased. In the early days of the Internet, the Usenet newsgroup alt.callahans was one of the largest non-pornographic networks in cyberspace, and spawned numerous spin-offs including two IRC channels and a location in Second Life—places where fans of the stories could bond and build community, not by discussing the stories, but by embracing the tenets that make the Callahan's Crosstime Saloon series so uniquely uplifting.

Yet for all its significance, the Callahan's series represents only one facet of Spider Robinson's writing. For the last three decades, Spider has produced at least one book a year, along the way garnering three Hugo Awards, a Nebula Award, a Locus Award, and several others, including the Robert A. Heinlein Medal for Lifetime Excellence—unsurprising, considering he's also the only writer to ever collaborate with Heinlein himself, posthumously completing the novel *Variable Star* from a 1955 outline. He's written the award-winning *Stardance* trilogy with his wife, been a guest at the White House, and written songs with musicians like David Crosby, Amos Garrett, and Todd Butler (the lyrics to which sometimes appear in the Callahan stories themselves).

Life, as Spider says, does not entirely suck—largely due to the preceding story.

**Looking back, what do you think still works well in this story? Why?**

My name, right up front under the title. It helped ensure its correct spelling on the check.

**If you were writing this today, what would you do differently? What are the story's weaknesses, and how would you change them?**

It's like asking what was ugly about my firstborn. At this remove, I can't think of a thing. Look how well she turned out . . .

**What inspired this story? How did it take shape? Where was it initially published?**

I had just flung a paperback across the room, snarling for the thousandth time in my life, "Hell, I could write better than that idiot!" I was sitting beside a sewer, protecting it from theft—I was night watchman over its construction site, in Babylon, New York—and I resumed thinking, as always when I'd run out of fiction, about where I'd rather be. The night before I had seen a Charles Boyer–Claudette Colbert film in which they were exiled Russian nobility, reduced to working as butler and maid for a family of pompous Brits . . . but late at night, when the master and mistress were abed, they would put on their ragged finery, drink champagne, and smash their glasses in the fireplace just like the Good Old Days.

Gee, I thought, it would be just great if there were a bar where they let you do that. That's where I'd rather be than here.

Of course . . . it would have to be a special sort of bar. With a special kind of customers, who could be trusted to hurl glassware around while loaded. And a very forgiving bartender. But boy, some interesting stories would probably get told there. . . .

Before me was a typewriter . . . and paper I didn't have to pay for, that only said "J. D. Posillico Construction Co." on one side . . . and hours of boredom before the end of my shift. The rest, as they say, is social studies.

When I was done, the resulting heap of stained paper looked, to me at least, just like a story manuscript, such as I imagined writers produced. I didn't expect that to fool an editor . . . but I did suddenly realize that if I sent it to one, he would have to send me a real rejection slip. With that, I could easily get laid. Tragic Figger of a Man, failed artist, genius undiscovered, etc. So the next day I went to the library, found *Writer's Market*, sussed out who paid the most for SF—*Analog* magazine—and decided it would have the most impressive rejection slips.

Editor Ben Bova screwed the whole thing up: instead of a rejection slip, he sent $400 and an invitation to lunch in the city. His first words to me were, "Does that bar of yours really exist? Because I'd sure like to go there." He printed "The Guy with the Eyes" in February 1973. In 2008, Ben and I shared the Robert A. Heinlein Medal for Lifetime Excellence.

**Where were you in your life when you published this piece, and what kind of impact did it have?**

I was just then out of college with a BA in English (after only 7 years), and having belatedly realized I didn't want to drive a cab, I was trying to figure out what I might do for a living when I grew up. The story's publication ensured that day would never arrive. Thank God: all I had come up with was journalism, which I discovered I hated, and folk music, which I loved but which ceased to exist as an occupation at just that moment in history. And guarding a sewer.

**How has your writing changed over the years, both stylistically and in terms of your writing process?**

The only stylistic change I've ever noticed myself came with the introduction of the word processor. Before then, I'd written everything longhand. Then during the brutal donkey labor of the typing process, I'd been motivated to cut like mad, losing words, sentences, even whole paragraphs or entire sub-plots. Then Jef Raskin created the personal computer. Nowadays, I just scroll my golden words past, and can't think of a reason in the world to cut any of them. Fortunately, if my readers noticed, they've apparently decided to keep their mouths shut and go along with the gag. Perhaps I ramble well. (P. G. Wodehouse has always been one of my favorite writers.)

Other than that, my style changes on a daily basis, depending on who I've been reading.

**What advice do you have for aspiring authors?**

Go back; it's a trap. After 35 straight years of sustained good luck and unbro-ken success, I'm as broke as when I started, paying off a mortgage, no savings, living from book to book, in a clearly dying industry. I'm 60 years old and I've bought one new car in my life. My TV has a cathode ray tube. Imagine how the less fortunate are doing. And from here on, things will be getting much, much worse: today's "audience" honestly believes anyone at all can write interest-ingly, and doesn't see why it should have to pay anyone to do so. They'll find out . . . but not necessarily before a generation of writers starves to death, like jazz musicians and stage actors.

On the other hand, I sleep when I'm tired, don't get up until I'm done, wear whatever I like, work when I feel the impulse, and get to spend as many of my waking hours as I want with my best friend, my wife. I have one important deadline a year. There are urgent professional reasons why I need to read lots of great books and listen to lots of superb music and watch lots of great mov-ies and smoke BC boo. I've become friends with people like Robert Heinlein, Theodore Sturgeon, Lawrence Block, Donald E. Westlake, Jef Raskin, Tom Robbins, John Varley, Paul Krassner, Stephen Gaskin, Cory Doctorow, and Amos Garrett. A few years ago, Laura Bush invited me and Jeanne to dinner with her and the old man, and brunch in the West Wing the next day. The other guests included Michael Connelly, George Pelecanos, Yevgeny Yevtushenko, and Bob Woodward. I'm allowed backstage at both Janis Ian and Crosby, Stills & Nash concerts; David and I collaborated on a song for Robert Heinlein. And I have managed to stay interesting to the most beautiful woman I ever saw for over thirty-five years; our first grandchild is due in five months. Life so far has not entirely sucked.

In return for all this, all I've had to do is stare at a blank monitor until beads of blood form on my forehead. And be willing to live on Scraped Icebox and Dishrag Soup sprinkled with fear.

It's going to get a lot harder from here on, though. Colleagues I consider my peers are going under. The traditional escape hatch for the failed fiction writer—journalism—is scrambling for survival itself. And the economy has no jobs for unskilled labor.

We need someone to reinvent the publishing industry for the Internet, we need a visionary to bring us the fabled New Business Model—that is, we need some rapacious fat bastard in a suit to figure out some bulletproof way to exploit us. My sincere advice to would-be writers today is exactly the advice I ignored myself 35 years ago: keep your day job. It took America nearly a decade to notice how incredibly boring reality TV was—and it still hasn't noticed how astonishingly boring talent-contest TV is—so it's going to take it a long time to notice how unbelievably boring all those blogs and twitters and amateur YouTubers are, and turn to professional storytellers again. When they do they'll probably want graphic novels.

For now, try something with more career potential. Like folk music, or modern dance, or experimental theater. It's no accident that my home has always been known as Tottering-on-the-Brink.

# Fragments of a Hologram Rose
## by William Gibson

T hat summer Parker had trouble sleeping.

There were power droughts; sudden failures of the delta-inducer brought painfully abrupt returns to consciousness.

To avoid these, he used patch cords, miniature alligator clips, and black tape to wire the inducer to a battery-operated ASP-deck. Power loss in the inducer would trigger the deck's playback circuit.

He brought an ASP cassette that began with the subject asleep on a quiet beach. It had been recorded by a young blonde yogi with 20-20 vision and an abnormally acute color sense. The boy had been flown to Barbados for the sole purpose of taking a nap and his morning's exercise on a brilliant stretch of private beach. The microfiche laminate in the cassette's transparent case explained that the yogi could will himself through alpha to delta without an inducer. Parker, who hadn't been able to sleep without an inducer for two years, wondered if this was possible.

He had been able to sit through the whole thing only once, though by now he knew every sensation of the first five subjective minutes. He thought the most interesting part of the sequence was a slight editing slip at the start of the elaborate breathing routine: a swift glance down the white beach that picked out the figure of a guard patrolling a chain-link fence, a black machine pistol slung over his arm.

While Parker slept, power drained from the city's grids.

The transition from delta to delta-ASP was a dark implosion into other flesh. Familiarity cushioned the shock. He felt the cool sand under his shoulders. The cuffs of his tattered jeans flapped against his bare ankles in the morning breeze. Soon the boy would wake fully and begin his Ardha-Matsyendra-something; with other hands Parker groped in darkness for the ASP deck.

Three in the morning.

Making yourself a cup of coffee in the dark, using a flashlight when you pour the boiling water.

Morning's recorded dream, fading: through other eyes, dark plume of a Cuban freighter—fading with the horizon it navigates across the mind's gray screen.

Three in the morning.

Let yesterday arrange itself around you in flat schematic images. What you said—what she said—watching her pack—dialing the cab. However you shuffle them they form the same printed circuit, hieroglyphs converging on a central component: you, standing in the rain, screaming at the cabby.

The rain was sour and acid, nearly the color of piss. The cabby called you an asshole; you still had to pay twice the fare. She had three pieces of luggage. In his respirator and goggles, the man looked like an ant. He pedaled away in the rain. She didn't look back.

The last you saw of her was a giant ant, giving you the finger.

Parker saw his first ASP unit in a Texas shantytown called Judy's Jungle. It was a massive console in cheap plastic chrome. A ten-dollar bill fed into the slot bought you five minutes of free-fall gymnastics in a Swiss orbital spa, trampolining through twenty-meter perihelions with a sixteen-year-old *Vogue* model—heady stuff for the Jungle, where it was simpler to buy a gun than a hot bath.

He was in New York with forged papers a year later, when two leading firms had the first portable decks in major department stores in time for Christmas. The ASP porn theaters that had boomed briefly in California never recovered.

Holography went too, and the block-wide Fuller domes that had been the holo temples of Parker's childhood became multilevel supermarkets, or housed dusty amusement arcades where you still might find the old consoles, under faded neon pulsing APPARENT SENSORY PERCEPTION through a blue haze of cigarette smoke.

Now Parker is thirty and writes continuity for broadcast ASP, programming the eye movements of the industry's human cameras.

The brown-out continues.

In the bedroom, Parker prods the brushed-aluminum face of his Sendai Sleep-Master. Its pilot light flickers, then lapses into darkness. Coffee in hand, he crosses the carpet to the closet he emptied the day before. The flashlight's beam probes the bare shelves for evidence of love, finding a broken leather sandal strap, an ASP cassette, and a postcard. The postcard is a white light reflection hologram of a rose.

At the kitchen sink, he feeds the sandal strap to the disposal unit. Sluggish in the brown-out, it complains, but swallows and digests. Holding it carefully between thumb and forefinger, he lowers the hologram toward the hidden rotating jaws. The unit emits a thin scream as steel teeth slash laminated plastic and the rose is shredded into a thousand fragments.

Later he sits on the unmade bed, smoking. Her cassette is in the deck ready for playback. Some women's tapes disorient him, but he doubts this is the reason he now hesitates to start the machine.

Roughly a quarter of all ASP users are unable to comfortably assimilate the subjective body picture of the opposite sex. Over the years some broadcast ASP stars have become increasingly androgynous in an attempt to capture this segment of the audience.

But Angela's own tapes have never intimidated him before. (But what if she has recorded a lover?) No, that can't be it—it's simply that the cassette is an entirely unknown quantity.

When Parker was fifteen, his parents indentured him to the American subsidiary of a Japanese plastics combine. At the time, he felt fortunate; the ratio of applicants to indentured trainees was enormous. For three years he lived with his cadre in a dormitory, singing the company hymns in formation each morning and usually managing to go over the compound fence at least once a month for girls or the holodrome.

The indenture would have terminated on his twentieth birthday, leaving him eligible for full employee status. A week before his nineteenth birthday, with two stolen credit cards and a change of clothes, he went over the fence for the last time. He arrived in California three days before the chaotic New Secessionist regime collapsed. In San Francisco, warring splinter groups hit and ran in the streets. One or another of four different "provisional" city governments had done such an efficient job of stockpiling food that almost none was available at street level.

Parker spent the last night of the revolution in a burned-out Tucson suburb, making love to a thin teenager from New Jersey who explained the finer points of her horoscope between bouts of almost silent weeping that seemed to have nothing at all to do with anything he did or said. Years later he realized that he no longer had any idea of his original motive in breaking his indenture.

The first three quarters of the cassette had been erased; you punch yourself fast-forward through a static haze of wiped tape, where taste and scent blur into a single channel. The audio input is white sound—the no-sound of the first dark sea . . . (Prolonged input from wiped tape can induce hypnagogic hallucination.)

Parker crouched in the roadside New Mexico brush at midnight, watching a tank burn on the highway. Flame lit the broken white line he had followed from Tucson. The explosion had been visible two miles away, a white sheet of heat lighting that had turned the pale branches of a bare tree against the night sky into a photographic negative of themselves: carbon branches against magnesium sky.

Many of the refugees were armed.

Texas owed the shantytowns that steamed in the warm Gulf rains to the uneasy neutrality she had maintained in the face of the Coast's attempted secession.

The towns were built of plywood, cardboard, plastic sheets that billowed in the wind, and the bodies of dead vehicles. They had names like Jump City and Sugaree, and loosely defined governments and territories that shifted constantly in the covert winds of a black-market economy.

Federal and state troops sent in to sweep the outlaw towns seldom found anything. But after each search a few men would fail to report back. Some had sold their weapons and burned their uniforms, and others had come too close to the contraband they had been sent to find.

After three months, Parker wanted out, but goods were the only safe passage through the army cordons. His chance came only by accident: Late one afternoon, skirting the pall of greasy cooking smoke that hung low over the Jungle, he stumbled and nearly fell on the body of a woman in a dry creek bed. Flies rose up in an angry cloud, then settled again, ignoring him. She had a leather jacket, and at night Parker was usually cold. He began to search the creek bed for a length of brushwood.

In the jacket's back, just below her left shoulder blade, was a round hole that would have admitted the shaft of a pencil. The jacket's lining had been red once, but now it was black, stiff and shining with dried blood. With the jacket swaying on the end of his stick, he went looking for water.

He never washed the jacket; in its left pocket he found nearly an ounce of cocaine, carefully wrapped in plastic and surgical tape. The right pocket held fifteen ampules of Megacillin-D and a ten-inch horn-handled switchblade. The antibiotic was worth twice its weight in cocaine.

He drove the knife hilt-deep into a rotten stump passed over by the Jungle's wood-gatherers and hung the jacket there, the flies circling it as he walked away.

That night, in a bar with a corrugated iron roof, waiting for one of the "lawyers" who worked passages through the cordon, he tried his first ASP machine. It was huge, all chrome and neon, and the owner was very proud of it; he had helped hijack the truck himself.

> If the chaos of the nineties reflects a radical shift in the paradigms of visual literacy, the final shift away from the Lascaux/Gutenberg tradition of a pre-holographic society, what should we expect from this newer technology, with its promise of discrete encoding and subsequent reconstruction of the full range of sensory perception?
>
> —Rosebuck and Pierhal,
> Recent American History: A Systems View.

Fast forward through the humming no-time of wiped tape—
—into her body. European sunlight. Streets of a strange city.

Athens. Greek-letter signs and the smell of dust . . .

—*and the smell of dust.*

Look through her eyes (thinking, this woman hasn't met you yet; you're hardly out of Texas) at the gray monument, the horses there in stone, where pigeons whirl up and circle—

—and static takes love's body, wipes it clean and gray. Waves of white sound break along a beach that isn't there. And the tape ends.

The inducer's light is burning now.

Parker lies in darkness, recalling the thousand fragments of the hologram rose. A hologram that has this quality: Recovered and illuminated, each fragment will reveal the whole image of the rose. Falling toward delta, he sees himself the rose, each of his scattered fragments revealing a whole he'll never know—stolen credit cards—a burned-out suburb—planetary conjunctions of a stranger—a tank burning on a highway—a flat packet of drugs—a switchblade honed on concrete, thin as pain.

Thinking: We're each other's fragments, and was it always this way? That instant of a European trip, deserted in the gray sea of wiped tape—is she closer now, or more real, for his having been there?

She had helped him get his papers, found him his first job in ASP. Was that their history? No, history was the black face of the delta-inducer, the empty closet, and the unmade bed. History was his loathing for the perfect body he woke in if the juice dropped, his fury at the pedal-cab driver, and her refusal to look back through the contaminated rain.

But each fragment reveals the rose from a different angle, he remembered, but delta swept over him before he could ask himself what that might mean.

# William Gibson

I n 1999, *The Guardian* called William Gibson "probably the most important novelist of the past two decades." The undisputed father of the
cyberpunk genre, having inspiring legions of authors, artists, and musicians from U2 to Sonic Youth, Gibson also teamed up with Bruce Sterling
to help found steampunk with *The Difference Engine*, which remains the
genre's best-known work. His debut novel, *Neuromancer*, was the first ever
to win science fiction's "triple crown"—the Hugo, Nebula, and Philip K. Dick
awards—and by 2007 had sold more than 6.5 million copies, as well as been
named one of the 100 best English-language novels written since 1923 by
*Time* magazine. He has been inducted into the Science Fiction Hall of Fame,
and awarded numerous honorary doctorates.

Yet to call William Gibson a science fiction author, or an author at all, is
to fundamentally miss the point. Though prose is his medium, Gibson is a
cultural lightning rod. Like many of the authors in this collection, he can be
credited with predicting any number of modern conventions (such as the
rise of reality television). Yet Gibson did not merely predict. Instead, the wild
imagination and tremendous popularity of his work at a crucial time in the
development of the Internet and Internet culture ran so deep as to make the
jump from prediction to causation, in fact shaping the very future he sought to
envision. Terms like *cyberspace, netsurfing, jacking in, ICE,* and *neural implants,*
as well as concepts from cybersex and online environments to meatpuppets
and the matrix—all were initially introduced by Gibson. In envisioning the
Internet and the information age, he gave us a language and iconography
with which to express ourselves, and the digital world we know is a direct
outgrowth of his art.

And he did it all without a modem or email address, on a typewriter from
1927.

In "Fragments of a Hologram Rose," the first story he ever finished, Gibson's
now-famous themes are already firmly in place, a dystopia of sprawling
high-tech slums and recorded stimulus. But no one, least of all Gibson,
could ever have predicted the indelible mark his tentative efforts would
leave on modern society.

**Looking back, what do you think still works well in this story? Why?**

This was not only the first story I published, but the first I completed. I literally hadn't yet learned how to move a character through simple narrative
space. That resulted in the invention of the memory-recording technology,
but it also forced me to work with the character's interiority. The capacity for
written depiction of character-interiority is what distinguishes prose fiction

from plays, screenplays, etc. So my lack of skill forced me to the core of prose, so to speak.

What I'm most aware of when look over this today is the hyper-specific focus on objects. I don't know what that's about. It's still a characteristic of my writing. I just don't know any other way to do it.

**If you were writing this today, what would you do differently? What are the story's weaknesses, and how would you change them?**

As with just about everything I've written, by the time I'm forced to let go of it, it feels like it's become what it is. I never think about revising published work. While it's being written, it's a process. On publication, it becomes an object.

**What inspired this story? How did it take shape? Where was it initially published?**

I was taking a course in science fiction at the University of British Columbia, in my senior undergraduate year. The teacher was Dr. Susan Wood. We were about the same age, and knew one another socially. I tried to get out of writing a term paper, and she cunningly suggested I turn in a piece of fiction instead. It proved hugely more difficult than any paper. She then insisted I submit it for publication.

I remember discovering that I could write very detailed, sometimes oddly evocative descriptions of objects relatively easily. I had to build on that.

It was published in a short-lived amateur magazine called *UnEarth*, which only considered unpublished writers. I think they paid $27.

**Where were you in your life when you published this piece, and what kind of impact did it have?**

I was married, not yet a parent, about to graduate, no idea as to future career other than definitely not wanting to teach. Given *UnEarth*'s great obscurity, nothing at all happened upon publication. I was somewhat underwhelmed, and didn't try writing any more fiction for a couple of years.

**How has your writing changed over the years, both stylistically and in terms of your writing process?**

It's gotten longer! Otherwise, I have a sneaking suspicion that it more closely resembles this first story, the longer I keep writing.

**What advice do you have for aspiring authors?**

Robert Sheckley gave me two very specific pieces of advice, on taking me to lunch in New York after buying "Johnny Mnemonic" for *OMNI* magazine.

Never, he said, sign a multi-book contract. And never buy that big old house that writers all seem to want to buy.

**Any anecdotes regarding the story or your experiences as a fledgling writer?**

If Susan Wood hadn't tricked me into writing this one, I'm not certain I'd have taken the step. I had a number of friends, early in my career, who did things like submitting story manuscripts behind my back, to markets I'd have been frightened to submit to (Susan was one of those as well, later) and I'm very grateful for that, as much as it made me want to scream at the time.

# A Long Way Back
## by Ben Bova

Tom woke slowly, his mind groping back through the hypnosis. He found himself looking toward the observation port, staring at stars and blackness.

*The first man in space,* he thought bitterly.

He unstrapped himself from the acceleration seat, feeling a little wobbly in free fall.

*The hypnotic trance idea worked, all right.*

The last thing Tom remembered was Arnoldsson putting him under, here in the rocket's compartment, the old man's sad soft eyes and quiet voice. Now 22,300 miles out, Tom was alone except for what Arnoldsson had planted in his mind for post-hypnotic suggestion to recall. The hypnosis had helped him pull through the blastoff unhurt and even protected him against the vertigo of weightlessness.

*Yeah, it's a wonderful world,* Tom muttered acidly.

He got up from the seat cautiously, testing his coordination against zero gravity. His magnetic boots held to the deck satisfactorily.

He was lean and wiry, in his early forties, with a sharp angular face and dark, somber eyes. His hair had gone dead white years ago. He was encased up to his neck in a semi-flexible space suit; they had squirmed him into it Earthside because there was no room in the cramped cabin to put it on.

Tom glanced at the tiers of instrument consoles surrounding his seat—no blinking red lights, everything operating normally. *As if I could do anything about it if they went wrong.* Then he leaned toward the observation port, straining for a glimpse of the satellite.

The satellite.

Five sealed packages floating within a three-hundred-foot radius of emptiness, circling the Earth like a cluster of moonlets. Five pieces sent up in five robot rockets and placed in the same orbit, to wait for a human intelligence to assemble them into a power-beaming satellite.

Five pieces orbiting Earth for almost eighteen years; waiting for nearly eighteen years while down below men blasted themselves and their cities and their machines into atoms and forgot the satellite endlessly circling, waiting for its creators to breathe life into it.

*The hope of the world,* Tom thought. *And little Tommy Morris is supposed to make it work . . . and then fly home again.* He pushed himself back into the seat. *Jason picked the wrong man.*

"Tom! Tom, can you hear me?"

He turned away from the port and flicked a switch on the radio console.

"Hello Ruth. I can hear you."

A hubbub of excitement crackled through the radio receiver, then the girl's voice: "Are you all right? Is everything . . ."

"Everything's fine," Tom said flatly. He could picture the scene back at the station—dozens of people clustered around the jury-rigged radio, Ruth working the controls, trying hard to stay calm when it was impossible to, brushing back that permanently displaced wisp of brown hair that stubbornly fell over her forehead.

"Jason will be here in a minute," she said. "He's in the tracking shack, helping to calculate your orbit."

*Of course Jason will be here,* Tom thought. Aloud he said, "He needn't bother. I can see the satellite packages; they're only a couple of hundred yards from the ship."

Even through the radio he could sense the stir that went through them.

*Don't get your hopes up,* he warned silently. *Remember, I'm no engineer. Engineers are too valuable to risk on this job. I'm just a tool, a mindless screwdriver sent here to assemble this glorified tinkertoy. I'm the muscle, Arnoldsson is the nerve link, and Jason is the brain.*

Abruptly, Jason's voice surged through the radio speaker, "We did it, Tom! We did it!"

*No,* Tom thought, *you did it, Jason. This is all your show.*

"You should be able to see the satellite components," Jason said. His voice was excited yet controlled, and his comment had a ring of command in it.

"I've already looked," Tom answered. "I can see them."

"Are they damaged?"

"Not as far as I can see. Of course, from this distance . . ."

"Yes, of course," Jason said. "You'd better get right outside and start working on them. You've only got forty-eight hours worth of oxygen."

"Don't worry about me," Tom said into the radio. "Just remember your end of the bargain."

"You'd better forget that until you get back here."

"I'm not forgetting anything."

"I mean you must concentrate on what you're doing up there if you expect to get back alive."

"When I get back we're going to explore the bombed-out cities. You promised that. It's the only reason I agreed to this."

Jason's voice stiffened. "My memory is quite as good as yours. We'll discuss the expedition after you return. Now you're using up valuable time . . . and oxygen."

"Okay, I'm going outside."

Ruth's voice came back on: "Tom, remember to keep the ship's radio open, or else your suit radio won't be able to reach us. And we're all here . . . Dr. Arnoldsson, Jason, the engineers . . . If anything comes up, we'll be right here to help you."

Tom grinned mirthlessly. *Right here: 22,300 miles away.*

"Tom?"

"Yes Ruth."

"Good luck," she said. "From all of us."

*Even Jason?* he wanted to ask, but instead said merely, "Thanks."

He fitted the cumbersome helmet over his head and sealed it to the joints on his suit. A touch of a button on the control panel pumped the compartment's air into storage cylinders. Then Tom stood up and unlocked the hatch directly over his seat.

Reaching for the handholds just outside the hatch, he pulled himself through, and after a weightless comic ballet managed to plant his magnetized boots on the skin of the ship. Then, standing, he looked out at the universe.

Oddly, he felt none of the overpowering emotion he had once expected of this moment. Grandeur, terror, awe—no, he was strangely calm. The stars were only points of light on a dead-black background; the Earth was a fat crescent patched with colors; the sun, through his heavily tinted visor, was like the pictures he had seen at planetarium shows, years ago.

As he secured a lifeline to the grip beside the hatch, Tom thought that he felt as though someone had stuck a reverse hypodermic into him and drained away all his emotions.

Only then did he realize what had happened. Jason, the engineer, the leader, the man who thought of everything, had made Arnoldsson condition his mind for this. No gaping at the universe for the first man in space, too much of a chance to take! There's a job to be done and no time for human frailty or sentiment.

*Not even that,* Tom said to himself. *He wouldn't even allow me one moment of human emotion.*

But as he pushed away from the ship and floated ghost-like toward the largest of the satellite packages, Tom twisted around for another look at Earth.

*I wonder if she looked that way before the war?*

Slowly, painfully, men had attempted to rebuild their civilization after the war had exhausted itself. But of all the things destroyed by the bombs and plagues, the most agonizing loss was man's sources of energy.

The coal mines, the oil refineries, the electricity-generating plants, the nuclear power piles . . . all shattered into radioactive rubble. There could be no return to any kind of organized society while men had to scavenge for wood to warm themselves and to run their primitive machines.

Then someone had remembered the satellite.

It had been designed, before the war, to collect solar energy and beam it to a receiving station on Earth. The satellite packages had been fired into a 24-hour orbit, circling the Earth over a fixed point on the Equator. The receiving station, built on the southeastern coast of the United States, saw the five units as a single second-magnitude star, low on the horizon all year, every year.

Of course the packages wavered slightly in their orbits, but not enough in eighteen years to spread very far apart. A man could still put them together into a power-beaming satellite.

If he could get there.

And if they were not damaged.

And if he knew how to put them together.

Through months that stretched into years, over miles of radioactive wilderness, on horseback, on carts, on foot, those who knew about the satellite spread the word, carefully, secretly, to what was left of North America's scientists and engineers. Gradually they trickled into the once-abandoned settlement.

They elected a leader: Jason, the engineer, one of the few men who knew anything about rockets to survive the war and the lunatic bands that hunted down anyone suspected of being connected with pre-war science.

Jason's first act was to post guards around the settlement. Then he organized the work of rebuilding the power-receiving station and a man-carrying rocket.

They pieced together parts of a rocket and equipment that had been damaged by the war. What they did not know, they learned. What they did not have, they built or cannibalized from ruined equipment.

Jason sent armed foragers out for gasoline, charcoal and wood. They built a ramshackle electricity generator. They planted crops and hunted the small game in the local underbrush. A major celebration occurred whenever a forager came back towing a stray cow or a horse or goat.

They erected fences around the settlement, because more than once they had to fight off the small armies of looters and anti-scientists that still roved the countryside.

But finally they completed the rocket . . . after exhausting almost every scrap of material and every ounce of willpower.

Then they picked a pilot: Thomas H. Morris, age 41, former historian and teacher. He had arrived a year before the completion of the rocket after walking 1,300 miles to find the settlement; his purpose was to organize some of the scientists and explore the bombed-out cities to see what could be salvaged out of man's shattered heritage.

But Tom was ideal for the satellite job: the right size—five-six and one-hundred thirty pounds; no dependents—wife and two sons dead of radiation sickness. True, he had no technical background whatsoever; but with Arnoldsson's hypnotic conditioning he could be taught all that it was necessary for him to know . . . maybe.

Best of all, though, he was thoroughly expendable.

So Jason made a deal with him. There could be no expeditions into the cities until the satellite was finished because every man was needed at the settlement. And the satellite could not be finished until someone volunteered to go up in the rocket and assemble it.

It was like holding a candy bar in front of a small child. He accepted Jason's terms.

The Earth turned, and with it the tiny spark of life alone in the emptiness around the satellite. Tom worked unmindful of time, his eyes and hands following Jason's engineering commands through Arnoldsson's post-hypnotic directions, with occasional radio conferences.

But his conscious mind sought refuge from the strangeness of space, and he talked almost constantly into this radio while he worked, talked about anything, everything, to the girl on the other end of the invisible link.

". . . and once the settlement is getting the power beamed from this contraption, we're going to explore the cities. Guess we won't be able to get very far inland, but we can still tackle Washington, Philadelphia and New York . . . plenty for us there."

Ruth asked, "What were they like before the war?"

"The cities? That's right, you're too young to remember. They were big, Ruth, with buildings so tall people called them skyscrapers." He pulled a wrench from its magnetic holder in the satellite's self-contained tool bin. "And filled with life. Millions of people lived in each one . . . all the people we have at the settlement could have lived on one floor of a good-sized hotel . . ."

"What's a hotel?"

Tom grinned as he tugged at a pipe fitting. "You'll find out when you come with us . . . you'll see things you could never imagine."

"I don't know if I'll come with you."

He looked up from his work and stared Earthward. "Why?"

"Well . . . Jason . . . he says there isn't much left to see. And it's all radioactive and diseased."

"Nonsense."

"But Jason says . . ."

Tom snorted. "Jason hasn't been out of the settlement for six years. I walked from Chicago to the settlement a year ago. I went through a dozen cities . . . they're wrecked, and the radioactivity count was higher than it is here at the settlement, but it's not high enough to be dangerous."

"And you want to explore those cities; why?"

"Let's just say I'm a historian," Tom answered while his hands manipulated complex wiring unconsciously, as though they belonged not to him but to some unseen puppeteer.

"I don't understand," Ruth said.

"Look—those cities hold mankind's memory. I want to gather up the fragments of civilization before the last book is used for kindling and the last machine turns to rust. We need the knowledge in the cities if we expect to rebuild a civilization . . ."

"But Jason and Dr. Arnoldsson and the engineers—they know all about . . ."

"Jason and the engineers," Tom snapped. "They had to stretch themselves to the breaking point to put together this rocket from parts that were already manufactured, waiting for them. Do you think they'd know how to build a city? Dr. Arnoldsson is a psychiatrist; his efforts at surgery are pathetic. Have you ever seen him try to set a broken leg? And what about agriculture? What about tool-making or mining or digging wells, even . . . what about education? How many kids your own age can read or write?"

"But the satellite . . ."

"The satellite won't be of any use to people who can't work the machines. The satellite is no substitute for knowledge. Unless something is done, your grandchildren will be worshipping the machines, but they won't know how to repair them."

"No . . ."

"Yes, Ruth," he insisted.

"No," she whispered, her voice barely audible over the static-streaked hum in his earphones. "You're wrong, Tom. You're wrong. The satellite will send us the power we need. Then we'll build our machines and teach our children."

*How can you teach what you don't know?* Tom wanted to ask, but didn't. He worked without talking, hauling the weightless tons of satellite package into position, electronically welding them together, splicing wiring systems too intricate for his conscious mind to understand.

Twice he pulled himself back along the lifeline into the ship for capsule meals and stimulants.

Finally he found himself staring at his gloved hands moving industriously within the bowels of one of the satellite packages. He stopped, suddenly aware that it was piercingly cold and totally dark except for the lamp on his helmet.

He pushed away from the unfinished satellite. Two of the packages were assembled now. The big parabolic mirror and two other uncrated units hung nearby, waiting impassively.

Tom groped his way back into the ship. After taking off his helmet and swallowing a couple of energy pills he said to the ship's radio:

"What time is it?" The abrupt sound of his own voice half-startled him.

"Nearly four a.m." It was Jason.

"Earth's blotted out the sun," Tom muttered. "Getting damned cold in here."

"You're in the ship?"

"Yes. It got too cold for the suit."

"Turn up the ship's heaters," Jason said. "What's the temperature in there?"

Tom glanced at the thermometer as he twisted the thermostat dial as far as it would go. "Forty-nine," he answered.

He could sense Jason nod. "The heaters are on minimum power automatically unless you turn them up. It'll warm you up in a few seconds. How's the satellite?"

Tom told him what remained to be done.

"You're not even half through yet." Jason's voice grew fainter and Tom knew that he was doing some mental arithmetic as he thought out loud. "You've been up about twenty hours; at the rate you're going you'll need another twenty-four to finish the job. That will bring you very close to your oxygen limit."

Tom sat impassively and stared at the gray metal and colored knobs of the radio.

"Is everything going alright?" Jason asked.

"How should I know? Ask Arnoldsson."

"He's asleep. They all are."

"Except you."

"That's right," Jason said, "except me."

"How long did Ruth stay on the radio?"

"About sixteen hours. I ordered her to sleep a few hours ago."

"You're pretty good at giving orders," Tom said.

"Someone has to."

"Yeah." Tom ran a hand across his mouth. *Boy, could I use a cigarette. Funny, I haven't even thought about them in years.*

"Look," he said to the radio, "we might as well settle something right now. How many men are you going to let me have?"

"Don't you think you'd better save that for now and get back to work?"

"It's too damned cold out there. My fingers are still numb. You could have done a better job on insulating this suit."

"There are a lot of things we could have done," Jason said, "if we had the material."

"How about the expedition? How many men can I have?"

"As many as you can get," the radio voice answered. "I promised I won't stand in your way once the satellite is finished and operating."

"Won't stand in my way," Tom repeated. "That means you won't encourage anyone, either."

Jason's voice rose a trifle. "I can't encourage my people to go out and risk their lives because you want to poke around some radioactive slag heaps."

"You promised that if I put the satellite together and got back alive, I could investigate the cities. That was our deal."

"That's right you can. And anyone foolish enough to accompany you can follow along."

"Jason, you know I need at least twenty-five armed men to venture out of the settlement . . ."

"Then you admit it's dangerous!" the radio voice crackled.

"Sure, if we meet a robber band. You've sent out enough foraging groups to know that. And we'll be travelling hundreds of miles. But it's not dangerous for the reasons you've been circulating . . . radioactivity and disease germs and that nonsense. There's no danger that one of your own foraging groups couldn't handle. I came through the cities last year alone, and I made it."

Tom waited for a reply from the radio, but only the hissing and crackling of electrical disturbances answered him.

"Jason, those cities hold what's left of a world-wide civilization. We can't begin to rebuild unless we reopen that knowledge. We need it, we need it desperately!"

"It's either destroyed or radioactive, and to think anything else is self-delusion. Besides, we have enough intelligence right here at the settlement to build a new civilization, better than the old one, once the satellite is ready."

"But you don't!" Tom shouted. "You poor damned fool, you don't even realize how much you don't know."

"This is a waste of time," Jason snapped. "Get outside and finish your work."

"I'm still cold, dammit," Tom said. He glanced at the thermometer on the control console. "Jason! It's below freezing in here!"

"What?"

"The heating unit isn't working at all!"

"Impossible. You must have turned it off instead of on."

"I can read, dammit! It's turned on as high as it'll go . . ."

"What's the internal thermometer reading?"

Tom looked, "Barely thirty . . . and it's still going down."

"Hold on, I'll wake Arnoldsson and the electrical engineers."

Silence. Tom stared at the inanimate radio which gave off only the whines and scratches of lightning and sun and stars, all far distant from him. For all his senses could tell him, he was the last living thing in the universe.

*Sure, call a conference,* Tom thought. *How much more work is there to be done? About twenty-four hours, he said. Another day. And another full night. Another night, this time with no heat. And maybe no oxygen, either. The heaters must have been working tonight until I pushed them up to full power. Something must have blown out. Maybe it's just a broken wire. I could fix that if they tell me how. But if it's not . . . no heat tomorrow night, no heat at all.*

Then Arnoldsson's voice floated up through the radio speaker: soft, friendly, calm, soothing . . .

The next thing Tom knew he was putting on his helmet. Sunlight was lancing through the tinted observation port and the ship was noticeably warmer.

"What happened?" he mumbled through the dissolving haze of hypnosis.

"It's all right, Tom." Ruth's voice. "Dr. Arnoldsson put you under and had you check the ship's wiring. Now he and Jason and the engineers are figuring out what to do. They said it's nothing to worry about . . . they'll have everything figured out in a couple of hours."

"And I'm to work on the satellite until they're ready?"

"Yes."

"Don't call us, we'll call you."

"What?"

"Nothing."

"It's all right, Tom. Don't worry."

"Sure Ruth, I'm not worried." *That makes us both liars.*

He worked mechanically, handling the unfamiliar machinery with the engineers' knowledge through Arnoldsson's hypnotic communication.

*Just like the pictures they used to show of nuclear engineers handling radioactive materials with remotely-controlled mechanical hands from behind a concrete wall. I'm only a pair of hands, a couple of opposed thumbs, a fortunate mutation of a self-conscious simian . . . but, God, why don't they call? She said it wasn't anything big. Just the wiring, probably. Then why don't they call?*

He tried to work without thinking about anything, but he couldn't force his mind to stillness.

*Even if I can fix the heaters, even if I don't freeze to death, I might run out of oxygen. And how am I going to land the ship? The takeoff was automatic, but even Jason and Arnoldsson can't make a pilot out of me . . .*

"Tom?" Jason's voice.

"Yes!" He jerked his attention and floated free of the satellite.

"We've . . . eh, checked what you told us about the ship's electrical system while Arnoldsson had you under the hypnotic trance . . ."

"And?"

"Well . . . it, eh, looks as though one of the batteries gave out. The batteries feed all the ship's lights, heat, and electrical power . . . with one of them out, you don't have enough power to run the heaters."

"There's no way to fix it?"

"Not unless you cut out something else. And you need everything else . . . the radio, the controls, the oxygen pumps . . ."

"What about the lights? I don't need them, I've got the lamp on my suit helmet."

"They don't take as much power as the heaters do. It wouldn't help at all."

Tom twisted weightlessly and stared back at Earth. "Well just what the hell am I supposed to *do?*"

"Don't get excited," Jason's voice grated in his earphones. "We've calculated it all out. According to our figures, your suit will store enough heat during the day to last the night . . ."

"I nearly froze to death last night and the ship was heated most of the time!"

"It will get cold," Jason's voice answered calmly, "but you should be able to make it. Your own body warmth will be stored by the suit's insulation, and that will help somewhat. But you must not open the suit all night, not even to take off your helmet."

"And the oxygen?"

"You can take all the replacement cylinders from the ship and keep them at the satellite. The time you save by not having to go back and forth to the ship for fresh oxygen will give you about an hour's extra margin. You should be able to make it."

Tom nodded. "And of course I'm expected to work on the satellite right through the night."

"It will help you keep your mind off the cold. If we see that you're not going to make it—either because of the cold or the oxygen—we'll warn you and you can return to the settlement."

"Suppose I have enough oxygen to just finish the satellite, but if I do, I won't have enough to fly home. Will you warn me then?"

"Don't be dramatic."

"Go to hell."

"Dr. Arnoldsson said he could put you under," Jason continued unemotionally, "but he thinks you might freeze once your conscious mind went asleep."

"You've figured out all the details," Tom muttered. "All I have to do is put your damned satellite together without freezing to death and then fly 22,300 miles back home before my air runs out. Simple."

He glanced at the sun, still glaring bright even through his tinted visor. It was nearly on the edge of the Earth-disk.

"All right," Tom said, "I'm going into the ship now for some pills; it's nearly sunset."

Cold. Dark and so cold that numbers lost their meaning. Paralyzing cold, seeping in through the suit while you worked. Crawling up your limbs until you could hardly move. The whole universe hung up in the sky and looked down on the small cold figure of a man struggling blindly with machinery he could not understand.

Dark. Dark and cold.

Ruth stayed on the radio as long as Jason would allow her, talking to Tom, keeping the link with life and warmth. But finally Jason took over, and the radio went silent.

*So don't talk,* Tom growled silently, *I can keep warm just by hating you, Jason.*

He worked through the frigid night, struggling ant-like with huge pieces of equipment. Slowly he assembled the big parabolic mirror, the sighting mechanism and the atomic convertor. With dreamy motions he started connecting the intricate writing systems.

And all the while he raged at himself: *Why? Why did it have to be this way? Why me? Why did I agree to do this? I knew I'd never live through it; why did I do it?*

He retraced the days of his life: the preparations for the flight, the arguments with Jason over exploring the cities, his trek from Chicago to the settlement, the aimless years after the radiation death of his two boys and Marjorie, his wife.

Marjorie and the boys, lying sick month after month, dying one after the other in a cancerous agony while he stood by helplessly in the ruins of what had been their home.

*No!* His mind warned him. *Don't think of that. Not that. Think of Jason, Jason who prevents you from doing the one thing you want, who is taking your life from you; Jason, the peerless leader; Jason, who's afraid of the cities. Why? Why is he afraid of the cities? That's the hub of everything down there. Why does Jason fear the cities?*

It wasn't until he finished connecting the satellite's last unit—the sighting mechanism—that Tom realized the answer.

One answer. And everything fell into place.

Everything . . . except what Tom Morris was going to do about it.

Tom squinted through the twin telescopes of the sighting mechanism again, then pushed away and floated free, staring at the Earth bathed in pale moonlight.

*What do I do now?* For an instant he was close to panic, but he forced it down. *Think,* he said to himself. *You're supposed to be a Homo Sapiens . . . use that brain. Think!*

The long night ended. The sun swung around from behind the bulk of Earth. Tom looked at it as he felt its warmth penetrating the insulated suit, and he knew it was the last time he would see the sun. He felt no more anger—even his hatred of Jason was drained out of him now. In its place was a sense of—finality.

He spoke into this helmet mike. "Jason."

"He is in conference with the astronomers." Dr. Arnoldsson's voice.

"Get him for me, please."

A few minutes of silence, broken only by the star-whisperings in the earphones.

Jason's voice was carefully modulated. "Tom, you made it."

"I made it. And the satellite's finished."

"It's finished? Good. Now, what we have to do . . ."

"Wait," Tom interrupted. "It's finished but it's useless."

"What?"

Tom twisted around to look at the completed satellite, its oddly-angled framework and bulbous machinery glinting fiercely in the newly-risen sun. "After I finished it I looked through the sighting mechanism to make certain the satellite's transmitters were correctly aimed at the settlement. Nobody told me to, but nobody said not to, either, so I looked. It's a simple mechanism . . . The transmitters are pointed smack in the middle of Hudson's Bay."

"You're sure?"

"Certainly."

"You can rotate the antennas . . ."

"I know. I tried it. I can turn them as far south as the Great Lakes."

A long pause.

"I was afraid of this," Jason's voice said evenly.

*I'll bet you were,* Tom answered to himself.

"You must have moved the satellite out of position while assembling its components."

"So my work here comes to nothing because the satellite's power beam can't reach the settlement's receivers."

"Not . . . not unless you use the ship . . . to tow the satellite into the proper orbital position." Jason stammered.

*You actually went through with it,* Tom thought. Aloud, he said, "But if I use the ship's engine to tow the satellite, I won't have enough fuel left to get back to Earth, will I?" *Not to mention oxygen.*

A longer pause. "No."

"I have two questions, Jason. I think I know the answers to them both but I'll ask you anyway. One. You knew this would happen, didn't you?"

"What do you mean?"

"You've calculated this insane business down to the last drop of sweat," Tom growled. "You knew that I'd knock the satellite out of position while I was working on it, and the only way to get it back in the right orbit would be for me to tow it back and strand myself up here. This is a suicide mission, isn't it, Jason?"

"That's not true . . ."

"Don't bother defending yourself. I don't hate you anymore, Jason, I understand you, dammit. You made our deal as much to get rid of me as to get our precious satellite put together."

"No one can force you to tow the satellite . . ."

"Sure, I can leave it where it is and come back home. If I can fly this ship, which I doubt. And what would I come back to? I left a world without power. I'd return to a world without hope. And some dark night one of your disappointed young goons would catch up with me . . . and no one would blame him, would they?"

Jason's voice was brittle. "You'll tow it into position?"

"After you answer my second question," Tom countered. "Why are you afraid of the cities?"

"Afraid? I'm not afraid."

"Yes, you are. Oh, you could use the hope of exploring the cities to lure me up here on this suicide-job, but you knew I'd never be back to claim my half of the bargain. You're afraid of the cities, and I think I know why. You're afraid of the unknown quantity they represent, distrustful of your own leadership when new problems arise . . ."

"We've worked for more than ten years to make this settlement what it is," Jason fumed. "We fought and died to keep those marauding lunatics from wrecking us. We are mankind's last hope! We can't afford to let others in . . . they're not scientists, they wouldn't understand, they'd ruin everything."

"Mankind's last hope, terrified of men." Tom was suddenly tired, weary of the whole struggle. But there was something he had to tell them.

"Listen, Jason," he said. "The walls you've built around the settlement weren't meant to keep you from going outside. You're not a self-sufficient little community . . . you're cut off from mankind's memory, from his dreams, from his ambitions. You can't even start to rebuild a civilization—and if you do try, don't you think the people outside will learn about it? Don't you think they've got a right to share in whatever progress the settlement makes? And if you don't let them, don't you realize that they'll destroy the settlement?"

Silence.

"I'm a historian," Tom continued, "and I know that a civilization can't exist in a vacuum. If outsiders don't conquer it, it'll rot from within. It's happened to Babylonia, Greece, Rome, China, even. Over and again. The Soviets built an Iron Curtain around themselves, and wiped themselves out because of it.

"Don't you see, Jason? There are only two types of animals on this planet; the gamblers and the extinct. It won't be easy to live with the outsiders, there'll be problems of every type. But the alternative is decay and destruction. *You've got to take the chance, if you don't you're dead.*"

A long silence. Finally Jason said, "You've only got about a half-hour's worth of oxygen left. Will you tow the satellite into the proper position?"

Tom stared at the planet unseeingly. "Yes," he mumbled.

"I'll have to check some calculations with the astronomers," Jason's voice buzzed flatly in his earphones.

A background murmur, scarcely audible over the crackling static.

Then Ruth's voice broke through, "Tom, Tom, you can't do this! You won't be able to get back!"

"I know," he said, as he started pulling his way along the lifeline back into the ship.

"*No!* Come back, Tom, please. Come back. Forget about the satellite. Come back and explore the cities. I'll go with you. Please. Don't die, Tom, please don't die . . ."

"Ruth, Ruth, you're too young to cry over me. I'll be all right, don't worry."

"No, it isn't fair."

"It never is," Tom said. "Listen Ruth, I've been dead a long time. Since the bombs fell, I guess. My world died then and I died with it. When I came to the settlement, when I agreed to make this flight, I think we all knew I'd never return, even if we wouldn't admit it to ourselves. But I'm just one man, Ruth, one small part of the story. The story goes on, with or without me. There's tomorrow . . . your tomorrow. I've got no place in it, but it belongs to you. So don't waste your time crying over a man who died eighteen years ago."

He snapped off his suit radio and went the rest of the way to the ship in silence. After locking the hatch and pumping air back into the cabin, he took off his helmet.

*Good clean canned air,* Tom said to himself. *Too bad it won't last longer.*

He sat down and flicked a switch on the radio console. "All right, do you have those calculations ready?"

"In a few moments . . ." Arnoldsson's voice.

Ten minutes later Tom reemerged from the ship and made his ghost-like way back to the satellite's sighting mechanism. He checked the artificial moon's position then went back to the ship.

"On course," he said to the radio. "The transmitters are pointing a little northwest of Philadelphia."

"Good," Arnoldsson's voice answered. "Now, your next blast should be three seconds' duration in the same direction . . ."

"No," Tom said, "I've gone as far as I'm going to."

"What?"

"I'm not moving the satellite any farther."

"But you still have not enough fuel to return to Earth. Why are you stopping here?"

"I'm not coming back," Tom answered. "But I'm not going to beam the satellite's power to the settlement either."

*"What are you trying to pull?"* Jason's voice. Furious. Panicky.

"It's simple, Jason. If you want the satellite's power you can dismantle the settlement and carry it to Pennsylvania. The transmitters are aimed at some good farming country, and within miles of a city that's still half-intact."

"You're insane!"

"Not at all. We're keeping our deal, Jason. I'm giving you the satellite's power, and you're going to allow exploration of the cities. You won't be able to prevent your people from rummaging through the cities now; and you won't be able to keep the outsiders from joining you, not once you get out from behind your own fences."

"You can't do this! You . . ."

Tom snapped off the radio. He looked at it for a second or two, then smashed a heavy-booted foot against the console. Glass and metal crashed satisfactorily.

*Okay,* Tom thought, *it's done. Maybe Jason's right and I'm crazy, but we'll never know now. In a year or so they'll be set up outside of Philadelphia, and a lot better for it. I'm forcing them to take the long way back, but it's a better way. The only way, maybe.*

He leaned back in the seat and stared out the observation port at the completed satellite. Already it was taking in solar energy and beaming it Earthward.

*In ten years they'll send another ship up here to check the gadget and make sure everything's okay. Maybe they'll be able to do it in five years. Makes no difference. I'll still be here.*

# Ben Bova

For more than half a century, Dr. Ben Bova has put the science in science fiction. A technical editor on Project Vanguard, the mission by which the United States successfully launched the second artificial satellite in response to the Soviet *Sputnik*, Dr. Bova never left the cutting edge of scientific knowledge, and neither has his writing. In his catalogue of more than 120 books, both fiction and nonfiction, Bova predicted the 1960s Space Race, solar power satellites, virtual reality, human cloning, stem cell therapy, the Strategic Defense Initiative of the 1980s, and countless other advancements which have either come to pass or are even now standing on our doorstep. He's the President Emeritus of the National Space Society, and a frequent commentator for both television and radio, with articles in such publications as *Scientific American* and *The New York Times*.

Yet as much as his ideas and breadth of knowledge have assisted him on his path, Ben Bova is known first and foremost for his writing and editing. A past president of the Science Fiction Writers of America, Ben Bova boasts a list of awards that read like a who's-who in science fiction: the John W. Campbell Memorial Award, the Isaac Asimov Memorial Award, the Robert A. Heinlein Award, and the 2005 Lifetime Achievement Award from the Arthur C. Clarke foundation "for fueling mankind's imagination regarding the wonders of outer space." After John Campbell's death, Bova took over editorship of *Analog Science Fiction*, the longest-running science fiction magazine in the world, and also spent time as the editor of *OMNI*, winning a grand total of six Hugo Awards for Best Editor. A teacher of science fiction and film at both Harvard and Hayden Planetarium in New York City, Bova writes to entertain, to educate, and to ensure that humanity's wonder continues to exceed its grasp—yet always with the science to back it up. Such meticulousness is evident even in his first published SF story, "A Long Way Back." Though not the first story he ever published—that honor going to several pieces published right after high school by *Campus Town*, a teenage magazine he helped run—nor the first SF story ever sold (which was lost forever when the magazine that bought it folded before printing it), "A Long Way Back" represents Bova's first foray onto the science fiction scene.

**Looking back, what do you think still works well in this story? Why?**

I think two technical points in the story have held up quite well: the idea that energy is the key to civilization and the idea of solar power satellites. Remember, this story was written some 10 years before Philip Glaser actually made the first technical proposal of the solar power satellite concept. The human conflict between Tom and Jason still holds up as well; it mirrors the larger conflicts between the haves and have-nots, and between the search for knowledge and the clinging to status-quo.

**If you were writing this today, what would you do differently? What are the story's weaknesses, and how would you change them?**

Of course, we know a lot more today than we did in 1960 about the realities of spacewalks and orbital construction. They are much more intricate than I depicted them in the story.

**What inspired this story? How did it take shape? Where was it initially published?**

"A Long Way Back" was published in 1960, in *Amazing Stories*, which was then edited by Cele Goldsmith. At this distance in time, I can't recall what inspired the story. I do remember that it was fairly easy for me to write: the words just seemed to flow out naturally. I offered it at the first Milford Science Fiction Writers' Workshop that I attended; it was received with faint praise.

**Where were you in your life when you published this piece, and what kind of impact did it have?**

I was married, with two adopted children, living in suburbia in the Boston area. I had just started a full-time "day job" as a science writer at the Avco Everett Research Laboratory, where I worked for the next 12 years, until I was selected to edit *Analog Science Fiction* magazine after the death of John W. Campbell. Publication of "A Long Way Back" started my career in writing for science fiction magazines. I soon had a cover story in *Amazing*, began to sell fiction to Campbell at *Analog*, and wrote a long series of nonfiction articles about extraterrestrial life for *Amazing*.

**How has your writing changed over the years, both stylistically and in terms of your writing process?**

I'm much more a novelist than a short-story writer. Somehow I find it easier, and more comfortable, to write novels than short fiction. Reading "A Long Way Back" so many years after it was published, I see that my style hasn't changed all that much. I still try to write clearly and naturalistically. I feel that, especially in science fiction, where there is so much for the reader to swallow, the writing style should be as easy to comprehend as possible.

**What advice do you have for aspiring authors?**

It's important—vital—to have something to say. Writers should get out and live in the real world, observe real people, learn the rhymes and rhythms of the way people speak and behave. Science fiction actually isn't about the future, or about technology, or about anything except human beings loving, hating, fearing, hoping. The characters may be in strange and alien surroundings, but good science fiction is first and foremost about people—the same as all good fiction.

**Any anecdotes regarding the story or your experiences as a fledgling writer?**

Well, shortly after "A Long Way Back" was published I received a phone call from Isaac Asimov. We both lived in the Boston area at that time and we were socially friendly. Isaac told me that Cele Goldsmith had asked him to write a nonfiction series for *Amazing* about extraterrestrial life. Isaac blithely told me that he informed Cele that he was too busy to do it, but his good friend Ben Bova would tackle the job, and Ben knew more about the subject than he (Isaac) did. I nearly dropped the phone and fainted. Isaac cheerfully explained that he would tell me everything he knew about extraterrestrial life, and surely I must know a thing or two that he didn't, so I would know more about the subject than he did! Cele did indeed ask me to do the series, Isaac did indeed tell me all he knew, and the series helped to establish my name in the science fiction audience.

# Possible to Rue
## by Piers Anthony

I want a pegasus, Daddy," Junior greeted him at the door, his curly blond head bobbling with excitement. "A small one, with white fluttery wings and an aerodynamic tail and—"

"You shall have it, Son," Daddy said warmly, absent-mindedly stripping off jacket and tie. Next week was Bradley Newton, Jr.'s sixth birthday, and Bradley, Senior had promised a copy of *Now We Are Six* and a pet for his very own. Newton was a man of means, so that this was no empty pledge. He felt he owed it to the boy, to make up in some token the sorrow of Mrs. N's untimely departure.

He eased himself into the upholstered chair, vaguely pleased that his son showed such imagination. Another child would have demanded something commonplace, like a mongrel or a Shetland pony. But a pegasus now—

"Do you mean the winged horse, Son?" Newton inquired, a thin needle of doubt poking into his complacency.

"That's right, Daddy," Junior said brightly. "But it will have to be a very small one, because I want a pegasus that can really fly. A full grown animal's wings are non-functional because the proportionate wing span is insufficient to get it off the ground."

"I understand, Son," Newton said quickly. "A small one." People had laughed when he had insisted that Junior's nurse have a graduate degree in general science. Fortunately he had been able to obtain one inexpensively by hiring her away from the school board. At this moment he regretted that it was her day off; Junior could be very single-minded.

"Look, Son," he temporized. "I'm not sure I know where to buy a horse like that. And you'll have to know how to feed it and care for it, otherwise it would get sick and die. You wouldn't want that to happen, would you?

The boy pondered. "You're right, Daddy," he said at last. "We would be well advised to look it up."

"Look it up?"

"In the encyclopedia, Daddy. Haven't you always told me that it was an authoritative factual reference?"

The light dawned. Junior believed in the encyclopedia. "My very words, Son. Let's look it up and see what it says about . . . let's see . . . here's *Opinion to Possibility* . . . should be in this volume. Yes." He found the place and read aloud. "'Pegasus—Horse with wings which sprang from the blood of the Gorgon Medusa after Perseus cut off her head.'"

Junior's little mouth dropped open. "That has got to be figurative," he pronounced. "Horses are not created from—"

"'. . . a creature of Greek mythology,'" Newton finished victoriously.

Junior digested that. "You mean, it doesn't exist," he said dispiritedly. Then he brightened. "Daddy, if I ask for something that does exist, then can I have it for a pet?"

"Certainly, Son. We'll just look it up here, and if the book says it's real, we'll go out and get one. I think that's a fair bargain."

"A unicorn," Junior said.

Newton restrained a smile. He reached for the volume marked *Trust to Wary* and flipped the pages. "'Unicorn—A mythological creature resembling a horse—'" he began.

Junior looked at him suspiciously. "Next year I'm going to school and learn to read for myself," he muttered. "You are alleging that there is no such animal?"

"That's what the book says, Son—honest."

The boy looked dubious, but decided not to make an issue of it. "All right— let's try a zebra." He watched while Newton pulled out *Watchful to Indices*. "It's only fair to warn you, Daddy," he said ominously, "that there is a picture of one on the last page of my alphabet book."

"I'll read you just exactly what it says, Son," Newton said defensively. "Here it is: 'Zebra—A striped horselike animal reputed to have lived in Africa. Common in European and American legend, although entirely mythical—'"

"Now you're making that up," Junior accused angrily. "I've got a picture."

"But Son—I thought it was real myself. I've never seen a zebra, but I thought— look. You have a picture of a ghost too, don't you? But you know that's not real."

There was a hard set to Junior's jaw. "The examples are not analogous. Spirits are preternatural—"

"Why don't we try another animal?" Newton cut in. "We can come back to the zebra later."

"Mule," Junior said sullenly.

Newton reddened, then realized that the boy was not being personal. He withdrew the volume covering *Morphine to Opiate* silently. He was somewhat shaken up by the turn events had taken. Imagine spending all his life believing in an animal that didn't exist. Yet of course it was stupid to swear by a horse with prison stripes . . .

"'Mule,'" he read. "'The offspring of the mare and the male ass. A very large, strong hybrid, sure-footed with remarkable sagacity. A creature of folklore, although, like the unicorn and zebra, widely accepted by the credulous. . . .'"

His son looked at him. "Horse," he said.

Newton somewhat warily opened *Hoax to Imaginary*. He was glad he wasn't credulous himself. "Right you are, Son. 'Horse—A fabled hoofed creature prevalent in mythology. A very fleet four-footed animal complete with flowing mane, hairy tail and benevolent disposition. Metallic shoes supposedly worn by the animal are valued as good luck charms, in much the same manner as the unicorn's horn—'"

Junior clouded up dangerously. "Now wait a minute, Son," Newton spluttered. "I know that's wrong. I've seen horses myself. Why, they use them in TV westerns—"

"The reasoning is specious," Junior muttered but his heart wasn't in it.

"Look, Son—I'll prove it. I'll call the race track I used to place—I mean, I used to go there to see the horses. Maybe they'll let us visit the stables." Newton dialed with a quivering finger; spoke into the phone. A brief frustrated interchange later he slammed the received down again. "They race dogs now," he said.

He fumbled through the yellow pages, refusing to let himself think. The book skipped rebelliously from Homes to Hospital. He rattled the bar for the operator to demand the number of the nearest horse farm, then angrily dialed "O"; after some confusion he ended up talking to "Horsepower, Inc.," a tractor dealer.

Junior surveyed the proceedings with profound disgust.

"Methinks the queen protests too much," he quoted sweetly.

In desperation, Newton called a neighbor. "Listen, Sam—do you know anybody around here who owns a horse? I promised my boy I'd show him one today. . . ."

Sam's laughter echoed back over the wire. "You're a card, Brad. Horses, yet. Do you teach him to believe in fairies too?"

Newton reluctantly accepted defeat. "I guess I was wrong about the horse, Son," he said awkwardly. "I could have sworn—but never mind. Just proves a man is never too old to make a mistake. Why don't you pick something else for your pet? Tell you—whatever you choose, I'll give you a matched pair."

Junior cheered up somewhat. He was quick to recognize a net gain. "How about a bird?"

Newton smiled in heartfelt relief. "That would be fine, Son, just fine. What kind did you have in mind?"

"Well," Junior said thoughtfully, "I think I'd like a big bird. A real big bird, like a roc, or maybe a harpy—"

Newton reached for *Possible to Rue*.

# Piers Anthony

A *New York Times* best seller many times over, Piers Anthony has been a major figure within the speculative fiction genre since the publication of his first novel, *Chthon*, in 1967, and its subsequent nominations for both Hugo and Nebula awards. Yet Anthony truly came into his own a decade later with *A Spell for Chameleon*, the first novel in the wildly popular Xanth series which is currently 34 books long and growing, its unique brand of lighthearted fantasy remaining a seemingly eternal staple of the genre.

With more than a hundred different novels and collections in print (including one title for each letter of the alphabet, from *Anthonoloy* to *Zombie Lover*), Piers Anthony is one of the most prominent and prolific SF writers of all time, and his work continues to inspire video games, board games, and as-of-yet unreleased films—as well as plenty of other authors. Yet while many fans consider *A Spell for Chameleon* the beginning for Piers Anthony, and scholars might correctly place *Chthon* as his first major appearance on the SF scene, the true origins of Anthony's career lie in a deceptively small story called "Possible to Rue."

**Looking back, what do you think still works well in this story? Why?**

I reread "Possible to Rue" 45 years later, and it strikes me as sharply written. The father-son dialogue remains apt, especially the aspect of the child seeming smarter than the parent. I like the ranges of the encyclopedia volumes, which eerily reflect the concerns of the father. And I like the insidious progression of seeming reality to fantasy. Anything looked up in this reference tends to become mythical. Where will it end? That's the concluding question. So I remain satisfied.

**If you were writing this today, what would you do differently? What are the story's weaknesses, and how would you change them?**

I think the story works as a teasing question, "What if?" I wouldn't change it.

**What inspired this story? How did it take shape? Where was it initially published?**

"Possible to Rue" was initially published in the April 1963 issue of *Fantastic* magazine. I believe the story was inspired by the way encyclopedias mark their volumes—AMERI to AUSTR, for example. Suppose such identifying alphabetical spans became more meaningful?

**Where were you in your life when you published this piece, and what kind of impact did it have?**

I was in my first trial year of staying home and writing, while my wife worked to support us. I owe my subsequent career to her support. Making that first sale was a terrific lift—but let's face it, the $20 I got for it wasn't enough to live on. Mainly it proved that I could write well enough to get published.

**How has your writing changed over the years, both stylistically and in terms of your writing process?**

I can't be sure how my writing has changed over the years, as I always tried to orient on the market I was trying for. I did move into novels, but for an economic reason: they paid more.

**What advice do you have for aspiring authors?**

Have a working spouse.

**Any anecdotes regarding the story or your experiences as a fledgling writer?**

One, with mixed emotions. For years my wife was the main breadwinner in our family, her income larger and more dependable. Then I started getting more successful. When she discovered that her whole annual income was enough to cover only the income tax on my income, she quit in disgust. She has not had to work since. I also tease my smart younger daughter, saying that for years I struggled to get rich enough to send her to college, and then she went on scholarship. Such are the problems of success. I recommend them to other writers interested in that situation.

# Craphound
## by Cory Doctorow

C raphound had wicked yard-sale karma, for a rotten, filthy alien bastard. He was too good at panning out the single grain of gold in a raging river of uselessness for me not to like him—respect him, anyway. But then he found the cowboy trunk. It was two months' rent to me and nothing but some squirrelly alien kitsch-fetish to Craphound.

So I did the unthinkable. I violated the Code. I got into a bidding war with a buddy. Never let them tell you that women poison friendships: in my experience, wounds from women-fights heal quickly; fights over garbage leave nothing behind but scorched earth.

Craphound spotted the sign—his karma, plus the goggles in his exoskeleton, gave him the advantage when we were doing 80 kmh on some stretch of back-highway in cottage country. He was riding shotgun while I drove, and we had the radio on to the CBC's summer-Saturday programming: eight weekends with eight hours of old radio dramas: "The Shadow," "Quiet Please," "Tom Mix," "The Crypt-Keeper" with Bela Lugosi. It was hour three, and Bogey was phoning in his performance on a radio adaptation of *The African Queen*. I had the windows of the old truck rolled down so that I could smoke without fouling Craphound's breather. My arm was hanging out the window, the radio was booming, and Craphound said, "Turn around! Turn around, now, Jerry, now, turn around!"

When Craphound gets that excited, it's a sign that he's spotted a rich vein. I checked the side-mirror quickly, pounded the brakes and spun around. The transmission creaked, the wheels squealed, and then we were creeping along the way we'd come.

"There," Craphound said, gesturing with his long, skinny arm. I saw it. A wooden A-frame real-estate sign, a piece of hand-lettered cardboard stuck overtop of the realtor's name:

EAST MUSKOKA VOLUNTEER FIRE-DEPT
LADIES AUXILIARY RUMMAGE SALE
SAT 25 JUNE

"Hoo-eee!" I hollered, and spun the truck onto the dirt road. I gunned the engine as we cruised along the tree-lined road, trusting Craphound to spot any deer, signs, or hikers in time to avert disaster. The sky was a perfect blue and the smells of summer were all around us. I snapped off the radio and listened to the wind rushing through the truck. Ontario is *beautiful* in the summer.

"There!" Craphound shouted. I hit the turn-off and down-shifted and then we were back on a paved road. Soon, we were rolling into a country fire-station, an ugly brick barn. The hall was lined with long, folding tables, stacked high. The mother lode!

Craphound beat me out the door, as usual. His exoskeleton is programmable, so he can record little scripts for it like: move left arm to door handle, pop it, swing legs out to running-board, jump to ground, close door, move forward. Meanwhile, I'm still making sure I've switched off the headlights and that I've got my wallet.

Two blue-haired grannies had a card-table set up out front of the hall, with a big tin pitcher of lemonade and three boxes of Tim Horton assorted donuts. That stopped us both, since we share the superstition that you *always* buy food from old ladies and little kids, as a sacrifice to the crap-gods. One of the old ladies poured out the lemonade while the other smiled and greeted us.

"Welcome, welcome! My, you've come a long way for us!"

"Just up from Toronto, ma'am," I said. It's an old joke, but it's also part of the ritual, and it's got to be done.

"I meant your friend, sir. This gentleman."

Craphound smiled without baring his gums and sipped his lemonade. "Of course I came, dear lady. I wouldn't miss it for the worlds!" His accent is pretty good, but when it comes to stock phrases like this, he's got so much polish you'd think he was reading the news.

The biddie *blushed* and *giggled*, and I felt faintly sick. I walked off to the tables, trying not to hurry. I chose my first spot, about halfway down, where things wouldn't be quite so picked-over. I grabbed an empty box from underneath and started putting stuff into it: four matched highball glasses with gold crossed bowling-pins and a line of black around the rim; an Expo '67 wall-hanging that wasn't even a little faded; a shoebox full of late sixties O-Pee-Chee hockey cards; a worn, wooden-handled steel cleaver that you could butcher a steer with.

I picked up my box and moved on: a deck of playing cards copyrighted '57, with the logo for the Royal Canadian Dairy, Bala Ontario printed on the backs; a fireman's cap with a brass badge so tarnished I couldn't read it; a three-story wedding-cake trophy for the 1974 Eastern Region Curling Championships. The cash-register in my mind was ringing, ringing, ringing. God bless the East Muskoka Volunteer Fire Department Ladies' Auxiliary.

I'd mined that table long enough. I moved to the other end of the hall. Time was, I'd start at the beginning and turn over each item, build one pile of maybes and another pile of definites, try to strategize. In time, I came to rely on instinct and on the fates, to whom I make my obeisances at every opportunity.

Let's hear it for the fates: a genuine collapsible top-hat; a white-tipped evening cane; a hand-carved cherry-wood walking stick; a beautiful black lace parasol; a wrought-iron lightning rod with a rooster on top; all of it in an elephant-leg umbrella-stand. I filled the box, folded it over, and started on another.

I collided with Craphound. He grinned his natural grin, the one that showed row on row of wet, slimy gums, tipped with writhing, poisonous suckers. "Gold! Gold!" he said, and moved along. I turned my head after him, just as he bent over the cowboy trunk.

I sucked air between my teeth. It was magnificent: a leather-bound miniature steamer trunk, the leather worked with lariats, Stetson hats, war-bonnets and six-guns. I moved toward him, and he popped the latch. I caught my breath.

On top, there was a kid's cowboy costume: miniature leather chaps, a tiny Stetson, a pair of scuffed white-leather cowboy boots with long, worn spurs affixed to the heels. Craphound moved it reverently to the table and continued to pull more magic from the trunk's depths: a stack of cardboard-bound Hopalong Cassidy 78s; a pair of tin six-guns with gunbelt and holsters; a silver star that said Sheriff; a bundle of Roy Rogers comics tied with twine, in mint condition; and a leather satchel filled with plastic cowboys and Indians, enough to reenact the Alamo.

"Oh, my God," I breathed, as he spread the loot out on the table.

"What are these, Jerry?" Craphound asked, holding up the 78s.

"Old records, like LPs, but you need a special record player to listen to them." I took one out of its sleeve. It gleamed, scratch-free, in the overhead fluorescents.

"I got a 78 player here," said a member of the East Muskoka Volunteer Fire Department Ladies' Auxiliary. She was short enough to look Craphound in the eye, a hair under five feet, and had a skinny, rawboned look to her. "That's my Billy's things, Billy the Kid we called him. He was dotty for cowboys when he was a boy. Couldn't get him to take off that fool outfit—nearly got him thrown out of school. He's a lawyer now, in Toronto, got a fancy office on Bay Street. I called him to ask if he minded my putting his cowboy things in the sale, and you know what? He didn't know what I was talking about! Doesn't that beat everything? He was dotty for cowboys when he was a boy."

It's another of my rituals to smile and nod and be as polite as possible to the erstwhile owners of crap that I'm trying to buy, so I smiled and nodded and examined the 78 player she had produced. In lariat script, on the top, it said, "Official Bob Wills Little Record Player," and had a crude watercolour of Bob Wills and His Texas Playboys grinning on the front. It was the kind of record player that folded up like a suitcase when you weren't using it. I'd had one as a kid, with Yogi Bear silkscreened on the front.

Billy's mom plugged the yellowed cord into a wall jack and took the 78 from me, touched the stylus to the record. A tinny ukelele played, accompanied by horse-clops, and then a narrator with a deep, whisky voice said, "Howdy, pardners! I was just settin' down by the ole campfire. Why don't you stay an' have some beans, an' I'll tell y'all the story of how Hopalong Cassidy beat the Duke Gang when they come to rob the Santa Fe."

In my head, I was already breaking down the cowboy trunk and its contents, thinking about the minimum bid I'd place on each item at Sotheby's. Sold individually, I figured I could get over two grand for the contents. Then I thought about putting ads in some of the Japanese collectors' magazines, just for a lark, before I sent the lot to the auction house. You never can tell. A buddy I knew had sold a complete packaged set of "Welcome Back, Kotter" action figures for nearly eight grand that way. Maybe I could buy a new truck . . .

"This is wonderful," Craphound said, interrupting my reverie. "How much would you like for the collection?"

I felt a knife in my guts. Craphound had found the cowboy trunk, so that meant it was his. But he usually let me take the stuff with street-value—he was interested in *everything*, so it hardly mattered if I picked up a few scraps with which to eke out a living.

Billy's mom looked over the stuff. "I was hoping to get twenty dollars for the lot, but if that's too much, I'm willing to come down."

"I'll give you thirty," my mouth said, without intervention from my brain.

They both turned and stared at me. Craphound was unreadable behind his goggles.

Billy's mom broke the silence. "Oh, my! Thirty dollars for this old mess?"

"I will pay fifty," Craphound said.

"Seventy-five," I said.

"Oh, my," Billy's mom said.

"Five hundred," Craphound said.

I opened my mouth, and shut it. Craphound had built his stake on Earth by selling a complicated biochemical process for non-chlorophyll photosynthesis to a Saudi banker. I wouldn't ever beat him in a bidding war. "A thousand dollars," my mouth said.

"Ten thousand," Craphound said, and extruded a roll of hundreds from somewhere in his exoskeleton.

"My Lord!" Billy's mom said. "Ten thousand dollars!"

The other pickers, the firemen, the blue haired ladies all looked up at that and stared at us, their mouths open.

"It is for a good cause." Craphound said.

"Ten thousand dollars!" Billy's mom said again.

Craphound's digits ruffled through the roll as fast as a croupier's counter, separated off a large chunk of the brown bills, and handed them to Billy's mom.

# Craphound

One of the firemen, a middle-aged paunchy man with a comb-over appeared at Billy's mom's shoulder.

"What's going on, Eva?" he said.

"This . . . gentleman is going to pay ten thousand dollars for Billy's old cowboy things, Tom."

The fireman took the money from Billy's mom and stared at it. He held up the top note under the light and turned it this way and that, watching the holographic stamp change from green to gold, then green again. He looked at the serial number, then the serial number of the next bill. He licked his forefinger and started counting off the bills in piles of ten. Once he had ten piles, he counted them again. "That's ten thousand dollars, all right. Thank you very much, mister. Can I give you a hand getting this to your car?"

Craphound, meanwhile, had re-packed the trunk and balanced the 78 player on top of it. He looked at me, then at the fireman.

"I wonder if I could impose on you to take me to the nearest bus station. I think I'm going to be making my own way home."

The fireman and Billy's mom both stared at me. My cheeks flushed. "Aw, c'mon," I said. "I'll drive you home."

"I think I prefer the bus," Craphound said.

"It's no trouble at all to give you a lift, friend," the fireman said.

I called it quits for the day, and drove home alone with the truck only half-filled. I pulled it into the coach house and threw a tarp over the load and went inside and cracked a beer and sat on the sofa, watching a nature show on a desert reclamation project in Arizona, where the state legislature had traded a derelict mega-mall and a custom-built habitat to an alien for a local-area weather control machine.

The following Thursday, I went to the little crap-auction house on King Street. I'd put my finds from the weekend in the sale: lower minimum bid, and they took a smaller commission than Sotheby's. Fine for moving the small stuff.

Craphound was there, of course. I knew he'd be. It was where we met, when he bid on a case of Lincoln Logs I'd found at a fire-sale.

I'd known him for a kindred spirit when he bought them, and we'd talked afterwards, at his place, a sprawling, two-story warehouse amid a cluster of auto-wrecking yards where the junkyard dogs barked, barked, barked.

Inside was paradise. His taste ran to shrines—a collection of fifties bar kitsch that was a shrine to liquor; a circular waterbed on a raised podium that was nearly buried under seventies bachelor pad-inalia; a kitchen that was nearly unusable, so packed it was with old barn-board furniture and rural memorabilia; a leather-appointed library straight out of a Victorian gentlemen's club; a solarium dressed in wicker and bamboo and tiki-idols. It was a hell of a place.

Craphound had known all about the Goodwills and the Sally Anns, and the auction houses, and the kitsch boutiques on Queen Street, but he still hadn't figured out where it all came from.

"Yard sales, rummage sales, garage sales," I said, reclining in a vibrating naughahyde easy-chair, drinking a glass of his pricey single-malt that he'd bought for the beautiful bottle it came in.

"But where are these? Who is allowed to make them?" Craphound hunched opposite me, his exoskeleton locked into a coiled, semi-seated position.

"Who? Well, anyone. You just one day decide that you need to clean out the basement, you put an ad in the *Star*, tape up a few signs, and voila, yard sale. Sometimes, a school or a church will get donations of old junk and sell it all at one time, as a fundraiser."

"And how do you locate these?" he asked, bobbing up and down slightly with excitement.

"Well, there're amateurs who just read the ads in the weekend papers, or just pick a neighborhood and wander around, but that's no way to go about it. What I do is, I get in a truck, and I sniff the air, catch the scent of crap and *vroom!*, I'm off like a bloodhound on a trail. You learn things over time: like stay away from Yuppie yard sales, they never have anything worth buying, just the same crap you can buy in any mall."

"Do you think I might accompany you some day?"

"Hell, sure. Next Saturday? We'll head over to Cabbagetown—those old coach houses, you'd be amazed what people get rid of. It's practically criminal."

"I would like to go with you on next Saturday very much Mr. Jerry Abington." He used to talk like that, without commas or question marks. Later, he got better, but then, it was all one big sentence.

"Call me Jerry. It's a date, then. Tell you what, though: there's a Code you got to learn before we go out. The Craphound's Code."

"What is a craphound?"

"You're lookin' at one. You're one, too, unless I miss my guess. You'll get to know some of the local craphounds, you hang around with me long enough. They're the competition, but they're also your buddies, and there're certain rules we have."

And then I explained to him all about how you never bid against a craphound at a yard-sale, how you get to know the other fellows' tastes, and when you see something they might like, you haul it out for them, and they'll do the same for you, and how you never buy something that another craphound might be looking for, if all you're buying it for is to sell it back to him. Just good form and common sense, really, but you'd be surprised how many amateurs just fail to make the jump to pro because they can't grasp it.

There was a bunch of other stuff at the auction, other craphounds' weekend treasures. This was high season, when the sun comes out and people start to clean out the cottage, the basement, the garage. There were some collectors in the crowd, and a whole whack of antique and junk dealers, and a few pickers, and me, and Craphound. I watched the bidding listlessly, waiting for my things to come up and sneaking out for smokes between lots. Craphound never once looked at me or acknowledged my presence, and I became perversely obsessed with catching his eye, so I coughed and shifted and walked past him several times, until the auctioneer glared at me, and one of the attendants asked if I needed a throat lozenge.

My lot came up. The bowling glasses went for five bucks to one of the Queen Street junk dealers; the elephant-foot fetched $350 after a spirited bidding war between an antique dealer and a collector—the collector won; the dealer took the top-hat for $100. The rest of it came up and sold, or didn't, and at end of the lot, I'd made over $800, which was rent for the month plus beer for the weekend plus gas for the truck.

Craphound bid on and bought more cowboy things—a box of super-eight cowboy movies, the boxes mouldy, the stock itself running to slime; a Navajo blanket; a plastic donkey that dispensed cigarettes out of its ass; a big neon armadillo sign.

One of the other nice things about that place over Sotheby's, there was none of this waiting thirty days to get a check. I queued up with the other pickers after the bidding was through, collected a wad of bills, and headed for my truck.

I spotted Craphound loading his haul into a minivan with handicapped plates. It looked like some kind of fungus was growing over the hood and side-panels. On closer inspection, I saw that the body had been covered in closely glued Lego.

Craphound popped the hatchback and threw his gear in, then opened the driver's side door, and I saw that his van had been fitted out for a legless driver, with brake and accelerator levers. A paraplegic I knew drove one just like it. Craphound's exoskeleton levered him into the seat, and I watched the eerily precise way it executed the macro that started the car, pulled the shoulder-belt, put it into drive and switched on the stereo. I heard tape-hiss, then, loud as a b-boy cruising Yonge Street, an old-timey cowboy voice: "Howdy pardners! Saddle up, we're ridin'!" Then the van backed up and sped out of the lot.

I got into the truck and drove home. Truth be told, I missed the little bastard.

Some people said that we should have run Craphound and his kin off the planet, out of the Solar System. They said that it wasn't fair for the aliens to keep us in the dark about their technologies. They say that we should have captured a ship and reverse-engineered it, built our own and kicked ass.

Some people!

First of all, nobody with human DNA could survive a trip in one of those ships. They're part of Craphound's people's bodies, as I understand it, and we just don't have the right parts. Second of all, they *were* sharing their tech with us—they just weren't giving it away. Fair trades every time.

It's not as if space was off-limits to us. We can any one of us visit their home-world, just as soon as we figure out how. Only they wouldn't hold our hands along the way.

I spent the week haunting the "Secret Boutique," AKA the Goodwill As-Is Centre on Jarvis. It's all there is to do between yard sales, and sometimes it makes for good finds. Part of my theory of yard-sale karma holds that if I miss one day at the thrift shops, that'll be the day they put out the big score. So I hit the stores diligently and came up with crapola. I had offended the fates, I knew, and wouldn't make another score until I placated them. It was lonely work, still and all, and I missed Craphound's good eye and obsessive delight.

I was at the cash-register with a few items at the Goodwill when a guy in a suit behind me tapped me on the shoulder.

"Sorry to bother you," he said. His suit looked expensive, as did his manicure and his haircut and his wire-rimmed glasses. "I was just wondering where you found that." He gestured at a rhinestone-studded ukelele, with a cowboy hat wood-burned into the body. I had picked it up with a guilty little thrill, thinking that Craphound might buy it at the next auction.

"Second floor, in the toy section."

"There wasn't anything else like it, was there?"

"'Fraid not," I said, and the cashier picked it up and started wrapping it in newspaper.

"Ah," he said, and he looked like a little kid who'd just been told that he couldn't have a puppy. "I don't suppose you'd want to sell it, would you?"

I held up a hand and waited while the cashier bagged it with the rest of my stuff, a few old clothbound novels I thought I could sell at a used book-store, and a *Grease* belt-buckle with Olivia Newton John on it. I led him out the door by the elbow of his expensive suit.

"How much?" I had paid a dollar.

"Ten bucks?"

I nearly said, "Sold!" but I caught myself. "Twenty."

"Twenty dollars?"

"That's what they'd charge at a boutique on Queen Street."

He took out a slim leather wallet and produced a twenty. I handed him the uke. His face lit up like a lightbulb.

It's not that my adulthood is particularly unhappy. Likewise, it's not that my childhood was particularly happy.

There are memories I have, though, that are like a cool drink of water. My grandfather's place near Milton, an old Victorian farmhouse, where the cat drank out of a milk-glass bowl; and where we sat around a rough pine table as big as my whole apartment; and where my playroom was the draughty barn with hay-filled lofts bulging with farm junk and Tarzan-ropes.

There was Grampa's friend Fyodor, and we spent every evening at his wrecking-yard, he and Grampa talking and smoking while I scampered in the twilight, scaling mountains of auto-junk. The glove-boxes yielded treasures: crumpled photos of college boys mugging in front of signs, roadmaps of far-away places. I found a guidebook from the 1964 New York World's Fair once, and a lipstick like a chrome bullet, and a pair of white leather ladies' gloves.

Fyodor dealt in scrap, too, and once, he had half of a carny carousel, a few horses and part of the canopy, paint flaking and sharp torn edges protruding; next to it, a Korean-war tank minus its turret and treads, and inside the tank were peeling old pinup girls and a rotation schedule and a crude Kilroy. The control-room in the middle of the carousel had a stack of paperback sci-fi novels, Ace Doubles that had two books bound back-to-back, and when you finished the first, you turned it over and read the other. Fyodor let me keep them, and there was a pawn-ticket in one from Macon, Georgia, for a transistor radio.

My parents started leaving me alone when I was fourteen and I couldn't keep from sneaking into their room and snooping. Mom's jewelry box had books of matches from their honeymoon in Acapulco, printed with bad palm-trees. My Dad kept an old photo in his sock drawer, of himself on muscle-beach, shirtless, flexing his biceps.

My grandmother saved every scrap of my mother's life in her basement, in dusty Army trunks. I entertained myself by pulling it out and taking it in: her Mouse Ears from the big family train-trip to Disneyland in '57, and her records, and the glittery pasteboard sign from her sweet sixteen. There were well-chewed stuffed animals, and school exercise books in which she'd practiced variations on her signature for page after page.

It all told a story. The penciled Kilroy in the tank made me see one of those Canadian soldiers in Korea, unshaven and crew-cut like an extra on "M*A*S*H," sitting for bored hour after hour, staring at the pinup girls, fiddling with a cross-word, finally laying it down and sketching his Kilroy quickly, before anyone saw.

The photo of my Dad posing sent me whirling through time to Toronto's Muscle Beach in the east end, and hearing the tinny AM radios playing weird psychedelic rock while teenagers lounged on their Mustangs and the girls sun-bathed in bikinis that made their tits into torpedoes.

It all made poems. The old pulp novels and the pawn ticket, when I spread them out in front of the TV, and arranged them just so, they made up a poem that took my breath away.

After the cowboy trunk episode, I didn't run into Craphound again until the annual Rotary Club charity rummage sale at the Upper Canada Brewing Company. He was wearing the cowboy hat, six-guns and the silver star from the cowboy trunk. It should have looked ridiculous, but the net effect was naive and somehow charming, like he was a little boy whose hair you wanted to muss.

I found a box of nice old melamine dishes, in various shades of green—four square plates, bowls, salad-plates, and a serving tray. I threw them in the duffel-bag I'd brought and kept browsing, ignoring Craphound as he charmed a salty old Rotarian while fondling a box of leather-bound books.

I browsed a stack of old Ministry of Labour licenses—barber, chiropodist, bartender, watchmaker. They all had pretty seals and were framed in stark green institutional metal. They all had different names, but all from one family, and I made up a little story to entertain myself, about the proud mother saving her sons' framed accreditations and hanging them in the spare room with their diplomas. "Oh, George Junior's just opened his own barbershop, and little Jimmy's still fixing watches . . ."

I bought them.

In a box of crappy plastic Little Ponies and Barbies and Care Bears, I found a leather Indian headdress, a wooden bow-and-arrow set, and a fringed buckskin vest. Craphound was still buttering up the leather books' owner. I bought them quick, for five bucks.

"Those are beautiful," a voice said at my elbow. I turned around and smiled at the snappy dresser who'd bought the uke at the Secret Boutique. He'd gone casual for the weekend, in an expensive, L. L. Bean button-down way.

"Aren't they, though."

"You sell them on Queen Street? Your finds, I mean?"

"Sometimes. Sometimes at auction. How's the uke?"

"Oh, I got it all tuned up," he said, and smiled the same smile he'd given me when he'd taken hold of it at Goodwill. "I can play 'Don't Fence Me In' on it." He looked at his feet. "Silly, huh?"

"Not at all. You're into cowboy things, huh?" As I said it, I was overcome with the knowledge that this was "Billy the Kid," the original owner of the cowboy trunk. I don't know why I felt that way, but I did, with utter certainty.

"Just trying to re-live a piece of my childhood, I guess. I'm Scott," he said, extending his hand.

*Scott?* I thought wildly. *Maybe it's his middle name?* "I'm Jerry."

The Upper Canada Brewery sale has many things going for it, including a beer garden where you can sample their wares and get a good BBQ burger. We gently gravitated to it, looking over the tables as we went.

"You're a pro, right?" he asked after we had plastic cups of beer.

"You could say that."

"I'm an amateur. A rank amateur. Any words of wisdom?"

I laughed and drank some beer, lit a cigarette. "There's no secret to it, I think. Just diligence: you've got to go out every chance you get, or you'll miss the big score."

He chuckled. "I hear that. Sometimes, I'll be sitting in my office, and I'll just *know* that they're putting out a piece of pure gold at the Goodwill and that someone else will get to it before my lunch. I get so wound up, I'm no good until I go down there and hunt for it. I guess I'm hooked, eh?"

"Cheaper than some other kinds of addictions."

"I guess so. About that Indian stuff—what do you figure you'd get for it at a Queen Street boutique?"

I looked him in the eye. He may have been something high-powered and cool and collected in his natural environment, but just then, he was as eager and nervous as a kitchen-table poker-player at a high-stakes game.

"Maybe fifty bucks," I said.

"Fifty, huh?" he asked.

"About that," I said.

"Once it sold," he said.

"There is that," I said.

"Might take a month, might take a year," he said.

"Might take a day," I said.

"It might, it might." He finished his beer. "I don't suppose you'd take forty?"

I'd paid five for it, not ten minutes before. It looked like it would fit Craphound, who, after all, was wearing Scott/Billy's own boyhood treasures as we spoke. You don't make a living by feeling guilty over eight hundred percent markups. Still, I'd angered the fates, and needed to redeem myself.

"Make it five," I said.

He started to say something, then closed his mouth and gave me a look of thanks. He took a five out of his wallet and handed it to me. I pulled the vest and bow and headdress out my duffel.

He walked back to a shiny black Jeep with gold detail work, parked next to Craphound's van. Craphound was building onto the Lego body, and the hood had a miniature Lego town attached to it.

Craphound looked around as he passed, and leaned forward with undisguised interest at the booty. I grimaced and finished my beer.

I met Scott/Billy three times more at the Secret Boutique that week.

He was a lawyer, who specialized in alien-technology patents. He had a practice on Bay Street, with two partners, and despite his youth, he was the senior man.

I didn't let on that I knew about Billy the Kid and his mother in the East Muskoka Volunteer Fire Department Ladies' Auxiliary. But I felt a bond with him, as though we shared an unspoken secret. I pulled any cowboy finds for him, and he developed a pretty good eye for what I was after and returned the favour.

The fates were with me again, and no two ways about it. I took home a ratty old Oriental rug that on closer inspection was a 19th century hand-knotted Persian; an upholstered Turkish footstool; a collection of hand-painted silk Hawaiiana pillows and a carved Meerschaum pipe. Scott/Billy found the last for me, and it cost me two dollars. I knew a collector who would pay thirty in an eye-blink, and from then on, as far as I was concerned, Scott/Billy was a fellow craphound.

"You going to the auction tomorrow night?" I asked him at the checkout line.

"Wouldn't miss it," he said. He'd barely been able to contain his excitement when I told him about the Thursday night auctions and the bargains to be had there. He sure had the bug.

"Want to get together for dinner beforehand? The Rotterdam's got a good patio."

He did, and we did, and I had a glass of framboise that packed a hell of a kick and tasted like fizzy raspberry lemonade; and doorstopper fries and a club sandwich.

I had my nose in my glass when he kicked my ankle under the table. "Look at that!"

It was Craphound in his van, cruising for a parking spot. The Lego village had been joined by a whole postmodern spaceport on the roof, with a red-and-blue castle, a football-sized flying saucer, and a clown's head with blinking eyes.

I went back to my drink and tried to get my appetite back.

"Was that an extee driving?"

"Yeah. Used to be a friend of mine."

"He's a picker?"

"Uh-huh." I turned back to my fries and tried to kill the subject.

"Do you know how he made his stake?"

"The chlorophyll thing, in Saudi Arabia."

"Sweet!" he said. "Very sweet. I've got a client who's got some secondary patents from that one. What's he go after?"

"Oh, pretty much everything," I said, resigning myself to discussing the topic after all. "But lately, the same as you—cowboys and Injuns."

He laughed and smacked his knee. "Well, what do you know? What could he possibly want with the stuff?"

"What do they want with any of it? He got started one day when we were cruising the Muskokas," I said carefully, watching his face. "Found a trunk of old cowboy things at a rummage sale. East Muskoka Volunteer Fire Department Ladies' Auxiliary." I waited for him to shout or startle. He didn't.

"Yeah? A good find, I guess. Wish I'd made it."

I didn't know what to say to that, so I took a bite of my sandwich.

Scott continued. "I think about what they get out of it a lot. There's nothing we have here that they couldn't make for themselves. I mean, if they picked up and left today, we'd still be making sense of everything they gave us in a hundred years. You know, I just closed a deal for a biochemical computer that's no-shit 10,000 times faster than anything we've built out of silicon. You know what the extee took in trade? Title to a defunct fairground outside of Calgary—they shut it down ten years ago because the midway was too unsafe to ride. Doesn't that beat all? This thing is worth a billion dollars right out of the gate, I mean, within twenty-four hours of the deal closing, the seller can turn it into the GDP of Bolivia. For a crummy real-estate dog that you couldn't get five grand for!"

It always shocked me when Billy/Scott talked about his job—it was easy to forget that he was a high-powered lawyer when we were jawing and fooling around like old craphounds. I wondered if maybe he *wasn't* Billy the Kid; I couldn't think of any reason for him to be playing it all so close to his chest.

"What the hell is some extee going to do with a fairground?"

Craphound got a free Coke from Lisa at the check-in when he made his appearance. He bid high, but shrewdly, and never pulled ten-thousand-dollar stunts. The bidders were wandering the floor, previewing that week's stock, and making notes to themselves.

I rooted through a box-lot full of old tins, and found one with a buckaroo at the Calgary Stampede, riding a bucking bronc. I picked it up and stood to inspect it. Craphound was behind me.

"Nice piece, huh?" I said to him.

"I like it very much," Craphound said, and I felt my cheeks flush.

"You're going to have some competition tonight, I think," I said, and nodded at Scott/Billy. "I think he's Billy; the one whose mother sold us—you—the cowboy trunk."

"Really?" Craphound said, and it felt like we were partners again, scoping out the competition. Suddenly I felt a knife of shame, like I was betraying Scott/Billy somehow. I took a step back.

"Jerry, I am very sorry that we argued."

I sighed out a breath I hadn't known I was holding in. "Me, too."

"They're starting the bidding. May I sit with you?"

And so the three of us sat together, and Craphound shook Scott/Billy's hand and the auctioneer started into his harangue.

It was a night for unusual occurrences. I bid on a piece, something I told myself I'd never do. It was a set of four matched Li'l Orphan Annie Ovaltine glasses, like Grandma's had been, and seeing them in the auctioneer's hand took me right back to her kitchen, and endless afternoons passed with my coloring books and weird old-lady hard candies and Liberace albums playing in the living room.

"Ten," I said, opening the bidding.

"I got ten, ten, ten, I got ten, who'll say twenty, who'll say twenty, twenty for the four."

Craphound waved his bidding card, and I jumped as if I'd been stung.

"I got twenty from the space cowboy, I got twenty, sir will you say thirty?"

I waved my card.

"That's thirty to you sir."

"Forty," Craphound said.

"Fifty," I said even before the auctioneer could point back to me. An old pro, he settled back and let us do the work.

"One hundred," Craphound said.

"One fifty," I said.

The room was perfectly silent. I thought about my overextended MasterCard, and wondered if Scott/Billy would give me a loan.

"Two hundred," Craphound said.

Fine, I thought. Pay two hundred for those. I can get a set on Queen Street for thirty bucks.

The auctioneer turned to me. "The bidding stands at two. Will you say two-ten, sir?"

I shook my head. The auctioneer paused a long moment, letting me sweat over the decision to bow out.

"I have two—do I have any other bids from the floor? Any other bids? Sold, $200, to number 57." An attendant brought Craphound the glasses. He took them and tucked them under his seat.

I was fuming when we left. Craphound was at my elbow. I wanted to punch him—I'd never punched anyone in my life, but I wanted to punch him.

We entered the cool night air and I sucked in several lungfuls before lighting a cigarette.

"Jerry," Craphound said.

I stopped, but didn't look at him. I watched the taxis pull in and out of the garage next door instead.

"Jerry, my friend," Craphound said.

"WHAT?" I said, loud enough to startle myself. Scott, beside me, jerked as well.

"We're going. I wanted to say goodbye, and to give you some things that I won't be taking with me."

"What?" I said again, Scott just a beat behind me.

"My people—we're going. It has been decided. We've gotten what we came for."

Without another word, he set off towards his van. We followed along behind, shell-shocked.

Craphound's exoskeleton executed another macro and slid the panel-door aside, revealing the cowboy trunk.

"I wanted to give you this. I will keep the glasses."

"I don't understand," I said.

"You're all leaving?" Scott asked, with a note of urgency.

"It has been decided. We'll go over the next twenty-four hours."

"But why?" Scott said, sounding almost petulant.

"It's not something that I can easily explain. As you must know, the things we gave you were trinkets to us—almost worthless. We traded them for something that was almost worthless to you—a fair trade, you'll agree—but it's time to move on."

Craphound handed me the cowboy trunk. Holding it, I smelled the lubricant from his exoskeleton and the smell of the attic it had been mummified in before making its way into his hands. I felt like I almost understood.

"This is for me," I said slowly, and Craphound nodded encouragingly. "This is for me, and you're keeping the glasses. And I'll look at this and feel . . ."

"You understand," Craphound said, looking somehow relieved.

And I did. I understood that an alien wearing a cowboy hat and six-guns and giving them away was a poem and a story, and a thirtyish bachelor trying to spend half a month's rent on four glasses so that he could remember his Grandma's kitchen was a story and a poem, and that the disused fairground outside Calgary was a story and a poem, too.

"You're craphounds!" I said. "All of you!"

Craphound smiled so I could see his gums and I put down the cowboy trunk and clapped my hands.

# Cory Doctorow

S atirized in the popular webcomic *xkcd* as the poster child for the "blo-gosphere," *New York Times* best seller Cory Doctorow has a reputation far greater than his relatively recent emergence into popular culture might suggest. A fellow of the Electronic Frontiers Foundation and the co-editor of *Boing Boing*, Cory Doctorow is a tastemaker and spokesman for an entire generation of geeks and techies. From his electronic podium, Doctorow has lobbied for liberalization of copyright laws, increased file-sharing, and the death of DRM, preaching that information deserves to be free. Moreover, he's not afraid to put his money where his mouth is, releasing electronic versions of his own books for free under a Creative Commons license, beginning with his first novel, *Down and Out in the Magic Kingdom*, which won the Locus Award.

Yet despite his personal celebrity and prodigious journalistic writings for publications such as *Popular Science*, *Make*, and *Wired*, it's Cory Doctorow's fiction that truly makes him stand out. An author of both short stories and nov-els, ranging from technology-driven hard science fiction to fairy-tale fantasy, Doctorow maintains a singular mastery of current trends, vernacular, and Internet culture, lending his stories a unique air of authenticity. His writings have won several Sunburst Awards, the John W. Campbell Memorial Award, and the Prometheus Award, and Doctorow himself won the 2007 Electronic Frontiers Foundation Pioneer Award for "the empowerment of individuals in using computers."

Along with his technological acumen, Doctorow has another widely known passion: a fascination with junk and kitsch that first reared its head in the story "Craphound." Though not technically his first publication, as he had sold several stories to semi-pro zines while still a teenager, "Craphound" represents Doctorow's first major sale, and is where he feels his writing career truly began.

**Looking back, what do you think still works well in this story? Why?**

The two things that were really going for the story were, one, the reverence for junk—and not the caliber of junk you get today, but junk when junk really meant something. We've been on this steady march of junk . . . when there was very little, everything got recycled and reused, but in that first blossoming after World War II, you got a really nice standard of junk. There were a lot of con-sumer goods, more than we could readily consume. We could improve stuff so fast that making it to last didn't make any sense—we started building things to fall apart. That was the golden age of junk. After the great deflowering of junk, when manufacturing in China and the Far East took off, it was replaced by a torrent of junk. We're rightfully nostalgic for that period when things were cheap but not hasty, when that specialness of being given a physical thing still remained. We were overwhelmed in 2005 or 2006. Physical objects have become kind of a burden, but back then they were still novelties.

The second thing that makes the story something you can really chew on is the mystery at the end. What is it that Craphound realizes? That the narrator realizes? What does it mean that this stuff is a story and a poem? It's a story that asks a lot of questions while evoking a lot of emotions.

**If you were writing this today, what would you do differently? What are the story's weaknesses, and how would you change them?**

If I were writing this today, I would have to tell the story of junk after this period. This was published before the World Trade Organization agreements and China's entry onto the manufacturing scene. It misses the big story of junk which was lurking just around the corner, more so than the nostalgia. I also think that one of the things that made that story so timely is that it hit at the dawn of eBay, a moment in North American cultural identity when suddenly the contents of every attic were available easily online. What was a lifelong quest became instantaneous gratification. In the past, you might spend ten years poking your head into second-hand bookstores searching for that one particular edition of a book you loved in first grade. Now it's ten seconds.

**What inspired this story? How did it take shape? Where was it initially published?**

This was originally published in *Science Fiction Age*, now sadly departed. Scott Edelman was the editor, and he had already hired me to write columns for him—a proto-blog about what was cool on the web—six times a year. That was back when they thought you could actually tell people about the web in print media. Scott had three amazing things going for him. First, he was sweet and nice to write for, and really responsive. Second, he was *fast*. Most editors in those days turned manuscripts around in the three hundred to five hundred a day range. If you'd written a manuscript that warranted a second or third read, it could take forever to hear back—the curse of being nearly good enough. Scott was good about turning it around more or less overnight, maybe in four or five days . . . and that from Canada! Last, Scott also paid *really* well—ten cents per word when most markets were paying four.

As for the inspiration, at the time I was living in this wonderful warehouse with two thousand square feet and a loft—an illegal rental, filled with a very bohemian community of artists and technological people. One of the things about all that space is that I was able to slowly fill it with all this junk I found at yard sales and things. I'd worked for several years at a great science fiction store called Bakka, and learned from the guy who lived in the apartment upstairs and worked as a picker. On slow days he would come down and spread out his finds for the day on the counter to show us.

**Where were you in your life when you published this piece, and what kind of impact did it have?**

I had always wanted to be a writer, and started selling to semi-pro markets when I was seventeen. Then I went to Clarion and hit a drought—I had about five years when I couldn't write anything. I'd gone from having some promising sales as a teenager to nothing, and was about to give up, when suddenly Scott and Gardner Dozois each bought a story within two weeks. Although it didn't change the world, "Craphound" was very well regarded, and it really set me back on my feet and got me writing again, recovered my confidence. A couple of years later I won the John W. Campbell Award. John Scalzi (another Campbell winner, who follows these things more than I do) says I'm the last one to win based on short stories rather than novels.

**How has your writing changed over the years, both stylistically and in terms of your writing process?**

My process is a lot less dependent on inspiration now. Inspiration is a shitty way to write. If you spend your life waiting for it while wanting to write for a living, you'll be a miserable bastard. Writing is something I do every day, a thousand words whether I feel like it or not. That's a much more sane approach. I think writers who rely on inspiration aren't very happy—the thing that makes their identity isn't in their control. I can't imagine a worse situation.

Style-wise, my plotting has really improved. That's something a lot of people said about my last book, *Little Brother*. My approach to plotting is: things always get worse. That gives you a reason to turn the page. The protagonist is reasonable and intelligent and trying to solve the problems, and it just keeps falling apart. It's a slow-motion car wreck.

**What advice do you have for aspiring authors?**

I've written this column more than once! Write a set amount every day. Finish what you write. Eschew ceremony, and don't get into habits—such as only writing when the children are asleep, or with a certain type of music playing—because you probably don't have control over them all the time. Don't let those external circumstances control you. Turn off your IM, or any real-time communications. Leave a little bit hanging at the end of every day: leave off in the middle of a sentence so that you've got a little bit to start you the next day, even if it's just the first five words.

**Any anecdotes regarding the story or your experiences as a fledgling writer?**

The thing that I remember most about being a new writer was the extent to which every tiny little victory was hoarded so carefully. If I got a positive review in a tiny zine, that was cause for celebration. That was something that went away after a little while. There comes a point where they stop being special in the same way. The first time your baby speaks, it's exciting. The millionth time, it might be annoying. (For the record, my daughter hasn't spoken yet.)

The advice I have for a lot of writers is: You may discover that success in writing isn't nearly as nice as you hope it would be. SF writers aren't widely regarded as important people. You might labor for 10 years as I did to make your first pro sale, and then after a few weeks, nobody cares anymore. I used to go to the bookstore and buy three copies of each magazine I was published in, hoping somebody would ask why, so I could say, "I have a story in it." But on the flip side, every now and again you discover a fan when you don't expect them. Once, when I was raising capital for a technology startup, it seemed like every venture capitalist I encountered was more impressed by my SF sales than my business plan . . .

# Highway 61 Revisited
## by China Miéville

She dreamt.

Dreamt of having normal eyes, a voice, and no hateful, loathsome Ultra-sight, the extra eye of far-seeing. Her brother, Peetra of the kill-stick, he did amer her. In that way, glad was she, glad she had the MindSpeak, and glad too that only Peetra was open to her secret tongue. Because though she was feared, even Non-amered now, if she so much as touched another mind, she would be cast out, and her strange octacles seccered away.

Sol cut the sky, awakening her. It glinted off her golden octacles: octacles without pupil or iris, just simple, glowing gold. She reached out tendrils of thought groping.

"Oh my brother Peetra of the kill-stick, do you sleep?"

"Oh my sister Alazbeph of the gold octacles, I sleep not, did your sleep-cycle pass with peace?"

"Oh brother my sleep-cycle passed without event as normal and without a scare-dream, did you have a peace-night or were scare-dreams unto you?"

"My sleep-cycle was a peace-night I thank you, oh my sister, I rise now."

She closed. Upon rising she looked at her pale, naked body, and sighed. Dressing, she thought, if the kill-stick was not I would not be here o they hate and fear me why why why?

The entrance to her casser was swept aside. She whirled round, gasping, but it was her brother. They hugged wunanuther.

"Bonmorn, my sister. Sol has rose, and my B'letts are problaty complete. I go now to Fredrig the blag smerth. Do you desire to companise me?"

"Oh my brother I do not know . . ."

"Fear not, sister mine. Jests and prencks contra you, I will ward off, and a thrown mizzle will not penetrate your far-sight. Companise me, serraplay?"

"If 'tis your wish my brother."

"'Tis my wish, oh sister, come."

They stepped out into the humid air and propered to Fredrigs smerthy. They could hear his hamm'r beating against the iyorn. As they ambuled along the ancient nigrer via, they passed near a group of people, Jesting and riddicling. As they went among the turb, a man muttered, "Begone, mutabitch, your kind of filth should dwell in the shit where you were spawned!"

Peetra's zord was out of his scab'rurd as the verbs were uttered. The life of the mascule lay in the temper of a young warrer.

"Insult again sister or late mother mine, Foulsod, and I seccrate your gizzard shall." The verbs came in a base growl from Peetra's thrax.

"Your pardoning, I orra indeed. Your sister is her own fem."

The zord was sheathed. Even at dorry-quatrer, Peetra was one of the Harwar-Sixchyun's best warrers, especialty since he had found the kill-stick in the wreckage of a Wartanck. He had errerd in the silvest, searching for game, when he had come across an old Wartanck, its great kill-stick pointed to the Elyzians. The place held great forebodeing for him, and he was inclined to proper away, but curiosness pushed him towards the Death-Vessel. Inside were dorr charred and decaying corr'pzes. He was just to proper, when he vidded a Novi object in a pile of burnt papyrer. He had picked it up and vidded it was a longe tube with a handle, and paucy leev'r at yoon end, and also another tube atop the magner yoon, with glazz lenzes. He vidded through them and realised they biggified things. Suddenly there was a "blang!" and a flazash of light, and the handle drived back-towards into his thrax. He viddiplussed at it in incrediblaty. He picked it up, gingerful, and vidded it all over. Then he propered back to the villij.

Since then, he had intelged how it proplelled paucy mizzles called "B'letts," and how to constract them. He had told the Blagsmerth how to constract them, the B'letts, and collected some novi ones every sizday. As he did hoday, on the quatry nonth of sunner.

"Bonmorn, Fredrig."

"Aaaah, Bonmorn, Bonmorn indeed Peetra. An Bonmorn to you, Alzabeph!"

Alzabeph smiled. In the whole sicky villij, she dellected Fredrig, even amered him, for he did not hate her. Once, she had in the silvest, and, other than Peetra, he alone had goned to sherch for her. And he had found her.

"Be the B'lettes parrered, Fredrig?"

"Yeay, up all the sleep-cycle I was, parerring them!" he said in Mocke Rue, "Take them! I am done with B'letts!"

"Aaaah, you're an amico, Fredrig."

"That I know! I be perfection itself!" He roared with laughter. "And," he said in a softer tone, "I have something for you, O Alzabeph." He held out to her a amerly, paucy silpha ring, set with couloured glazz. She was very touched, and glowing tears d3dripped down her cheeks. She looked at the ring and putted it on her indacs finger. She hugged Fredrig.

"Ooo, found a ald lad'l by the poowel. Meltened it down, to make a brazilett for Elan, then found a paucy bit left over," he explained, "and the gryn glazz was from an old boott'l I found."

"Anyway, here's the B'letts." He handed Peetra a small wooded bok, frull of paucly B'letts. "Take caution!" he added. "The small rooj mark on a paucy lot, indicates a novi idea of me. I hollowed and filled them with sticleback poisent! A graze will cause Mort!"

"This is an idea indeed! Very novi. Bon, Bon! Gratias, gratias!" said Peetra in wonder. He filled the kill-stick with a poisent B'lett.

"Bon bye, Fredrig, and gratias again." They turned, and begunned the ambler back.

"My sister, I need to proper on a hunt in silvest, for meat. I shall be returned presently."

"Bon O brother here I shall wait."

She went to her casser, holding all the time, mai soon he passed beyond her range. She sat on a cheyr, and began to write a poem. She had practised writing since she was paucy. She did it with a scratchy knibb on stiff papyrer.

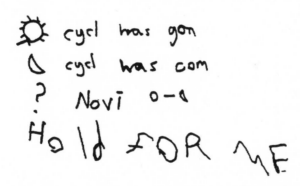

Her writing became blurred as she weepded. Suddenly a rough voice yelled, "Get up, Mutabitch. Get up on your foul legs!" She vidded up in incrediblaty. A turb of angry mascules and fems, led by the mascule who had insulted her earlier. He grabbed her brown hair and yankded her up. "Get up, I said!" She opened her mouth in pain. He threw her into the turb where dorr more mascules grabbed and threr her into the via. She got up and tried in vain to proper but they grabbed and holded her. The premier mascule grabbed her shift, and ripped it down the midian, so it fell straight down. She gasped and tried to pull her rukers about her, but the mascules held her. The mascule grabbed her, and while the other dorr held her, he beat her with knotted rope, and approached her with mort in his octacles and was about to entrer her when she, in despration threw her mind around.

Altheworld flinched involuntarily, but one mascule, in another part of the villij, vidded up from his work, grabbed a novily forged zord and ran off. He did not intellge why.

A roar of rage shook the Turb.

"No!" Fredrig smashed through. "No! Not that a masculine warrer, of the Harwar-Sixchyun could attack," his octacles strayed to the red weals across her corr'pz, "and, and beat and ravage a defencless fem? I SAY NO!"

With rage and power oozing from his every pore, he swung the zord. Fredrig was a plusmuscular mascule, with his work, and with additional rage-power, the zord swung down and with a noise like a spade in wet turf, it bit the kneck, crated the spinalerl column, and passed through to the other side. The head of her attacker rolled off Alzabeph, and the mort octacles viddiplused at her in accusation. The bllod ozzed sluggishly from the kneck, dien suddenly fountained forth, cover her in rooj fluid.

"Go, fem. Quickly! Into the silvest! Get a zord and protectashield from my forj. I join you shall soon!"

She propered. As she did so, she heard sounds of battle from the square. She entered Fredrig's place, grabbed the nearest zord and protectashield, and propered.

Peetra comed back deoectedly. A mal trip. Nothing mai . . . what was that?

"Peetra! I help need!" He heard Fredrig's voice, and the clashing of metal meeting metal. He propered, cocking his kill-stick.

"Haar!" A Blang echoed in the air and yoon of the attackers fell mort.

"I come, Fredrig!"

"Non, fool, proper! Your sister is endangered!"

"What?"

"The foulsods attacked her! She propered to the silvest."

"Come, dien!"

With a last slash they propered down the via to the silvest, grabbing protectashields from Fredrig's forj.

She propered. Thorns ripped across her Newd corr'pz, drawing more bllod adding the now solidificating on her. With a start, saw a plant ahead. With thorns as well, but these waved invitingly, with no breeze! She knew this was a mutobramble. Yoon scratch, and all the network of stems would imprison her, drawing vital body salts with their thorns.

She turned, and whimpered with sick fear. Voices approached. She crouched and listened.

"Cheer up, amico. We will find her soon!"

"Oh no please."

"But Fredrig, we've sherched for yorncks, and no . . ."

With a sob and blast of intelliging, she leaped in front of her brother.

They ambuled, as they had done for the whole sol-cycle, it seemed . . .

"O brother, do you receive the noise of burdds?"

"Yes, sister."

"She talks, does she?" Since they had told him, Fredrig could not get over her MindSpeak.

"It is a sound to make yoon glad."

"It is. But do not let any pack you." Suddenly a squirrel darted in front of them. They backed away nervously.

"Haa . . . I see . . . Muta . . . Gold eye . . . help me . . ." the squirrel stammered.

"Whaat?" she thought. "How does it know . . . ?"

Peetra raised the kill-stick and the squirrel scuttled off.

"It came too close. Mort unto you those tall'ns give."

Later in the eve they came to a starg, evil horns glinting in the lunalight, "Hhhu, Nnnooo kkihlll mmmere I yooo ammiiiccooo. . ." and Peetra shot him.

"Good eating for us, catiousness take though. The venn'm sac lie beneath the prongs." They made flame, and enroasted the corr'pz.

"I had a novi idea!" said Fredrig. He milked the venn'm sacs, and let the light bleur liquid dripple over the zords.

"Tis baneful," he said grimly, "but the need is ours."

That night, they took turns to sentinard. As Peetra did so, he heard a paucy russle. He rose, speedily.

"Who beeth there? Who?" he demanded angerfully. Another russle answered him.

"Who is there?" He yelled.

"Nyaar, kill . . . !" a hoarse voice screamed, and quatrey vulv'vreens leapt into sight. Their tails swished and thrumped the ground, menacingly. "Mmeeeeaaatt!" said yoon. "Gruun . . . Hungggerrful!" screamed the same yoon. They all holded clubbers in their forepands. They advanced.

With a yell, yoon attacked Alzabeph. She dodged, and full of savaery, sheathed her zord in the beestee, then gasped with horror. The blood stained her zord. The vulv'vreen choked as the starg venn'm took effect. The others were not so lukful. The last thing Alzabeph vidded before the clubber hit the back of her kneck, was Fredrig and Peetra falling. Then the sleep of nonconshusfullness hit her.

The premier thing that Peetra vidded as he woke, was the kindly looking old mascule beinding over him concernfully.

"Ah. Awake. Yes." The mascule nodded his head wisenessfully. "No. Don't move. Too tired. Tough fight. Yes."

"Who . . . ?"

"Philipson. James B. At . . . erm . . . your service, Sir!" The masculer tongue was novi, with novi verbs, and strange pauses. But it was understandable. "Ah. One moment. Yes. Friends. Your Friends wake." And he approached the other dorr, lying some distance away. Peetra saw he was in a plus large casser. But their host was speaking:

"Now. Yes. Hello. I am James Philipson. I am your friend. Or amico. As you say. You, I suppose, are wondering how you are . . . here. Yes?" They murmered assent.

"Yes. I also, erm, have. A gun, yes. I have one. And the were wolves are . . . dead. Yes. But now. Important. Who are . . . you?" he asked. He looked at Alzabeph, who shook her head helplessly.

"She no voice has. Radioness clogs her tongue," explained Peetra.

"Ah. Yes. Of course, a mutant." His voice softened. "Poor girl."

"We are of the warrer tribe, the Harwar-sixchyun . . ."

"That will do. Tell me, is there a road in your village?"

"R-road?"

"I mean, via?"

"Yes. A nigrer yoon, with a blanch line dividing it."

"Ah . . . I see. Do you know where the name Harwar-sixchyun comes from?"

"No."

"Ah. Well. Many years ago, the world was full of people. Powerful people. With fantastic engines, music, and a magical life source, called Elektrersiti. With this power, they could do almost anything. But. They made another power. Called Nyookliah power. Stronger than Elektrersiti. But more deadly. With an evil effect, and side-power, called Radioactervisness, which warped, and killed people. They made big bombs, which are like huge bullets, which burst over big places. These bombs were full of Radioactervisness. 'Defence.' Now. At that time, the world was split up. Into big countries. Where we are, was called Ham'riga. We were ruled by an Evil sorcerer, called Ronaltarraycun. He had one big enemy called 'The Red Warriors of the Sorfiet Unified.' They were led by Shrerninkhof. Ronaltarraycun had a bad woman as an ally from across the water, from the isles of Britaly. She was known as the 'woman of iron.' But her true name was Murgisfatshur. One day the two evil sorcerers ganged against the valiant red warriors. They thew big bombs. So the red warriors threw them back. They ruined the Earth.

"That was a thousand years ago. We have lost civilization. But I cling to it. My name you see. From a true civilized name. Oh, and of names . . . the 'Harwar-Sixchyun' comes from this. In those days, they had magic riding things, of iron and steel, called 'automobiles.' These ran on big vias called roads. The bigger road were called 'Highways' and these were numbered. You, Peter. Count to ten . . . sorry, dizz."

"Yoon, dorr, trey, quatry, sank, siz, set, och, non, dizz."

"You see. The tongue has been perverted. Anyway. Back then, they said 'Sizzy-yoon,' as 'Sixty-one,' and used it as foundations for the village. And you, my dear Alzabeph. Ah," his voice was soft. "Yes. You see, today, still, there are bomb remnants, occasionally, radioactervisness finds its way to a mother's womb, and does its evil deed. You are a victim. But do not fear. I think . . . you will prevail." He turned to address them all.

"But now, I have something serious to say. I have searched for such followers. You shall do great work!"

All could sense that he was excited about something. He leaned forward eagerful.

"You . . ." A sigiter whistled through an open freetrer. "Hhnaaa . . ." He made an Evil sound as the styel tipped cap't penetred his Luvorgan, ceasing the neverstop pumping.

Fredrig and Peetra grabbed their zords. Alzabeph hesited. Since the vulv'vreen died at her rukers, she had been sick at the thought. More Mort, she stand could not . . .

But it vidded as though she would be spared. Instead of ripping and secreting for meat, the vulv'vreens rushed away . . . Gleenessfully.

"Appears it not, amicae, he was the target of their evil? Aaah, but life is sweet, it takes mort to realize how plus so," stated Fredrig, mournessly.

"But we should get on," said Peetra, "Sleep-cycle approaches."

They stepped onto the road.

As they approached the setting sol, the last lines of her unfinished poem ran through Alzabeph's mind:

"Sol-cycle has gone.
Sleep-cycle has come.
What will new day hold for me?
Whateverso beit,
Bon or non,
I will accept it, Joyfully . . ."

# China Miéville

**B**ritish author China Miéville made a splashy entrance in 1998 with his first novel, *King Rat*, which was nominated for Bram Stoker and International Horror Guild awards, and quickly followed up with *Perdido Street Station*, which won the Arthur C. Clarke and British Fantasy awards and introduced readers to his popular world of Bas-Lag. Since then he has gone on to win both awards again, as well as a Locus Award, and been nominated for a host of others with each new novel he publishes.

Both on the page and off it, China Miéville isn't afraid to rattle a few cages in striving for change and progress. Describing his own work as "weird fiction," Miéville is viewed by many as a spokesman for the New Weird literary movement, attempting to broaden modern fantasy and help steer the genre away from the Tolkien pastiches that sometimes characterize it. His novels often contain strong political threads—unsurprisingly, seeing as Miéville holds a Ph.D. in international law. Outspoken and politically active himself, Miéville has stood for the House of Commons for the Socialist Alliance, and even published a book-length version of his doctoral thesis, *Between Equal Rights: A Marxist Theory of International Law*, though he is careful to stress that he does not expect anyone to actually read it.

When this anthology was originally compiled, Miéville was asked if he would allow the inclusion of "Looking for Jake," the story that all online and print sources at the time named as his first published work. Instead, he responded with "Highway 61 Revisited," a childhood tale so obscure that only he still remembered it, and which had never been collected since its original publication in 1986. It is precisely this sort of discovery—and the generous authorial commentary that accompanies it—which was the original inspiration for *Before They Were Giants*.

**Looking back, what do you think still works well in this story? Why?**

It's a little difficult to say whether anything in particular "works well," because when you're dealing with stories written by child writers, I think the rules genuinely are different. Funnily enough, I was just in Warwick University (where I teach creative writing), doing a lesson on Jane Gaskell's book *Strange Evil*, and we were talking about exactly this, because she wrote it when she was 14. We were also discussing Daisy Ashford's book *The Young Visiters* (*sic*), from when she was nine. The thing is that what those pieces of writing have, I think, at their best, is a sort of reasonably unmediated relationship with their own obsessions.

What I like about this story, still, is that it is a bit pell-mell, completely in itself. There's very little "face" in children's writing. I also still like the invented language, and the animals that desperately try to talk to the characters. And I like the politics, with some reservations (I was never the kind of Stalinophile that story would suggest—I was just trying to answer *Rambo*-esque propaganda by making the usual baddies the goodies). But I like the fact that there's a kind of wide-eyed but heartfelt politics to it. And RonaltaRaycun, or however I spelled it—the odd spellings, punnings, etc. still work for me.

**If you were writing this today, what would you do differently? What are the story's weaknesses, and how would you change them?**

Nothing. I think the story is a perfect jewel in which nothing needs changing . . . right?

Speaking as an adult writer, there are 10,000 things wrong with this story. Its plot is, um, cursory. Its characterization is, uh, broad-brush. Its theme is, well, not the *most* original. Its embedded politics are, say, a tad naive. Its attitudes to women are, shall we say, somewhat sickly sacralizing. Etc.

I was twelve. I. Was. *Twelve*.

That doesn't mean I'm ashamed of it. I'm not, at all. I have vast affection for this story. I love the language, I love the gusto, I love that I gave a shit about it, I love that it has a sense of the sort of weird that I always loved, I love the first sentence, I love that it includes a non-Roman pictographic alphabet. But yeah, it has a flaw or two. I doubt Hollywood will come doorknocking.

**What inspired this story? How did it take shape? Where was it initially published?**

This story is a combination of two influences that I hadn't actually had directly. Someone had described to me the book *Riddley Walker* by Russel Hoban, which is post-apocalyptic but written in a new language, and I hadn't read it yet (I did, but not for many years) but thought it was a great idea, so tried to do my own version. And the title, "Highway 61 Revisited," was obviously the Bob Dylan song, but it was set by a teacher—I hadn't heard the song, and didn't for many years. So that story is a naive and sincere triangulation between two important cultural touchstones that I had never actually encountered.

So we got set the assignment by an English teacher, who gave us the title, and as I say, I riffed off the idea of this book that I'd heard about—I was reading *loads* of post-apocalypse fiction, loved the shit out of it—and thought about this highway in the middle of a post-apoc tribe. When my teacher got it and really liked it, he entered it for this competition, which was run in conjunction by the publisher Macmillan and the stationers chain in the UK, WH Smith, called the Young Writers of the Year, which was kind of a big competition for children writers during the '80s. And it ended up after a long time being one of the prize winners, and the prize was a check and publication in this anthology that they put out every year of all the winners. So I guess technically it doesn't count as a *sale*, but a prize. Am I still eligible for this anthology? Can I stay?

**Where were you in your life when you published this piece, and what kind of impact did it have?**

That's an interesting question. It's difficult to know, exactly, because it was such a long time ago. But I think—I *think*, I hope I'm not post-facto reconstructing—that it was the kind of validation that probably made me think I could actually do this a bit.

Having said which . . . I don't recall it having an *explicit* impact like that in my head. I don't remember sitting down and thinking, "this is it, I can/ must/will be a writer, this proves it." I'm not saying I didn't say that to myself, but I don't remember it. But I think I kind of metabolized it as something really great, that changed the way I thought about what I was doing. And also because a lot of the reviews of the book singled the story out, which was lovely—although in truth, I think that was partly because many of the reviewers were not SF readers, so the story probably looked more original to them than maybe it was. Fuck it, they can't take it back now. Tough.

For all of this, though, you have to remember that I didn't relate to this as a "sale." From that point of view, my first "sale" happened just over 10 years ago, and *that* had the kind of impact we're talking about, because that was what I wanted to do. "Highway 61 Revisited" was more foundational, I think, in a different way. When I sold *King Rat*, it was incredibly exciting. And almost immediately afterward I sold a short story called "Looking for Jake," which much later became the title story to my short story collection. Though I'd sold KR earlier, it was LFJ that appeared first, in an anthology. And seeing it appear, that was the point at which I started to think: holy shit.

The thing with selling a novel is that there tends to be a long turnaround time, so you're intensely excited when you make the sale, but then there's another year before the motherfucker appears, by which time it's not exactly anti-climactic—the appearance of the book is incredible—but it is a little mediated.

**How has your writing changed over the years, both stylistically and in terms of your writing process?**

I'm a terrible person to talk to about "process." I know people are very interested in it, and writers get asked about it a lot, but I'm just not systematic enough to be able to answer it very much. I'm not one of those writers that writes from 9:00 to 12:00 every day. Some days or weeks I won't do anything on fiction. But when I *do* write fiction, which is what I like doing most, of course, I tend to do it in very intense, very long bursts. I work for two, three, four weeks, six to seven days a week, between nine and twelve hours a day, and am extremely antisocial. That's my preferred method of working. But that's just the actual typing stuff. There's also the scribbling in notebooks, the thinking up ideas, etc., and that might happen on the top of a bus or whatever. So I can only answer the question very vaguely. I'm not very rigorous about method. I *am*, though, rigorous about the method of the narrative itself. I never write anything without a very strong sense of the total shape of a narrative—a pretty coherent and careful plan of the book's architecture. The idea of "just starting and seeing what happens" brings me out in hives with anxiety.

In answer to the question about style: I've become more conscious of the writing, more aware of it at a formal level. Which I think makes me a better writer, but also makes it harder, because you up your own game, and you try harder. So for example, I'm very aware of lots of the flaws of *Perdido*. It's very undisciplined. Which, perhaps or perhaps not ironically, is part of what those people who like it like about it. That isn't illegitimate—there can be something very winning about undisciplined writing, up to a point. But I am getting much more disciplined as I get older.

I'm also very interested in deliberately experimenting with style. *Iron Council* is written in a very different style from *Perdido* and *The Scar*—I was very consciously trying to do something with the style. I think it's one reason that *Iron Council* is less popular with a lot of readers. I'll also say—and I hope this doesn't sound defensive, because people have every right to their reactions—that that's also why for me it is without question my favorite of those three books. That experimentation at the level of prose, which I acknowledge did ask certain things of the reader that the other books didn't necessarily do, is something I'm really proud of. And I think in general that the project of trying to experiment, do things differently, is interesting. My latest book, *The City & The City*, is very different again, and written in a voice that I hope is extremely different from any of the others published so far. Obviously, you've no right to expect readers necessarily to like all of the stuff you do, if you're interested in experimenting with those changes, but I hope it makes for a more interesting trajectory overall, and even if people don't care for one particular book so much, I hope ultimately it makes the whole thing more interesting for the reader, as well as the writer.

**What advice do you have for aspiring authors?**

I think it can actually be quite helpful to get critique and feedback from someone who comes from a very different writing tradition than you. A lot of my students write what I think of as mainstream "literary" fiction, and I think it's very, very helpful for me to see what people from that tradition are working on, and very helpful for them to get feedback from someone with a rather different eye from their main readers.

I would say that for me, the advice would probably be very nuts and bolts stuff. Think about the structure of your book before you start writing it. The more you can plot in advance, the easier it will be to write the chapters as they come up, without drifting or getting baggy. If you can write a few hundred words every day, let alone a thousand or two thousand, you *will* finish the book before all that long. The trick is to not for a second let yourself know you're writing a novel, or it's easy to panic. You're just trying to get a thousand words done. Just a thousand. Then another thousand. That's all. Nothing to see here. No novel. No sirree, nothing that big.

If you plan in advance and think about the structure, you'll have a reasonably clear idea of what chapter has to come after what has to come after what, so the writing of each of those one to five thousand words needn't be a giant deal, because you don't have to agonize about what to do next. You just refer to your grid/wheel/plan/outline/etc.

**Any anecdotes regarding the story or your experiences as a fledgling writer?**

The only one that comes to mind is talking once to M. John Harrison, the toweringly brilliant writer of the Viriconium series, which had a huge influence on me. He's always been very hardcore about his writing—has taken it absolutely seriously, has bent his whole life toward it—and doesn't have a lot of time for those not prepared to. We were talking one day, and I said something about, "Oh, I really, really hope I can live on writing full-time, it would be so amazing."

And he said, "You can live on writing full-time. But you might have to be prepared to live without certain luxuries. Like a fridge."

And he meant it. Scared the bejeezus out of me. Luckily, I never had to do without a fridge—I thought I was going to be an academic, and after my second book, *Perdido Street Station*, I was able to work full-time as a writer. But I was halfway through the Ph.D. when that happened, and I finished the Ph.D., so when everyone turns their back on me, I hope I can trundle back into academia.

# In Pierson's Orchestra
## by Kim Stanley Robinson

*The dead shall live, the living die,*
*and Music shall untune the sky.*

Hallway to hallway to hallway I flit, like a bat in a mine. The lights are dimmed and the halls are empty, eerie gray slots. I cast long shadows from low light to light as I move along, next to the wall. I can feel my upper arms slide wetly against my ribs, and my heart's *allegro* thumping. A voice within me sneers: "Time for your diamond, junkie."

Dead sober will I see him, I promise myself again. My hand shakes and I put it back in my pocket. Familiar halls now, and I slow down as if the air is getting thicker; still in color-blind greys, and the air is perhaps filled with dust, or smoke. It is past time for my next crystal. I have not slept for five days, I am continuing on the drive of my decision.

Home. VANCOUVER CONSERVATORY, the tall door announces. I turn the knob, give the door a push to get it started. It opens. I slip through, silently cross the entrance floor. Pierson's hologramic statue stares down at me, a short ruby-red figure transparent in the dim light. I circle him warily, alive to his presence in the shadows between me and the ceiling. Hallways, again; then another door, the door: sanctum sanctorum. You remember the old animated film *Fantasia*? Suddenly I am Mickey Mouse, in Dukas' *The Sorcerer's Apprentice*, about to interrupt the sorcerer over his cauldron. A deep bell clangs from the main hall and I jump. Midnight: time for the breaking of vows. I knock on the door, a mistake; I have the privilege of entering without knocking; but no, I have lost all that, I have revoked all that. An indistinct shout arrives from inside.

I push the door open and a slice of white light cuts into the hallway. In I go, blinking.

The Master is under the orchestra, on his back, tapping away cautiously at the dent in the tuba tubing. The dent occurred at the end of the last grand tour, when one of the workmen helping to move it onto a rollcart tripped and kicked the tuba with his steel-tipped boot.

The Master looks up, white eyebrows rising like a bird's crest. "Eric," he says mildly, "why did you knock?"

"Master," I say shakily, my resolve still firm, "I can no longer be your apprentice."

Watch that sink in, like a hot poker in snow. He edges out from under the orchestra, stands up; all slowly, so slowly. He is old. "Why is this, Eric?"

I swallow. I have a lie all prepared, I have considered it for hours and hours; it is absurd, impossible. Suddenly I decide to tell him the truth. "I am addicted to nepanathol."

Right before my eyes his face turns deep red. "You what?" he says, then almost shouts, "I don't understand!"

"The drug," I explain, "I'm hooked."

Has the shock been too much for him? He trembles. He gets it out, calm and clear. "Why?"

It is so complex. I shrug. "Master," I say, "I'm sorry."

With a convulsive jerk he throws the hammers in his hand, and I flinch; they hit the foam lining of the wall without a sound, then click against each other as they fall.

"You're sorry!" he hisses, and I feel his contempt. Why does one always whisper in this room? "You're sorry! My God, you'd better be more than sorry! Three centuries, eight masters of the orchestra, you to be the ninth and you break the line for a drug? The greatest artistic achievement of all time—" he waves toward the orchestra, but I refuse to look at it—"you choose nepanathol above it? How could you do it? I'm an old man, I'll die in a few years, there isn't time to train another musician like you—and you'll be dead before I will!" True enough, in all probability. "I will be the last Master," he cries out, " and the Orchestra will be silenced!"

With the thought of it he twists and sits down cross-legged on the floor, crying. I have never seen the Master cry before, never thought I would. He is not an emotional man.

"What have I done?" Echoless shrieks. "The Orchestra will end with me and they will say it's my fault, that I was a bad Master—"

"You are the best of them," I get out.

He turns on me. "Then why? *Why?* How could you do this?"

I would have been the ninth Master of Pierson's Orchestra. The heir to the throne. The crown prince. Why indeed? Such a joke.

As from a distance I hear myself. "Master," I say, "I will stop taking the drug."

I close my eyes as I say it. For an old man's sake I will go through the withdrawal from nep. I shake my head, surprised at myself.

## In Pierson's Orchestra

He looks up at me with—what is it, craftiness? Is he manipulating me? No. It's just contempt. "You can't," he mutters angrily. "It would kill you."

"No," I say, though I am by no means sure of this. "I haven't been addicted long enough. A few hours; eight, maybe; then it will be over." It will be short; that is my only comfort. A very real voice inside me is protesting loudly: "What are you *doing?*" Pain. Muscle cramps, memory confusion, memory loss. Nausea. Hallucinations. A high possibility of sensory damage, especially to the ears, sense of smell, and eyes. I do not want to go blind.

"Truly?" the old man is saying. "When will you do this?"

"Now," I say, ignoring the voice inside. "I'll stay here, I think," gesturing toward the Orchestra but still not looking in its direction.

"I too will stay—"

"No. Not here. In the recording booth, or one of the practice rooms. Or go up to your chambers, and come back tomorrow."

We look at each other then, old Richard and young Eric, and finally he nods. He walks to the tall door, pulls it open. He turns his head back. "You be careful, Eric," he says.

I nearly laugh, but am too appalled. The door clicks shut, and I am alone with Pierson's Orchestra.

I can remember the first time I saw the Orchestra, in Sydney's old sailboat of an opera house, around the turn of the century when my mother and I were living there. It was a special program for young people, and the Master—the same one, Richard Wolfgang Weber Yablonski, an old man even then—was playing pieces to delight the young mind: I can remember the *1812 Overture*, Moussorgsky's *Pictures at an Exhibition*, De Bruik's *Night Sea*, and Debussy's *Claire de Lune*. The *Claire de Lune* was a shock; used to my mother's quick, workmanlike version. I barely recognized the Master's; slow, simple, the solo piano supported at times by the strings; he started each phrase hesitantly, and exaggerated the rests, so that I felt as if the music had never been played before; that it was the results of the blue lights striking the fantastic tower of blue circles and glints, and long blue curves.

After the performance a few children, the ones being considered for the apprenticeship, came forward to talk with the Master. I walked down the aisle, my mother's palm firm in the middle of my back, barely able to pull my eyes from the baroque monster of wood and metal and glass, to the mere mortal who played the thing. He spoke to us for a while, quietly, of the glories of playing an entire orchestra by oneself, watching our faces.

"And which did you like better," he asked, "*Pictures at an Exhibition* played on the piano, or with the full orchestral arrangement?"

"Orchestra," cried a score of voices.

"Piano," I said, hitting a sudden silence.

"Why?" he asked politely, focusing on me for the first time. I shrugged nervously; I couldn't think, I truly didn't know; fingers digging into my back, I searched for it—

It came to me. "Because," I said, "it was written for piano."

Simple. "But do you not like Ravel's arrangement?" he inquired, interested now.

I thought. "Ravel changed a rough Russian piano score into a French romantic orchestration. He changed it." Oh, I was a bright kid, no doubt about it, back in those days when I spent five hours a day at the keyboard and three in the books—and one in the halls, one desperately short hour, five o'clock to six o'clock every day in the halls burning up a day's pent-up frustration—

"Have you compared the scores?" the Master asked me.

"Yes, Master, they are very similar. It is the instrumentation that makes the difference."

The Master nodded his head, seeming to consider this. "I believe I agree with you," he said.

Then the talk was over and we were on our way home. I felt sick to my stomach. "You did good," my mother said. I was nine years old.

And here I am ten years later, sick to my stomach again. That is, I think I am. It is difficult to tell what is happening in my body—past time for my next crystal, that's sure. The little twinges of dependence are giving me their warning, in the backs of my upper arms. At least it will be short. "Just like sex," I remember an addict saying in a high-pitched voice. "Short and sweet with the climax at the end." His friend nodded and flashed fingers at him.

I turn to the Orchestra. "Imagine all of the instruments of a full symphonic orchestra caught in a small tornado," an early detractor said of it, "and you will have Pierson's invention." The detractor is now forgotten, and few like him exist now; age equals respectability, and the Orchestra now has three hundred years' worth. An institution.

And imposing enough: eleven meters of instruments suspended in air, eleven meters of twisted brass and curved wood, supported by glass rods only visible because of the blue and red spotlights glinting from them. The cloud of violas, the broken staircase of trombones; a truly beautiful statue. But Pierson was a musician as well as a sculptor, a conductor as well as an inventor, and a genius to boot: an unfortunate combination.

I move to the piano opening and slide onto the bench. The glass depression rods cover the keys so that it is impossible to play the piano from here; I must move up to the control booth. I do that, using the glass steps behind the cellos. Even the steps are inlaid with tiny French horn figures. Incredible. It is as if I were seeing everything in the Orchestra for the first time. The control booth, suspended in the center of the thing, nearly hidden from the outside; I am astounded by it. As always, I sit back in the chair and look at the colors: keyboards, foot pedals, chord knobs, ensemble tabs, volume stops, percussion buttons, keyboards, keyboards; strings yellow, woodwinds blue, brass red, percussion brown—

. . . then the Master, waiting outside the Orchestra to listen, shouts "Play!" impatiently, and I jump and begin the lesson. "Play!" he shouts as I sit watching the clarinets rising. "Play! What are you doing? You cannot just sit and look at the Orchestra," he tells me emphatically, "until you have learned to play it," and even as he tells me he is looking at the Orchestra himself, watching the dark browns reflect out of the golds and silvers; but then, he can play it—

. . . I hit one of the tabs with my toe, the tympani roll tab, hit *tempo* and *sustain* keys and boom, suddenly the B flat tympani fill the room, sticks a blur in the glass arms holding them. I long to hold the drum sticks and become the rhythm myself, to see the vibrations in the sound surface and feel them in the pit of my stomach; but to play that roll in Pierson's Orchestra I just slide a tab to a certain position and push another one down with my toe, so I stop pushing the tab down and there is instant silence.

I do not feel well. The clean red and blue dots in the metal surfaces have become prisms—I blink and they are dots again. Water in my eyes, no doubt. I look at all the keyboards surrounding me. Just a fancy organ is all it is.

I remember when I was learning to play the trumpet, and the triumph it was to play high C. I left all three valves open and pushed the mouthpiece against my lips so hard I could feel the  little white ring that would show when I took the horn away which is the wrong way to play high notes, but I had a weak embouchure—and forced a thin stream of air through my clamped lips to hear a high G, surely the highest note in my power. But then my stiff fingers pushed down the first two valves, I tightened my lips an impossible notch further, and the note slid up to an A as the valves hit their stops; quickly then, I lifted my right forefinger and reached a B. And then finally, before I ran out of air, with my eyes closed and my face contorted and my lips actually hurting, I lifted the middle valve and was magically playing a C, high C; a weak, scratchy note that soon dissolved into dry air rasping through the brass tubes; but a high C nevertheless. It was an achievement.

I touch a small piece of red plastic. A small plastic gate opens in a hollow plastic tube, compressed air forces its way through a wire-banded pair of plastic lips into one of the four trumpets, then winds its way through the tubes, and emerges from the bell as a pure, impossibly high E, two full steps above the highest note I ever played. I turn off the note. "Great, Pierson," I say aloud. "Great."

I begin playing Vivaldi's Oboe Concerto in F, ignoring the starts of pain that flare like struck matchheads in my arms and legs and neck. I play all sixty strings with my left hand, snapping down chord tabs until as I play the first violin part, the second violins, the violas, the cellos, the basses— they all automatically follow. Passages where they are not in unison have been rearranged, or, if vital, will be played with great difficulty on the individual keyboards below the control. Percussion and brass use the same method, but are played by my feet unless especially difficult. In this way the entire concerto is played leaving the right hand free to play the oboe solo as it runs over the background, a kitten on a marble staircase. The whole process requires intense concentration, which I am not giving it—I am playing quite poorly—and the ability to divide one's attention four or five ways without becoming confused; but still, four or five ways, not one hundred and ten.

I swing down the basses' keyboard so I can play it with my feet. I indulge my bad habit and watch my feet as I play, big toes trapped and pointing downward under the pressure of the other toes, bouncing over the yellow keys and creating low bowed notes that expand out of the rising spiral of big, dark bodies behind me. My arches cramp, and in my guts something twists. I can't remember the music—the conductor's score that threaded through my head is gone. I can no longer play. Sweat is breaking out of my face and arms, and the Orchestra is slowly spinning, as it does in concerts—

. . . I am waiting for Mikel and JoAnne to arrive so we can leave for the concert. I am at the battered old upright piano that I brought from my mother's house right after the funeral, playing Ravel's *Pavanne* and crying at it. I laugh bitterly at my ability to act, unsure as always if my emotions are real, or feigned for some invisible audience in a theater wrapped around my head; and I think, ignoring the evidence blinking before me: I can call them up at will when I'm miserable enough!

Mikel and JoAnne walk in, laughing like wind-chimes. They are both singers in Vancouver's Opera, true artists. They light up some Baygolds and we smoke and talk about *Tslitschitche*, the quartet we are going to hear. The conversation slows, Mikel and JoAnne look at each other:

"Eric," Mikel says, "JoAnne and I are going to drop crystals for the concert." He holds out his hand. In his palm is a small clear crystal that looks like nothing so much as a diamond. He flips it into the air, catches it in his mouth, swallows it, grins. "Want to join us?" JoAnne takes one from him and swallows it with the same casual, defiant toss. She offers one to me, between her fingers. I look at her, remembering what I have heard. Nepanathol! I do not want to go blind.

"Are you addicted?" I ask. They shake their heads.

"We restrict ourselves to special occasions," JoAnne explains. They laugh. The idea of it—

"Hell," I say, "give me one." I hit notes on the piano; C,G, G G sharp, G—B,C; and put a crystal in my mouth. It has no taste. I swallow it—

Hallucinations. For a moment there I was confused. I get back onto the stool and regret moving so quickly. Nausea is making me weak. I try playing some Dixieland, an avocation of mine of which the Master disapproves and in which I am (perhaps as a result) quite knowledgeable. It is difficult to play the seven instruments all at once—clarinet, trumpet, trombone, banjo, piano, drums, bass (impossible, actually; watch the tapes take down eight-bar passages and replay them when *repeat* buttons are pushed; often playing the Orchestra requires skills usually possessed by sound engineers), so I drop all of them but the front line.

The trombone is a fascinating thing to watch! Unable to anticipate the notes as human players do, the glass arms of the Orchestra move the slide about with an incredible, mechanical, inhuman speed. I am playing the Jack

Teagarten solo to *St. Louis Blues,* and I am hitting wrong notes in it. I switch to the clarinet solo which is, to my surprise, the solo from *The Rampart Street Parade* (you see how they fit together?) and quit in resignation. I hate to play poorly.

"All you have to do to stop this," the voice says out loud, and then I finish it in my head, *is to get home and swallow a nep crystal.* Without a moment's thought I slip off the stool: my knees buckle like closing penknives and I crash into the bank of keyboards, fall to the floor of the booth. In the glass floor are inlaid bass and treble clef signs. After a while I pull myself up and am sick in the booth's drinking fountain. Then I let myself drop back to the floor.

I feel as sick after vomiting as before, which is frightening.

"Do, do something," the voice says, "don't just look at it." At what? I ask. I pull out the celesta keyboard just before me, the bottom one in the bank. I look up at the ornate white box that is the instrument, suspended in the air above me, dwarfed by the grand piano beside it. The celesta: a piano whose hammers hit steel plates rather than wires. I run my finger along a few octaves and a spray of quick bell-notes echoes through the chamber.

I try a Bach Two-Part Invention, a masterpiece of elegance that properly belongs on the harpsichord. My hands begin to play at different tempos and I can't stop it; frightening! I stop playing, and to aid my timing I reach a shaky right hand up and start the metronome, an antique mechanical box that struck Pierson's fancy at about eighty. An upside-down pendulum, visually surprising because it seems to contradict the laws of gravity rather than agree with them as a normal pendulum does.

I begin the Invention again, but the tempo is too fast for me (I usually play it at 120); the notes become a confused mass, sounding like church bells recorded and replayed at a much higher speed.

The gold weight on the metronome's arm reflects a part of my face (my eyes) as it comes to its lowest point on the left side. And my heart—certainly my heart is beating in time with the metronome's penetrating, woodblock-struck, rhythmic *tock*.

And just as undeniably the metronome is speeding up. Impossible, for the weight has not moved on the arm, yet true; at first it was an *andante tock . . . tock,* and now it is a good march tempo, *tock, tock*; and my heartbeat *a tempo* all the way. With each pulse small specks of light are exploding and drifting like tiny Chinese lanterns across my eyes. I can feel the quick pulses of blood in my throat and fingers. I am scared. The *tocks* are now an *allegretto tocktocktock.* I lift my finger up, a terrible weight, and stick it into the flashing silver arc with the gold band across its center. The metronome stops.

I begin breathing again. My heart begins to slow down. A true hallucination, I think to myself, is very disturbing. After a time I push the celesta keyboard back into its nook and try to stand up. My legs explode. I grasp the stool. Cramps, I think in some cold corner of my mind, watching the limbs flail about. I knead the bulging muscles with one hand and keep shifting to find a more comfortable position; it occurs to me with a start that this is what the phrase "writhing in agony" describes; I had thought it was just a literary figure.

The cold corner of my mind disappears, and that was all that was left—

I come to and the cramps are gone. They feel like they are on the verge, though. If I don't move, I think I will be all right. I wish it were closer to the end.

I can see my reflection in the tuba's dented bell. A sorry-looking spectacle, disheveled and pale. The features are architecturally distinct. I can quite clearly see the veins below my eyes. The reflection wavers, each time presenting me with a different version of my face. Some are dome-foreheaded and weak-chinned; some have giant hooked noses; others are lantern-jawed and have pointy heads. Some are half-faced—

. . . I am trying to keep in step with the rest of the Children's Orchestra, now being temporarily transformed for the Tricentennial celebration into a marching band. A marching band: in the old days they used to dress musicians in uniforms and have them walk through the streets in ranks and files, playing tunes to the tempo of their steps. I can conceive of nothing more ridiculous, as I struggle under the weight of a Sousaphone, a tuba stretched into a circle so that it can be carried while marching. There are no pianos in a marching band, obviously. Fuming at the treatment a child prodigy receives, I puff angrily into the huge mouthpiece and watch my reflection sway back and forth in the curved brass surface. The conductor is scurrying about the edges of the group, consulting the *Parade Manual* in his hand and shouting, "Watch your diagonals! Watch those diagonals!" Next to me Joe Tanaka (he is a cellist, drafted as I have been) says, "If God meant us to play and walk at the same time, he'd have had us breathe through our ears." The halls force us to make a ninety-degree turn and there is chaos. "Step small on the inside!" the conductor is shouting. Each rank looks like a game of crack-the-whip. "Halt!" the conductor shrieks. Still breaking up at Tanaka, I cannon into the girl in front of me and three or four of us go down in a tangle. In the midst of the cries and recriminations I look at the crumpled Sousaphone bell and see the lower half of my face reflected: big mouth, no eyes—

I have a terrific headache. I reach up to the stool and grab it; my hand closes on nothing and I look again; at least six inches off. I must get up on the stool. Arms move up, feet grope for purchase, all very slowly. I move with infinitesimal slowness, as a child does when escaping his house at night to run the halls. Head to seat, knee to footbar, I stop to get used to the height, watching the fireworks display in my eyes. My hands never stop trembling now.

Now I am up and seated on the stool. I remember a film in which a man was buried to the neck in the tidal flats, at low tide. A head sitting on wet, gleaming sand, looking outward: the image is acid-etched on the inside of my eyelids.

*Do something.* I pull out the French horn and oboe keyboards for Handel's *Children's Prayer.* "These are the instruments with colds," the Master once said in a light moment. "The horn has a chest cold, the oboe a head cold." Handel is too slow. I switch to scales, C, F, B flat, E flat, A flat, D flat; bead, bead; every good boy deserves favor, each good boy does fine; then the minors, harmonic and melodic—

. . . "Drop that sixth," she yells from the kitchen, "harmonic not melodic. Play me the harmonic now."

Again—

"Harmonic!"

Again.

She comes in, grabs my right hand in hers, hits the notes. "Third down, sixth down, see how it sounds spooky? Do it now."

Again. "Okay, do that twenty times, then we'll try the melodic."

I stop playing minor scales, my heart pounding. I collect the oddball keyboards seldom played—glockenspiel, contrabassoon, harp, alto clarinet—and become bored with them even as I gather them. I am sick again in the drinking fountain. Certainly I have been in the Orchestra for a long time. A walk about the room would be nice, but I fear it is beyond me. I am very near the end, one way or another. The tide is rising. De Quincey and Cocteau lied to me—there is no romance in withdrawal, in the experience itself, none at all. It is no fun. It hurts.

There is a knock at the door. In it swings, slow as an hour hand. A short man struts through the doorway. Tied to his middle is a small bass drum, and welded to the top of the drum is a battered trumpet, its mouthpiece waving about in front of his face. Beside the mouthpiece is a harmonica, held in place by stiff wires wrapped around his neck. In his right hand is a drumstick, in his left hand is an old clacking percussion device (canasta) and between his knees are tarnished cymbals, hanging at odd angles. He looks as scruffy as I feel. He marches to a spot just below me, lightly beating the drum, then halts and brings his knees together sharply. When the din dies down he looks up and grins. His face has a reddish tint to it, and I can see through his nose.

"Who are you?" I ask.

"John Pierson," he replies, "at your service." Suddenly I see the resemblance between the disreputable character below me and the statue high in the outer entryway. "And you?" he says to me. His hair is tangled.

"Eric Johann Vivaldi Wright."

"Ah-ha! A musician."

"No," I tell him, "I just operate your machine."

He looks puzzled. "Surely it takes a musician to operate my machine?"

"Just a button-pusher. Did you really build this thing?" Time stretches out. We are speaking in a dead silence, stillness. There are long pauses between phrases.

"I did."

"Then it's all your fault. You're the cause of the whole mess," I say down to him, "you and your stupid vulgar monstrosity! When you erected this heap," I ask him, tapping a glass upright sharply with my foot, "were you serious?"

"Certainly," he replies, nodding gravely. "Young man," he says, emphasizing every third or fourth word with a rimshot, "you have Completely Missed the Point. You claim Too Much for my Work. With my invention it is Possible for One Man to play extremely Complex pieces by Himself. That is All. It is merely a rather Complicated musical Instrument, able to create Beautiful Music."

"No way, old man," I say, "it's an imitation orchestra is what it is, and pretty poor job it does, too. For example" (I have run through this so many times before): "If Beethoven's *Third* were to be played, which one could do it better, your Orchestra or the Quebec Philharmonic?"

"Quebec, undoubtedly, but—"

"Okay, then. All you've done is turned a sublime group achievement into a half-assed egotistical solo."

"No, no, no, no, no," he exclaims, rimshots for every "no." "The invention is an imitation of an orchestra, only in the same way a one-man band was an imitation of a band, eh?" He winks suggestively. "In other words, not at all. A one-man band was not to be judged for anything except his own individual performance. It is a fallacy to become comparative." He takes off and makes a revolution around the Orchestra, playing "Dixie" on the trumpet and pounding the bass drum, and filling all the rests with the cymbals. It sounds horrible. Back again. "Entertaining, no? Contributions?" He grins. "A one-man band was a great institution."

"Maybe," I say, "but none of them ever claimed to be musicians."

"They most certainly did! Someone who makes music, young man, is a musician. This purist attitude, this notion of artistic integrity that you have, has blinded you. Art with a capital A! What nonsense! Music is noise that entertains, that makes one feel good. My instruments can do that as well as any."

"No it can't," I almost shout. "Wrong! This *instrument* can't make music as well as the instrument that is in an orchestra, that takes a hundred and ten people to play it. Your instrument is just showmanship, and I am an artist. There is no shame in being a purist."

"Bah!" he says. "A purist is just someone living a hundred years in the past. You would have scoffed at the integrity of the organ had you been around at its invention, or the synthesizer."

"A purist," I say, "just likes to see things done right." I trace the other line down, following arguments like fugues. "And if you're going to build a solo instrument that makes a lot of sounds, why not work with synthesizers?"

"Because," he explains, waving the drumstick about, "this is prettier. Isn't that reason enough? Christ! You purists are so refined. If you are to play my instrument you must change the way you think of yourself.

"You can't change the way you are."

"You most certainly can! What could be simpler? Listen: you want the music to be played as written, as well as possible. Fine. That is admirable. My instrument does not make much of a symphonic orchestra, it is true, even though the simplifications made are your fault and not the machine's; but that is not what I built it to be, believe me! It has its own artistic integrity, and you must find it. If you do not like simplifying orchestral arrangements, don't! Play something else! If you can find nothing that seems suitable, write something yourself! I don't suppose anyone has shown you my compositions for the instrument? No? Ah, well, they never did think much of me as a composer." He brightens. "Enjoy yourself in that little booth, eh? Have you ever done that? It's quite easy."

I look around at the banks of keyboards. "It's just like putting on a show," I mutter.

"So? Then put on a show! It's a great, showy machine when you get to know it. Of course, you don't know it very well, yet." He smiles a crafty smile. "I took nineteen years to build it," he says, "and it would only take two or three to put it together. There's more to it than meets the eye." He turns to leave, shimmering his familiar transparent red. He walks to the door and stops. "Play it," he says, "don't just look at it. Play it with everything in you." He leaves. The door closes.

So here I am, a young man frying in a hallucinogenic withdrawal, suspended in this contraption like a fly trapped in the web of a spider frying in a hallucinogenic withdrawal . . . You've seen pictures of those poor tangled webs that drugged spiders make in labs? That is what Pierson's Orchestra would look like in two dimensions, from any side. A glass hand, a tree reaching up in a swirl of rich browns and silvers and prisms. Music doesn't grow on trees, you know. The cymbals are edged with rainbows.

Most certainly I have been suffering delusions. It is easy afterward to say that a conversation with a man dead three centuries is an illusion, but while it is happening, it is hard to discount one's senses. Damage is being done in my brain; it is as if I can feel the individual cells swelling and popping. I am very sick. There is little to do but sit and wait it out. Surely it is near the end—in a sudden flash I see the Orchestra as a giant baroque cross upon which I am draped . . . but no. It is a fantasy, one I can recognize. I am afraid of those I can't recognize.

"Just like sex," the deaf man said, "climax at the end." I wait. Time passes. *Pop pop pop* . . . like swollen grains of rice. Something must be done. Might as well play the damn thing. Put on a show.

I'm not convinced by you, Pierson! Not a bit!

I begin arranging the keyboards into concert position, my hands shoving them about like tugboats pushing big ships. Dispassionately I watch my hands shake. The cold corner of my mind has taken over and somehow I am outside the nausea. I am seeing things with the clarity you have when you are extremely hungry, or tired past the point of being tired. Everything is quite clear, quite in focus. I have heard that drowning men experience a last period of great calm and clarity before losing consciousness. Perhaps the tide is that high now. I cannot tell. Oh, I am tired of this! Why can't it be over? Bach's "Rejoice, Beloved Christians," the baritone playing the high line. The passages come to me clean and sharp now. I find it hard to keep my balance; everything is overexposed. I am swaying. I close my eyes. A Chopin Nocturne. Against the black field of my eyelids' insides there is a marvelous show of lights, little colored worms that burst into existence, crawl across my vision and disappear. Behind the lights are barely discernible patterns, geometric tapestries that flare and contract under the pressure of my eyelids. The music is intertwined with this odd mandala; when I clamp my eyes hard there is a sudden rush of blue geometry with a black center, with it a roll of tympani, shrieking of woodwinds and the strings fitting quickly and surely into the fantastic blue patterns that blossom before me. Mozart's Concerto in G, as effortlessly as if I were the conductor and not the performer. Above it rises a trumpet solo, my own improvisation, arching high above the structure of the concerto. My interior field of vision clears and becomes a neutral color, grey or dull purple. Ten clear lines run across it in sets of five. The score. As I play the notes they appear, in long vertical sets as in a conductor's score. They move off to the left as if the score were on a conveyor belt. Excellent. Half-notes, quarter-notes in the bass clef; long runs of sixteenth-notes in the treble, all look like the sun shining through pinholes in a dark sheet of paper. The concerto flows into Beethoven's Fifth Symphony, with a transition that pleases me. As far as I can tell the score is perfectly accurate. I am playing brilliantly, with enough confidence to throw grace notes of my own about in passages of great speed. I think, "It would be nice to have the cellos playing their counterpoint here," and then I hear the cellos making their quick departure from the rest of the strings. My fingers are not doing it. Play it with everything you have. The Finale of the Third, every single instrument achingly clean and individual. Nineteen years, Pierson, is this what you mean?

The Orchestra is the extension of what I want to hear.

I move into realms of my own, shifting from passage to passage, playing what I always wanted to hear; half-remembered snatches, majestic crescendos that you wake up from in the middle of the night, having dreamed them, and wish you could recapture; the architecture of Bach, the power of Beethoven, the beauty of Mozart, the wit and transitions of de Baik. All a confusion, all a marvel. Think it in your head and hear the Orchestra play it. The performer the instrument, the instrument a part of the performer. Pierson, what have you done?

Music. If you are at all alive to it you will have heard passages that bring a chill to your back and a flush of blood to your cheeks; a physical response to beauty. A rush. The music I am playing now is the very distillation of that feeling. It soars out and for the first time I hear echoes in this room, it is that powerful. The score no longer consists of musical notation; it is an impressionistic fantasy of a musical score, the background a deep blood red, the notes sudden clusters of jewels or long flows of colors I can't identify even as I see them; yet see them, most certainly. The drums are pounding, strings rushing and jumbling, awash in a wave of *fortissimo* brass shouts, not blaring—the horns of the Orchestra cannot blare—but at their highest volume, triumphant—

. . . triumphant she is as I ascend the dais I can see her face and she is strained and ecstatic as if in labor for to her I am being born again and throughout the investiture all I can see is her bright face before me unto her a Master is born—

. . . and masterful, chaotic yet perfectly calculated. The score is a *mille fleurs* of twisted colors, falling, falling, the notes are falling. I open my eyes and find that they are already stretched wide open; a rush of red, red is all I see, a blinding waterfall of molten glass cascading down, behind it a thousand suns.

I awake from a dream in which I was . . . in which I was . . . walking through hallways. Talking with someone. I cannot remember.

I am lying on the glass floor of the booth, I can feel the bas-relief of the clef signs. My mouth feels as if it had been washed in acids, which I suppose it has. My legs. My left hand is asleep. I have been poured from my container, my skeleton is gone. I am a lump of flesh. I move my arm. An achievement.

"Eric," comes the Master's voice, high-pitched in its anxiety. It is probably what awakened me. His hand on my shoulder. He babbles without pause as he helps me out of the Orchestra. "I just got back, you're all right, you're all right, the music you were playing, my God, magnificent, here, here, watch out, you're all right, my son—"

"I am blind," I croak. There is a pause, a gasp. He holds me in his arms, half carries me onto a cot of some sort, muttering in a strained voice as he moves me about.

"Horrible, horrible," he keeps saying. "Horrible." It is age-old. Lose your sight, and learn to see. I blink away tears for my lost vision, and cannot see myself blink.

"You will make a great Master," he says firmly.

I do not answer.

And after a long pause—

"Yes," I say, wishing he understood, wishing there was someone who understood, "I think it will."

# Kim Stanley Robinson

T here's a strange perception among some writers and critics that genre fiction, especially science fiction and fantasy, is somehow different from "literature." Despite the fact that many novels now universally regarded as classics began as Victorian soap-operas (Dickens, anyone?), speculative fiction's tendency to focus on ideas rather than characterization or symbolism leads some scholars to turn up their noses and condemn the whole genre as "mere entertainment."

Authors like Kim Stanley Robinson throw a monkey wrench into such arguments. Often categorized as a writer of "literary science fiction," Robinson is a student of language first and foremost, having studied English and literature all the way through a Ph.D., and unafraid to display his mastery of it. Best known for his widely praised Mars Trilogy, in which a longstanding passion for the Red Planet resulted in one of the most popular terraforming sagas of all time, Robinson has also produced the post-apocalyptic Three Californias trilogy, *Antarctica*, *The Years of Rice and Salt*, and the global-warming series Science in the Capitol. Often dealing with highly relevant environmental and social justice themes, in which scientists manage to triumph while still fundamentally acting like scientists, his works have picked up two Hugo and Nebula awards, the World Fantasy Award, the John W. Campbell Memorial Award, and no less than six Locus awards.

The story in this collection, "In Pierson's Orchestra," eventually evolved into the novel *A Memory of Whiteness*. But in 1976, long before the story's novelization or the successes of books like the Mars Trilogy, there was only a young grad student, and a fortuitous Clarion application . . .

**Looking back, what do you think still works well in this story? Why?**

I think the structuring of the story is quite strong, maybe because it is simple and conforms to the Aristotelean unities of time and place, as if it were a play. The protagonist's past is filled in neatly in this structure, again as it would be if the story were being staged, almost. This kind of structural success had to have been almost purely an accident. In terms of the content, the attempt to write about music is always doomed, but here it becomes part of a more general out-of-body experience like a shaman voyage, and the description of that transcendence has a certain rhetorical lift and carry to it—the first of many tries at describing such states in my work. There is also a little bit of life knowledge about piano teaching that got into the story, from my childhood with my mom. Little touches there are right because I knew what I was talking about. There were very few things you could say that about at the time I wrote that story, so to an extent it represents the power (often exaggerated) of the phrase "write what you know."

**If you were writing this today, what would you do differently? What are the story's weaknesses, and how would you change them?**

Well this is very hard to imagine. After I wrote *The Memory of Whiteness* as a continuation of this story, using this story as the first chapter, I understood that writing about music just can't be done very well; the two are simply too different, so that what can be said about music doesn't capture the actual experience of listening to music. So from that time (1983) on, I have not written about music except very incidentally. In the case of this story, music would be too important to leave out. If I were to write it today, I wouldn't write it. That would also save me having to confront the story's weaknesses, for instance its ignorance of drug addiction and withdrawal.

**What inspired this story? How did it take shape? Where was it initially published?**

I went to a Yes concert and watched Rick Wakeman play a synthesizer bank with which he could sound like an entire orchestra. It struck me that a physicalization of this electronic sound would make a beautiful statue as well as instrument. My grandfather was an organ player among other instruments, and I had enjoyed pulling the various stops on his organ and listening to the sounds it would make. So these experiences gave me the context for the idea to come to me, I'm sure.

At the time I had the idea for the story, I was beginning to add short story writing classes to my poetry classes at UC San Diego. I was in my junior year of college there, and over the previous year had become very intent on writing, mostly poetry, but with short fiction included almost from the start. At the same time I was discovering science fiction as a reader. I was reading a lot of New Wave science fiction and I found it really exciting. The future of the arts was now something science fiction was interested in, and the stories were filled with avant-garde techniques from the high Modernist period of the 1920s and 30s, which was another body of work I was discovering at that time. I was doing a lot of reading and writing, and all my life I listened to music while working; really at my house music was playing all the time. So it all came together in the winter of 1972, and I distinctly remember writing the first draft of this story by hand at my parents' house, in my old bedroom, over the Christmas break, and finishing the final few scenes in a single day, and re-reading the pages and realizing that I had done something better than I had ever managed before. As I had written stories off and on since I was about twelve, this feeling was among other things a distinct surprise.

**Where were you in your life when you published this piece, and what kind of impact did it have?**

Where I was when I sold it is the interesting part. I had sent the story in as my submission story to the Clarion writer's workshop, in the spring of 1974, and I had been accepted into the workshop, but had been unable to attend for personal reasons. When I wrote to tell the Clarion people that, they wrote back and said they were sorry and hoped I could attend the next year or some later time. I hoped so too, and forgot about it; spent much of that summer in the Sierras, and in August of 1974 took off from a backpacking trip direct for Boston, where I was going to start at Boston University as a graduate student in English. As I drove east on Highway 80 I called my parents from time to time, and I stopped late one afternoon in Rawlings, Wyoming, to call them from a gas station phone booth. My mom answered and told me a letter had arrived for me from Damon Knight. I had her open it and read it to me, and in it Damon said he had read and liked my Clarion submission story, and would like to buy it for *Orbit*. I was amazed. I drove on that evening with Beethoven's Third playing very loudly. I stopped for the night at the rest stop on the continental divide, which in those days (I hope still) was marked by a stupendously tall statue of Lincoln's head. This seemed a very appropriate magical sign to me, and I laid out in my sleeping bag in the parking lot next to my car, and by a street lamp read Fritz Leiber's "Gonna Roll the Bones" in Ellison's *Dangerous Visions*, and afterward lay there awake for a good part of the night.

Publication itself was not at all as memorable. It took a long time before it came out in *Orbit 18*; I think it was 1976. After that I was truly a published writer, and that was nice to think and to tell people. Also, it made me think of myself as a writer earlier than I might have otherwise, and to throw myself into all my efforts with that project in mind, and to enjoy everything that happened as part of the process of becoming a writer. In that sense Damon's generosity had a huge impact on my life.

**How has your writing changed over the years, both stylistically and in terms of your writing process?**

That's hard to say. So much has changed. It's like looking back two or three reincarnations; I have a tenuous sense of connection with that person. Also it's not really fair to compare yourself to a beginner. I'm a better writer now, but it's been thirty-five years of continuous work on the problem, so I'd better be. As for my writing process, I still work in much the same way; I get an idea, write a quick rough draft, revise it many times.

**What advice do you have for aspiring authors?**

Learn a day job and keep it for money and raw material for fiction; vary the pacing in your stories; schedule your writing time into your weekly schedule; finish stories; send them out; read widely; try pastiches and parodies; read poetry and write it too.

# Destroyers
## by Greg Bear

You are the man who destroys churches?" I asked, poising my pencil over a clean sheet of note paper.

"Yes," said the young, pleasant-looking man before me. "I do."

"And what are your reasons for destroying churches?" I scribbled as he spoke.

"Reasons? There are many. Let's see . . . mmm. Yes, for one, churches have sought to hold people under their power for centuries, even eons. They have sought to impress their often archaic ideas on people by any and all means—though force, mingling of societies, legislations, anything." He smiled as I wrote. "You are doing an article?"

"Perhaps," I replied. "When did you go before the computer to be licensed?"

"Four months ago. There was a long line of people, many different complaints and ideas. Some were licensed; most weren't. These fools who wish to exterminate a neighbor because he cracks his egg at the small end get nowhere with the computer, of course. It only accepts legitimate—and well worded—queries for licenses, of course."

"And you destroy synagogues, monasteries, and temples?"

"Of course."

"But not the Buildings of the New Religion?"

"No, I have no complaint against them."

"Thank you," I said.

He acknowledged with a smile and handshake. "When you get your article finished, send me a copy of the magazine. I would enjoy seeing what you write."

"Very well," I replied. "If I sell it."

"Oh, no doubt you will, if you're any writer at all. Many people are interested in church-destroyers these days."

I left the church-destroyer's office and went downtown on my next mission. I thought deeply on what the c.d. had said, and came to many interesting conclusions. They were transferred to my notebook as soon as I grasped them.

I entered the office of the communist-destroyer. In my notebook I made sure not to confuse him with the church-destroyer when I abbreviated. I put him down as cm.d.

"What can I do for you?" he asked. He was a thin man with large eyes and nervous skin, with a face which can be described only as loose. He did not smile, but he did not frown, either.

"You destroy communists?" I asked, pencil over notebook.

"Yes. Every damn one of them. Why?" Did I detect a hint of a frown? No . . . perhaps just a minor throat irritation. I prepared to switch on my shield, just in case.

"I write," I replied. "Articles, stories, books, and such."

"Oh. Be careful when you leave the building, my friend. There is a man down the street a ways who destroys writers." His eyes flashed.

"I am a government writer," I said, and produced the small counterfeit card. "To continue. Why do you destroy communists?"

"Because they wish to take us all over. They're clever, too, and they could do it if it wasn't for us."

"There is a group?"

"Naturally. It isn't too large, of course—" he lied, obviously—"but it's enough to keep them from getting too strong all at once."

"How do you tell a communist?" I scribbled furiously.

"Normally we get calls from people who report their neighbors or something. Then we check out the reports—there's a stiff penalty in hitting normal people, of course—and move in if they're valid. You'd be surprised how many false reports we get. Probably the communists do it themselves, give reports, I mean—just to get at us." His face was red. He spoke in a tense voice. I readied one free finger over my shield switch.

"Fine. Thank you very much, and success."

He smiled weakly and opened the door for me. "Careful of that writer-destroyer!" he warned and I shook my head.

I took the monorails to Jayark-Mirie and noted with interest that two men shot each other on car 34-c. I wondered who they were even now, but nobody ever finds out unless one of the destroyers isn't really a destroyer. If he's a normal person, they raise quite a fuss.

In Jayark, two men started battling it out on the streets and everybody automatically flipped on their shields. I believe only one man was killed that time, but I didn't really notice.

I interviewed the conservative-destroyer in his home.

"You destroy conservatives?" I asked.

"Yes, mm hmm. Conservatives, John Birchers, Nazis, and so on. You a writer?"

I nodded. "Why?" I asked.

"Why? Why what?"

"Why do you destroy conservatives?"

"Because they think they're right and no one else is. I can't stand that. It makes me sick."

"Why didn't you become a church-destroyer, or a communist-destroyer, or somebody like that?"

"I only have one choice of license and occupation, of course. I chose this one—don't know really why. I just dislike old fogies with polluted brains functioning at half mast in reverence for the dear departed good old days."

"Thank you."

The last person I interviewed was the atheist-destroyer. He was an aged gentleman, dressed in a trim gray suit and carrying a fine cherry cane with gold tip. He had a sour face and a frown of the true avenger.

"You kill atheists?"

"I kill atheists." He had a rough, grating voice sounding like gravel tinking on windows.

"Why?"

"Because it's God's law. They hate all honest religioners, they do, and anyone who doesn't think like them is nuts. In their opinion, of course. Bunch of twisted punks, all of them." I thanked him and left the house. The monorail trip back to Brighton was quick and silent, giving me little time to organize my notes. I did that when I arrived at my hotel.

I spent three hours re-wording and correcting and doing the final draft. Then I sent my report and query into the computer.

I received my license today, along with the blank entrance form for purchasing a weapon.

I'm licensed to destroy destroyers.

# Greg Bear

S ince the 1970s, Greg Bear has been publishing short stories and novels that attempt to answer deep and abiding questions regarding
both science and culture. Though occasionally branching into fantasy and horror, the hard science fiction for which he is best known has
addressed everything from viral evolution to overpopulation and the Fermi
paradox, and his short story (and later novel) "Blood Music" has been
credited as the first appearance of nanotechnology in science fiction. Along
the way, he's picked up three Hugo Awards, a John W. Campbell Award, a
Robert A. Heinlein Award, and a whopping five Nebula Awards—one of
only two authors ever to win a Nebula in every category. The scientific rigor
within many of his stories has been praised by the prestigious research
journal *Nature*, and that same devotion to cutting-edge fact and plausible
extrapolation has led him to serve on political and scientific action com-
mittees and advisory boards for everyone from Microsoft to the U.S. Army,
the CIA, and the Department of Homeland Security.

Though his short stories began appearing regularly in major science fiction
venues three decades ago—and his artwork several years before that—Bear's
little-known first step into the field saw print several years prior, while the
author himself was still in high school.

**Looking back, what do you think still works well in this story? Why?**

The shorter a story is, the more difficult it is to write—but for me, as a young-
ster, this one was remarkably easy. Even at the age of fifteen, the culture of
intolerance and bigotry of the mid-sixties had affected me strongly, and the
story even today packs a bit of that old punch.

**If you were writing this today, what would you do differently? What are
the story's weaknesses, and how would you change them?**

I'd probably just rewrite it, which would likely make it twice as long.

**What inspired this story? How did it take shape? Where was it initially
published?**

I wrote it in 1966—so long ago I don't remember the specific circumstances.
Around that time, I was visiting Los Angeles with my cousin Dan Garrett and
dropping by Forry Ackerman's house to chat and see his collection. Forry
suggested I try sending stories to Robert Lowndes, who was editing a number of magazines—very low-budget, small saddle-staple productions for

Health Knowledge Publications, including *The Magazine of Horror* and *Famous Science Fiction*. I thought the logo for *The Magazine of Horror* was a little too gruesome—I was quite the style worry-wart back in those days—and drew up a scratchboard sample of an alternate cover, which Lowndes graciously thanked me for, but said that the logo's original dripping blood no doubt helped sales. I then submitted "Destroyers" to him, and to my shock, almost immediately he accepted it. It was published in 1967, and I was paid 10 dollars—and somewhere, I still have a copy of that check. I fondly remember dropping by Readerama in Grossmont Center in San Diego to buy copies of my first publication—with high school buddies in tow. Stephen King, incidentally, published his first story in *The Magazine of Horror*.

**Where were you in your life when you published this piece, and what kind of impact did it have?**

I was a kid. I had been submitting stories to magazines for three years at that point—and the sale knocked me for a loop. It also impressed my parents. I don't remember lording it over my high school English teachers, but I'm sure that was at the back of my thoughts! However, I wouldn't sell another story for four years, so that balanced things out.

**How has your writing changed over the years, both stylistically and in terms of your writing process?**

It's gotten a little better.

**What advice do you have for aspiring authors?**

Keep writing! Don't get hung up on one story or one book. A career is rarely made by one achievement.

**Any anecdotes regarding the story or your experiences as a fledgling writer?**

I could try to imagine my teachers dealing with a student who had already professionally published a story, but who refused to do the assigned homework—how do you get through to such a character?

# Out of Phase
## by Joe Haldeman

T rapped. From the waterfront bar to a crap game to a simpleminded ambush in a dead-end alley.

He didn't blame them for being angry. His pockets were stuffed with their money, greasy crumpled fives and tens. Two thousand and twenty of their hard-earned dollars, if his memory served him right. And of course it did.

They had supplied three sets of dice—two loaded, one shaved. All three were childishly easy to manipulate. He let them win each throw at first, and then less and less often. Finally, he tested their credulity and emptied their pockets, with ten sevens in a row.

That much had been easy. But now he was in a difficult position. Under the transparent pretext of finding a bigger game, the leader of the gang had steered him into this blind alley, where five others were hiding in ambush.

And now the six were joined in a line, advancing on him, pushing him toward the tall Hurricane fence that blocked the end of the alley.

Jeff started pacing them, walking backwards. Thirty seconds, give or take a little, before he would back into the fence and be caught. Thirty seconds objective . . .

Jeff froze and did a little trick with his brain. All the energy his strange body produced, except for that fraction needed to maintain human form, was channeled into heightening his sensory perceptions, accelerating his mental processes. He had to find a way out of this dilemma, without exposing his true nature.

The murderous sextet slowed down in Jeff's frozen eyes as the ratio of subjective to objective time flux increased arithmetically, geometrically, exponentially.

A drop of sweat rolled from the leader's brow, fell two feet in a fraction of a second, a foot in the next second, an inch in the next, a millimeter, a micron . . .

Now.

A pity he couldn't just kill them all, slowly, painfully. Terrible to have artistic responsibility stifled by practical obligations. Such a beautiful composition.

They were frozen in attitudes ranging from the leader's leering, sadistic anticipation of pleasure (dilettante!), to the little one's ill-concealed fear of pain, of inflicting pain, to Jimmy's unthinking, color-blinded compulsion to take apart, destroy . . . ah, Jimmy, slave of entropy, servant of disorder and chaos, I will make of you an epic, a saga.

I *would*, that is. I *could*.

But Llarvl said . . .

That snail. Insensitive brute.

Next time out I'll get a supervisor who can *understand*.

But next time out, I'll be too old.

Even now I can feel it.

Damn that snail!

The ship hovered above a South American plantation. People looked at it and saw only the sky beyond. Radar would never detect it. Only a voodoo priest, in a mushroom trance, felt its presence. He tried to verbalize and died of a cerebral occlusion.

Too quick. Artless.

Llarvl was talking to him. "Bluntly, I wish we didn't have to use you, Braxn." His crude race communicated vocally, and the unmodulated, in-and-out-of-phase thought waves washed a gravelly ebb and flow of pain through Braxn's organ of communication. He stored the pain, low intensity that it was, for contemplation at a more satisfactory time.

He repeated: "If only we had brought someone else of your sort, besides your father, of course. Shape-changers are not such a rarity." He plucked out a cilium in frustration, but of course felt no pain. Braxn was too close; sucked it in.

"A G'drellian poet. A poet of pain. Of all the useless baggage to drag around on a survey expedition . . ." He sighed and ground his shell against the wall. "But we have no choice. Only two bipeds aboard the ship, and neither of them is even remotely mammalian. And the natives of this planet are acutely xenophobic. Hell, they're *omni*phobic. Even harder to take than you, worthy poet.

"But this is the biggest find of the whole trip! The crucial period of transition—they may be on the brink of civilization; still animals, but rapidly advancing. Think of it! In ten or twenty generations they'll be human, and seek us, as most do. We've met thousands of civilized races, more thousands of savage ones; but this is the first we've found in transition. Ethnology, alien psychology, everything"—he shuddered—"even your people's excuse for art, will benefit immeasurably."

Braxn made no comment. He hadn't bothered to form a speech organ for the interview. He knew Llarvl would do all the talking anyway.

But he had been studying, under stasis, for several hours. Knowing exactly what needed to be done, he let half his body disintegrate into its component parts and started to remold them.

First the skeleton, bone by thousandth bone; the internal organs, in logical order, glistening, throbbing, functioning; wet-red muscle, fat, connective tissue, derma, epidermis; smooth and olive, fingernails, hair, small mole on the left cheek.

Vocal cords, virgin, throb contralto: "Mammalian enough?"

"Speak Galactic!"

"I said, 'Mammalian enough?' I mean, would you like them bigger," she demonstrated, "or smaller?"

"How would I know?" snapped Llarvl, trying to hide his disgust. "Pick some sort of statistical mean."

Braxn picked a statistical mean between the October and November Playmate of the Month.

With what he thought was detached objectivity, Llarvl said, "Ugly bunch of creatures, aren't they?" About one hundred million years ago, Llarvl's race had one natural enemy—a race of biped mammals.

With a silvery laugh, Braxn left to prepare for planetfall.

Braxn had studied the Earth and its people for some ten thousand hours, subjective time. She knew about clothes, she knew about sex, she knew about rape.

So she appeared on Earth, on a dirt road in South America, without a stitch. Without a blush. And her scholastic observations were confirmed, in the field, so to speak, in less than five minutes. She learned quite a bit the first time; less the second. The third time, well, she was merely bored.

She made him into a beautiful . . . poem?

She made him into a mouse-sized, shriveled brown husk, lying dead by the side of the road, his tiny features contorted with incredible agony.

She synthesized clothes, grey and dirty, and changed herself into an old, crippled hag. It was twenty minutes before she met another man, who . . .

Another dry husk.

Braxn was getting an interesting, if low, opinion of men, Bolivian farmers in particular; so she changed herself into one. The shoe on the other foot, she found, made things different, but not necessarily better. Well, she was gathering material. That's what Llarvl wanted.

She waited for a car to come by, reverted to the original voluptuous pattern, disposed of the driver when he stopped to investigate, took his form and his car, and started on her world tour.

Braxn tried to do everything and be everyone.

"He" was, in turn, doctor, lawyer, fencing coach, prostitute, auto racer, mountain climber, golf pro. He ran a pornography shop in Dallas, a hot dog stand at Coney Island, a death-sleep house in Peking, a Vienese coffeehouse, the museum at Dachau. He peddled Bibles and amulets, Fuller brushes and heroin. He was a society deb, a Bohemian poet, a member of Parliament, a *cul-de-jatte* in Monaco.

For operating expenses, when he needed small sums, he wove baskets, sold his body, dived for pennies, cast horoscopes.

Hustled pool.

The sweat drop had moved a hundredth of an inch. Must stop wasting time, but it's so hard to concentrate when it feels like you have all the time in the universe.

Braxn knew that he could remain in this state only a few more minutes (subjective) before he was stuck in it permanently. On the ship he could spend as much time as he wanted in mental acceleration, but here there was no apparatus to shock him out of it before trance set it. The trance would go on for more than a thousand years, such was his race's span of life. But to the six hoods he would age and die in a few seconds, reverting to his original form for an invisible nanosecond before dissolving into a small grey mound of dust.

He was seeing in the far infrared now, and definition was very poor. He switched to field recognition. The dull animals confronting him had dim red psionic envelopes, except for the one in agony, whose aura was bordered with coruscating violet flashes.

Electromagnetic. The ion fog around the leader's watch glowed pale blue. Leakage from the telephone and power lines made kaleidoscopic patterns in the sky. His back felt warm.

Warm?

He switched to visual again and searched the people's eyes for reflections. There—the little scared one—his eyes mirrored the fence, the Hurricane fence. Spaced with ceramic insulators . . .

He started to slow down his mind, speed up the world. The drop inched, fell to the ground with slow purpose; struck and flowered into tiny droplets.

Sound welled up around him.

"—eezuz Christ, he must be scared stiff!"

Braxn stumbled back toward the electrified fence, manufacturing adrenaline to substitute for his spent strength. His stomach knotted and flamed with impossible hunger. He received the pain and cherished it.

The leader advanced for the kill, bold and cocky, switchblade in his right hand, his left swinging a bicycle chain like a stubby lariat.

Braxn secreted a flesh-colored, rubbery coating over his body and, on top of that, a thin layer of saline mucus.

"Come, Retiarius!" he croaked.

"Huh?" The leader faltered in his advance, too late.

Braxn grabbed the bicycle chain and the fence simultaneously. There was a low, sixty-cycle hum, and the hood crumpled to the ground. He looped the chain around the scared one's neck and pulled him into the fence. Three to go.

The others had stopped, bewildered. Braxn, gaining strength at the expense of his temporary body, snatched the nearest one and hurled him into the fence. Another started to run, but Braxn used the chain as a bolo and brought him down. He dragged him screaming to the fence and shoved his face into it.

The only one left was Jimmy.

"Jimmy-baby!" The dim giant stood his ground, trying to understand what had happened, too sure of his own strength to be really afraid. He took a tentative step forward.

Now. The more fantastic, the better. He could do anything in front of this oaf.

Braxn kept the rubbery coating, but altered its reflective properties. Now it was flesh-colored to Jimmy. He kinked his hair, flattened his nose, broadened his lips, started to swell in height and breadth.

He was becoming a carbon copy of Jimmy—more true in the man's eyes than any photograph could be, for the specifications were coming from his own dim brain.

Thus the biceps were a bit larger, the face a little meaner, than the lying mirror would reflect. The teeth were square and white, and instead of the ugly mole on his check there was an incredibly virile scar that lanced down to his chin, catching the corner of his mouth in a perpetual arrogant sneer. He laughed, deep and hollow, mirthless.

"Whassa matter, you? Y'seen me before?"

Jimmy stood transfixed, a bewildered smile decorating his vacant face.

"Nuthin' faze you, Jim?" Braxn looked at the big Negro and cracked his knuckles. He let one finger fall off. It hit the ground, changed into a centipede, and scurried off. Jimmy followed its progress with awe. He looked up to his double again, smile gone, eyes narrowing.

Braxn dropped the patois. "Watch closely, Jimmy. You've got fear in you, like anybody else, and I think I know where to find it."

The strong, manly face blurred for an instant and came back into focus. The scar was a puffy infected seam that defiled a face no longer vigorous or handsome. It pulled down the lower lip to expose a yellow canine. The face was lined with a delicate tracery of worry and pain, the grooves growing deeper and more complex in front of Jimmy's horrified eyes.

The hair, sprinkled with grey, grew white and was gone except for a dirty stubble on the twisted, knobby chin. Face as body wasted away; wrinkled parchment stretched tight over a leering death mask.

Bloodshot eyes clot with rheum, cataracts cloud and blind them, the lids close and collapse inward and the body—real only in the minds of two disparate creatures—was mercifully dead.

The brown skin darkened further and released its life grip on the ancient body; the body puffed up again in macabre burlesque of its younger brawn. It lived again for a short time as maggots fed on its putrescence.

Then a dry, withered husk again, still standing upright; the last vestiges of skin and flesh sloughed off to reveal a brown-stained skeleton filled with nameless cobwebs. It collapsed with a splintering clatter.

On top of the pile of grey dust and bones, the yellow skull glared balefully at Jimmy for a long moment, and then, piece by piece, the whole grisly collection started to reassemble itself.

Before the clatter of Jimmy's footstep's had faded, his alter ego was whole and well again. The black-skin molecules had become charcoal-grey-Brooks-Brothers-suit molecules and Braxn, the very model of the young man on his way up.

Braxn scanned the still forms around him and found that they were all still unconscious. One, the little one, was dead. Probing further, Braxn dissolved a blood clot, patched an infarction, and shocked the still heart back into action. Pity to spoil good art—he liked the combination of cause and effect and dumb luck causing only the harmless one to die. Survival of the fittest, eugenics will out, and all that. With a mental shrug, Braxn walked off to find a cab.

"Oh, enter, by all means." Llarvl slipped into the Survey Chief's cabin with trepidation. He was in for a bad time.

The chief, who looked like a cross between a carrot and a praying mantis, got right to the point. "Llarvl, your reports stopped coming in several cycles ago. From this I infer that either a.) your scout is dead, not likely; b.) he got disgusted with your asinine questions, rather more likely; or c.) he went on one of his blasted binges and is busily turning the autochthones into quatrains and limericks. I find this last alternative the most probable, if the least palatable. He *is* a G'drellian, an adolescent at that. Do you know what that means?"

"Yes, sir, it means that he's in the aesthetic stage of . . ."

"It *means* he should have been locked up before we got within a parsec of this primitive world.

"But, sir, after his initial experiments he stopped killing them. Why, I *made* him stop. He might have drawn attention to himself."

"Your devotion to objectivity is most commendable."

"Thank you, sir."

"It shows that you know and appreciate the first rule of contact." He pressed a stud, and one wall became transparent. He gestured at the busy scene beneath them. "Are they aware of our presence?"

"Our course not, sir. That *is* the first law."

"Tell me, Llarvl. What sort of radiation would you suppose their eyes are sensitive to?"

The captain's addiction to obliqueness was most exasperating. "Well, sir, since their planet goes around a yellow star, their organs of vision are sensitive to a narrow band of radiation centered around the 'yellow' wavelengths."

The captain scraped his thorax with a claw. Llarvl interpreted this as applause. His race had forgotten sarcasm eons before the captain's had invented fire.

"You are a good study, Llarvl."

"Thank you, sir."

"So we make our ship transparent in these wavelengths, at great expenditure of power."

"Yes, sir. So the natives' development won't be influenced by premature knowledge of . . ."

". . . and with similar expenditure of power, we extend this transparency down into the longer wavelengths. Why do we do this, Llarvl?

The little ethnologist was perplexed. Even the lowliest cabin boy could answer these questions.

"Why, of course, sir, it's to make the ship invisible to radar detection. Only it's not really invisible, it's just that the local implicit coefficient of absorption becomes asymptotic with . . ."

"Llarvl"—the captain sighed—"I learned one of those creatures' words the other day; and I suppose you've run into it now and then: catechism."

"Yes, sir," Llarvl squirmed.

"Now as far as I can tell, though I'm not a man of learning myself, this is a form of stylized debate; wherein one person asks a series of questions, whose answers are so simple that they brook no disagreement or misinterpretation. These answers, forced, as it were, upon the hapless interrogatee, lead to an inevitable conclusion, which gains a spurious validity through sheer tautological mass. Is that fairly accurate?"

Llarvl paused a second to retrieve the sentence's verbs, as the captain had mischievously, if appropriately, switched from English to Middle High German.

"Yes, sir, very accurate."

"Well, then"—the captain gave a gleaming metallic smile—"to borrow another of their delightfully savage concepts, the *coup de grace*. How did we know that they had radar, long before we came into its range?"

"Radio broadcasts, sir, and television."

"Which means?"

"Mass communications, sir."

"Which means?"

"Sir, I'm aware of . . ."

"You're aware of the fact that our arty friend could gain control of this planetwide network, and, in a matter of seconds, destroy almost every intelligent being on the planet. Or worse, reduce them to gibbering animals. Or perhaps worse still, increase their understanding of themselves beyond the threshold . . ."

"Yes, sir." Llarvl could fill in the blanks.

"Then get out of here and let more capable minds deal with the situation."

"Yes, sir." The ethnologist started to scuttle toward the door.

"And Llarvl . . . remember that your captain, like most of the members of this expedition, normally communicates mind to mind, and can read your surface thoughts even when they are not verbalized."

"Yes, sir," he said meekly.

"Your captain may be a 'pompous martinet,' yes, but really, Llarvl: 'a vegetable that walks like a man'? Racism is, I think, singularly inappropriate in an ethnologist. Make an appointment with the psychiatric staff."

"Yes, sir."

"And on your way down, check at the galley and see if Troxl has a couple of years' work for you to do."

The captain watched the disconsolate creature scurry out, and settled down at his desk. He passed a claw over a photosensitive plate.

"Computer," he thought.

"Here, Captain."

"Where the hell is that G'drellian poet?"

The machine thought a low hum. "I can't find him. He must be generating a strong block. You know a G'drellian can synthesize 'dummy' thought waves exactly out of phase with his natural pattern, and by combining the two patterns . . ."

"How do you know he isn't just on the other side of the planet?" A computer will talk on one subject forever, if you let it.

"Using the planet's satellites as passive reflectors, I can cover 80 percent or more of the planet's surface, and by integrating the fringe effects from . . ."

"I believe you. Then tell me; where is his old goat of a father?"

"Mediating in the meat locker, in the form of a large stalagtite, as he has been, I might add, ever since you . . ."

"All right! Have Stores send me up a winter outfit. I'll have to go and try to blackmail him into telling me where his blasted progeny is."

Give me a thousand humorless ethnologists, thought the captain to himself; give me a thousand garrulous computers, but spare me the company of G'drellians. Even on G'drell, they confine the adolescents to one island, to work out their poetry on worms and insects and each other.

A survey expedition needs a G'drellian, of course; a mature one to solve problems beyond the scope of the computer, but—

Damn that Brohass! He must have known he was gravid when he volunteered for the trip. How do you deal with these creatures, who seem to live only to torment other people with their weird, inscrutable sense of humor? Brohass knew he would undergo fission, knew his offspring would reach adolescence in midvoyage, and probably contrived to send the ship to a planet where . . .

The captain's reverie was broken by the robot from Stores. "The clothing you requested, sir."

"Put it on the hook there." The robot did so and glided out of the room.

I should have had it delivered to the locker, thought the captain; clothing was tantamount to obscenity to many of the crew members, and one must maintain dignity . . .

"Yes, one must, mustn't one," thought the computer.

"Will you go do something useful?" The captain threw up a block in time to miss the reply. He jerked the clothes off the hook and strode out of his cabin, letting out occasional thoughts about the ancestry, mating, habits, etc., of the machine that was the ship's true captain.

"Fasten your seat belts, please." The slender stewardess swayed down the aisle, past a young man with a handsome, placid face and a Brooks Brothers suit. "Landing at Kennedy International in three minutes."

Braxn did as told, shifting the heavy attaché case from his lap to the floor. Two hundred pounds of gold bullion would buy a great deal of prime time.

They landed uneventfully. Braxn took a helicopter to the Pan American Building, went down to the 131st floor, and into an office with gold leaf on the frosted-glass entrance, proclaiming Somebody, Somebody, and Somebody, Advertising Counselors.

He came out two hundred pounds lighter, having traded the gold for one minute of time, nine o'clock Saturday night (an hour away), on all of the major radio and television networks. A triumph of money over red tape, his commercial would be strictly live, with no chance of FCC interference. And his brand of soap would certainly make the world a cleaner place for a person to live in.

Alone.

The captain donned his thermal outerwear and entered the massive locker. Sure enough, there was a huge blue stalagtite suspended from the ceiling. He addressed it.

"Brohass," he thought obsequiously, "would you serve your captain?"

The huge icicle fell and splintered into several thousand pieces. They reassembled into a creature who looked rather like the captain.

"What would you do to me if I said 'no'?"

"That's ridiculous," said the captain, somewhat emboldened by facing a familiar shape. "No one can do anything to harm you."

"All right, that settled, will you please *go* and let me get back to my conversation."

Curious in spite of himself, the captain asked, "Who are you conversing with? You don't generally think with the other crew members."

"My father has found a particularly humorous ninth-order differential equation; he is explaining it to me, and I would like to devote all of my energy to understanding."

The captain shivered, not just from cold. Brohass's father had been dead for thirty years. But half of him would live as long as Brohass lived; a quarter would live as long as Braxn, and so on down the line. It was unsettling to more mortal beings that a G'drellian maintained an autonomous existence, within his descendants, for tens of thousands of years after physical death. Whether a G'drellian would ever die completely was problematical. None yet had.

"This won't take much of your time. I want you to locate Braxn and give him a message."

"Why can't you find him yourself?

"It's a rather large planet, Brohass, and he's thrown up a strong communication block."

"We're on a planet? Which one?"

The captain thought a long string of figures. "They call it 'Earth.'"

"I'm afraid I'm unfamiliar with it. Please open your mind and let me extract the relevant details."

The captain did so, with chagrin. Brohass could easily have asked the computer, but his people were born voyeurs, and never would pass up a chance to probe another's mind.

"Interesting, savage—I can see why he was drawn to it. Incidentally, your treatment of Llarvl was shameful. In his place, *you* would have lost control of my son just as quickly.

"And your knowledge, captain, of the people on this planet, is encyclopedic, but imperfect. You misunderstand both catechism and tautology, you used the expression *coup de grace* where *coup de theatre* would have been more fitting, and your Middle German would send a Middle German into convulsions. Furthermore, you *are* an ambulatory vegetable.

"To your credit, however, you were correct in assessing my son's plans. He is now in possession of a minute of 'time,' as they say, on the planet's communication network.

"Funny idea, that; beings possessing time rather than the other way around . . ."

"Brohass!"

"Captain?"

"Aren't you going to do anything?"

"Interfere with my child's development?"

"He's going to *kill* several billion entities!"

"Yes . . . he probably is. Mammals, though. You have to admit they'd probably never make anything of themselves, anyhow."

"Brohass! You've got to stop him!"

"I'm pulling your spindly leg, captain. I'll talk to him. Just once, just once I would like to have a captain who could take a joke. You know, you vegetable people are unique in the civilized universe in your . . ."

"How much time do you have?"

"Oh, two thousand three hundred thirty-eight years, four days and . . ."

"No, no! How much time before Braxn gets on the air?"

"If Braxn got on the air, he would fall to the ground, even as you and I."

The captain made a strangling noise.

"Oh, don't bust a root. I have several seconds yet." Brohass reverted to his native formlessness and sent a piercing tendril of thought through his son's massive block.

"Braxn! This is your father. Will you slow down just a little bit?"

Braxn concentrated, and the bustling studio slowed down and froze into a tableau of suspended action. "Yes, Father. Is there something I can help you with?"

"Well, first, tell me what you're doing in a television studio."

"At the minute of maximum saturation, I'm going to broadcast the Vegan death-sign. That's all."

"That's all. You'll kill everybody."

"Well, not everybody. Just those who are watching television. Oh, yes, and I've worked out a phonetic equivalent for simultaneous radio transmission. Get a few more that way, if it works."

"Oh, I'm sure you can do it, son. But, Braxn, that's what I wanted to think to you about."

"You're going to try to think me out of it."

"Well, if you want to put it that way . . ."

"I bet that joke of captain put you up to it."

"You know that that vegetable who walks like a man . . ."

"Hey; that's a good one, Father. When'd you—"

"—neither he nor anyone else on this tin can could make me do anything that I . . ." Brohass sighed. "Look, Braxn. You're poaching on a game preserve. Worse, shooting fish in a barrel. With a fission bomb, yet. How can you get any aesthetic satisfaction out of that?"

"Father, I know that quantity is no substitute for quality. But there are so *many* here!"

"—and you want to be poet laureate, right?" Brohass snorted mentally.

"There's something wrong in that? This will be the biggest epic since Jkdir exterminated the . . ."

"Braxn, Braxn; my son—you're temporizing. You know what's wrong, don't you? Surely you can feel it."

Braxn fell silent as he tried to think of a convincing counterargument. He knew what was coming.

"The fact is that you are maturing rapidly. It's time to put away your blocks—sure, you can go through with this trivial exercise. But you won't be poet laureate. You'll be dunce of the millennium, prize buffoon. You're too old for this nonsense anymore; I know it, you know it, and the whole race would know it eventually. You wouldn't be able to show your mind anywhere in the civilized universe."

He knew that his father was telling the truth. He had known for several days that he was ready for the next stage of development, but his judgment was blinded by the enormity of the canvas he had before him.

"Correct. The next stage awaits you, and I can assure you that it will be even more satisfying than the aesthetic. You have a nice planet here, and you might as well use it as the base of your operations. The captain is easily cowed—after I assure him that you no longer wish to, shall we say, immortal-ize these people in verse, he'll be only too glad to move on without you. We'll be back to pick you up in a century or so. Good-bye, son."

"Good-bye, Father."

The filament of the green light on the camera facing him was just starting to glow. He had something less than a hundredth of a second.

Extending his mental powers to the limit, he traced down every network and advertising executive who knew of the deal he had made. From the minds of hundreds of people he erased a million memories, substituting harmless ones. Two hundred pounds of gold disappeared back into thin air. Books were balanced.

Everyone in the studio had the same memory: Five minutes ago a police-escorted black limousine screeched to a halt out front, and this man, familiar face lined and pale with shock, stormed in with a covey of Secret Service men and commandeered the studio.

Braxn filled out his face and body with paunch. The man who owned this face died painlessly, as soon as Braxn had assimilated the contents of his brain. The body disappeared; his family and associates "remembered" that he was in New York for the week.

A finger of thought pushed into another man's heart and stopped it. Convincing—he was overworked and overweight, anyhow. But to be on the safe side, Braxn adjusted his catabolism to make it look as if he had died ten minutes earlier. He manufactured appropriate cover stories.

All this accomplished, Braxn let time resume its original rate of flow.

The light winked green. A voice offstage said, "Ladies and gentlemen"—what else could one say—"the, uh, vice president of the United States."

Braxn assumed a tragic and weary countenance. "It is my sad duty to inform the nation . . ."

Nine stages in the development of a G'drellian, from adolescence to voluntary termination.

The first stage is aesthetic, appreciation of an Art alien to any human, save a de Sade or a Hitler.

The second stage is power . . .

# Joe Haldeman

J oe Haldeman has a mixed relationship with writing advice, and for good reason—having sold the first two stories he ever wrote to *Galaxy* and *The Twilight Zone*, and his first novel to the first publisher he showed it to, Haldeman is living proof that sometimes you can succeed right out of the gate, with nothing more than raw talent and effort. Yet as a longstanding writing teacher everywhere from MIT to the prestigious Clarion writers' workshops, Haldeman still does his best to teach the rest of us just what it is about his own writing that has brought him such success.

And success it is, by anyone's standards. The science fiction classic *The Forever War*, published just three years after his mainstream debut novel *War Year*, won the Hugo, Nebula, and Ditmar awards, and is held up along-side Heinlein's *Starship Troopers* by many fans as the best science fiction war novel of all time, drawing heavily on Haldeman's own wartime experiences as a combat engineer in Vietnam. It sequel, *The Forever Peace*, won the Hugo, Nebula, and John W. Campbell awards—the first such "triple crown" in more than two decades. Along the way, Haldeman's authored more than thirty other books and graphic novels, picking up several more Hugos and Nebulas, multiple Rhyslings for SF poetry, a World Fantasy Award, and the James Tiptree, Jr. Award, making him one of the most respected and criti-cally acclaimed writers in the genre.

Yet even the best have to start somewhere, and before the military service that would come to influence Haldeman's most famous works, there was "Out of Phase," in which a young author introduces us to the myriad and fascinating alien races inside his head . . .

**Looking back, what do you think still works well in this story? Why?**

I guess most of the humor holds up. And the horror. (It was written before I went to Vietnam, interestingly enough, though rewritten afterward.)

**If you were writing this today, what would you do differently? What are the story's weaknesses, and how would you change them?**

I couldn't write this story today, because I'm not 23 years old anymore. If I were to write a similar story, it would be more tightly focused; there are a few pages where I obviously didn't know where the story was going. But that doesn't mean that I can go to those pages and fix them, because the flawed passages generated the rest of the story, for better or for worse. The actual rewrite of "Out of Phase" is the novel *Camouflage*, written some thirty years later.

**What inspired this story? How did it take shape? Where was it initially published?**

The story was inspired by a writing class deadline. It started with a detailed description of a pool game, which I later cut, at editor Fred Pohl's suggestion. It was initially published in *Galaxy* magazine.

**Where were you in your life when you published this piece, and what kind of impact did it have?**

I'd just gotten back from Vietnam. The army gave you 30 days' "compassionate leave," and one thing I did with the time was retype the two SF stories I'd written in my last semester in college, and send them out. (The other one, "I of Newton," eventually wound up as an episode on *Twilight Zone*.) It sold in a couple of months, and I realized that writing would be an important part of my life, if not a significant source of income.

**How has your writing changed over the years, both stylistically and in terms of your writing process?**

My writing has gotten smoother, if not easier. I write almost every day, which was not true in the very beginning.

**What advice do you have for aspiring authors?**

Listen to advice but don't take it.

**Any anecdotes regarding the story or your experiences as a fledgling writer?**

An almost impossible coincidence . . . when this story was supposed to come out, August 1969 (for the September issue), we were traveling around in Mexico. We headed up toward St. Louis for the World Science Fiction Convention. Checked dozens of convenience stores and drug stores driving up through Texas and Oklahoma; no one had the current *Galaxy*. When I got to the convention, I found out why—the whole print run of the issue was stranded in a freight yard in New Jersey, so the magazine would go out to distributors late or not at all. I was devastated, of course; no one at the con saw my maiden effort.

Driving home to College Park, Maryland, we stopped one night to camp at Hungry Mother State Park in Virginia. There was one other camper, a guy who was sitting at a picnic table, reading a magazine in the light of a Coleman lantern.

It was the September 1969 *Galaxy*. I got all excited and told him I had a story in it. He thought I was nuts, but did agree that my driver's license identified me as Joe Haldeman.

# The Coldest Place
## by Larry Niven

In the coldest place in the solar system, I hesitated outside the ship for a moment. It was too dark out there. I fought an urge to stay close by the ship, by the comfortable ungainly bulk of warm metal which held the warm bright Earth inside it.

"See anything?" asked Eric.

"No, of course not. It's too hot here anyway, what with heat radiation from the ship. You remember the way they scattered away from the probe."

"Yeah. Look, you want me to hold your hand or something? Go."

I sighed and started off, with the heavy collector bouncing gently on my shoulder. I bounced too. The spikes on my boots kept me from sliding.

I walked up the side of the wide, shallow crater the ship had created by vaporizing the layered air all the way down to the water ice level. Crags rose about me, masses of frozen gas with smooth, rounded edges. They gleamed soft white where the light from my headlamp touched them. Elsewhere all was as black as eternity. Brilliant stars shone above the soft crags; but the light made no impression on the black land. The ship got smaller and darker and disappeared.

There was supposed to be life here. Nobody had even tried to guess what it might be like. Two years ago the Messenger VI probe had moved into close orbit about the planet and then landed about here, partly to find out if the cap of frozen gasses might be inflammable. In the field of view of the camera during the landing, things like shadows had wriggled across the snow and out of the light thrown by the probe. The films had shown it beautifully. Naturally some wise ones had suggested that they were only shadows.

I'd seen the films. I knew better. There was life.

Something alive, that hated light. Something out there in the dark. Something huge . . ."Eric, you there?"

"Where would I go?" he mocked me.

"Well," said I, "if I watched every word I spoke I'd never get anything said." All the same, I had been tactless. Eric had had a bad accident once, very bad. He wouldn't be going anywhere unless the ship went along.

"Touché," said Eric. "Are you getting much heat leakage from your suit?"

"Very little." In fact, the frozen air didn't even melt under the pressure of my boots.

"They might be avoiding even that little. Or they might be afraid of your light." He knew I hadn't seen anything; he was looking through a peeper in the top of my helmet.

"Okay, I'll climb that mountain and turn it off for awhile."

I swung my head so he could see the mound I meant, then started up it. It was good exercise, and no strain in the low gravity. I could jump almost as high as on the Moon, without fear of a rock's edge tearing my suit. It was all packed snow, with vacuum between the flakes.

My imagination started working again when I reached the top. There was black all around; the world was black with cold. I turned off the light and the world disappeared.

I pushed a trigger on the side of my helmet and my helmet put the stem of a pipe in my mouth. The air renewer sucked air and smoke down past my chin. They make wonderful suits nowadays. I sat and smoked, waiting, shivering with the knowledge of the cold. Finally I realized I was sweating. The suit was almost too well insulated.

Our ion-drive section came over the horizon, a brilliant star moving very fast, and disappeared as it hit the planet's shadow. Time was passing. The charge in my pipe burned out and I dumped it.

"Try the light," said Eric.

I got up and turned the headlamp on high. The light spread for a mile around; a white fairy landscape sprang to life, a winter wonderland doubled in spades. I did a slow pirouette, looking, looking . . . and saw it.

Even this close it looked like a shadow. It also looked like a very flat, monstrously large amoeba, or like a pool of oil running across the ice. Uphill it ran, flowing slowly and painfully up the side of a nitrogen mountain, trying desperately to escape the searing light of my lamp. "The collector!" Eric demanded. I lifted the collector about my head and aimed it like a telescope at the fleeing enigma, so that Eric could find it in the collector's peeper. The collector spat fire at both ends and jumped up and away. Eric was controlling it now.

After a moment I asked, "Should I come back?"

"Certainly not. Stay there. I can't bring the collector back to the ship! You'll have to wait and carry it back with you."

The pool-shadow slid over the edge of the hill. The flame of the collector's rocket went after it, flying high, growing smaller. It dipped below the ridge.

A moment later I heard Eric mutter, "Got it." The bright flame reappeared, rising fast, then curved toward me.

When the thing was hovering near me on two lateral rockets I picked it up by the tail and carried it home.

"No, no trouble," said Eric. "I just used the scoop to nip a piece out of his flank, if so I may speak. I got about ten cubic centimeters of strange flesh."

"Good," said I. Carrying the collector carefully in one hand, I went up the landing leg to the airlock. Eric let me in.

I peeled off my frosting suit in the blessed artificial light of the ship's day.

"Okay," said Eric. "Take it up to the lab. And don't touch it."

Eric can be a hell of an annoying character. "I've got a brain," I snarled, "even if you can't see it." So can I.

There was a ringing silence while we each tried to dream up an apology. Eric got there first. "Sorry," he said.

"Me too." I hauled the collector off to the lab on a cart.

He guided me when I got there. "Put the whole package in that opening. Jaws first. No, don't close it yet. Turn the thing until these lines match the lines on the collector. Okay. Push it in a little. Now close the door. Okay, Howie, I'll take it from there . . ." There were chugging sounds from behind the little door. "Have to wait till the lab's cool enough. Go get some coffee," said Eric.

"I'd better check your maintenance."

"Okay, good. Go oil my prosthetic aids."

"Prosthetic aids"—that was a hot one. I'd thought it up myself. I pushed the coffee button so it would be ready when I was through, then opened the big door in the forward wall of the cabin. Eric looked much like an electrical network, except for the gray mass at the top which was his brain. In all directions from his spinal cord and brain, connected at the walls of the intricately shaped glass-and-soft-plastic vessel which housed him, Eric's nerves reached out to master the ship. The instruments which mastered Eric—but he was sensitive about having it put that way—were banked along both sides of the closet. The blood pump pumped rhythmically, seventy beats a minute.

"How do I look?" Eric asked.

"Beautiful. Are you looking for flattery?"

"Jackass! Am I still alive?"

"The instruments think so. But I'd better lower your fluid temperature a fraction." I did. Ever since we'd landed I'd had a tendency to keep temperatures too high. "Everything else looks okay. Except your food tank is getting low."

"Well, it'll last the trip."

"Yeah. 'Scuse me. Eric, coffee's ready." I went and got it. The only thing I really worry about is his "liver." It's too complicated. It could break down too easily. If it stopped making blood sugar Eric would be dead.

If Eric dies I die, because Eric is the ship. If I die Eric dies, insane, because he can't sleep unless I set his prosthetic aids. I was finishing my coffee when Eric yelled. "Hey!"

"What's wrong?" I was ready to run in any direction.

"It's only helium!"

He was astonished and indignant. I relaxed.

"I get it now, Howie. Helium II. That's all our monsters are. Nuts."

Helium II, the superfluid that flows uphill. "Nuts doubled. Hold everything, Eric. Don't throw away your samples. Check them for contaminants."

"For what?"

"Contaminants. My body is hydrogen oxide with contaminants. If the contaminants in the helium are complex enough it might be alive."

"There are plenty of other substances," said Eric, "but I can't analyze them well enough. We'll have to rush this stuff back to Earth while our freezers can keep it cool."

I got up. "Take off right now?"

"Yes, I guess so. We could use another sample, but we're just as likely to wait here while this one deteriorates."

"Okay, I'm strapping down now. Eric?"

"Yeah? Takeoff in fifteen minutes, we have to wait for the ion-drive section. You can get up."

"No, I'll wait. Eric, I hope it isn't alive. I'd rather it was just helium II acting like it's supposed to act."

"Why? Don't you want to be famous, like me?"

"Oh, sure, but I hate to think of life out there. It's just too alien. Too cold. Even on Pluto you could not make life out of helium II."

"It could be migrant, moving to stay on the night side of the pre-dawn crescent. Pluto's day is long enough for that. You're right, though; it doesn't get colder than this even between the stars. Luckily I don't have much imagination."

Twenty minutes later we took off. Beneath us all was darkness and only Eric, hooked into the radar, could see the ice dome contracting until all of it was visible: the vast layered ice cap that covers the coldest spot in the solar system, where midnight crosses the equator on the black back of Mercury.

# Larry Niven

For nearly half a century, Larry Niven has been a major force in the science fiction community, both on and off the page. Perhaps best known for his 1971 novel *Ringworld*, as well as collaborations like *The Mote in God's Eye* and *Lucifer's Hammer* with Jerry Pournelle, Niven has won five Hugo Awards, a Nebula, and a Locus Award, and been nominated for numerous others. Along with his original work, he's also crossed media boundaries and written extensively for various science fiction shows such as *Land of the Lost*, *Star Trek: The Animated Series*, and *The Outer Limits*, as well as forging into comic books with DC's Green Lantern (and "Man of Steel, Woman of Kleenex," the now-infamous essay that dares to address the physics of Superman's sex life). Not content to restrict himself to fiction, Niven has used his scientific extrapolation and critical eye to advise the U.S. Department of Homeland Security, as well as Ronald Reagan during the years of the Strategic Defense Initiative.

Along the way, Niven has contributed several big ideas to science fiction as a whole, from the stripped-down Dyson Sphere that gave *Ringworld* its name to the carefully crafted races of his Known Space universe and the various maxims known as "Niven's Laws" to SF fandom. Despite its relative brevity, "The Coldest Place," with its Big Science premise, Known Space setting, and strange but plausible "alien," retains a uniquely Niven flavor.

**Looking back, what do you think still works well in this story? Why?**

It's the characters. I used them to better purpose in a later story, "Becalmed in Hell." And it's the puzzle—courtesy of Isaac Asimov. In an article he wrote that the night side of Mercury was likely the coldest place in the solar system, with no sunlight ever (as in his "The Dying Night"). This seemed counterintuitive, but hey.

**If you were writing this today, what would you do differently? What are the story's weaknesses, and how would you change them?**

First, I'd leave out the pipe. An astronaut who smokes now seems silly. Second, I'd have to use a crater at Mercury's pole to get anything like a "coldest place." Even so, it's hard to believe it's that cold. Third—there's not much action. I'd get Howie and Eric in trouble.

**What inspired this story? How did it take shape? Where was it initially published?**

It was inspired by the Asimov article, and took shape all in one tortured sitting: I wasn't yet skilled at writing. Frederik Pohl selected it for *Worlds of If*, a magazine now defunct, which published a novice's story in every issue.

**Where were you in your life when you published this piece, and what kind of impact did it have?**

It was my first sale, for $25 in 1960s money. That was all I needed to convince me that I was a writer. My family stopped bugging me to get a job. I was bemused, but not dismayed, when Mercury turned out to be something other than what I'd imagined.

**How has your writing changed over the years, both stylistically and in terms of your writing process?**

I like to think I've gotten better. Even so, writing isn't easier. I see more that needs improving. Also, it sometimes feels like I've used up all the good ideas.

**What advice do you have for aspiring authors?**

You work indoors and there's no heavy lifting. It's a good life, but it's sometimes lonely. Try collaborating; but remember, some of the best can't collaborate at all.

**Any anecdotes regarding the story or your experiences as a fledgling writer?**

This story was obsolete before it was printed. Some Russkis showed that Mercury had a thin atmosphere derived from the solar wind (protons = hydrogen.) Atmospheres conduct and circulate heat. Not much later the planet was shown to be rotating with respect to its Sun. There's no "where midnight crosses the equator on the black back of Mercury."

But Fred never asked for the money back.

# Mirrors and Burnstone
## by Nicola Griffith

Jink brushed a fingertip over the wall before her. It was smooth and smelled strange. A cloud unwound itself from the spring moon and silver light pinned her to the turf.

Motionless, she breathed slow and deep. This was unexpected. Just after dawn that day she and Oriyest had studied the clouds, decided they would stay heavy the whole night.

Cloud slid over the moon's face once more and Jink gauged their denseness and speed, judging the time it would take to sing open the warehouse doors.

It should be safe.

She waited ten heartbeats until the night was once more thick and black, then ghosted along the smooth wall until she reached the glass doors. The floor hummed beneath her feet. To one side, the square of press-panel gleamed. She ignored it. Word had spread through the journeywomen: to press at random in the hope of opening the doors sent a signal to Port, that Outlandar centre of noise and light that had appeared on their world this season. She would sing the doors open.

She composed herself, back straight and legs slightly spread. She sang softly and listened with attention reflected vibration, adjusting here, compensating there. She stopped to test her work.

Almost. Four more fluting notes and the doors hissed open.

At her tread, lights clicked on automatically, making her blink. The doors slid closed. Under her bare feet, the foamplast was hard and cold. She hardly noticed, amidst the alien sights and smells: containers, sacks and crates; mechanisms standing free under thick coats of lubricant. She scented this way and that, laid a hand in wonder on a bulging sack. There was enough food here to feed herself and Oriyest for seasons . . .

Jink was thoughtful. What did the Outlandar intend with such stores? The building was on grazing lands accorded seasons ago to Oriyest and herself. By that token, they were due a small portion of the goods stored. But what did the Outlandar know of such things? She looked at the largest store of food she had seen in her life. They would not miss a pouchful.

She squatted to examine a sack. It was not tied but sealed in some way unknown to her. She slipped her knife from her neck sheath and hefted it. It would be a shame to spoil such fine material, but there was no other way. She slid the blade down the side of the sack.

"Stop right there."

Jink froze, then looked slowly over her shoulder. Mirrors. She had heard of such.

The figure in the slick, impact-resistant suit was pointing something at her. A weapon. It motioned her away from the sack.

"Move very slowly," the voice said, "lie down on your belly, hands above your head." The figure also mimed the instructions.

Jink could not tell if the voice was female or male. It came flat and filtered through the mirror-visored helmet. Nor did the suit give any indication. She did as she was told. The Mirror relaxed a little and holstered the weapon. A second Mirror stepped into view, levering up his visor. He looked down at Jink. "Hardly worth the bother, Day," he said and spat on the floor. Day, the first Mirror, shrugged and unclipped her helmet.

"You know what they said: every, repeat, every intruder on Company property to be apprehended and brought to Port. We let this one go and some hard-nosed lieutenant hears of it, bang goes all that accumulated R&R. Or worse."

Jink listened hard, understanding most of the words but making little sense of the whole. She held herself still when Day squatted down by her head.

"Don't be scared. You'll come to no harm from us."

Jink said nothing. She sensed no violence in the Mirror but would take no risks.

"She doesn't understand a word, Day. Just get her on her feet and I'll call a pickup."

He raised her left wrist to his mouth and spoke into the com strapped there. Jink heard the indifference, the boredom in his voice as he recited a string of numbers to Port Central. Day leaned and casually hauled Jink to her feet.

Jink breathed slowly, stayed calm. Day's gloved fingers were still curled loosely round her elbow. The Mirror turned to her partner.

"All okay?"

"Yeah. Be ten, fifteen minutes."

"Want to wait outside?"

"No." He stamped his boots on the floor. "It's cold enough in here. We'd freeze out there."

Jink wondered at that. Cold? It was spring.

The Mirror eyed Jink, in her shift. "Skinny thing, isn't she?"

"They all look the same," Day said. "Like wisps of straw."

# Mirrors and Burnstone

Jink held her silence but thought privately that the Mirrors were as graceful as boulders.

She felt a faint disturbance, a wrongness in the foamplast beneath her feet. She tried to listen, stiffening with effort.

Day must have felt her captive's muscles tense and tightened her grip. "Don't try anything, skinny. The doors are locked good this time." She tapped the key box on her hip. "Besides, now we've reported you, we'd have to hunt you down even if you did escape. Which isn't really likely. No," she said easily, "you just keep quiet and behave and in a few days you'll be back with your family. Or whatever."

Jink was not listening. Did the Mirrors not feel it? Burnstone, going unstable beneath their feet. When she spoke, her voice was harsh with fear. "Leave. Now."

Day looked at her. "Well, it speaks. You're a sly one." She did not seem perturbed. "The pickup'll be a few minutes yet. There's no rush."

"No. We have to leave now." She did not pull free of the tight hand around her arm but turned slowly to Day, then the other Mirror.

"We stand on burnstone. We must be very, very careful. Tread like flies on an eggshell."

"What's she talking about, Day?"

"Don't know. Sounds . . ." She looked hard at Jink's strained face. "What's burnstone?"

"Beneath the soil. A stone that burns. If you hit it too hard, or dig near it, you let—"

She heard a noise from the other Mirror. She turned. He was lighting a cigarillo.

"No!"

But it was too late. The match strip, still alight, was already falling from his fingers. Jink moved.

While the Mirrors were still hearing her shout, she pushed away Day's grip with a strength they did not know she possessed. Even before the tiny spark hit the ground, she was running. Straight towards the glass doors.

"Hey! Stop! You'll . . ." Day fumbled for the key box.

Jink crossed her arms over her head and dived through the glass.

Day cursed and ran towards the shattered door. There was blood everywhere.

Jink knew she was hurt but she had no thought in her mind but running. She ran with all her strength. She heard the soft whump of the erupting fireball just before the edge of expanding air caught her and tumbled her head over heels. She rolled but the force of the explosion drove her straight into an outcrop of rock. Her thoughts went runny and red. Pain all over. She hung on to consciousness, forced herself to her feet. After the fireball, there were always a few minutes before the burn really took hold. She stumbled back towards the remains of the warehouse.

A quick glance told her that the other Mirror was dead. She stepped over shards of glass and pieces of smouldering plastic to where Day lay; she was unconscious but breathing. Jink could not see much wrong with her. Hissing against the pain, she bent and grasped the Mirror's suit at the neck seal, hauled Day across the grass. Her hands ached with the effort. She dragged the unconscious Mirror behind the same rocks she had crashed into earlier. There was shelter enough only for one. Day would have to stay here and Jink would run for it.

She rolled Day close to the rock as she could, tucking the flopping arms away. Day's wristcom blinked green. Jink hesitated, then squatted. She unfastened the strap and the com dropped into her palm. Despite her dizziness, she took three quick breaths and looked back into her memory, forcing it to be clear. Once again, she watched the Mirror touch two buttons, then speak. She opened her eyes. Pressed the buttons.

"PORT CENTRAL." The voice was flat, tinny. Jink held the com close to her mouth, as she had seen the Mirror do.

"Burnstone," she croaked. The flames had caught at her throat.

"PORT CENTRAL," the voice repeated.

"Burnstone," Jink said, fighting spinning nausea, "your Mirrors have started a burn!"

"WHO IS THIS. NAME AND NUMBER."

Jink looked at it. The voice tried another tack.

"WHERE ARE YOU."

"I'm—a building. A store building."

"WHERE. COORDINATES."

"It—I know nothing of your numbers." Blood dripped down her back from between her shoulderblades. She blinked, focussed. "The storehouse lies beneath the moon's path as she travels across the sky from your Port to the horizon. The wind blows from my left as I face . . . as I face . . ."

"PLEASE GIVE DIRECTIONS."

A great wave of pain swept over her.

"The clouds above are thick and soft. One holds the shape of a woman's face. One yet to pass overhead is a tree, the trunk short and strong."

"REPEAT. PLEASE GIVE DIRECTIONS."

Jink fought the urge to shout at the stupid voice. She was giving the best directions she knew. One had only to look at the sky and follow. She tried again.

"The grass here is . . ."

"GET OFF THE AIR YOU LUNATIC. WE ARE TRACING THIS CALL AND GOD HELP YOU WHEN YOU SOBER UP IN THE LOCKHOUSE. WE'RE SENDING A PICKUP TO—"

"But one is already coming," Jink said, trying to remember if she had already said that. "It must not land. Its weight will only make the burn worse. You must tell it not to land."

The voice shouted something but Jink ignored it.

"It must not land," she repeated. She was feeling very ill.

The ground was hot to the touch. There was danger of an extrusion. Port would not listen. Day was as safe as possible. She had to get away.

She dropped the wristcom and started walking. Vaguely, she realized that her arms and legs were red with her own blood. She kept moving. A walk, a shambling trot, a walk again. Every step counted.

She fell. The slight jar was enough to send her drifting off into nothingness.

When she woke it was dawn. She was sick and cold but her mind was clearer. The gaping cut that ran from between her shoulder to midway down her back had stopped bleeding. Her skin felt raw. From behind the hummock of grass where she lay she could hear Mirrors shouting, the rumble and clank of heavy machinery. Company had sent people to fight the burn.

Jink eased herself into squatting position and watched for a while.

They were doing it all wrong. The machine was tearing at the soil, lifting it out in huge chunks and dumping them in piles. Figures in suits and masks walked in a line, spraying foam. Jink found it difficult to understand their stupidity. Had no one told them that the only way to deal with burnstone was to leave well alone? All this walking and digging aggravated the burn.

She ran towards a black suit, grabbed the arm. "Stop," she shouted, "you must stop."

The man turned. A Mirror Captain. Jink's hair was singed and she was crusted with dried blood. The Mirror turned his head slightly, and called to another black-suited figure.

"Lieutenant!"

"Sir?"

"Take this native to the medic. Find out what she's doing here, how on god's earth this thing started."

"Sir." She looked at Jink. "Can you walk?"

"Yes. But there is no time."

She swayed and the lieutenant reached out, intending to steady her. Jink backed away.

The lieutenant flipped up her visor. Perhaps the native would be reassured at the sight of her face. She reached out again, but hesitated. There was so much blood. How could she tell where was safe to touch?

Jink closed her eyes, listened with her whole body. She could feel the burn-paths now. One heading north, one slightly eastwards, downslope, towards Oriyest. Nearby, an extrusion of hot rock bubbled from the ground. She heard the Captain yelling for his Mirrors to smother it. She opened her eyes, caught the lieutenant's arm.

"Listen to me. Your . . . foam. It keeps the heat in. It feeds the burn. You must not. The digging it—" She did not know the outland word. "It . . . angers the burn, prods it to greater ferocity. You must not. Leave it."

"Lieutenant!" the Captain snapped. The lieutenant spun round guiltily. "I told you to take the native to the medic."

"Sir." She hesitated. "Sir, she was speaking of the burn. The fire, sir. Maybe we should listen. She seemed most certain that—"

"Lieutenant, the girl has a lump on her head the size of an egg. She is concussed, suffering from shock and weak from loss of blood. Even if she were talking sense, which I very much doubt, would it be fair to keep her here in this condition?"

"I . . . no, sir."

"The medic, lieutenant."

"Yes, sir."

Jink did not stay to listen further. She had tried, but now there was Oriyest to think of. She ran.

The Captain bit back an oath. "No, lieutenant. Let her go. We've enough to worry about here."

Midmorning. Jink jogged over the familiar rise.

Where was the flock? Neither sight nor smell gave any clue. She cupped her hands around her mouth.

"Oriyest!"

The call echoed and was still. She ran on. She came to a great outcrop of rock that towered above her like a bank of stormcloud.

"Oriyest!"

The rocks echoed back her shout, and something else. The herd bird flapped heavily overhead.

"Clan!"

The herd bird hesitated, made another overpass. Jink smothered her impatience, forced herself to sink slowly into a crouch on the grass. She knew she smelled of burnstone and blood. Clan would be nervous. She waited.

The herd bird spread his leathery wings and sculled air, landing an arm's length away. He did not fold his wings and his crest stayed erect. Jink made no move.

Slowly, cautiously, he sidled nearer. Jink watched his beak slits flaring as he sampled the air. He hopped closer. Jink spat in her palm, rubbed it against the grass to wash away blood and burn smells. She reached out an inch at a time. Clan lowered his head but did not hop away. Her fingertips brushed his pectorals. He huffed. She scratched at the soft down around his keelbone. He began to croon.

"Where's the flock, Clan? And Oriyest?"

He grumbled in his throat, then flapped and hopped a few paces towards the rocks. Jink levered herself to her feet and followed slowly.

Oriyest had left her a message, a satchel of food and a waterskin. Jink read the message first, picking up the pebbles one by one and dropping them in her pouch. The message stones, rounded and smooth from generations of use, were one of Oriyest's treasures.

She ate cautiously, uncertain of her stomach, and thought hard. The message said that Oriyest had felt the burn and had taken the flock to their safeplace. Jink was to join her there as soon as possible. If Jink was injured, then she was to send Clan to the flock and Oriyest would come to her. If neither Jink nor Clan came to the flock within three days, Oriyest would journey to the store building and then if necessary to Port Central itself in search of her.

## Mirrors and Burnstone

Message stones did not allow for subtlety of tone but Jink could well imagine Oriyest's grim face as she placed those particular pebbles. She sighed, wishing Oriyest was beside her now.

She shook nuts and dried fruit into one hand and clucked encouragingly at Clan. He sidled over on stiff legs and neatly picked up the offering. When he had finished, Jink pulled him to her. She pointed his head in the direction of the safeplace and scratched at his keelbone.

"Find Oriyest, Clan. Oriyest." She pressed her cheek onto his skull and hummed the findflock command twice, feeling the bone vibrate. She pushed him. In an ungraceful clutter of legs and wings he hauled himself into the air. Jink watched him flap northward, then lay down on her stomach. She was very tired.

It was afternoon and she could not expect Oriyest before nightfall, some time before the burnpath crept its soft, dangerous way here. She thought of the Outlandar store building; anger at their stupidity stirred sluggishly at the back of her mind. She had heard rumours of their ignorance but to be faced with its enormity was something else. Outlandar ignorance would cost them vast areas of pastureland, destroyed in the burn. Even if a good portion survived, the area would be unstable for seasons. Burnstone was like that. She had heard of one seam that had smouldered for generations before sighing into ash.

The Outlandar respected nothing. According to the last journeywoman teller to share a fire with herself and Oriyest, the strangers had triggered a handful of burns already. Still they did not learn. Were they capable of it?

Jink stretched, grimacing as the new scar on her back tugged awkwardly. It was healing well but strength was slow to return.

She hunkered down again. The youngling on the grass before her would not live: the flock was birthing before time. The long run from the rock to the safeplace ahead of the burn had shocked the young from their mothers' wombs before they were grown enough to live. Jink looked at it sadly. Even as she watched, it stopped breathing.

On the way down the hill she caught the echoes of Oriyest's singsong commands to Clan as they herded the flock into the gully for the evening. They met at the bottom. Oriyest, stripped to the waist, looked at Jink.

"The little one died?"

"Yes."

Oriyest sighed. "Flenk dropped two. Both dead. I buried them by the creek."

Jink did not know what to say. Flenk was their best producer. If she dropped badly . . . "The others?"

"I don't know." They began walking back to the shaly overhang where they had been camping since their flight from the burn. "They seem sound. If only one or two drop tomorrow then we'll be over the worst. And we will have been lucky."

Her voice was not bitter, now was not the time for such things. The flock must be seen to first. After that there would time to think. Then they would send out the message cord.

T'orre Na found them five days after they sent the cord. The three women sat around their fire, dipping hard dry bread into the stewpot. The sky was clear, bright with stars and the moon's shining three-quarters face. T'orre Na ate the last mouthful and settled back expectantly. This time, the journeywoman was here not to tell but to listen.

The fire popped. Jink added another stick.

"I worry, T'orre Na," she said.

The journeywoman looked from Jink's smooth brow to Oriyest's calm eyes. "Not about your flock."

"No. And yes. We were lucky. We lost less than two handfuls. This time."

"Ah." T'orre Na nodded to herself. She stripped the bark from a twig and began to pick her teeth, waiting for Jink to continue.

"The Outlandar understand nothing. Much of our grazing is destroyed and will take seasons to re-grow. Do they take heed? No. Their hearts and minds are closed to us. Closed to our land, to what eases it, what angers it."

Oriyest looked at T'orre Na. "Perhaps they have not been taught to listen to the right things."

"Is that what you wish, Oriyest? Jink?" The journeywoman tossed her stick into the fire. "You want the Outlandar to learn to hear?"

"Something must be done."

"Indeed." She paused. "It would not be easy."

"Nor impossible, T'orre Na." Jink leaned forward. "I have spoken of the two Mirrors—Day and Lieutenant—who would have listened. And Captain, too, was not unkind, just . . ."

"Over filled with small things."

"Yes," Jink said, surprised. That was it exactly. His mind had been heaving with little things that meant nothing to her: numbers and quotas, money, promotion, service record . . . She shook her head to free it from those hard, incomprehensible thoughts.

"They are all the same," T'orre Na said softly. "I have been to their Port and I have seen."

Jink and Oriyest said nothing. Not far away they heard one of the flock shifting over the rocky ground, sending pebbles scattering along the gully. There was an enquiring low from another, then silence.

"They should be made to hear," Jink said finally. T'orre Na looked at Oriyest who looked right back. The journeywoman sighed.

"Very well. What will you ask for?"

Jink pondered. The usual penalty for triggering a burn was double the amount of destroyed land from the wrongdoer's holdings. But the Outlandar had no land to give.

"We will ask a hearing. As our reparation price we will demand that the Outlandar listen to us. Listen and hear. We will teach about burnstone. We will demand to learn what it is they want from us, why they came here and put their store buildings on our grazing lands. And when we know more, we will ask more."

Oriyest looked at the journeywoman. "Will you help us?"

T'orre Na looked from Oriyest's steady gaze to Jink. They would do it anyway, without her. "I'll help."

Day was startled when she saw them. Natives were a very rare sight inside Port, and here were two of them, making straight for where she sat at the bar. She recognized one of them as her skinny captive. As they approached, she marvelled at how such a frail-looking thing could have dragged her, in full armour, all the way to the shelter of that rock. But she must have done. There was no other explanation.

"Greetings, Mirror."

"Hello." She lifted her helmet off the stool next to her. "Uh, sit down."

Oriyest nodded. They sat. Day cleared her throat.

"You shouldn't be here. Technically, you're an escapee." She felt awkward.

"Will you help us?" Jink asked.

"Well, sure. But all you have to do is lose yourself. Leave Port. No one'll think to chase you up."

The other one seemed amused. "You mistake us, Mirror."

The skinny captive, Jink, laid a hand on her arm. "Listen to us," she said. "If you can help, we would thank you. It costs nothing to listen, Mirror Day." Day blinked. "Will you hear us?"

"Go ahead."

The other one spoke. "I am Oriyest. Jink and I tend our flock. Some seasons are good, some are not so good, but we expect this and we survive. This would have been a good season but for the burn you and your companion started." Her brown eyes were intent on Day's. "When you built your store place on our land, we thought: it is not good grazing land they have chosen; perhaps the Outlandar do not know of our custom of permission and barter; we will not make complaint. This has changed."

"Now wait a minute. That land is Company land."

"No."

"Yes. God above, the whole planet is Company land!"

"No." Oriyest's eyes glittered like hard glass beads. "Listen to me, Mirror Day, and hear. Seven seasons ago we petitioned the journeywomen. The land between the two hills of Yelland and K'thanrise, between the river that runs to the sea and the rocks known as Lother's Finger, was deemed to be ours to use until we no longer have need of it."

Day had never thought about natives owning things. "Do you have any of that recorded?"

Jink frowned. "Recorded?"

"Yes. Recorded on a disc or in a— No, I don't suppose you would. Anything written down?" She looked at their blank faces. "Here." She pulled a pad and stylus from her belt. Wrote briefly. "See?"

Jink looked at the marks on the pad thoughtfully. "This is a message?"

"Of sorts. Do you have any, uh, messages saying the land is yours?"

"Our messages last long enough to be understood. Then . . ." Jink shrugged.

Day drummed her fingers on the bar. There must be some way they recorded things. She tried again.

"How would you settle a dispute?" She groped for words. "What would happen if another herder moved onto your land and claimed it?"

"They would not do that. Everyone knows that land is for our use. If they need more land, they have only to ask."

"But how would they know the land is yours? You could be lying."

Day caught Oriyest looking at her as though she were stupid. "If a herder thought that through some madness I spoke an untruth," she said, slowly, distinctly, "a journeywoman would be summoned. She would speak the right of it."

"But how would she know?"

Jink gestured impatiently. "How does anyone know anything? We remember."

"But what if a journeywoman forgot?"

"Journeywomen do not forget." Her voice was suddenly flat, cold. She leaned towards the Mirror and Day found herself afraid of the alien presence before her.

"There is a life between us, Mirror Day. I ask you once again: will you aid us?"

Day was afraid. She was made more afraid by the fact that she did not understand what she was afraid of. She licked her lips. "If a journeywoman will speak for you . . ." She hesitated but neither Jink nor Oriyest stirred. "If that's your law then I'll see what I can do." Day wished she had another drink. "Look, I can't do much. I'm only a Mirror. But I'll find out who can help you. I can't guarantee anything. You understand?"

"We understand." Oriyest nodded once. "I will bring the journeywoman." She slid from her stool and was gone.

"Will she be long?"

"Not very long."

"Long enough for a drink," Day muttered to herself. She raised a finger to the bartender, who poured her another beer. She stared into her glass, refusing to look at Jink. The minutes passed. Now and then she raised her head to glance at her helmet on the bar. The doorway was reflected in its mirror visor. Men and women came and went, mostly Mirrors snatching an hour's relaxation between shifts.

Maybe she should just cut and run. She couldn't afford to get mixed up in a natives' rights campaign. Her promotion to sergeant was due in about eight months. Maybe even a transfer. But if Company got wind of all this . . . Then she remembered the look in Jink's eyes, the way she had said: There is a life between us. Day shuddered, thinking of her own reply: I'll see what I can do. In some way she did not fully understand, she realized that she was committed. But to what? She sipped her beer and brooded.

When Oriyest entered with the cloaked journeywoman, Day deliberately took her time to swing her stool round to face the natives.

The woman standing next to Oriyest seemed unremarkable. Day had expected someone more imposing. She did not even have the kind of solemn dignity which Day, over the years and on various tours of duty, had come to associate with those of local importance.

The journeywoman slipped her hood from her head, smiled and held out her hand earth-style. "I am named T'orre Na, a viajera, or journeywoman."

Automatically, Day drew herself upright.

"Officer Day, ma'am." She had to stop herself from saluting. She broke into a sweat. She would never have been able to live that down. Saluting a native . . .

T'orre Na gestured slightly at their surroundings. "Can you speak freely here?"

"Yes." Day glanced at the time display on her wristcom. Most of the Mirrors would be back on shift in a few minutes and the main damage, being seen with the natives in the first place, was already done. They sat in a corner booth. Day wanted another beer but wondered if alcohol would offend the journeywoman. To hell with it. "I'm having another beer. Anything I can get any of you?"

T'orre Na nodded. "A beer for myself, Officer Day." T'orre Na turned to Jink and Oriyest. "Have you sampled Terrene beer? No? It's good." She laughed. "Not as strong as feast macha but pleasant all the same."

The beer came. All four drank; T'orre Na licked the foam from her lips with evident enjoyment.

Day spoke first. "As I've already said, to Jink and Oriyest, I can't do much to help."

"Officer Day, I believe that you can. Tell me, what is the normal complaints procedure?"

"There isn't one. Not for n— the indigenous population."

"What procedure, then, would you yourself use if you had cause for complaint?"

"Officially, all complaints from lower grades get passed to their immediate superiors, but," Day leaned back in her chair and shrugged, "usually the complaints are about senior officers. Company doesn't have much time for complaints."

T'orre Na pushed her glass of beer around thoughtfully. "Not all Outlandar are Company," she said.

Day frowned. "What do you mean?"

"The Settlement and Education Councils' representative."

"Courtivron, the SEC rep? You're mad," Day said. "Look, you just don't know how things work around here."

"Explain it to us then, Mirror," said Oriyest.

"It's too complicated."

Oriyest's voice remained even. "You insult us, Mirror."

That brought Day up short. Insult them?

T'orre Na leaned forward. "Officer Day," she said softly, "you are not the first Outlandar with whom I have had speech. Nor will you be the last. We are aware that we need more knowledge, that is why we ask for your help. Do not assume that ignorance is stupidity. And do not assume that my ignorance is total. I understand your . . . hierarchies. You have merely confirmed my guesses so far."

Day did not know what to think.

"The information we need is simple. Jink met a lieutenant she thinks would help us. We need to find her."

"What's her name?"

"We don't know. We have her description." T'orre Na nodded at Jink.

"Tall, a handwidth taller than yourself, Mirror Day. Eyes light brown with darker circles round the rim of the iris. Thin face. Pale skin with too many lines for her seasons." Jink looked at Day. "I judge her to be younger than yourself. Square chin, medium lips with a tilt in the left corner. Her hair is this colour," she pointed to the wood-effect table top, "and is not straight. It's longer than yours. She has no holes in her ears for jewellery. You know such a one?"

Day nodded. Lieutenant Danner. The one on accelerated promotion. By the time Day made staff sergeant, or the heady heights of lieutenant, Danner would be a commander. At least.

T'orre Na was watching her. "Will this lieutenant listen?"

"Yes. Lieutenant Danner will listen to anyone."

"You do not approve."

"No. She's too young, too unprofessional."

"Too willing to listen."

Day opened her mouth then shut it again. The journeywoman's tone had said: what is wrong with listening? Just as Jink had said earlier. Day felt her world tilting. These crazy natives were confusing her, never reacting the way they should. The sooner she got rid of them the better.

"I'll find the lieutenant."

They were all crowded into Lieutenant Danner's living mod. Jink shifted uncomfortably. The space was too small for two, let alone five. T'orre Na and the lieutenant sat cross-legged on the bed, Oriyest sat on the floor, and Day stood at parade rest by the doorport. Jink herself perched on the sink in the bathroom niche, the only place left. She felt like a spare limb. Day had made the introductions but it was mainly the journeywoman and the lieutenant who spoke.

"What point, then, shall I put forward to the SEC rep, T'orre Na? The necessity for concrete reparation, or the implementation of an education programme regarding burnstone?"

Oriyest answered. "Both," she said.

Annoyingly, the lieutenant looked to T'orre Na for confirmation. T'orre Na did not oblige. The lieutenant was forced to respond to Oriyest.

"I'm not really sure that both matters should be raised at the same time."

"Why?"

"Because of the way bureaucracy works."

"Is your bureaucracy so stupid it can only think upon one thing at a time?"

Jink watched Day carefully school her expression to hide her amusement. The lieutenant grimaced.

"Not precisely. If, only if, the SEC rep decides to pass on your complaint, things will be made difficult if the complaint encompasses more than one area. That will mean the involvement of more than one sub-committee, which will lead to delays."

"The difficulty, then, is one of time?" Oriyest asked.

"Yes, exactly."

Oriyest smiled. "Well then. There is no rush. Speak of both."

"I don't believe you understand the kind of timescales involved here." She turned to face T'orre Na. "Even supposing I went out that door now, this minute, and that Courtivron decided without pause for thought to continue with this action, and even supposing his superiors on Earth agreed to back us, which is by no means certain, that would just be the beginning. Evidence would have to be assembled, shipped out—it might even mean going off-planet for these two," she nodded at Oriyest and Jink. "After that there'll be delays for feasibility reports and if, at long last, it's all agreed, then there are advisory bodies to be formed, supervisory employees to be selected . . . And during all this, Company will be blocking and fighting everything. They have planetsful of lawyers."

Neither T'orre Na nor Oriyest seemed perturbed. Jink was barely listening; the small space felt as though it was crowding in on her. Day's expression was politely attentive but Jink had a feeling that the Mirror's thoughts were elsewhere.

"At the minimum," the lieutenant was saying, "we are talking of three or four years. At the maximum . . . who knows. Ten years? Twelve?"

When T'orre Na merely nodded, the lieutenant looked exasperated.

"Do you know how long a year is?"

"We are familiar with your reckoning. Are you familiar with ours? No," she waved a hand to dismiss the lieutenant's nod, "I don't speak of how many of our seasons there are in one of your years. I speak of deeper things. You think of us as passive creatures. We are not. We have been learning, watching. I know your customs, your attitudes, your food. Your beer." She grinned at Day, who seemed startled but grinned back. "How much do you know of us?"

"Much." The lieutenant's cheeks were flushed. "I know you all came originally from Earth, a long time ago. I've read articles on your culture, your art, the structure of your society—"

"And dismissed it. Look at me, Hannah. How do you see me? As a child? A primitive you wish to study for your amusement? Look at my hand." T'orre Na held out her hand and Hannah did as she was ordered. "This hand can birth children, this hand can weave, sow crops and harvest them. This hand can make music, build a dwelling. This hand could kill you." T'orre Na spoke quietly. "Look well at this hand, Outlandar. Do you truly believe that the owner of this hand would allow herself to be treated as nothing?"

The journeywoman's eyes were deep and black.

Day stared at T'orre Na, realizing she had never seen so much strength in a person before. Her breath whistled fast and rhythmic as in combat alert; the lieutenant might take exception to what could be a threat. Once, on Earth, she had seen a spire of red rock towering up over a desert. From a distance, it had seemed fragile but up close its massiveness, the strength of its stone roots had been awe-inspiring.

Gradually, her breathing slowed and relaxed: there would be no violence. A child kicking a mountain was not violence, merely futility.

The lieutenant was pale but kept her voice steady. "What are you going to do?"

T'orre Na smiled slightly. "What we are doing now. Seek ways to educate you. Will you help us?"

"Yes."

Jink stood up. "I have to leave," she said. "It's too small in here. I can't breathe."

"We can speak somewhere bigger if you prefer."

"No, Oriyest. You know what I know. Speak for us both."

Danner cleared her throat. "Officer Day."

Day straightened to attention. "Ma'am?"

"Escort Jink wherever she wishes to go. Be back here within two hours. You will be needed to escort the journeywoman and her companions to the perimeter of the camp."

"Understood, ma'am."

She palmed the door plate and they stepped over the raised sill. "I need no escort," Jink said as soon as the door hissed closed behind them.

"I know. Neither of us has any choice." She hesitated. "If you want, I'll leave you, meet you here again in a couple of hours." She waited while Jink considered it. "But I'd rather show you something of Port. I . . ." She hesitated again. "I still haven't thanked you for . . . coming back. When the burnstone went."

Jink waited.

"Thank you," Day said. "You saved my life."

Jink just smiled and touched her on the arm. They walked in silence past the canteens and kitchen.

"What would you like to see first?"

"The place where you heal the sick. If you have one."

Day raised her eyebrows. "The hospital?" She had expected Jink to ask to see the space shuttles.

"Have I said something wrong?"

"No. You just surprised me. Again." Jink nodded. "You're so . . . different."

"But of course. Come. Show me the hospital."

Clan snorted and butted Jink as she pulled the flatbread from the cooking stone. She tossed him a piece. He huffed in disgust; it was too hot to eat. Oriyest and T'orre Na were already spooning beans into their bread.

"When will you move?" the journeywoman asked.

"When the younglings are sturdy enough to keep up with the rest of the flock," Jink said over her shoulder. "Ten days, maybe less."

"We'll journey to Jink's clan land," Oriyest said, "they have spare grazing. After the hot season we'll hear of other land we can use?"

"Yes." T'orre Na nodded. "We will be swift."

They were silent a while, eating.

"The burn could have been worse," Oriyest said at last. "We went to see it, yesterday. Three seasons, no more, and we can return."

"So. Good news."

"Yes." Jink stretched, watching her long evening shadow. "We took Day to see." She looked sideways at T'orre Na. "She is learning to think of larger things, that Mirror."

The journeywoman nodded approvingly. "Learn from each other. It will be needed."

Oriyest put down her bread, plucked idly at the grass. "She would like to help us move the flock. When the time comes. We told her yes."

T'orre Na looked thoughtfully at Jink, smiled as she saw the flush creeping up the herder's cheeks.

"Ah, so that's how it is." She laughed, touched Jink's hair. "Such friendships are good, but stay mindful of your differences. Both of you."

They nodded. T'orre Na yawned. "Now, I must sleep."

"A song before dreaming?" Jink held her pipe out to the journeywoman. T'orre Na gestured for her to keep it.

"Play something soft. I will sing."

So Jink played, a low quiet melody, and T'orre Na sang of hills, of air, of patience. Oriyest, banking the fire before they slept, joined in to harmonize.

# Nicola Griffith

Nicola Griffith is a writer. She is also—in the most laudatory sense possible—a complete badass. Before immigrating to the United States from her native Yorkshire, England, she earned money arm-wrestling in bars, teaching self-defense classes, and fronting a decidedly aggressive band called Janes Planes. When she did decide to immigrate—and was subsequently denied—the resulting legal battle was so intense as to result in a new law, with the U.S. State Department declaring it was "in the National Interest" for her to live in the States. The case even appeared on the front page of the *Wall Street Journal*, where Nicola's victory was used as an example of the United States' declining moral standards.

Not surprisingly, Nicola's writing is equally revolutionary. Through such formative novels as *Ammonite* and *Slow River*, as well as her co-edited *Bending the Landscape* anthology series, Nicola has become one of the foremost voices for societal Others in genre fiction, winning the James Tiptree, Jr. Award, the World Fantasy Award, the Nebula Award, and a total of six Lambda Literary Awards for work exploring LGBT themes—a tendency evident even in her very first story.

**Looking back, what do you think still works well in this story? Why?**

I like the varied pacing. I like the juxtaposition of raw new settlement and age-old landscape. I like the characters—a mix of old and young, wise and foolish, innovative and patient. I love Jink's stubbornness and idealism, Day's final willingness to accept another worldview, Danner's determination to be a good officer. Also, I'm irrationally fond of the herdbird.

**If you were writing this today, what would you do differently? What are the story's weaknesses, and how would you change them?**

I would cut all the vaguely ESP stuff. In *Ammonite* I turned it into a biological process, a side effect of the Jeep virus. Here, in what turned out to be the prequel story, it's utterly unthoughtout, and new-agey clichéd. I don't know what I was thinking. Perhaps I'd just finished reading something by Marion Zimmer Bradley . . .

**What inspired this story? How did it take shape? Where was it initially published?**

It grew from a dream: fireball; slight, skinny thing rescuing a person in armor; running across an overcast plain. When I woke up I wanted to know who or what the skinny thing was, and what happened next.

At this point—1986—I'd been an unconscious writer, scribbling away with a fountain pen on lined paper. "Mirrors and Burnstone" was different. I approached it carefully, consciously (though still by hand). When I finished and read it over, I thought, Oh, this is a real story; I want to send it out for publication; I'll have to learn to type. So for my birthday I begged my parents for, and got, the money for a used typewriter. After much deliberation I chose an IBM Selectric. I set out to teach myself to type. I borrowed a book—and two days later found myself becoming annoyed when I couldn't touch-type flawlessly. "Mirrors" is seven thousand words long; no matter how many hours I banged at those keys, I couldn't produce a decent-looking typescript. Finally a friend of mine couldn't stand it anymore and offered to type it for me. She did such a fine job (thanks, Maggie, wherever you are) that when I sold the story a few months later to *Interzone* (the contract is dated October 1987; I made £238) the typesetter sent me a letter telling me it was the cleanest piece of fiction he had ever seen. My first sale; my first fan letter. I grinned a lot.

**Where were you in your life when you published this piece, and what kind of impact did it have?**

I was 25 or 26 when I wrote it in 1986. I was 28 when it was published, in *Interzone* 25, in autumn 1988. My very first professional publication. It attracted a little attention: a piece about it appeared in the *Hull Daily Mail*. (I don't remember how or why, exactly—but I suspect I sent out a press release; I had spent years as a community organizer, self-defense teacher, and lead singer in a band; I understood the value of publicity.) Some local fans contacted me to say Hi, and welcome to the fold. I thought it was a little weird but I said Hi back. Then I learnt there was a group of SF fans in Leeds. They wanted to make friends, too. Making friends involved, in Hull, the ritual viewing of taped *Star Trek: The Next Generation* episodes (which I'd never seen), and, in Leeds, the consumption of lots of beer and discussion of literary SF. A whole new world.

David Pringle, the editor of *IZ*, asked me to write some fiction for the Warhammer fiction anthologies he was putting together. I leapt at the chance. I wrote two novellas and a short story, and learned even more about writing consciously and professionally to deadline—instead of looking pale and artistic while waiting for inspiration to strike.

As a result of meeting people and writing the Warhammer stuff I was invited to my first convention, Mexicon (II, I think, though it could have been III) and sat on my first panel, something to do with the portrayal of women in science fiction as Other, interchangeable with aliens. (This is now a rather hoary subject, but at the time it was all new to me. I was thrilled; I resolved to take my task seriously.) So there I was, on stage, everything proceeding smoothly until the moderator, Sherry Coldsmith, asked me to tell the audience a little about the aliens in "Mirrors and Burnstone." I opened my mouth—I was prepared, totally prepared, with snippets of theory, quotes from critics; oh, I was going to stun them with my erudition—but before I could say one word I was stuck dumb by the realization that the aliens—Jink and Oryest and T'orre Na—were women. At that realization, the whole plot of a novel dropped like a screen menu into my head and started scrolling. I thought my eyes would burst and my teeth fly out. I sat mute. A year later, when I had moved to the US, I started writing that novel, and it turned into *Ammonite.*

**How has your writing changed over the years, both stylistically and in terms of your writing process?**

I'm much, much better at it. I spend much more time on it (writing is my only source of income). Yet my major concerns are the same: landscape and how it reflects the characters moving through it, and the human paradox of difference and sameness. I'm still utterly besotted with world-building, though now it's exotic and/or historical rather than futuristic. I write novels—I honestly think I'm better at long form fiction than short; it's just the way my mind works.

**What advice do you have for aspiring authors?**

Do the work. There are no shortcuts, no funny handshakes, magic bullets, or secret decoder rings. It's not about who you know (or even who knows you). It's about the work. Do the work, don't skip any of the steps. Patience is your friend. So is faith: at some point in every project, you look about you and you're surrounded by dust; behind you nothing but dust, ahead of you nothing but dust. You have to believe that if you just keep going, that dust will turn into story. It always does. Also, treat everyone around you like a real human being. You never know when that weird creepy fan you just told to fuck off will become the most powerful editor in science fiction.

# Just a Hint
## by David Brin

It was exactly seven A.M. when Federman finished typing the last data entry. The small console flashed a confirmation and, several miles away, the central processor began correlating the results of the previous evening's observation run.

Federman winced as he stretched in the swivel chair, his spine cracking. Age seemed to make every strain and pop a cruel reminder, as if decay were audibly calling out its territoriality.

The classical music station playing on his desktop radio began an update of the morning's headlines.

The weather would be beautiful over most of the country. The chance of rain in the nearby area was less than twenty percent. The current probability estimate for the likelihood of nuclear war this year still hovered around twenty percent also.

Liz Browning backed in, pushing the door open with one foot as she balanced a cardboard tray with coffee, doughnuts, and the morning newspaper.

"Good," she said, laying her load down on his desk. "I knew you could finish without me. I don't know how you stay up all night reducing data without getting hungry. I just had to get some food!"

As a matter of fact, Federman had started noticing a growling emptiness in his stomach almost the moment the last figure had been typed. If his graduate student had been glad to let him finish alone, he was just as happy she had brought back the goodies.

"It's love, Liz. Anyone who stays up all night has to be in love . . . in this case with astronomy. Either that or he's crazy or in the army."

Elizabeth Browning grinned ironically, leaving crinkled smile lines around her eyes. Her straight brown hair was braided behind her back.

"Or it means he wants to beat Tidbinbila into print with that new pulsar analysis. Come on, Sam. Outside it's already a beautiful day. Let's let some light in here." She went to the window and pulled the heavy drapes aside. A bolt of brilliant sunshine came crackling in. She didn't even wince as she leaned forward to open the window, but Federman covered his eyes.

"Cruel youth," he moaned. "To bring these spotted hands and time-wracked limbs before the searching gaze of day."

"Aw, come on, Sam. You and I both know there's no such quotation. Why do you keep making up fake Shakespeare?"

"Perhaps I'm a poet at heart?"

"You're a scoundrel and a rogue at heart. That's why I'm so incredibly pleased with myself for latching onto you as a research advisor. Everybody else may be losing their grants as the military budget increases, but you know how to finagle enough funding to keep the radio astronomy program here going. My biggest hope is that I can learn your techniques."

"You'll never learn them as long as you fail to understand why I make up Bard-isms." Federman smiled.

Liz pointed a finger at him, then thought better of it.

"Touché," she said. "I'll enroll in Lit. 106 next term. Okay? That is, if there's still a world then."

"Are we in a pessimistic mood today?"

Liz shrugged. "I shouldn't be, I suppose. Every spring it seems there's less smog and other pollution. Remember that eyesore wrecking yard on Highway Eight? Well, it's gone now. They've put in a park."

"So nu? Then what's wrong?"

She threw the morning paper over to his side of the desk. "*That's* what's wrong! Just when we seem about to make peace with nature, they're step-ping along the edge of war! There were demonstrations on campus yesterday . . . neither side listening to the other, and neither side willing to concede a single point. I tell you, Sam, it's all I can do to keep from hiding in my work and letting the world just go to hell on its own!"

Federman glanced at the paper, then looked up at his assistant. His expres-sion was ironic.

"Liz, you know my feelings about this. Radio astronomy is not discon-nected from the problems of war and peace of Earth. It may, indeed, be intimately involved in the solution."

The sophont had no nose, but he did have a name. If one started there and kept listing his attributes one would find him quite a bit more human than not. The things his species had in common with the dominant race of Earth would have surprised them both almost as much as the differences, but the most important of each has already been mentioned.

He had no nose. His name was Fetham.

"No!" he cried out in the language of confrontation. He pounded a four-fingered fist on his desktop. "Are you mad? Mad! What do you mean, the funds are needed elsewhere? The legislature agreed by almost unanimous vote. Full, permanent, emergency funding!"

The smaller being with no nose was named Gathu. He held up his hand in a newly discovered version of the Gesture of Placation directed at the Optic Nerve.

"Please, Academician! Please remember that those votes were taken years ago. There is a new Assembly now. And since the public health situation has deteriorated . . ."

"The problem I am trying to solve!"

" . . . it has fallen on the leadership to seek out new sources of finance for medical research. Surely you know that we applaud your efforts. But it seemed more and more a shot in the dark."

Fetham's prehensile ears waved in agitation.

"Of *course* it's a shot in the dark! But isn't it worth it? There may be a race out there that has been through what we now face. With the entire world threatened, our very survival in question, shouldn't we make an effort to contact them?"

The government representative nodded. "But you have another two years in your appropriation, have you not? And by husbanding your funds you might make them last longer."

"Idiots!" Fetham hissed. "Why, the first beamed message will reach my first target star only this year! It will take more years for their reply to reach us, barring any delay in interpreting the message!

"Are *all* governments as stupid as ours?"

Gathu stiffened. His ridge crest waved in suppressed irritation.

"You may, of course, emigrate to any other nation you wish, Academician. The international Concords give you the right to establish yourself as a citizen of any system of government found under our sun.

"Shall I arrange to have the papers sent over? Perhaps you'll have better luck . . ."

Gathu's voice trailed off, for Fetham had raised his hands in the Gesture of Supreme Disgust and fled the room.

Federman stared at the ceiling while he tilted back in his swivel chair. "You know, someone once told me that the true definition of genius was the ability to suddenly see the obvious."

Liz Browning stopped packing long enough to pick up her coffee cup. The stained newspaper was open to a page of boldface headlines and photos of armed men.

"Do you mean that the answer may just be staring us in the face? Are you saying that we're stupid?"

"Not stupid. Obstinate, perhaps. We hold on to our basic assumptions tenaciously, even when they are about to kill us. It's the way human beings work.

"For instance, did you know that for years Europeans thought tomatoes were poisonous? No one bothered to test the assumption.

"Even the most daring and open of us can't question an assumption until he becomes *aware* of it! When everyone accepts a paradigm it never becomes a topic of conversation. There must be thousands, *millions*, of things like that which men and women never even notice because they don't stand out from the background."

Liz shook her head.

"You don't have to belabor the point. Every sophomore has thought about that at one time or another. And it's certainly happened that some genius has leapt out of the bathtub, screaming 'Eureka!' and gone on to tell everybody of the new way to do things."

She tapped the newspaper.

"But this isn't as easy as that. Our problem of world survival is made up of several hundred million tiny problems, each with all the complexity of a living person. There's no underlying simplicity to war and politics, much as Marxists and others dream of finding one. They only make matters worse with simplistic claims and pseudologic."

Federman sat up straight and rested both palms on the desk. He looked at Liz seriously.

"The idea is that we may have missed something basic."

He stood up quickly, and instantly regretted it as his heart pounded to make up for the shift in blood pressure. For a moment, the room lost its focus.

Deliberately, to keep Liz from becoming concerned, he picked his way around the clutter of books and charts on the floor and rested his shoulder against the window frame.

Brisk, cool spring morning air flooded in, carrying away the stale odors of the night. There was a sweet, heavy smell of new-mown grass.

On its way to him the breeze toyed with the branches of aspen and oak trees and the waving wheatfields in the valley several miles away. A low pride of cumulus clouds drifted overhead, cleanly white.

In the distance he could see a gleaming Rapitrans pull into the station at the local industrial park. Tiny specks that were commuters wandered away from the train and slowly dispersed into the decorously concealed factories that blended into the hills and greenery.

It was, indeed, a beautiful day.

Birds were singing. A pair flew right past his window. He followed them with his eyes until he saw that they were building a nest in the skeleton of what was to have been a new hundred-meter radio telescope.

There was a rumbling in the sky. Above the high bank of clouds a formation of military transports made a brief glint of martial migration. The faint growling of their passage had become an almost daily occurrence.

Federman turned away from the window. Inside, except where the brilliant shaft of light fell, there appeared to be only dimness. He spoke in the general direction of his friend and student.

"I was only thinking that maybe we've been missing the forest for the trees. It might be something so simple . . . something another culture with a different perspective might . . ."

"Might what, Sam?" Liz's voice had an edge to it. "If there ever *were* peaceful cultures on Earth, they didn't have the other half of the solution—a way to keep from getting clobbered by the other guy who *isn't* peaceful! If they did have that answer too, where are they now?

"Look at the world! Western, Asian, African, it makes no difference which culture you look at. They're all arming as fast as they can. Brushfire wars break out everywhere, and every month the Big Blow doesn't happen makes worse the day when it does!"

Federman shrugged and turned to look out the window again.

"Maybe you're right. I supposed I'm just wishing for a *deus ex machina*." His eyes lovingly converted the abandoned, unfinished dish outside.

"Still, we've done so well otherwise," he went on. "The simple problems with obvious answers are all being solved. Look at how well we've managed to clean up the environment, since people found out about the cancer-causing effects of pollution in the seventies and eighties. Sure, there was inertia. But once the solution became obvious we went ahead and did the logical thing to save our lives.

"I can't escape the feeling, though, that there's a similar breakthrough to be made in the field of human conflict . . . that there's some *obvious* way to assure freedom and dignity and diversity of viewpoint without going to war. Sometimes I think it's just sitting there, waiting to be discovered, if only we had just a hint."

Liz was silent for a moment. When she spoke again it was from the other edge of the window. She too was looking out at the spring morning, and at the armed convoy in the sky.

"Yes," she said softly. "It would be nice. But to be serious, Sam, do you really think you could get any more funding than you've already got, to do your spare-time search for radio messages from space? And even if you were successful, do you think the Big Blow would wait long enough for us to decipher a message, then send one of our *own*, and eventually ask complex questions on sociology?"

She shook her head. "Would they be similar enough to us to understand what we'd be asking? Do you really think we're missing something so fundamentally simple that just a hint over the light-years would make that much difference?"

Federman shrugged. His gaze remained fixed on the skeleton in the yard.

The scientist with no nose looked out over his city. For a long time he had fretted and fumed beneath the great dish antenna; then he had gone for a walk around the edge of the research center compound.

Years ago these hills had been suburbs. Now factories belched smoke into the air on all sides. The sight cheered him slightly. He could never look at such an obvious sign of progress and prosperity for long and stay in a black mood.

There were so many other things to be proud of, too.

After the invention of atomic weapons, before he was born, his parents' generation had finally found the motivation to do the obvious and abolish war. The method had been there all along, but no one had been sufficiently motivated before. Now the fruits of peace were multiplying throughout the world.

Two automobiles for everyone! Fast, efficient stratospheric transport! Quick-foods easily dispensed from fluorocarbon-driven aerosol cans! The licentious luxury of lead-lined dinnerwear!

All of this was good. Peace and prosperity.

But the Plague had then come among them, soon after the last war, and now affected almost everyone. Lung ailments, skin cancer . . . that horrible sickness that struck the mercury and bismuth mines . . . the death of the fisheries.

Huge sums were spent to find the microorganisms responsible for this rash of diseases. Some were found, but no germs yet that could account for the wide range of calamities. Some scientists were now suggesting a pathogen smaller than a virus.

Fetham looked up. Gathu. The government representative had followed him outside.

"I am sorry I shouted," Fetham said slowly. The other being-with-no-nose did the equivalent, for his species, of a forgiving nod. Fetham gave a handturn of thanks.

"It's just that I was hoping the Others might know something . . . something that would help us understand."

Gathu was sympathetic.

"I know, Academician. But honestly, what could they tell us about our problems—especially biological problems—even if you did succeed in making contact?

"If they exist at all, they live on a completely different world, with different body chemistry. How could they give us knowledge that would help us defeat this Plague?"

Fetham performed a gesture that conveyed the meaning of a shrug. His large and very subtle ears filtered out the brash, ever-present noise of traffic, yet allowed him to hear the whistling of the wind through the silted, murky sky.

Suddenly he had a totally irrelevant thought.

*I wonder where the birds are? They used to be all over this part of the city. I never noticed that they had gone, until now.*

"I suppose," he sighed. "I suppose I was hoping for just a hint . . ."

# David Brin

Having achieved a Ph.D. in physics and a postdoctoral fellowship at the California Space Institute and the Jet Propulsion Laboratory, *New York Times* best seller David Brin is uniquely qualified to write the hard science fiction for which he is best known. Since the 1980 publication of his first novel, *Sundiver*, Brin has gone on to win a host of accolades including multiple Hugo, Locus, and John W. Campbell Awards. In addition to the Uplift series, which began with *Sundiver* and remains his most popular work to date, Brin also gained notoriety with novels like 1989's *Earth* (which accurately foreshadowed global warming, cyberwarfare, and the Internet as we know it today); *The Postman*, a critically acclaimed post-apocalyptic novel that spawned a major motion picture from Kevin Costner; and *Foundation's Triumph*, in which he undertook the weighty responsibility of tying up all the loose ends in Isaac Asimov's classic series.

In many ways, David Brin's work emphasizes the speculative nature of SF, and often blurs the boundaries between fiction and prediction. As a result, he has written extensive nonfiction such as *The Transparent Society*, which won the American Library Association's Freedom of Speech Award, and is a regular television commentator and consultant for organizations concerned with the future, from the U.S. Defense Department to corporations like Google. In "Just a Hint," Brin gives us a look at those early attempts to extrapolate from current trends and human nature to catch a glimpse of the future.

**Looking back, what do you think still works well in this story? Why?**

It is about an irony that does not change . . . the fact that our preconceptions control what we are able to think about. Some of our current problems may have answers that we simply haven't thought of. That's why it is important to compare notes with other people. And, when it comes to *big* preconceptions, those "others" may live very far away.

**If you were writing this today, what would you do differently? What are the story's weaknesses, and how would you change them?**

Today, I would probably mention the Fermi Paradox—the mystery of why we've not heard nor seen any signs of aliens—and that would be wrong in the case of this simple story. Which is just fine the way it is.

**What inspired this story? How did it take shape? Where was it initially published?**

It's a little *"Analog*-style" think piece, more about the idea than the characters or plot or language. Hence, of course, it was first published in *Analog*.

**Where were you in your life when you published this piece, and what kind of impact did it have?**

I was finishing graduate school at UCSD in astrophysics. I had already published *Sundiver*. After that, I received my first rejection slip for a story. So this sale came as welcome news. It meant I wasn't just a one-sale wonder!

**How has your writing changed over the years, both stylistically and in terms of your writing process?**

One grows, learns a thousand tricks and how to avoid a zillion errors. Still, there's nothing like that verve and thrill when you just start out down this long road.

**What advice do you have for aspiring authors?**

A vast topic! I've distilled a long litany of advice at http://www.davidbrin.com/advice.htm.

# A Sparkle For Homer
## by R. A. Salvatore

Horatio Hairfoot was a most respectable halfling. In fact, his friends and neighbors in Inspirit Downs, a village in the easy land most centered in The World, called him Homer, which is a fair compliment, I might tell you, implying all the lovely homely things associated with respectable halflings: plentiful meals (Horatio preferred eight a day, thank you, Breakfast, Brunch, Lunch, Late-afternoon-snack, Dinner, Supper, Before-bed-to-quiet-the-belly, and, of course, the inevitable Midnight-raid-the-larders); sitting by the hearth, toasting his toes; and sitting on the side of the hill, blowing smoke rings at the lazily passing clouds. Yes, most respectable villagers spent most days off their feet. They could watch their toes wiggle that way—that is, when their bellies hadn't gotten too round for such enjoyable sights as wiggling toes!

Horatio rolled and stretched in his slumber, twisted about and worked his diminutive frame every which way in search of elusive comfort. Finally, he caught something sharp in the small of his back and that woke him with a start. He remembered at once where he was, and that awful thought sent him burrowing back under the shelter of his blanket, which simply could not cover both his head and toes at the same time.

"Let's go, lazy one!" barked the too-awake voice of Bagsnatcher Bracegirdle, a not-too-respectable at all sort of halfling. "Bags" had a bit o' the dwarf in him, so it was said, and a fondness for adventure that kept him out of Inspirit Downs more than in. Indeed, he was a burly one, nearly as muscled as a dwarf, though of course he had no beard, and he bragged openly about dragon fights and goblin wars and other sorts of things that others loved hearing about, but generally scorned. On those occasions when Bags was in town, and always in the Floating Cloud Tavern, few went too near to him, but many remained within earshot of his continual spoutings. So it had come as quite the surprise, you can imagine, when Mayor Faltzo Furstockings announced that his tender and most respectable, if not overly cute, daughter Tippin and Bagsnatcher Bracegirdle would be wed on mid-summer's morning.

Oh, the rumors flew wide and thick that day, I tell you! Some said that Bags had come into a fortune along in his adventuring and had promised Mayor Faltzo that he would settle down. There was talk of a dowry—they called it a bribe—paid by Bags to the mayor. Others, looking for a bit more fun out of the unexpected announcement, claimed that Mayor Faltzo had an inkering for adventuring himself, and that Bags and he would start off soon after the honeymoon on a most extraordinary journey. Whatever the intent, the news came unexpectedly, as I have told you, and so too, especially to Horatio, did Bags's proclamation that Horatio Homer Hairfoot would stand beside him as his Best Halfling.

Horatio hardly knew Bags, had never even talked to the adventuresome fellow as far as he could remember, and being named as that one's Best Halfling set off a whole new round of whispers, these speaking of most unpleasant things, like "yearning for a dragon fight," concerning Horatio. None of them were true, of course; Homer had earned his nickname in heart as well as in reputation. To this day, no one knows exactly why Bags chose Homer, not even Bags probably, but most tavern-philosophers have come to agree that the wayward adventurer just wanted a most respectable fellow by his side to add the right flavor to the extraordinary wedding.

All in all, being named as Best Halfling had been an unwelcomed declaration to Homer, and sitting on the rocky, sloping ground, sore in a dozen places and his belly rumbling in protest of the bland and not-so-plentiful food, Homer's glare at Bagsnatcher's back was not a pleasant one! He had accepted the invitation to stand beside Bags, of course, not much choice is given in these matters (not if one intends to remain respectable). Homer figured that if he could afterward stay low-key enough, the damage to his reputation would heal in a year or so, though he knew that he would hear a whispered laugh at his back every now and again, whenever he chanced a visit to the Floating Cloud. If, however, Homer could have imagined the trouble his acceptance would land him in, he would have become ill, or broken his foot, or done anything else that would have allowed him to bow out gracefully, so to speak.

For now Homer had his own adventure, it seemed, and he did not like it, not one bit. A chill and moist wind blew in with the dawnslight, making the creaks all the more prominent in Homer's backbone. The night had been crystal clear—far in the west and far below, the traveling companions had spotted the lights of Inspirit Downs—but now the mist hung thick as dwarven ale.

"A fine day to be climbing over hard rocks," grumbled Homer before he even got all the way out of his tangled blankets. The sarcasm in his voice was even more evident now than it had been on the previous three days of his trek, though it was quite lost on Bags, thoroughly pleased by the morning, foggy or not, and by the adventure in general.

"We'll be picking our paths careful, is all," Bags snorted in reply. "There's just the one way to go, ye know—up!" He chuckled and swatted Homer playfully on the back. Homer took it with a grunt and did well to hide his cringing at Bag's dwarven-flavored accent, an accent that only reminded Homer of his predicament.

"Up," Homer echoed grimly. Now he cast a scornful look at his companion, barely more than a dark silhouette in the thick fog. "You do not have to enjoy this so much!"

Bags chuckled in reply, understanding, but hardly accepting, the respectable fellow's gloom. "'Ere, go on yerself," said Bags. "I'm the one what's injured here, bein' a newlywed and all! Should be back with me best girl, not up here leading yerself into a fine and, if we're lucky, dangerous journey! Ye get a bargain, by me seeing! Ye get an adventure easily bought 'n handed right to ye!"

Homer did not reply, realizing that he and Bags saw things simply too differently for him to explain this point of view. Homer did want to throttle Bags for his claims of being the "injured one," though, for it was Bags, and Bags alone, who had landed them here. The wedding had gone splendidly, but the reception was quite another matter. The unusual circumstances had provided a good deal of mirth to the whole town, and the gathering had howled even louder when Bags, tipping his twelfth mug of black dwarven mead (another testament that he had a "bit o' the dwarf in him," for none but a dwarf or dwarf-kin could put down even an eight pack of that stuff without being put down himself!), made a somewhat crass and undeniably stupid remark about his soon-coming adventures with his new wife. Always the protective father, Mayor Falzo had promptly invented a "vital" mission, and Bags, without ever remembering it, had promptly volunteered, and had volunteered, too, to take his Best Halfling and best buddy Homer along with him.

So here they were, Homer miserable and Bags three days married and with his waiting wife miles away. Back in the town they were all laughing, Homer knew, for even Tippin Furstockings-Bracegirdle, always ready to join in on the fun, had thought the whole thing hilarious.

"We'll be reaching the summit this day, by me guess," Bags remarked after they had silently, and sullenly for Homer, eaten their breakfast.

"To find a stone," Homer grumbled.

"*The* stone," the adventuresome fellow corrected with a gleam in his pale gray eyes. "If the rumors hold to true, the heart stone o' the One Mountain's sitting at the top for our plucking! Such a gem'd be worth many thousands o' gold coins, I don't mind telling ye!" Bags rubbed his hands eagerly together, and if he missed his new wife in the least, Homer could not see it. "Heart stone!" he declared.

"Hearth stone would be better," Homer muttered under his breath. His family was well off, and Homer saw no need for any adventures, however they might add to the treasury. Besides, Homer knew it, even if Bags was too blinded by the thought of excitement to see it, that Mayor Faltzo's sudden proclamation that the heart stone was just sitting out in the open atop the One

Mountain was only just a ruse. Rumors of that fabled stone had been tossed about for years, centuries even, and if anyone had ever actually seen it, then no one had seen him see it, if you understand my meaning.

"Ofttimes the greatest treasures be sittin, for the grabbing right in front of us, lad," Bags replied to Homer's obvious disbelief. "Just waiting for to be plucked!"

Homer narrowed his eyes and firmed up his hairless jaw at Bag's choice of words, a similar phrase to the one Bags had used at the wedding reception, the one that had landed them in this lousy adventure in the first place.

Bags gave up against that unrelenting stare, a vile grimace that only an underfed and uncomfortable halfling could properly produce. "Might be we'll catch sight of a dragon," Bags growled, stealing every bit of Homer's bluster, and pulled his weapon off his backpack to heighten the other's terror. It was a curious thing, unlike any weapon Homer had ever seen (not that he had seen many), with a hammer head on one side, an ax head on the other, and a cruel barbed spear tip topping the whole of it off. Bags just called it his banger-chopper-thruster and left it for his enemies to see what it could do. Whatever it might have been, it looked unwieldingly heavy to Homer, and even he—though not inclined to magic—could sense the powerful enchantments on the thing. Homer should have been comforted to have one who could wield the weapon well standing beside him, but the mere sight of the thing unnerved him and turned his stomach so that it made him think that eating might not be a very fine thing.

Homer stood up then and looked all about, a futile attempt in the wall of fog. Before he could begin to grumble about the weather, though, Bags scooped up his pack and started off at a quick pace. Homer swallowed his complaints, and then, when he realized that he was alone, swallowed his fear and ran off to follow.

They made good headway, despite the mist, but even though the dawn soon moved fully into day, the gloom only increased. Soon the companions couldn't see each other, couldn't even see their own furry feet.

"We shall tumble down to our deaths," Homer moaned at Bags's back.

Bags, ever alert, was too engaged to respond to the comment. The ground had become soft under his feet, springy as a thick bed of moss, a curious fact since they had left the trees and most other vegetation far behind. Also, the ground had leveled off, though Bags had noted no upcoming flat regions along the chosen trail when they had set camp the night before. Instinctively, his experienced hands went to his banger-chopper-thruster. With a word to the magical weapon, "Foe-faces," he enacted a blue faerie light along the weapon's multiple heads. But the glow only reflected off the pressing fog back in his face, and though he was not a tall creature, and though he stooped to get even lower, Bags could not even discern the nature of the ground beneath him.

Homer came rushing up then, having lost sight of Bags when Bags dipped low, and bounced off his sturdy companion and tumbled down in a heap.

"You should warn me when you plan to stop!" the respectable halfling cried. Poor Homer was quite unnerved, and you would be too, I should guess, if you were half a head more than three feet tall, with a belly wider than your shoulders, and caught in a strange fog on a strange mountain, expecting a dragon to swoop down at you, or a ghoul to jump in your face, or a wolf to snap at your behind, or a million other things, terrible things, that were said to happen on adventures. Even a low-flying bird could pose a threat to one of Homer's stature!

Again Bags let the comment pass. They were in the Wilds, after all, and should take every step with measured caution. Bags could not believe that Homer, however inexperienced, would be so reckless as to run up all of a sudden, with not a hint of a warning. Shaking his head, he hoisted Homer to his feet, placed one of Homer's hands squarely on his hip, and told him to stay quiet and not let go for any reason.

A short time later, the wind kicked up and the fog thinned for just a moment. Bags was indeed relieved to see that the summit of the mountain, above them on the left, had grown much closer, though the sight only reminded Homer of his aversion to places higher than his top cupboard. Bags slapped his banger-chopper-thruster across his open palm and proclaimed, "This day'll see the end of our road!"

Homer glanced around nervously at the echoing blasts of the adventuresome halfling's cry. The ground was still soft, something quite out of the ordinary, or a bigger and thicker patch of moss than Homer had ever heard of. And, Homer, most respectable, as I have said, understood well enough that "out of the ordinary" inevitably signaled trouble. But Bags, undaunted, pounded on, no longer giving his unusual surroundings a second thought. He wanted to get to the summit, find the stone, and get back to Tippin (and to thousands of gold pieces!).

When another wind gust thinned the mist again a few minutes later, though, even determined Bags began to understand clearly that something was not as it should be and took pause. The mountaintop was still on their left, and still not high above them, but it was much farther away.

"How is this?" Homer cried, letting go of his companion and nearly swooning. He wandered right by Bags, eyes fixed on the curious sight, then caught himself after a moment and turned back, seeing the blue faerie light of Bags's enchanted weapon and, behind it, the shadow of a burly halfling.

"Take ye not another step," Bags whispered. Before Homer could begin to ask why, the end of a rope slapped into his chest and fell at his feet. "Tie it about yer waist," Bags instructed.

"Where are we?" Homer demanded in a high-squeal, much like a pig that sees the farmer's cleaver and knows that a holiday meal is not far off. Homer was thinking that Bags knew something that he did not, and trying to catch up with the reasoning, he looked helplessly back in the direction of the mountaintop. The opaque veil had returned.

Bags walked by him then, again taking up the lead and starting out at a slow and cautious pace. He did indeed have his suspicions, but they seemed too outlandish to be taken seriously or to be shared at that time. "Keep yer steps right behind me own," he explained to his flustered companion.

"Steps?" Homer replied defiantly. "Confusticate your own steps." Then he sat down, "Plop!" and crossed his soft arms over his chest, taking care to look dangerous and not to let his arms rest casually on his belly.

"Ye mean to sit here?" Bags asked, curious and somewhat amused.

"And if I do?"

"Then keep the rope," Bags said, beginning to loosen his end. "I'll come back for ye if I can, and if I cannot, well . . ."

Homer was up and moving, though grumbling with every step.

They went on slowly for a few minutes, and then Bags had his answers. He heard Homer shriek out and then the rope went taut so suddenly that it nearly pulled him from his feet. Bags stumbled forward and knew by the dropping angle of the line that he would soon join his companion in the fall. His dwarf-like, corded muscles pulled hard, and luckily he caught his balance in the nick of time. Then Bags scrambled along cautiously, following the lead to a hole in the spongy ground, or more particularly to a hole in the cloud island. Peering through the inconstant fog, he made out Homer's frantically flailing form, dangling free, a mile or two above the flat farmlands.

"Ahah!" Bags called at the confirmation that they were indeed on a cloud. "Now we're getting somewhere!"

"Getting?" Homer stuttered, barely able to breathe, let alone speak. Homer had thought adventures most unpleasant things before they had ever started out, if you remember. He had liked a soft hearth chair, or a hard kitchen chair, or the soft grass of a gentle hill beneath his bum. Now, hanging free, except for the pinching tight rope about his waist, he . . . well, you can imagine his face accurately enough, I should guess—eyes popping wide, mouth opening and closing weirdly to catch gulps of air, and a general expression that would make a respectable fellow shudder just to hear described about on another, much less wear himself.

For all of his complaining about Bagsnatcher Bracegirdle (and Homer would complain about that one till the end of his long days!), Homer was glad to have one so capable and strong beside him at that time. Bags pulled and hauled with all his strength, then caught hold of helpless Homer, who had come up upside down, by the toes and pulled him back onto the soft, but tangible ground.

"Where are we?" Homer finally demanded again after several unsuccessful attempts to spit out any words.

"On a cloud," Bags replied calmly. "Haven't ye learned that yerself?"

Homer's reply came out once again as an undecipherable gurgle and he toppled, and would have gone through the hole again had Bags not caught him.

"A cloud," Bags explained when Homer awoke many minutes later, "with holes in it." He helped his reluctant companion, mostly by the threat of leaving him once again, unsteadily to his feet. "And drifting afar o' the mountain."

"Then where are we to go?" Homer demanded in a broken, squeaky voice.

Bags shrugged and started off. "Any way's as good as another," he muttered. "Just keep a firm hold on that rope!" Homer hardly needed to be reminded.

They had just started off across the bouncy surface when the fog cleared again briefly.

"Another mountain!" Homer cried hopefully, seeing a gigantic form rising before them. "Quickly, before the cloud drifts beyond it."

Bags wasn't in so much of a hurry. He, too, had seen the mound, but he wasn't so certain of Homer's identification. The One Mountain was so named because it was the only thing larger than a hillock for many, many miles. Homer trotted past him and continued on, though, and for all his strength, the burly fellow could hardly hope to slow his excited, and terrified, companion. He put his banger-chopper-thruster over one shoulder, just in case, and checked the knot of the rope around his waist. With Homer rushing along blindly, building so much momentum, Bags had to wonder what useful purpose the rope might serve if his companion flew headlong into a hole.

"Loyalties," the adventuresome Bags muttered and secured the knot.

The next time the wind thinned the mist, Homer skidded to an abrupt stop. Looming before him was no mountain, though certainly it was mountain-sized, but a castle, carved of smooth marble. Unable to tear his eyes from the spectacle, the stunned halfling lumbered on, coming to a stop before a door that stood fully twenty feet high.

"Not a dwarf's home," Bags remarked, coming up behind Homer.

Homer's glare showed that he did not enjoy the sarcasm. He reached up as high as he could and jumped, but came nowhere close to the crystal doorknob. Even so, Bags slapped him on the arm for the attempt.

"Once did a wise man note that often there be a better way to enter a giant's home than by the front door," Bags remarked. His simple logic reminded Homer of many things, most notably, the danger, and the timid fellow promptly slapped himself on the arm, just for a good measure.

Bags started off then, around the base of the castle, pointedly giving a sharp tug on the rope as soon as the slack tightened. Halfway around the immense building, the companions found a high window.

"A better way in," Bags remarked with a wink and a smirk. When Homer realized his companion's intent, he cast a doubtful gaze and started quickly away, only to be dragged back, cursing ropes with every passing foot.

Short of stature and with plump hands, halflings are not the best of climbers. But though the blocks of the wall were well fitted by a giant's estimation, cracks that seemed tiny to the hands of a giant proved to be ample holds, even perches, for Bags. Just a few short minutes later, though Homer was still far below, Bags peeked in the great window. He had come to a bedroom, huge but nearly filled by a gigantic canopied bed, a desk that he could have used as a lean-to, and a wardrobe large enough to serve as a gathering hall for half of Inspirit Downs. A mural-sized painting hung on the wall opposite Bags, a marvelous work depicting handsome, blue-skinned giants dancing through the mist swirls of their cloud world.

When he was convinced that the room was empty, Bags swung in and secured the rope to a leg of the huge desk. Too amazed by the quality of the furnishings, he didn't wait for poor Homer to catch up. He crept up to the room's wooden door and cracked it open, looking out on a high and wide corridor of red-veined marble, lined by statues and paintings and lighted by a crystalline chandelier that glittered with a thousand candles. A second door stood across the way, a third twenty feet down the wall from that, and a fourth marked the end of the corridor, where it took a sharp bend.

Still seeing no signs of the castle's inhabitants, Bags crept back to the window. Homer sat frozen twenty feet below, staring down into the mist and shaking his head in disbelief.

"Are ye coming then?" Bags called down to him.

"No," Homer replied evenly.

"Yes!" Bags corrected and he heaved and tugged on the rope until his reluctant companion was pulled to the windowsill. Still Homer did not move, not, that is, until Bags pointedly untied the knot about the desk leg and dropped the rope loosely to the floor.

"Have yerself a fine drop," the burly fellow said, and before he finished the statement, Homer was long past him, peering out the bedroom door. Bags promptly resecured the knot of the desk, just to keep their escape route open.

"Lots to check in here," Bags said, but Homer, suddenly entranced (now that he had solid footing again under him), was too busy staring at the hallway's magnificent chandelier to even hear him. Before he realized what he was doing, Homer had dropped the rope off his waist, slipped across the hallway, and put his ear to the closest door.

Footsteps—big footsteps.

But not from beyond the door, Homer realized, coming out of his enchantment. He looked down the corridor just as a tremendous boot appeared around the bend. Homer looked desperately back to the bedroom, but realized he couldn't make it without being seen, and realized that Bags wasn't close enough to help him this time. He pushed through the unknown door, hoping that no other giants waited within.

"Homer?" Bags called softly when he looked up from the desk drawer and realized that his companion had moved away. Too curious to worry, Bags scaled the huge desk, wondering why in the Nine Hells giants would need a desk. The size of the quill pen he found made him earnestly hope he never encountered the bird from which it had been plucked! Likewise, the ink well could have held enough ale to keep even Bags content for a month!

Other giant-sized artifacts littered the desktop and filled the central, topmost drawer, including a leather bag that seemed more suited to the hands of a man, or a halfling, than to a giant.

"Ho, ho, thee dost indeed speaketh simply theeee most marvelous things!" squealed a high-pitched, but undeniably giant voice from the hallway. That the giant could speak was enough of a surprise to Bags, but the dignified, almost haughty tone of the statement nearly floored the halfling. Remembering his immediate predicament, though, he snatched up the bag, swung down from the desk, and rushed to the wardrobe, diving inside.

"Wit is indeed a blessing of the gods," a deeper voice replied. Bags held his breath when he heard the two giants enter the room and close the wooden door behind them. A single, unnerving thought came into focus then: the rope.

He heard the bedsprings creak, and hoped that the giants would retire without noticing. He clutched his banger-chopper-thruster tightly, though, suspecting that he would soon have to put it to use. "Homer?" he asked quietly, suddenly remembering his companion.

The thought was stolen a second later though, in the boom of a giant's voice. "What ho!" called the deeper-voiced colossus. "Intruder!"

"Oh, dear," piped the higher voice—from the bed, Bags guessed. "Not now, I pray thee! Alert someone else and be done with it."

"That chicken-stealing . . ."

"Goose-stealing," the higher voice corrected.

"That goose-stealing peasant boy!" the deeper voice boomed. Bags followed the resounding thumps of the giants footsteps to the desk and then to the window.

"Didst he retrieve the beans?" the higher voice squealed, almost in desperation. Bags looked down curiously at the beans in the bag and scratched his hairless face, wondering what marvelous artifact he might have stumbled upon. You or I in Bags's situation would have stayed put right then, and wisely so, and let the giants go off on their wild goose chase, or wild goose-stealer chase, as the case may be. But Bags was of a different mind-set than you or I, and most people and every halfling, too. Always was that rascal thinking of bards' songs and cunningly trapped treasure chests and other sorts of dangerous things, and at that moment, Bags was thinking too that he owed some loyalty to fragile Homer, wherever that one might be. The last thing on Bag's mind sitting in that dark wardrobe was sitting tight and letting events pass him by.

Now was the time for action.

At first, Homer thought he had jumped into a bear cave and it took his best effort not to rip out a revealing scream. As soon as he realized that the furs pressing in all about him were no longer attached to their original owners, Homer relaxed and pushed his way blindly through the long and narrow closet, and soon came to the other door on this side of the hallway. He cracked it open and looked back to the bedroom. The wooden door was closed, but Homer could still hear the giants speaking within. Should he go back and check things out? he wondered, remembering his companion. Homer realized then that he admired Bags, even if he did not particularly like him, and he boldly strengthened his resolve to go and see if he might help out. He straightened his belt, tucking his belly back under it, and almost took the first step.

But then, singing down the far end of the corridor caught Homer's attention, a song as sweet as a morning dove's, though obviously much louder. Also, a sweet fragrance wafted down to titter, tantalizingly, under Homer's nose, an aroma of springtime and newly blossomed flowers.

"Bags can handle them," the enchanted (and relieved) Homer told himself, and before his loyalty could argue back, his curiosity had his ear pressed against the far door in the hallway. The volume told him that the singer was probably a giant, but Homer had never heard of a lark, much less a giant, that could carry a tune so very well.

There was a keyhole high above him and, fortunately, a stately, high-backed chair against the wall beside the door. Homer glanced all about, then scrambled up the chair. Drawing one deep breath to steady himself, he peered in through the keyhole and saw . . . nothing.

"Confusticate it," Homer mumbled under his breath, for apparently the key was set into the lock on the other side.

He reached up cautiously and grasped the doorknob, meaning to use it for support as he slipped his hand inside the lock and fumbled about. Unknown to him, though, the door was not locked, and as soon as he leaned forward, the knob turned under his weight and the door swung in.

You can imagine the look on the giantess's face, sitting in her claw-footed bathtub with bubbles all about her a dozen feet from the door and staring back at the helpless halfling, dangling, kicking, from her doorknob. But you cannot, I assure you, fully appreciate the expression on Homer's face when the blue-skinned giantess, all spectacular, fresh-smelling, and abundantly curvy, eighteen feet of her, jumped up, twisting and moving her arms about in a futile attempt to cover her bigger-than-life, bigger-than-Homer's-wildest-dreams, naked body.

Bags took a deep breath and slapped his banger-chopper-thruster across his open palm. "The gods of battle be with me," he growled and burst through the door, hoping that his estimation of the giants' whereabouts would prove accurate.

The giantess, wearing a satiny, lace-trimmed peignoir, sprawled languidly across the bed; her companion stood at the window, leaning out and looking out for some clue as to the identity of the intruder.

Though he had spent many seasons in the Wilds, battling all sorts of nasty things, Bags had never before seen humanoids of this size. Fearlessly, the rugged halfling ignored the shock and followed through with his original battle plan. He charged the bed first, swatting out one, and then a second, canopy support with his banger. The heavy canopy dropped down on the reclining female like some giant net before she even had time to scream.

Bags paid her no more heed at that moment. He charged the other giant, arriving just as the towering humanoid spun about in surprise.

Bags barely knew where to hit the thing; it was simply too tall for him to hope of getting in a critical strike. Always ready to improvise, he slammed, again with the banger section, down on the giant's toes.

"YEEEEOWW!" the giant howled, and grasped at his foot and hopped up into the air. "You chicken-stealing . . ."

"Goose-stealing," came a muffled correction from under the canopy.

Bags wasn't hearing any of it. Now using his thruster, he charged ahead, driving the stooping giant backward. Unbalanced and too startled to respond, the giant recoiled, and tumbled out of the window. More agile than his size would indicate, the giant did manage to grab the rope as he fell, but his momentum was simply too great and the act only snapped off the desk leg securing the rope's other end, and it followed him in his drop.

Bags watched the giant plummet down into the misty shroud, then reappear above the fog for an instant on his first bounce. Thinking himself quite clever, the hobbit spun back toward the bed, spinning his weapon about to bring the chopper ominously to bear.

The giantess had risen and had managed to rip one of her arms through the canopy's cloth. But her thrashing had only tightened the cloth's hold on her and she stumbled and fell, hopelessly entangled.

Bags's warrior instincts told him to rush up and finish her. He might have done it, though the idea of killing a female, even a female giant, did not please him. Bags was no slaughtering warrior, no matter how he blustered about his adventures in the Floating Cloud in Inspirit Downs. He had always preferred the thieving style of adventuring; that way, no one really got hurt, least of all himself! Now he found himself in a dilemma, though. Could he dare to leave a giantess unharmed behind him? Before he could work things out, a shriek from down the hall caught his attention.

"Eeek! A mouse!" the naked giantess in the bathtub squealed. "Somebody step on it! Kill it! Kill it! Hit it with a broom!" She squirmed and twisted, kicking up bubbles every which way.

Homer had not lived an adventurous life, but in The World, so full of spice and variety, he had witnessed (or thought he had witnessed) many wondrous spectacles. But the flummoxed fellow had never seen anything to match the magnificence of the sight before him now. He tried to babble out an apology for his intrusion, or a warning for the giantess to be silent, or anything at all.

Whatever he was trying to say, the giantess could only guess, for his words came out as simply, "Hummina hummina."

While Homer hung transfixed from the crystal doorknob, the giantess leapt into action. She scrambled out the back side of the tub and grasped it in her huge hands. Giant muscles corded and flexed (and poor Homer verily swooned at the sight, dropping down to the floor and barely holding his balance) as the great lady hoisted the side of the tub.

Hundreds of gallons of soapy water poured out under Homer, knocking him from his feet.

The snarling giantess came on, flipping the tub right over the prone Homer. Then, though he couldn't have hoped to lift the tub anyway, the giantess sat down atop it and started calling for her husband.

Hopelessly trapped, Homer just rolled to a sitting position in the soapy puddle and put his back to the side of the tub. He should have been thinking of a plan of action, but he could not shake the image of the giantess, of the suds rolling wide and long around her curves.

"Coming, Homer!" Bags roared, charging down the corridor, his banger-chopper-thruster waving high above his head, readied to throw.

"Oh, dear," the giantess replied to the yell, and she rolled off the far side of the tub just as the wild-eyed halfling loosed his weapon.

Bag's aim was almost always perfect, but he, too, became a bit distracted at the sight of the naked and soapy giantess, and the throw came in just a tad low. The heavy weapon slammed into the side of the metal bathtub with a resounding "BOOOOING!" A stunning, deafening peal that shook even the incredible image of the giantess from the mind of poor Horatio Hairfoot.

Unable to slow on the slick floor, Bags slid in heavily against the tub. His weapon lay on the ground beside him and he quickly scooped it up. Seeing the frantic, and embarrassed, giantess making no move toward him, and guessing the fate of his reluctant companion, Bags slipped the thruster part under the edge of the tub. With a great heave, Bags brought the side up and Homer, recognizing the scruffy, fur-lined boots of his rescuer, quickly scrambled out.

"Are you unharmed?" Bags asked, truly concerned.

"Huh?" was Homer's reply. He wiggled a slender finger into his still-vibrating ear.

Alarms rang out all through the castle. In the doorway down the other end of the first corridor appeared the tangled giantess, dragging the bed behind, and the thunder of a dozen giant boots resounded down the corridor to the side of the bathroom.

"Run away!" Homer cried. He looked around, confused, at how distant his own words sounded.

"But we're heroes, lad!" Bags protested. "Run? From mere giants? Whate'er might the bards write?"

Though Homer, again wiggling a finger in his ear, could hardly hear his companion, he read Bags's lips well enough to understand the protest. "Our epitaphs," he remarked, then he was off. He stopped at the bathroom door, though, and turned back to the huddled giantess. Again wanting only to apologize, Homer managed to utter, "Thank you."

The giantess crinkled her surprisingly delicate features, covered herself as best she could, and looked around for a broom.

Bags came into the corridor casting a scornful glare at the back of his retreating companion. "Heroes!" he muttered grimly, and he set his feet firmly and started down the side passage, his banger-chopper-thruster waving menacingly.

Then a half-dozen eighteen-foot-tall (and nearly as wide), blue-skinned giants, wielding the biggest swords and clubs that Bags had ever seen, appeared from around another bend.

"To Hell with the bards!" Bags gasped and he set off after Homer, whose respectability so suddenly seemed an admirable trait.

"Oh, no, you don't!" the bed-dragging giantess sneered at Homer. The deafened fellow barely heard her, but words didn't seem necessary at that moment. The giantess rushed out from the bedroom and Homer recoiled.

The bed caught sideways in the door, abruptly ending the giantess's charge. The remaining canopy supports snapped off after the initial jolt, and the giantess tumbled headlong. Homer took off at once. He leapt atop the back of the giantess and ran right over her, scrambling and diving over and around the blocking bed.

Bags came next, leaping the prone giant in a single bound, then dipping a shoulder and bowling right into the bed. He promptly bounced off and landed on his butt in the middle of the hallway. Growling in defiance, the halfling took up his weapon and charged headlong, tearing and chopping wildly.

"Finesse," Homer remarked sarcastically when his companion crashed through amid a snowstorm of feathery mattress filling.

"Finesse, Bagsnatcher style." Bags promptly and proudly replied without missing a beat.

"The rope?" Homer asked, noticing the broken desk and the missing leg.

Bags shrugged helplessly and charged to the window, scrambling up to the sill, the thunder of giant boots fast approaching the doorway behind him.

"Climb?" asked Homer, terrified, but moving up to join his companion.

"Sort of," Bags tried to explain. Thinking an action worth a thousand words (and not having the time for a thousand words), he grabbed Homer by the collar and heaved him over and out. Then Bags leapt after his dropping companion, hoping the cloud to be as pillowy as he remembered.

"I will pay you back for that one day!" Homer, puffing angrily, promised fiercely when he and Bags had finally stopped bouncing. Bags let the threat go without reply, not having the time to pause and debate the issue just then.

Great horns sounded all throughout the giant castle.

"Where do we go?" Homer, suddenly timid again, cried.

Bags threw his hands out wide and ran off into the mist. "Any way," he answered as the castle disappeared into the fog behind them. "Just beware of . . ."

"Holes!" Homer cried, and Bags spun about just as Homer dropped from sight. The adventurous fellow dove to his belly, thinking his companion doomed.

But fat little fingers, grasping wildly at the edge of cloud stuff, showed Bags differently. "Holes," he agreed, hoisting Homer back up to the cloud.

"Long way down," Homer remarked weakly, trying futilely to smile.

"But sure it be a beautiful day!" Bags replied, trying to brighten things up.

Homer was glad to realize that his hearing had returned, but he really didn't appreciate Bags's lame attempt at levity, not with a horde of angry giants chasing them! "But how are we to escape?" he asked.

"There must be some way," Bags replied, turning serious. "Might that the cloud'll find the top of another mountain." He looked back toward the castle. "Or might it be that the giants possess something . . .

"Beans!" Bags cried suddenly.

"Beans?"

Bags produced the leather bag and waved it at Homer's uncomprehending stare. Then, as Bags revealed the small sack's contents and handed one bean to Homer, Homer's expression turned curious. Legends of the properties of magical beans were not so uncommon.

"Surely, it cannot . . ." Homer began, but now the giants had apparently come out of the castle and the cry of "Release the beast!" took away any logical protests he might have had.

"Plant it!" Bags yelled at Homer.

Homer dropped a bean onto the cloud and stood back, seeming confused.

"Not on the cloud!" Bags cried.

"Over here!" yelled a giant, homing in.

"Then where?" Homer pleaded, positively flummoxed.

Bags dropped to his knees and blew with all his breath, waving his hands as he did to try to clear away the fog. "Down here," he explained, pointing into the hole.

Homer dropped down and peered through the hole, nearly swooning from the dizzying height. Far, far below, the farmlands of Windydale, a human settlement on the back side of the One Mountain, east of Inspirit Downs, loomed lush and green.

"Down there?" Homer asked, unbelieving.

Bags nodded frantically.

"But the prevailing winds," Homer protested. "And the drift of the cloud, combined with the time-lapse of the falling bean . . ."

Bags shot Homer his most incredulous look, and the helpless halfling shrugged and dropped the bean. It plummeted from sight, lost in the wide view of the wide world.

"Sneaking rats!" boomed a giant. The companions jumped up and spun around to find themselves helplessly surrounded by a dozen armed and armored giant warriors.

A long moment of uneasy silence passed as the two sides took a measure of each other.

"So, what d'ye think the bards'll put in our epitaphs?" Bags asked Homer off-handedly.

The giants started to circle, gradually closing in. Suddenly, though, the cloud began to shake violently. Barely able to keep their footing, the giants and the companions watched in amazement as a huge green stalk burst up through the hole and rolled up lazily into the air.

"Beans!" Bags and Homer shouted together, and not waiting to hold a lengthy discussion over their good fortunes, they sprang onto the beanstalk and slipped down under the cloudy fog.

Their descent was rapid, but their troubles were far from over. A brave giant started down after them, and even more disturbing, "the beast" soon appeared under the far rim of the cloud.

"Now I'm knowing where they get their writing utensils," Bags muttered grimly when the gigantic, eaglelike bird, with talons suitable for snatching full-grown cattle, swooped into view, bearing the largest giant of all, and still another giant warrior besides that, on its black-feathered back.

The monstrous bird rushed past the friends, the wind of its great wings nearly pulling them from their tentative perch.

Farmer Griswald Son-o'-Jack was not very happy when the magical beanstalk roared up and overturned his chicken coop, sending his prized hens fluttering in every direction. Nor was Griswald overly surprised, certainly not as surprised as you or I might have been, for he had heard of such trouble-bringing plants in his day—from his father, repeatedly, when he was a young boy. Indeed, there was a saying among Griswald's family, founded on solid experience, so it's said:

> *Cows for beans is folly;*
> *Sow's ear, no purse of silk.*
> *Better off to keep the cow*
> *And barter with the milk.*

That was a pretty common saying among the farmers in those lands in those days, and a pretty respectable one as well (since trading a valuable cow for beans usually will lead one to woe).

Griswald looked up at the sky, where the stalk disappeared into a cloud and where the outline of a huge bird could be seen rushing back and forth past it.

Griswald's farmhands appeared then, bearing axes and knowing what must be done. On a nod from their boss, they set to chopping.

The largest giant, driving the huge eagle, swooped the bird in low beneath the companions, and his lesser giant companion sprang out into the beanstalk.

"The way is blocked!" Homer cried, looking down at the formidable obstacle, and then up again to the descending giant above.

"Not for long," Bags promised. He put his back to the stem and found a secure foothold. Then he took aim with his banger-chopper-thruster, putting it in line with the blocking giant's head.

Looking up at the wild fires burning in the halfling's blue eyes, the giant realized the potential for some serious pain. "Please, good gentlesir, do not do that," he begged.

"Hold yer words, foul giant!" Bags roared, acting the hero once again. "Brave are ye in advantage, but ye've not reckoned with the likes of Bagsnatcher Bracegirdle, son o' Brunhilda Bracegirdle! Know that yer evil heart'll beat no more!"

"Evil!" cried the largest giant as the eagle swooped by yet another time. "Why, I take that as a most uncalled-for insult!"

"Give it to them good, King Cumulonimbus!" yelled the giant on the stalk high above.

"But you, diminutive one," the eagle-rider continued. "I see well enough what demeanor your most harsh actions bespeak! Whilst I admit curiosity as to how two halflings (for that is what you are, I believe) might"—his voice faded and then came again a moment later as the eagle banked through a wide and distant turn—"I'll not wait to hear your lies!" The great bird came in again, and now the king leveled a barbed lance at poor, shivering Homer.

"Ye're a giant!" Bags huffed, unafraid—of course, the lance wasn't aimed at him. "Thus are ye marked as evil!"

"Er, Bagsnatcher," interjected Homer, looking pointedly at the point. "Perhaps this is not the time for name-calling." Homer thought his suggestion an excellent one, and indeed it was, but his whisper was lost in the continuing banter between the blustery halfling and the giant king.

"We most certainly are not!" the giant roared. "But thou hast come to us as thieves! Thus I proclaim you to be evil!"

"I am not!" Bags shouted back, stamping his foot against the beanstalk, which nearly dislodged him. With a mighty heave—for a halfling—of his free arm, Bags sent his banger-chopper-thruster head over handle at the approaching menaces. The weapon caught the eagle square in the head, and the bird squawked out a piercing cry and spiraled out of control.

The giant king, suddenly losing all interest in spearing the halfling, dropped his lance and leapt out, catching the beanstalk in a tentative hold just above his lowest companion, between the giant and poor Homer.

If big King Cumulonimbus had any intention of parlaying, or of attacking, at that point, his words were lost in the first shudders of the blows from the farmers' axes.

The giant looked around pleadingly at the trail of black feathers, but the great eagle was not to be found.

"Not evil?" Homer asked the king.

"Nor are you?" Cumulonimbus, clutching more desperately now, replied hopefully.

"Pray, might I suggest that we carry on this conversation back up at the cloud?" called the highest giant, who had already begun his ascent. The stalk creaked in protest as the farmer's axes continued their work.

Homer abruptly shifted his posture and looked for handholds above him. Hearing a growl to the side, he turned to see Bags, now with a knife between his teeth, working his way down toward the giant king.

"Lef the bards seft their phens to pharchmenth!" the wild-eyed fellow lisped. "Vhat gwories we'll be findin' dis' day!"

"Shut up, Bags!" Homer snapped. "And put the knife away!"

Bags cast a wounded glance at his companion. "Dey're giants," he argued around the knife blade. "An' giants er ephil thins. We must vanquisht dem—rule oft heroes!"

As if in response, the stalk suddenly rolled out wide.

"Polly!" screamed the giant king. The eagle swooped out of a nearby cloud, meaning to come to the call of its master. But the bird hesitated when it saw the warrior, now secure in his footing and holding the tip of a readied throwing knife.

"Come on, birdie!" he roared.

"Shut up, Bags!" both Homer and King Cumulonimbus yelled together. "And put the knife away!"

Bags looked doubtfully at Homer and at the giant king. On his adventures in the Wilds, Bags had learned a simple rule concerning monsters from which he could not flee: kill them before they kill you. But with the beanstalk obviously heading down, that rule somehow simply didn't seem to apply. With an embarrassed shrug, Bags stuffed the knife back between his teeth.

The eagle glided in.

"Might I offer thee the hospitality of my table?" King Cumulonimbus said to the companions as he and the other giant sprang out onto the great bird's back. The third giant had already disappeared back up through the mist of the cloud. "Please. Thou must come and meet my beautiful wife, Queen Cirrostratus."

Homer, a sudden sparkle in his eyes, looked hopefully over to Bags.

"I'll not dine wif giants!" the stubborn fellow protested around the steel-bladed knife. The beanstalk creaked and fell.

"I shall see that those words are etched on your epitaph!" Homer promised as he tumbled. King Cumulonimbus caught him by the toes and pulled him on the bird.

"Epitaph," Bags muttered, spitting out the knife as he plummeted. "Sure that I'm beginning to hate that word."

They caught him about a mile down. Out of breath, Bags offered no speech of gratitude when he climbed onto the eagle's back to take a seat between Homer and the two giants.

But neither did he waggle his little fist in protest.

"And could you later set us down back on that mountain?" Homer was asking, pointing off into the distance. "A little mission concerning a certain stone, you know."

"Oh, the heart stone," replied King Cumulonimbus. "Only a rumor, of course. We only just inquired into it ourselves."

"Of course," said the other giant, noting the incredulous stares they exchanged. "Why else would we come in so low, where any vermin might . . ."

The murderous look that came immediately to the sturdy fellow's eyes stuck the words right in the callous giant's throat. "Where any noble adventurers," he prudently corrected, "might wander onto our cloud?"

"Then no sense'n going back to the mountain." Bags beamed, suddenly remembering his waiting bride and willing to put aside all of his stubborn prejudices concerning the giants. What a tale he'd have to tell in the Floating Cloud that night! "Right after supper, then, ye can put us down in Inspirit Downs, thank ye, the town on th'other side of the mountain."

But Homer wasn't so certain that they would be getting back so soon. He had a hunch that he had already met King Cumulonimbus's wife and if his suspicions held true, Homer figured that he could spend a week, at least, just enjoying her company.

If your travels of The World ever bring you near to Inspirit Downs, you might consider stopping in to hear the tale of the cloud giants told one more time.

Don't go to the Floating Cloud, though, to hear Bagsnatcher's nightly recounting. That fellow's as full of bluster as ever, and his tales of his heroic struggles in the castle are lengthy and boring, and ultimately untrue.

You might find Horatio, though, sitting on the side of a hill, shooting smoke rings up at passing clouds. They don't call him Homer anymore in Inspirit Downs, and hardly ever refer to him as "most respectable." Not that Horatio minds; the memories, he figures, one in particular, are well worth the dent in his reputation.

A few kind words and a block of pipeweed should get Mr. Hairfoot to tell you about his one great adventure, and he'll tell it pretty well (though he won't go into details about the giant queen and the claw-legged bathtub; he's too much the gentle fellow for that!). You should be able to imagine that part well enough for yourself, though, by the depth of the sparkle that inevitably comes to Horatio's eyes.

# R. A. Salvatore

No author has done more to popularize shared-world fiction than R. A. Salvatore. With the creation of his signature character, the dark elf Drizzt Do'Urden, in the second Forgotten Realms novel for Dungeons & Dragons, Salvatore started a wildfire that has burned steadily ever since. Along with further tie-in novels for D&D and Star Wars, he's also published numerous creator-owned series such as The DemonWars Saga, the Spearwielder's Tales, and the Crimson Shadow series. Of the more than 50 books he currently has in print, 18 of them have been *New York Times* best sellers, totaling more than 10 million copies sold. And with his highly detailed action scenes and classic roleplaying-game flavor, Salvatore's name is ubiquitous among fans of both fantasy and gaming alike.

Though Salvatore launched his career with the Forgotten Realms novel *The Crystal Shard* in 1988, "A Sparkle for Homer" represents his first foray into short fiction, and epitomizes the fast-paced, high-adventure fantasy for which he's known.

**Looking back, what do you think still works well in this story? Why?**

The charm of it. I fear that we're losing the charm of fantasy. As we profess our grittiness and willingness to let the bad guys win or as we "gray down" the heroes, we are pushing aside a very important paradigm of escapist fantasy fiction: the good feeling. I'm not saying this lightly, and certainly not calling for a Polyanna genre, but there remains room on those many shelves for a tale that fills you with a sense of adventure, a sense of heroism and a feeling at the end that things got a little bit, or a lot, better.

**If you were writing this today, what would you do differently? What are the story's weaknesses, and how would you change them?**

I never follow this kind of reasoning and won't answer. When I had the chance to rewrite my first novel before its reprint with Del Rey, I read the book and cringed often. Some of the ideas were so dated—the Bermuda Triangle angle for example—and quite honestly, some of the mechanics were less than perfect. But I didn't change a thing. Novels and stories are a snapshot in time, both reflective of the world around them and indicative of where the author was when he/she wrote the piece. Rewriting is cheating everyone.

**What inspired this story? How did it take shape? Where was it initially published?**

This was initially a story about Drizzt and Wulfgar, my signature characters in the Forgotten Realms. I wrote it for *Dragon* magazine, but to my surprise, they rejected it. I really liked it, though, and so when this opportunity came up, I sent it to Brian Thomsen at Warner Books. He liked it and put it in the anthology *Halflings, Hobbits, Warrows and Wee Folk*. To my ultimate satisfaction, the story got great reviews—I still needle the *Dragon* editor about that whenever I hear from her. It's all good-natured, of course. One man's steak is another's hamburger, and it's all perfectly valid.

**Where were you in your life when you published this piece, and what kind of impact did it have?**

It was early on, but I had a few books published already. The most important thing for me was that this anthology got me out of Lake Geneva again, and with some well-known New York writers like Craig Shaw Gardner. It was quite a thrill being in print beside some of those folks. I don't know that it had an effect on my career other than that, but I got to publish a story I really enjoyed writing.

**How has your writing changed over the years, both stylistically and in terms of your writing process?**

In ways good and bad. Mechanically, I can fly through now with little problem. I think in terms of story structure and tightness, I'm better now, as well. But experience brings a cost, I fear, and I have to battle the downside all the time. When I first started, there was an energy there that couldn't be contained. I had to write—all the time! I can draw a sports analogy: when I was twenty-five, I could run up and down the court for an hour without a gasp. Now at fifty, that court seems awfully long, doesn't it? Of course, I'm smarter now, and I know how to cheat.

**What advice do you have for aspiring authors?**

Boy, this is a tough one. My general advice remains the same: if you can quit, then quit. If you can't quit, you're a writer. This has to come from inside; you have to have stories clawing at the inside of your skin, demanding release. If the actual writing isn't like that, this business will destroy you in short order. On a more specific and pragmatic note, things are changing very quickly in the publishing business, and anyone trying to break in had better understand those changes and be on the front end of the wave. A couple of years ago, I would never have recommended self-publishing, for example, but now I'm hearing that some folks are having success with that. Using the Internet, conventions and local markets, these authors are building a following and that then attracts a publisher. Getting published the old fashioned way—sending a manuscript to a publisher—seems like a dead end right now.

Again, I'm shooting half-blind here. I've been writing contracted books for a lot of years and haven't been on the market.

**Any anecdotes regarding the story or your experiences as a fledgling writer?**

I still giggle when I think about the biggest break I ever got, the luckiest choice: the creation of Drizzt Do'Urden. When auditioning for the Forgotten Realms' second novel, the only written reference I had was the first novel, Douglas Niles' excellent *Darkwalker on Moonshae* (I still love that book). In that book, the only maps portrayed the Moonshae Isles, a small cluster of small islands that afforded no room for stories that didn't at least touch upon the dominant characters Doug had created. Nothing of substance could happen there without Doug's heroes knowing about it.

So when I wrote the sample chapter for my audition, I used one of Doug's characters to introduce Wulfgar, the protagonist of my book, and then get out of the way, as I didn't want to use Doug's character. Soon after, TSR explained that they didn't want me to set my book on the Moonshaes, which confused me because all I saw other than them was ocean. However, they had decided that I would write the book. So they sent me the maps of the Forgotten Realms, this vast, sprawling world. After a couple of weeks of back-and-forth, figuring out which game designers and which writers were doing books and modules in various parts, I exiled myself to this tiny strip of land as far out of the way as I could get, and decided that would be Icewind Dale.

I thought no more about it and went about trying to flesh out the outline of the book when, while sitting at my day job (I was a financial analyst at the time), I got a call from Mary Kirchoff, my editor. Mary had a problem. She was going into a marketing meeting to "sell" my book to the sales team, but since I was now thousands of miles from the Moonshaes, and since Doug was writing sequels to his book, I needed a new sidekick for Wulfgar.

"No problem," I said. "I didn't want to use anyone else's characters anyway."

"I'm going in to sell the book and I need a new sidekick for Wulfgar," Mary replied.

"No problem. I'll get back to you next week."

"No, you don't understand. I've got a meeting on your book and I need that sidekick."

With a sigh, I answered, "Okay, it's almost lunch time. I'll try to come up with something during the break."

"No, Bob," came her exasperated reply. "I'm standing outside the room where the others are waiting because I'm late for a meeting about your book, and I need a sidekick for Wulfgar."

"A black elf," I blurted a moment later (the drow used to be called "black elves," not "dark elves").

"A drow?" I could hear the hesitance in her voice.

"Yeah, a drow ranger. That'll be cool. No one's done that before."

"There's probably a reason for that, Bob."

"No, no, it will work. A drow ranger, a good black elf."

She was late for the meeting and couldn't stand there arguing with me, so she just said, "Okay, since it's a sidekick character, I'll let you get away with it. What's his name?"

Without hesitation, without having any idea of why or how or anything else, I said, "Drizzt Do'Urden of Daermon N'a'shezbaernon, the Ninth House of Menzoberranzan."

"What?"

"I don't know!"

"Can you spell that?"

"Not a chance."

And it was true. I had no idea of how that happened, of where that idea came from. I had never thought about a drow character, had never played one in a game, or anything like that. I knew not what a "Daermon N'a'shezbaernon" might be, or what a "Menzoberranzan" was or why this was the ninth house. It just happened. Poof. Out of the blue.

Changed my life.

Poof.

# The Boys
## by Charles Stross

The boys scuttled over the concrete slab like cockroaches, exoskeletons a dull bronze in the orange glare that passed for daylight. A dense mist concealed rocks and ankles and a corpse. The roar of a police carrier echoed through the trees, a pulsing racket of authority: the boys didn't care. By the time the patrol arrived the corpse was brain-dead, stripped of eyes and kidneys and viscera as well as bionics. The boys had left their incestuous joke with the corpse; a noose.

Darkness descended on the area, a protective screen for the armoured hovercraft as it swept through the gap in the forest, cruising slowly between fungus-streaked biomass modules. Among the video surfaces that lined the cabin the Hunter sat bolt upright; her scanscreens scintillated as she focused on the partially dismembered cadaver.

"Boys; he's been dead for half an hour." The constables flinched and whined; she noticed them and moderated her voice. They were sensitive units, too valuable to waste.

"Nothing here," she told the autopilot. "Get the skull, then take us home."

The small noises of relief were drowned by the roar of the fans. Some of the cyborged dogs muttered and scratched their implants as the carrier turned and rumbled back towards the castle. In the wake of the hovercraft the cobblestones were darker than before, by an increment of congealing blood.

The castle, a perfect cube with edges a kilometer long, shone with an ominous red glow that filtered through the grime of centuries. The degenerate bioforms of the landscape twisted away from the laser-veined monolith of lunar basalt; nerve-trees bubbled into fatty shapes and creeping acantho-pods bristled as they crept past. The clouds above it reflected the glow, megawatts of energy expended in a display of power. The ceiling of the world, a continuation of the floor by any other name, hung thirty kilometers overhead, masked by clouds: cylindrical storms and spiral winds induced by convection from the algae-fogged solar windows were the predominant weather pattern. The world existed in a soyuz-shell; Translunar Seven, the Islamic Corporate Shogunate, had seen better days.

The view from the incoming drifter would have been spectacular if anyone had bothered to experience it. The pod closed in on the habitat slowly, waiting to be picked up by a tug as it drifted past. Its self-sustaining ecosystem basked in the glare of sunlight, pulsing out a call sign to the tracking systems of the Shogunate. At a range of a hundred kilometers the orbital nation was a slowly rolling wall of grey metal and ceramic. Outlying parabolic light farms provided a hook for the eyes, stationary mylar mirrors focused on geodesic domes that could contain anything from algae tanks to laser cells. Thin stems of plastic fastened them to the hub regions at either end of the colony. They were huge, kilometers in diameter, as were the solar windows set into the wall of the world. The drift pod was a bacillus approaching a brontosaur.

To say that nobody was there to experience the view would be an error. There were the pod's native bionics and their supportive life-system, and more—a human cargo. Nike was a fully gender-identified female human; she had all the right complement of arms, legs and sensory organs, which was not mandatory. Coming from Troy-Jupiter, where lots of things called themselves human, this was quite a surprise. But Nike wasn't bothering about the scenery; she was worrying about customs.

"You're still set on going in?" asked the pod persona, an expert system that called itself Valentin Zero.

"Maybe." Nike stared into inner space, mirrored contact lenses turning her eyelids into projection screens for video nodes in her optic nerves. "I may just go through with this. I may. Just."

She ground to a halt, thoughtfully, remembering what it had been like when she had been there before. A modified wasp buzzed to a six-point landing on her left arm, abdomen curved to inject. Its lance slid out and penetrated her skin, extending feathery biosensors into her peripheral circulation.

"Spying again, Valentin?" She opened her eyes and looked at the wasp. Its metallic carapace shone with black and red stripes, tiny alphanumerics embossed on its wings.

"I can never tell what you're thinking," said the program. "It makes me nervous." Nike tried an experimental grin, her face twisting into a semblance of spontaneity.

"When you're like that," complained Valentin, "you're unreadable."

"If I do go," she said, "do you think I should continually signal my intentions with my anatomy?" This time the facial expression was more natural; heavy irony. Her face resembled her body; slim, pared-down, like something designed for speed rather than comfortable habitation.

"You ported into that brain, badly, if you think you can convince anyone you're human if you don't look spontaneous. You don't have to tell everyone what you're going to do; just make them think they know."

She snorted. "How long is it since you were human, Valentin?"

The pilot sounded surprised. "Me, human? What do you take me for? A potential defector?"

The wasp picked up traces of neuropeptides that warned of danger. "Don't be alarmed," she said, "but if I thought that, I'd have to kill you. I need you here." Mirrors slid across her eyeballs, a deliberate snub to conversation. The wasp took wing in a vindictive whine of chitin, leaving a bead of blood oozing from her skin. It flew to a nearby neuroplant with off-yellow tendrils as fat as her fingers that dug their way into the hull of the drifter pod, and offered biochemical homage.

"I've made up my mind," she said. "I'm going."

Valentin didn't reply. There was a gentle thumping from outside the pod, followed by a barely perceptible return to acceleration, unfelt for six weeks; the tug had latched on.

Nike returned to her customs video briefing.


"If we accept your application for citizenship you must accept our semiotics. If we accept your physiology you must accept our commensal bacteria. If we accept your psychodynamics you must accept our law."

The customs official stared at her with phased-array eyes, cruciform wings of black synthetic retinae. It was a robot, and not a well-maintained robot; it recited by rote, sounding bored.

"Repeat after me: Death to the imperialist Zionist ronin, the lackeys of neo-humanist cladisticians, and the discorporate running-dog zaibatsu. I swear to follow the decree of the Hezbollah and the shogun in all things, to abide by the shari'a, to follow humility and modesty as a law for the rest of my natural life, and to refrain from acts of treason against the corporation . . ."

Nike recited the oath expressionlessly. The syllables were stale in her mouth; she'd memorized them during the two-day immigration. Then she walked through the exit of the customs hall. Her feet ached from months of free fall. The black cross of the robots' retinal array tracked her as far as the path into the forest before losing interest and swiveling back to the entry gates.

Mist swirling at ankle-level obscured roots looped to catch unwary feet, pits of rotting vegetation hollowed out by subsidence, other unseen hazards. Videomice crouched in the boles of trees, grooming their paws, faces almost obscured by the black buttons of their eyes. Nike proceeded without guidance; the customs briefing had hinted that there had been political changes unnoted by the immigrant-processing module over the past two centuries. A faint rumble drifted from the distance, menacing in the twilight as the colony precessed towards nightfall.

The videomice were the eyes and ears of the Hunter, but there were too many of them to monitor simultaneously. Nike ignored them, relying on the prickling of her neck to tell her when one of them was belching a coded data packet to the castle: her close-cropped hair was wired for microwaves. She guessed that there were other watchers in the forest, other eyes, and it scared her. Traffic control had confirmed that no one had visited the Corporate Shogunate for a good six years now, and no one had left it for over a decade. If anyone human was left alive, Nike would be the subject of intense surveillance. She stumbled occasionally and paused to brush branches out of her way as she followed the trail into the woods that blanketed the colony interior. She was right; other eyes were watching her.

Boys drifted like ghosts, moving in silence across the open spaces. Their choreography was uncanny, plotted by computer for a ballet corps of cyborgs. The ground beneath their feet was a bare surface of white ceramic that curved away to either side until it submerged beneath a layer of earth; it was the naked hull, exposed by erosion. Every ten metres a grey pole stood, festooned with branching sensors and small pumps, a trellis left over from the soil-support system. Ecological vandalism had stripped it bare in this area, a kilometer-wide strip of sterility near the equator. Darkness had fallen across it an hour ago and the people of the night were rising.

The Hunter watched them on a screen in the safety of the castle. Reclining in a throne of skulls hung with nutrient tubes and neural jacks, she looked akin to those she observed; pale, with the fleshlessness of a rapidly-growing child and the synthetic skin of the ageless. The resemblance was due purely to design convergence. The Hunter—her title was as good as her name—was not a boy. To be a boy was a gesture of fanaticism, and the Hunter was hardly a fanatic. Not any more.

"What are they doing now?" The voice came from above and behind her head. She watched the screen with the intensity of a sniper.

"They appear to be constructing something . . ." The Hunter paused to consult her throne of brains. "A gallows."

"Why?"

The Hunter thought for a while. "It's an archaic device used for punitive purposes. The victim is suspended by a rope for some time—it looks uncomfortable. Possibly dangerous if no spinal bypass is installed."

"Who is the object of this device?" The voice sounded bored. It probably knew already and was testing her.

"That's not clear, yet."

"Keep me informed." The voice vanished as rapidly as it had manifested itself, and the Hunter shuddered. She had a fear of that voice, conditioned by a century of ignorance. No-one had met the Shogun face to face and told the tale within living memory. Her memory. The Shogun was an enigma. It might not even exist; or it might . . .

The twilight ritual of the boys played itself out. One of their own, out on the white plain, was stripped of his exoskeleton; they bound his hands behind his back with a cord of red silk. It was impossible to tell if he struggled—those who surrounded him were too strong for unamplified muscles to resist. Up went the rope, the prisoner on the polished teakwood scaffold, the drop

## The Boys

. . . The Hunter watched, fascinated. Centripetal acceleration dragged the twitching feet out, deviating from the vertical. *There's something nasty in the world*, she realized, as infrareds observed the body cooling. The boys left an hour before she admitted to herself that what she'd witnessed was not a punishment but an execution. The absolutism of age. *They cannibalized one of their own*, she wondered; *why? Have the boys become so jaded that they gamble with their own lives?* And, dawning slowly in her mind: *I don't understand this any more.*

The house was so well camouflaged that Nike almost stumbled into it before she realized what it was. It lay among the trees, concealed by a dense thicket of ivy; its owner waited for her outside.

"You're the immigrant," he said; "I'm Ben."

"Nike." She watched him closely, noted dark skin but no cranial hair.

"Winged victory? Or the missile?" When he spoke he held his head on one side. "Never mind. You'll be wanting somewhere to stay while you find out what it's like here. You'll be wondering why I'm offering that. I'll tell you; we don't see many strangers."

"How many of you are there?" she asked.

He shrugged. "Maybe five hundred, maybe less. Nobody counts. There's the boys, the servants of the Shogunate, a few civilian groups who keep quiet. And the neuroplants, who total about six million posthumous intelligences."

For a moment Ben looked like something else; infinitely weary, lines engraved on his face like tribal scars concealing eyeball-tracked weapons systems. It passed; Nike concentrated on the smell of his skin, the pheromones he exuded. They smelt so natural that he might have been a prehistoric subsistence farmer or test pilot. There was a sense of archaic simplicity about him.

"Do you eat?" she asked.

The Hunter dug through her collection of spare skulls in search of an appropriate memory, in response to a desperate urge to understand. She found one, long-jawed with the baroque horns of an extinct fashion. The motions were instinctive by now; she plugged it into her throne by a fat nerve trunk and felt the alien emotions expand her perceptions. The skull had been poorly maintained, isolated in sensory deprivation for the better part of the century; the personality had ablated away to a core of memories and a gnawing loneliness.

She remembered being a he: experienced at second hand the stars beyond the window of a cramped cargo drifter between worlds, the waves of vapour churning at the edges of the red spot as mining drones scooped up megatons of methane from the Jovian atmosphere. That wasn't right; she carried on searching. Later she remembered arriving at Translunar Seven shortly before the revolution. Being caught up in the confusion and arrested by the Hezbollah, undergoing the terror of forcible decapitation. This was too recent;

she wanted somewhere in between. Tried to remember. What had it been like in Troy-Jupiter two hundred years ago?

The agonies this brain had been squeezed through made her wince. It was easy for a Hunter to fall into the trap of thinking of her memories as something more than a cunning source of information, of trying to relate to the dead minds in the boneyard. She hunted and eventually found what she was looking for, partially obscured by the pain of a bizarre and self-destructive marriage.

A memory of what it was like before the revolution, before she had become a Hunter.

The house vomited pre-digested morsels into the feeding trough. As Nike and Ben ate, she tried to assess the situation. It was worse than she'd expected; the palace wasn't far from dead. An unseen ruler who might not even exist, a dissident faction with unspeakable habits, and a dying periphery of humans.

"They shut down half the farms a century ago," said Ben, "and most of the rest forty years later. There wasn't enough demand on the manufacturing capacity to justify running it all. Nobody needs anything—the die-backs left a vast overcapacity. And the city's a playground for the boys so nobody lives there anymore."

He shoveled in another handful of food. "You came at the wrong time."

Nike watched him silently for a while, fascinated. She wondered if she'd met him years ago; so many of her memories from the early days had been wiped to make room for new experiences that she couldn't be sure.

He finished eating.

"Just what *did* you come here for?" he asked.

"To take over," she said. "We need this space. What's your interest?"

He grinned, face in shadow from the sunduct in the roof. "I'm a neutral. I have no interest in conflict."

"So?" she asked.

"The question is what you can do for us," he added. "Who are you?"

Her eyes flashed, reflecting the night with mirrored venom. "I'm your missile, the forerunner. My people are coming and they need a vacant biosphere. Don't stand in our way."

"I'm not," he remonstrated mildly. "But the boys are. And the Shogun might."

"Yes," she said. "Just what are these boys? And who is this Shogun?"

"That," he replied, "is something I expected you to know already."

The Hunter stared at the screen until the pain in her eyes forced her to blink furiously, tears trickling down her cheeks. It was hard to bear, this sense of her humanity being reduced to a cypher by isolation. The feeling that she'd been locked in her role for too long while the boys played their blood-games in the forest. Sometimes she sent out for a warm skull to scan for the wet sensations of dying; she couldn't remember her name but she felt that if she concentrated on it for long enough it would return . . . she was close to an overload with time. It had been too many years since she had been merely human. *Damn, damn,* she whispered to herself in a monotonous litany; *why do I keep forgetting what it was like?* There was no answer; there never was.

All she knew was that she couldn't get a grip on her emotions. There'd been a time, not so long ago in historical terms, when she had possessed a blindingly important purpose for which she had sacrificed her freedom to be anywhere but here. The purpose might have been connected with the Shogun or the boys; it had faded into the cobwebs of neurones that died and were replaced by the longevity programs. To those who knew the signs she was as old as the artificial hills. She knew that it had meant everything to her; once she'd been willing to die for it. But she couldn't remember. All that she knew was the voice from behind her throne, and the boys.

Three grey cylinders the size of mice drifted in free fall, jostling in the thin breeze along the axis of the world. One of them was capped at each end by a blue, very human eye. Another sprouted two surreal ears, perfect fleshy miniatures that merged seamlessly with the cylinder. The third had no discernable sense organs, but from a crack in its flank grew an almost perfect stem of convolvulus. The bindweed curled and twisted, loosely holding the other two cylinders in its green coils. A wasp coasted nearby, red-banded and bearing stenciled cyrillic insignia on its wings; five kilometers below, the cotton-wool swathes of cloud veiled the floor of the world. Valentin Zero had smuggled his cortex modules into the shogunate as seeds disguised in Nike's gut. Reaching the free-fall zone via the sewage system, the modules had matured and grown rapidly by preying on wind-born organisms; the wasp was one of many infiltrators sweeping the world for news.

As darkness fell, the twittering code-pulses from the videomice quietened; Valentin tuned in on the steady, low-powered grumble of the neuroplants, the tok-tokking of a factory talking to its robots, the crackling of poorly shielded bionics hooked into the soil-support system. The microwave traffic was richer and more compressed than sonic communication, echoing back and forth along the eighty-kilometer cylinder. But Valentin was listening for a single delicate pulse-train; the side-band transmission from Nike's eyeballs.

This situation interested him, inasmuch as anything could hold his attention these days; the ins and outs of betrayal, of wheels within wheels and subordinates who were superiors. Valentin Zero was an expert system wired for espionage, and his current mission was to monitor Nike. She was so old as to be almost obsolete: old enough to have been here before. His sensorium ghosted through winds of data—the life-blood of even the most seriously injured orbital republic—until he finally locked onto a signal that looked right. It was faint, but the coding matched his key; he locked on and submerged in the transmission, saw what Nike was seeing.

The wall of the house caved in soundlessly, blood spurting from arteries buried in the walls, followed by a spasm as the floor shuddered and died. A release of sphincters flooded the food trough. A boy stepped through a ragged rent in front of her; his left arm was coated to the elbow with a smooth sheen of gore, the chainsaw semi-retracted and murderous. His bronze exoskeleton exposed white skin and atrophied genitals, a wildly ecstatic smile beneath a cowlick of brown hair. The running lights on his spinal carapace were blinking green and violet pips, as membranes slid down across Nike's eyes and a targeting display flashed a red crosshair surrounded by flickering digits across his face.

"Hello," he said, and tittered. Ben sat where he was, very still, eyes narrowed; Nike felt her perception compress into a point on the boy's forehead, a point that could be made to explode.

"Hello," she replied. The boy frowned, as if disappointed.

"You're not scared," he complained, "and you're not dead. What are you?" He pouted with a transsexual sullenness that struck her as grotesquely overdone.

"I'm a visitor," she replied. "What are you?"

"I'm a Boy," he said, smiling suddenly; "I've come—"

"He's come to negotiate their surrender," said Ben. The boy flared again, mercurially angry.

"You shut up, old man! That's for me to tell. It's not true, anyway."

Ben shut up, his face blank. Nike felt as if the ground was dissolving beneath her feet. She'd pegged Ben as a non-participant, but this boy seemed to know something that she didn't.

"What have you got to tell me?" she asked, nerves alive with unease.

"Merely to enquire after your health and your diplomatic patronage," said the boy, sniffing disdainfully. With uncharacteristic lack of theatrical presence he scratched under one arm. "But the old man of the monolith's got to you already, I see!"

"The monolith?" she asked, tracking Ben with her peripheral vision. He sat as still as a rock.

"The castle . . . the claw of the Shogun. We've been trying to get him to call off the Hunter for decades, haven't we?" The boy glanced at Ben pointedly; Ben rocked slowly back and forth. The boy grimaced. "Observe the Shogun: ruler of the world, patron of the ongoing revolution, supreme systems coordinator of the digitized districts, etcetera. We've been trying to get him to do his job since he ran away fifty years ago, but he refuses."

"Why?" she asked, wondering to whom she should address the question.

"Because I'm not ready to let the boys do what they were designed to do," said Ben, not looking at her: "I'm not prepared to digitize the entire human biomass of the System to suit a political goal. When we designed the boys—"

"—Who were 'we'?" she butted in, gripped by a sense of déjà vu.

"The Turing Front, the society for synthetic intelligence. The Islamic Corporate Shogunate was an experimental deployment for the revolution; fanatical cyborgs. Some of them were the wild boys and some of them were less obvious, like the Hunters. They knew that when they died they'd be preserved in the transputer array; their job was to forcibly integrate all reactionary elements. Very successful, I might add: most of the neuroplants in this world are part of the mind-support system. But it didn't work out too well." Ben paused, head bowed; the boy looked at him accusingly.

"The ecosystem needed a firm hand in control and began to shut down," said the boy. "We stayed on in hope of finding transport to another world where we could integrate, but evidently there was a quarantine pact; all the exfiltrators lost contact. And then Ben reprogrammed that blasted Hunter—the only surviving one, we exported all the other clones—on our collective ass to keep us from getting enough slack . . ." He shook his alloy-framed head. "Unless those early cadres succeeded, the revolution was an abortion. Any idea how many humans want to be digitized without the initial demonstration?"

Nike looked at him enigmatically. "Yes," she said; "I have. I've seen it at first hand."

"Why are you here?" asked the boy.

Nike shrugged. "My people aren't very popular out there," she said. "We need somewhere to go; the New Cladists are pushing in everywhere, and politically we've lost ground so heavily that unless we find a closed habitat we'll be forced to condense in order to prevent mass defections."

"New Cladists?" said Ben. "What are they?"

"Human revenants, technically adept at manipulating biosystems," she replied. It was so tiring, being on edge like this: even the wild boys didn't seem threatening enough to justify keeping her defenses on edge. "We just can't compete." A soft rain was falling outside, pattering through the hole in the wall.

"And who are you?" probed the boy, looking for completeness.

"Can't you guess?" she complained. "You've had it easy with your smug mind-games and your revolution; don't you see?" The wind ghosted through the house like the soul of history, ruffling her hair. "We tried to carry the revolution through outside the closed habitat, we fought for a century . . ." She stared into reflective distances, eyes like dark mirrors, resembling her mind.

". . . but they didn't want us."

The Hunter was wandering, adrift in an ocean of despair, when she came across Valentin Zero. Her video surfaces were locked into the sonic images of a fruit bat in free fall; when she saw something unusual, she tensed instinctively. Could it be a boyish thing, here in the axial zone? A surge of conditioned reflexes drowned her nervous system in adrenalin and hatred; but as the bat approached the object it resolved into three components, all too small. Her skulls couldn't find a meaning for it. Drifting into a close approach, she noted three cylinders and a bushy twirl of vegetation. Modified axons in the bat's ears recognized high-frequency emissions, the fingerprint of molecular-scale processors; it had to be intelligent.

*Hello unidentified structure,*" she squeaked through the ultrasonic larynx of the bat. "Talk to me."

The structure began to rotate, sluggishly; the bat picked up another object, the vibrating flight surfaces of an insect. An eye swam into view, shielded by a triangular leaf. The bat screamed; something was scanning down its nervous system, tying to locate the Hunter's interface.

*"Who are you?"* said the cluster of grey cylinders, words burning tracks of silvery pain through the mind of the bat. *"Visualize yourself."* The Hunter framed an image and transmitted it, waited as the intruder scanned it.

*"Nike,"* broadcast Valentin; *"What are you doing here?"*

Then there was silence, as high above the castle the Hunter remembered who she had been.

# Charles Stross

W

hen first approached, Charles Stross was reluctant to allow his freshman effort to be included in *Before They Were Giants*. Yet there can be no question that he deserves to be here. Starting out his career as a freelance writer, during which time he invented several iconic monsters for Dungeons & Dragons (such as the death knight, the slaad, and the githyanki—a race surreptitiously borrowed from George R. R. Martin) and did extensive work as a technology journalist, in the last 10 years Stross has traded in such pursuits as well as day jobs as a computer programmer and certified pharmacist in favor of publishing no less than 20 critically acclaimed novels and short story collections. His work has received the Hugo Award, two Locus Awards, a Sidewise Award, and several others, along with a host of nominations, and he shows no signs of slowing down anytime soon.

While Stross himself may not see many connections between his early work and the newer books, devotees of his hard science fiction will no doubt notice one thread that binds them: a gonzo, no-holds-barred approach to SF, in which new ideas are a dime a dozen, and the sheer density of conjecture and cutting-edge concepts dare the reader to try and assimilate them all at once.

**Looking back, what do you think still works well in this story? Why?**

Truth be told, I don't even want to re-read the story. I wrote it off as juvenilia and a learning exercise years ago.

**If you were writing this today, what would you do differently? What are the story's weaknesses, and how would you change them?**

I wouldn't write a story like this today.

Let me anatomize: it's a simple conceptual one-shot (William Burroughs meets William Gibson). It's poorly executed, the characterization doesn't work terribly well, it's overly influenced by what I was reading at the time (*Schismatrix* by Bruce Sterling), and doesn't say anything really interesting or useful.

**What inspired this story? How did it take shape? Where was it initially published?**

I wrote it in 1985, aged 21, on my first word processor, largely for the feel of the style. I was very much still learning the craft at the time, and I'd have done better to have left it in the small press/workshop zine I was frequenting at the time—this being pre-Internet, a lot of what happens on critters.org today, writers learning their craft through workshops, took place on paper in workshop zines that were circulated to members for criticism—but instead I sent it to *Interzone*. And for some reason, *Interzone*'s editors liked it. (I think they were wrong, with an extra 23 years of perspective, but there's no accounting for taste.)

**Where were you in your life when you published this piece, and what kind of impact did it have?**

It was a huge morale boost; surely fame, fortune, and a multi-book contract were just around the corner!

So I kept on writing and kept on submitting short stories. It only took me another 15 years to sell a novel.

**How has your writing changed over the years, both stylistically and in terms of your writing process?**

I think my writing has changed immensely—I'm not the same guy I was when I was less than half my current age! I've spent 13 of the past 18 years writing for a living, so I'm a lot more in control of my technique. I've had a lot more life experience, so I know a bit more about characterization. And I'm a lot more aware of what I'm doing at the level of narrative structure, plot, theme, and so on.

More importantly, I shook off the initial cyberpunk infection (it bit hard, if you were in your late teens/early twenties in the 1980s) and began looking a bit more deeply at the society around me. SF tends to reflect our concerns about the present on the silver screen of the future; cyberpunk (with its designer labels, black leather and chrome, and large multinationals) was very much a movement rooted in the early 1980s. I don't need a movement to hand me a cognitive map of my own near-future these days: I just need to go online and look around to see any number of really weird phenomena that are changing the way we live.

**What advice do you have for aspiring authors?**

Keep writing, keep finishing stories, send them out—and listen to what comes back.

Try and fine-tune your bullshit detector so that you can tell the difference between useful criticisms and idiotic ones. (Most of the time people who criticize your work do so honestly, and you can learn a lot from them; but sometimes they're just trying to fuck with your head for their own reasons.)

Oh, and don't pick fights with critics. That's *really* important.

**Any anecdotes regarding the story or your experiences as a fledgling writer?**

## The Boys

Only this: *Interzone* published "The Boys," and for some reason SF illustrator Pete Lyon was commissioned to do a cover painting for that issue, based on the story. Guess who bought the painting, a couple of years later? (Unfortunately the media he used degrade somewhat with UV exposure, so I don't currently have it on display. But then again, it's kind of creepy . . . like the original story.)

# Ginungagap
## by Michael Swanwick

A bigail checked out of Mother of Mercy and rode the translator web to Toledo Cylinder in June Industrial Park. Stars bloomed, dwindled, disappeared five times. It was a long trek, halfway around the sun.

Toledo was one of the older commercial cylinders, now given over almost entirely to bureaucrats, paper pushers, and freelance professionals. It was not Abigail's favorite place to visit, but she needed work and 3M had already bought out of her contract.

The job broker had dyed his chest hairs blond and his leg hairs red. They clashed wildly with his green cache-sexe and turquoise jewelry. His fingers played on a keyout, bringing up and endless flow of career trivia. "Cute trick you played," he said.

Abigail flexed her new arm negligently. It was a good job, but pinker than the rest of her. And weak of course, but exercise would correct that. "Thanks," she said. She laid the arm underneath one breast and compared the colors. It matched the nipple perfectly. Definitely too pink. "Work outlook any good?"

"Naw," the broker said. A hummingbird flew past his ear, a nearly undetectable parting of the air. "I see here that you applied for the Proxima colony."

"They were full up," Abigail said. "No openings for a gravity bum, hey?"

"I didn't say that," the broker grumbled. "I'll find—hello! What's this?" Abigail craned her neck, couldn't get a clear look at the screen. "There's a tag on your employment record."

"What's that mean?"

"Let me read." A honeysuckle flower fell on Abigail's hair, and she brushed it off impatiently. The broker had an open-air office, framed by hedges and roofed over with a trellis. Sometimes Abigail found the older Belt cylinders a little too lavish for her taste.

"Mmp." The broker looked up. "Bell-Sandia wants to hire you. Indefinite term one-shot contract." He swung the keyout around so she could see. "*Very* nice terms, but that's normal for a high-risk contract."

"High risk? From B-S, the Friendly Communications People? What kind of risk?"

The broker scrolled up new material. "There." He tapped the screen with a finger. "The language is involved, but what it boils down to is they're looking for a test passenger for a device they've got that uses black holes for interstellar travel."

"Couldn't work," Abigail said. "The tidal forces—"

"Spare me. Presumable they've found a way around that problem. The question is, are you interested or not?"

Abigail stared up through the trellis at a stream meandering across the curved land overhead. Children were wading in it. She counted to a hundred very slowly, trying to look as if she needed to think it over.

Abigail strapped herself into the transition harness and nodded to the technician outside the chamber. The tech touched her console, and a light stasis field immobilized Abigail and the air about her while the chamber wall irised open. In a fluid bit of technological sleight-of-hand, the translator rechanneled her inertia and gifted her with a velocity almost, but not quite, that of the speed of light.

Stars bloomed about her, and the sun dwindled. She breathed in deeply and—

—was in the receiver device. Relativity had cheated her of all but a fraction of the transit time. She shrugged out of harness and frog-kicked her way to the lip station's tugdock.

The tug pilot grinned at her as she entered, then turned his attention to his controls. He was young and wore streaks of brown makeup across his chest and thighs—only slightly darker than his skin. His mesh vest was almost in bad taste. But he wore it well, and looked roguish rather than overdressed. Abigail found herself wishing she had more than a cache-sexe and nail polish on—some jewelry or makeup, perhaps. She felt drab in comparison.

The starfield wraparound held two inserts routed in by synchronous cameras. Alphanumerics flickered beneath them. One showed her immediate destination, the Bell-Sandia base *Arthur C. Clarke*. It consisted of five wheels, each set inside the other and rotating at slightly differing speeds. The base was done up in red-and-orange supergraphics. Considering its distance from the Belt factories, it was respectably sized.

Abigail latched herself into the passenger seat as the engines cut in. The second insert—

*Ginungagap, the only known black hole in the sun's gravity field, was discovered in 2023,* a small voice murmured. *Its presence explained the long-puzzling variations in the orbits of the outer planets. The* Arthur C. Clarke *was*

"Is this necessary?" Abigail asked.

"Absolutely," the pilot said. "We abandoned the tourist program a year or so ago, but somehow the rules never caught up. They're very strict about the regs here." He winked at Abigail's dismayed expression. "Hold tight a minute while—" His voice faded as he tinkered with the controls.

*established forty years later and communications with the Proxima colony began shortly thereafter, Ginungagap*

The voice cut off. She grinned thanks. "Abigail Vanderhoek."

"Cheyney," the pilot said. "You're the gravity bum, right?"

"Yeah."

"I used to be a vacuum bum myself. But I got tired of it, and grabbed the first semipermanent contract that came along."

"I kind of went the other way."

"Probably what I should have done," Cheyney said amiably. "Still, it's a rough road. I picked up three scars along the way." He pointed them out: a thick slash across his abdomen, a red splotch beside one nipple, and a white crescent half obscured by his scalp. "I could've had them cleaned up, but the way I figure, life is just a process of picking up scars and experience. So I kept 'em."

If she had thought he was trying to impress her, Abigail would have slapped him down. But it was clearly just part of an ongoing self-dramatization, possibly justified, probably not. Abigail suspected that, tour trips to Earth excepted, the *Clarke* was as far down a gravity well as Cheyney had ever been. Still, he did have an irresponsible boyish appeal. "Take me past the net?" she asked.

Cheyney looped the tug around the communications net trailing the *Clarke*. Kilometers of steel lace passed beneath them. He pointed out a small dish antenna on the edge and a cluster of antennae on the back. "The loner on the edge transmits into Ginungagap," he said. "The others relay information to and from Mother."

"Mother?"

"That's the traditional name for the *Arthur C. Clarke*." He swung the tug about with a careless sweep of one arm, and launched into a long scurrilous story about the origin of the nickname. Abigail laughed, and Cheyney pointed a finger. "There's Ginungagap."

Abigail peered intently. "Where? I don't see a thing." She glanced at the second wraparound insert, which displayed a magnified view of the black hole. It wasn't at all impressive; a red smear against black nothingness. In the starfield it was all but invisible.

"Disappointing, hey? But still dangerous. Even this far out, there's a lot of ionization from the accretion disk."

"Is that why there's a lip station?"

"Yeah. Particle concentration varies, but if the translator were right at the *Clarke*, we'd probably lose about a third of the passengers."

Cheyney dropped Abigail off at Mother's crewlock and looped the tug off and away. Abigail wondered where to go, what to do now.

"You're the gravity bum we're dumping down Ginungagap." The short, solid man was upon her before she saw him. His eyes were intense. His cache-sexe was conservative orange. "I like the stunt with the arm. I'm Paul Girard. Head of external security. In charge of your training. You play verbal Ping-Pong?"

"Why do you ask?" she countered automatically.

"Don't you know?"

"Should I?"

"Do you mean now or later?"

"Will the answer be different later?"

A smile creased Paul's solid face. "You'll do." He took her arm, led her along a sloping corridor. "There isn't much prep time. The dry run is scheduled in two weeks. Things will move pretty quickly after that. You want to start your training now?"

"Do I have a choice?" Abigail asked, amused.

Paul came to a dead stop. "Listen," he said. "Rule number one. Don't play games with *me*. You understand? Because I always win. Not sometimes, not usually—always."

Abigail yanked her arm free. "You maneuvered me into that," she said angrily.

"Consider it part of your training." He stared directly into her eyes. "No matter how many gravity wells you've climbed down, you're still the product of a near-space culture—protected, trusting, willing to take things on face value. This is a dangerous attitude, and I want you to realize it. I want you to learn to look behind the mask of events. I want you to grow up. And you will."

*Don't be so sure.* A small smile quirked Paul's face as if he could read her thoughts. Aloud, Abigail said. "That sounds a little excessive for a trip to Promixa."

"Lesson number two," Paul said. "Don't make easy assumptions. You're not going to Proxima." He led her outward—down the ramp to the next wheel, pausing briefly at the juncture to acclimatize to the slower rate of revolution. "You're going to visit spiders." He gestured. "The crewroom is this way."

The crewroom was vast and cavernous, twilight gloomy. Keyouts were set up along winding paths that wandered aimlessly through the workspace. Puddles of light fell on each board and operator. Dark-loving foliage was set between the keyouts.

"This is the heart of the beast," Paul said. "The green keyouts handle all Proxima communications—pretty routine by now. But the blue . . ." His eyes glinting oddly, he pointed. Over the keyouts hung silvery screens with harsh grainy images floating on their surfaces, black-and-white blobs that Abigail could not resolve into recognizable forms.

"Those," Paul said, "are the spiders. We're talking to them in real time. Response delay is almost all due to machine translation."

In a sudden shift of perception, the blobs became arachnid forms. That mass of black flickering across the screen was a spiderleg and that was its thorax. Abigail felt an immediate primal aversion, and then was swept by an all-encompassing wonder.

"Aliens?" she breathed.

"Aliens."

They actually looked no more like spiders than humans looked like apes. The right legs had an extra joint each, and the mandible configuration was all wrong. But to an untrained eye they would do.

"But this is—how long have you—why in God's name are you keeping this a secret?" An indefinable joy arose in Abigail. This opened a universe of possibilities, as if after a lifetime of being confined in a box someone had removed the lid.

"Industrial security," Paul said. "The gadget that'll send you through Ginungagap to *their* black hole is a spider invention. We're trading optical data for it, but the law won't protect our rights until we've demonstrated its use. We don't want the other corporations cutting in." He nodded toward the nearest black-and-white screen. "As you can see, they're weak on optics."

"I'd love to talk . . ." Abigail's voice trailed off as she realized how little-girl hopeful she sounded.

"I'll arrange an introduction."

There was a rustling to Abigail's side. She turned and saw a large black tom-cat with white boots and belly emerge from the bushes. "This is the esteemed head of Alien Communications," Paul said sourly.

Abigail started to laugh, choked it back in embarrassment as she realized that he was not speaking of the cat. "Julio Dominguez, section chief for translation." Paul said. "Abigail Vanderhoek, gravity specialist."

The wizened old man smiled professorially. "I assume our resident gadfly has explained how the communications net works, has he not?"

"Well—" Abigail began.

Domniguez clucked has tongue. He wore a yellow cache-sexe and matching bow tie; just a little too garish for a man his age. "Quite simple, actually. Escape velocity from a black hole is greater than the speed of light. Therefore, within Ginungagap the speed of light is no longer the limit to the speed of communications."

He paused just long enough for Abigail to look baffled. "Which is just a stuffy way of saying that when we aim a stream of electrons into the boundary of the stationary limit, they emerge elsewhere—out of another black hole. And if we aim them *just so*"—his voice rose whimsically—"they'll emerge from the black hole of our choosing. The physics is simple. The finesse is in aiming the electrons."

The cat stalked up to Abigail, pushed its forehead against her leg, and mewed insistently. She bent over and picked it up.

"But nothing can emerge from a black hole," she objected.

Dominguez chuckled. "Ah, but anything can fall in, hey? A positron can fall in. But a positron falling into Ginungagap in a positive time is only an electron falling out in negative time. Which means that a positron falling into a black hole in negative time is actually an electron falling out in positive time—exactly the effect we want. Think of Ginungagap as being the physical manifestation of an equivalence sign in mathematics."

"Oh," Abigail said, feeling very firmly put in her place. Three white moths flittered along the path. The cat watched, fascinated, while she stroked its head.

"At any rate, the electrons do emerge, and once the data is in, the theory has to follow along meekly."

"Tell me about the spiders," Abigail said, before he could continue. The moths were darting up, sideward, down, a chance ballet in three dimensions.

"The *aliens*," Dominguez said, frowning at Paul, "are still a mystery to us. We exchange facts, descriptions, recipes for tools, but the important questions do not lend themselves to our clumsy mathematical codes. Do they know of love, do they appreciate beauty? Do they believe in God, hey?"

"Do they want to eat us?" Paul threw in.

"Don't be ridiculous." Dominguez snapped. "Of course they don't."

The moths parted when they came to Abigail. Two went to either side; one flew over her shoulder. The cat batted at it with one paw. "The cat's name is Garble," Paul said. "The kids in Bio cloned him up."

Dominguez opened his mouth, closed it again.

Abigail scratched Garble under the chin. He arched his neck and purred all but noiselessly. "With your permission," Paul said. He stepped over to a keyout and waved its operator aside.

"Technically you're supposed to speak a convenience language, but if you keep it simple and nonidiomatic, there shouldn't be any difficulty." He touched the keyout. "Ritual greetings, spider." There was a blank pause. Then the spider moved, a hairy leg flickering across the screen.

"Hello, human."

"Introductions: Abigail Vanderhoek. She is our representative. She will ride the spinner." Another pause. More leg waving.

"Hello, Abigail Vanderhoek. Transition of vacuum garble resting garble commercial benefits garble still point in space."

"Tricky translation," Paul said. He signed to Abigail to take over.

Abigail hesitated, then said, "Will you come to visit us? The way we will visit you?"

"No, you see—" Dominguez began, but Paul waved him to silence.

"No, Abigail Vanderhoek. We are sulfur-based life."

"I do not understand."

"You can garble black hole through garble spinner because you are carbon-based life. Carbon forms chains easily, but sulfur combines in lattices or rosettes. Our garble simple form garble. Sometimes sulfur forms short chains."

"We'll explain later," Paul said. "Go on, you're doing fine."

Abigail hesitated again. What do you say to a spider, anyway? Finally, she asked, "Do you want to eat us?"

"Oh, Christ, get her off that thing," Dominguez said, reaching for the keyout.

Paul blocked his arm. "No," he said. "I want to hear this."

Several of the spiderlegs wove intricate patterns. "The question is false. Sulfur-based life derives no benefit from eating carbon-based life."

"You see," Dominguez said.

"But if it were possible," Abigail persisted. "If you *could* eat us and derive benefit. Would you?"

"Yes, Abigail Vanderhoek. With great pleasure."

Dominguez pushed her aside. "We're terribly sorry," he said to the alien. "This is a horrible, horrible misunderstanding. You!" he shouted to the operator. "Get back on and clear this mess up."

Paul was grinning wickedly. "Come," he said to Abigail. "We've accomplished enough here for one day."

As they started to walk away, Garble twisted in Abigail's arms and leapt free. He hit the floor on all fours and disappeared into the greenery. "Would they really eat us?" Abigail asked. Then amended it to, "Does that mean they're hostile?"

Paul shrugged. "Maybe they thought we'd be insulted if they *didn't* offer to eat us." He led her to her quarters. "Tomorrow we start training for real. In the meantime, you might make up a list of all the ways the spiders could hurt us if we set up transportation and they are hostile. Then another list of all the reasons we shouldn't trust them." He paused. "I've done it myself. You'll find that the lists get rather extensive."

Abigail's quarters weren't flashy, but they fit her well. A full starfield was routed to the walls, floor, and ceiling, only partially obscured by a trellis inner-frame that supported foxgrape vines. Somebody had done research into her tastes.

"Hi." The cheery greeting startled her. She whirled, saw that her hammock was occupied.

Cheyney sat up, swung his legs over the edge of the hammock, causing it to rock lightly. "Come on in." He touched an invisible control, and the starfield blueshifted down to a deep erotic purple.

"Just what do you think you're doing here?" Abigail asked.

"I had a few hours free," Cheyney said, "so I thought I'd drop by and seduce you."

"Well, Cheyney, I appreciate your honesty," Abigail said. "So I won't say no."

"Thank you."

"I'll say maybe some other time. Now get lost. I'm tired."

"Okay," Cheyney hopped down, walked jauntily to the door. He paused. "You said 'later,' right?"

"I said *maybe* later."

"Later. Gotcha." He winked and was gone.

Abigail threw herself into the hammock, redshifted the starfield until the universe was a sparse smattering of dying embers. Annoying creature! There was no hope for anything more than the most superficial of relationships with him. She closed her eyes, smiled. Fortunately, she wasn't currently in the market for a serious relationship.

She slept.

She was falling . . .

Abigail had landed the ship an easy walk from 3M's robot laboratory. The lab's geodesic dome echoed white clouds to the north, where Nix Olympus peeked over the horizon. Otherwise all—land, sky, rocks—was standard-issue Martian orange. She had clambered to the ground and shrugged on the supply backpack.

Resupplying 3M-RL stations was a gut contract: easy but dull. So perhaps she was less cautious than usual going down the steep rock-strewn hillside, or perhaps the rock would have turned under her no matter how carefully she placed her feet. Her ankle twisted and she lurched sideways, but the backpack had shifted her center of gravity too much for her to be able to recover.

Arms windmilling, she fell.

The rockslide carried her downhill in a panicky flurry of dust and motion, tearing her flesh and splintering her bones. But before she could feel pain, her suit shot her full of a nerve synesthetic, translating sensation into colors: reds, russets, and browns, with staccato yellow spikes when a rock smashed into her ribs. So that she fell in a whirling rainbow of glorious light.

She came to rest in a burst or orange. The rocks were settling about her. A spume of dust drifted away, out toward the distant red horizon. A large jagged slab of stone slid by, gently shearing off her backpack. Tools, supplies, airpacks, flew up and softly rained down.

A spanner as long as her arm slammed down inches from Abigail's helmet. She flinched and suddenly events became real. She kicked her legs, and sand and dust fountained up. Drawing her feet under her body—the one ankle bright gold—she started to stand.

And was jerked to the ground by a sudden tug on one arm. Even as she turned her head, she became aware of a deep, profound purple sensation in her left hand. It was pinioned by a rock not quite large enough to stake a claim to. There was no color in the fingers.

"Cute," she muttered. She tugged at the arm, pushed at the rock. Nothing budged.

Abigail nudged the radio switch with her chin. "Grounder to Lip Station," she said. She hesitated, feeling foolish, then said, "Mayday. Repeat, Mayday. Could you guys send a rescue party down for me?"

There was no reply. With a sick green feeling in the pit of her stomach Abigail reached a gloved hand around the back of her helmet. She touched something jagged, a sensation of mottled rust, the broken remains of her radio.

"I think I'm in trouble." She said it aloud and listened to the sound of it. Flat, unemotional—probably true. But nothing to get panicky about.

She took quick stock of what she had to work with. One intact suit and helmet. One spanner. A worldful of rocks, many close at hand. Enough air for—she checked the helmet readout—almost an hour. Assuming the lip station ran its checks on schedule and was fast on the uptake she had almost half the air she needed.

Most of the backpack's contents were scattered too far away to reach. One rectangular gaspack, however, had landed nearby. She reached for it but could not touch it; squinted but could not read the label on its nozzle. It was almost certainly liquid gas—either nitrogen or oxygen—for the robot lab. But there was a slim chance it was the spare airpack. If it was, she might live to be rescued.

Abigail studied the landscape carefully, but there was nothing more. "Okay, then, it's an airpack." She reached as far as her tethered arm would allow. The gaspack remained a tantalizing centimeter out of her reach.

For an instant she was stymied. Then, feeling like an idiot, she grabbed the spanner. She hooked it over the gaspack. Felt the gaspack move grudgingly. Slowly nudged it toward herself.

By the time Abigail could drop the spanner and draw in the gas pack, her good arm was blue with fatigue. Sweat running down her face, she juggled the gaspack to read its nozzle markings.

It was liquid oxygen—useless. She could hook it to her suit and feed in the contents, but the first breath would freeze her lungs. She released the gaspack and lay back, staring vacantly at the sky.

Up there was civilization: tens of thousands of human stations strung together by webs of communication and transportation. Messages flowed endlessly on laser cables. Translators borrowed and lent momentum, moving streams of travelers and cargo at almost (but not quite) the speed of light. A starship was being readied to carry a third load of colonists to Proxima. Up there, free from gravity's relentless clutch, people lived in luxury and ease. Here, however . . ."

"I'm going to die." She said it softly and was filled with wondering awe. Because it was true. She was going to die.

Death was a black wall. It lay before her, extending to infinity in all directions, smooth and featureless and mysterious. She could almost reach out an arm and touch it. Soon she would come up against it and, if anything lay beyond, pass through. Soon, very soon, she would *know*.

She touched the seal to her helmet. It felt grey—smooth and inviting. Her fingers moved absently, tracing the seal about her neck. With sudden horror, Abigail realized that she was thinking about undoing it, releasing her air, throwing away the little time she had left . . .

She shuddered. With sudden resolve, she reached out and unsealed the shoulder seam of her captive arm.

The seal clamped down, automatically cutting off air loss. The flesh of her damaged arm was exposed to the raw Martian atmosphere. Abigail took up the gaspack and cradled it in the pit of her good arm. Awkwardly, she opened the nozzle with the spanner.

She sprayed the exposed arm with liquid oxygen for over a minute before she was certain it had frozen solid. Then she dropped the gas pack, picked up the spanner, and swung.

Her arm shattered into a thousand fragments.

She stood up.

Abigail awoke, tense and sweaty. She blueshifted the walls up to normal light, and sat up. After a few minutes of clearing her head, she set the walls to cycle from red to blue in a rhythm matching her normal pulse. Eventually the womb-cycle lulled her back to sleep.

"Not even close," Paul said. He ran the tape backward, froze it on a still shot of the spider twisting two legs about each other. "That's the morpheme for 'extreme disgust,' remember. It's easy to pick out, and the language kids say any statement with this gesture should be reversed in meaning. Irony, see? So when the spider says that the strong should protect the weak, it means—"

"How long have we been doing this?"

"Practically forever," Paul said cheerfully. "You want to call it a day?"

"Only if it won't hurt my standing."

"Hah! Very good." He switched off the keyout. "Nicely thought out. You're absolutely right: it would have. However, as a reward for realizing this, you can take off early *without* it being noted on your record."

"Thank you," Abigail said sourly.

Like most large installations, the *Clarke* had a dozen or so smaller structures tagging along after it in minimum maintenance orbits. When Abigail discovered that these included a small wheel gymnasium, she had taken to putting in an hour's exercise after each training shift. Today, she put in two.

The first hour she spent shadow-boxing and practicing savate in heavy-gee to work up a sweat. The second hour she spent in the axis room, performing free-fall gymnastics. After the first workout, it made her feel light and nimble and good about her body.

She returned from the wheel gym sweaty and cheerful to find Cheyney in her hammock again. "Cheyney," she said, "this is not the first time I've had to kick you out of there. Or even the third, for that matter."

Cheyney held his palms up in mock protest. "Hey, no," he said. "Nothing like that today. I just came by to watch the raft debate with you."

Abigail felt pleasantly weary, decidedly uncerebral. "Paul said something about it, but . . ."

"Turn it on, then. You don't want to miss it." Cheyney touched her wall, and a cluster of images sprang to life at the far end of the room.

"Just what is a raft debate, anyway?" Abigail asked, giving in gracefully. She hoisted herself onto the hammock, sat beside him. They rocked gently for a moment.

"There's this raft, see? It's adrift and powerless, and there's only enough oxygen on board to keep one person alive until rescue. Only there are three on board—two humans and a spider."

"Do spiders breathe oxygen?"

"It doesn't matter. This is a hypothetical situation." Two-thirds of the image area were taken up by Dominguez and Paul, quietly waiting for the debate to begin. The remainder showed a flat spider image.

"Okay, what then?"

"They argue over who gets to survive. Dominguez argues that he should, since he's human and human culture is superior to spider culture. The spider argues for itself and its culture." He put an arm around her waist. "You smell nice."

"Thank you." She ignored the arm. "What does Paul argue?"

"He's the devil's advocate. He argues that no one deserves to live and they should dump the oxygen."

"Paul would enjoy that role." Abigail said. Then, "What's the point to this debate?"

"It's entertainment. There isn't *supposed* to be a point."

Abigail doubted it was that simple. The debate could reveal a good deal about the spiders and how they thought, once the language types were done with it. Conversely, the spiders would doubtless be studying the human responses. *This could be interesting*, she thought. Cheyney was stroking her side now, lightly but with great authority. She postponed reaction, not sure whether she liked it or not.

Louise Chang, a vaguely high placed administrator, blossomed in the center of the image cluster. "Welcome," she said, and explained the rules of the debate. "The winner will be decided by acclaim," she said, "with half the vote being human and half alien. Please remember not to base your vote on racial chauvinism, but on the strengths of the arguments and how well they are presented." Cheyney's hand brushed casually across her nipples; they stiffened. The hand lingered. "The debate will begin with the gentleman representing the aliens presenting his thesis."

The image flickered as the spider waved several legs. "Thank you, Ms. Chairman. I argue that I should survive. My culture is superior because of our technological advancement. Three examples. Humans have used translation travel only briefly, yet we have used it for sixteens of garble. Our black-hole technology is superior. And our garble has garble for the duration of our society.

"Thank you. The gentlemen representing humanity?"

"Thank you, Ms. Chairman." Dominguez adjusted an armlet. Cheyney leaned back and let Abigail rest against him. Her head fit comfortably against his shoulder. "My argument is that technology is neither the sole nor most important measure of a culture. By these standards dolphins would be considered brute animals. The aesthetic considerations—the arts, theology, and the tradition of philosophy—are of greater import. As I shall endeavor to prove."

"He's chosen the wrong tactic," Cheyney whispered in Abigail's ear. "That must have come across as pure garble to the spiders."

"Thank you. Mr. Girard?"

Paul's image expanded. He theatrically swigged from a small flask and hoisted it high in the air. "Alcohol! There's the greatest achievement of the human race!" Abigail snorted. Cheyney laughed out loud. "But I hold that neither Mr. Dominguez nor the distinguished spider deserves to live, because of the disregard both cultures have for sentient life." Abigail looked at Cheyney, who shrugged. "As I shall endeavor to prove." His image dwindled.

Chang said, "The arguments will now proceed, beginning with the distinguished alien."

The spider and then Dominguez ran through their arguments, and to Abigail they seemed markedly lackluster. She didn't give them her full attention, because Cheyney's hands were moving most interestingly across unexpected parts of her body. He might not be too bright, but he was certainly good at some things. She nuzzled her face into his neck, gave him a small peck, returned her attention to the debate.

Paul blossomed again. He juggled something in his palm, held his hand open to reveal three ball bearings. "When I was a kid I used to short out the school module and sneak up to the axis room and play marbles." Abigail smiled, remembering similar stunts she had played. "For the sake of those of us who are spiders, I'll explain that marbles is a game played in free-fall for the purpose of developing coordination and spatial perception. You make a six-armed star of marbles in the center . . ."

One of the bearings fell from his hand, bounced noisily, and disappeared as it rolled out of camera range. "Well, obviously it can't be played here. But the point is that when you shoot the marble just right, it hits the end of one arm and its kinetic energy is transferred from marble to marble along that arm. So that the shooter stops and the marble at the far end of the arm flies away." Cheyney was stroking her absently now, engrossed in the argument.

"Now, we plan to send a courier into Ginungagap and out the spiders' black hole. At least, that's what we say we're going to do.

"But what exits from a black hole is not necessary the same as what went into its partner hole. We throw an electron into Ginungagap, and another one pops out elsewhere. It's identical. It's a direct casual relationship. But it's like the marbles—they're identical to each other and have the same kinetic force. It's simply not the same electron."

Cheyney's hand was still, motionless. Abigail prodded him gently, touching his inner thigh. "Anyone who's interested can see the equations. Now, when we send messages, this doesn't matter. The message is important, not the medium. However, when we send a human being in . . . what emerges from the other hole will be cell for cell, gene for gene, atom for atom identical. *But it will not be the same person.*" He paused a beat, smiled.

"I submit, then, that this is murder. And further, that by conspiring to commit murder, both the spider and the human races display absolute disregard for intelligent life. In short, no one on the raft deserves to live. And I rest my case."

"Mr. Girard!" Dominguez objected, even before his image was restored to full-size. "The simplest mathematical proof is an identity: that A equals A. Are you trying to deny this?"

Paul held up the two ball bearings he had left. "These marbles are identical too. But they are not the same marble."

"We know the phenomenon you speak of," the spider said. "It is as if garble the black hole bulges out simultaneously. There is no violation of continuity. The two entities are the same. There is no death."

Abigail pulled Cheyney down, so that they were both lying on their sides, still able to watch the images, "So long as you happen to be the second marble and not the first." Paul said. Abigail tentatively licked Cheyney's ear.

"He's right," Cheyney murmured.

"No, he's not," Abigail retorted. She bit his earlobe.

"You mean that?"

"Of course I mean that. He's confusing semantics with reality." She engrossed herself in a study of the back of his neck.

"Okay."

Abigail suddenly sensed that she was missing something. "Why do you ask?" She struggled into a sitting position. Cheyney followed.

"No particular reason." Cheyney's hands began touching her again. But Abigail was sure something had been slipped past her.

They caressed each other lightly, while the debate dragged to an end. Not paying much attention, Abigail voted for Dominguez and Cheyney voted for Paul. As a result of a nearly undivided spider vote, the spider won. "I told you Dominguez was taking the wrong approach," Cheyney said. He hopped off the hammock. "Look, I've got to see somebody about something. I'll be right back."

"You're not leaving now?" Abigail protested, dumbfounded. The door irised shut.

Angry and hurt, she leapt down, determined to follow him. She couldn't remember ever feeling so insulted.

Cheyney didn't try to be evasive; it apparently did not occur to him that she might follow. Abigail stalked him down a corridor, up an inramp, and to a door that irised open for him. She recognized that door.

Thoughtfully, she squatted on her heels behind an untrimmed boxwood and waited. A minute later, Garble wandered by, saw her, and demanded attention. "Scat!" she hissed. He butted his head against her knee. "Then be quiet, at least." She scooped him up. His expression was smug.

The door irised open and Cheyney exited, whistling. Abigail waited until he was gone, stood, went to the door and entered. Fish darted between long fronds under a transparent floor. It was an austere room, almost featureless. Abigail looked, but did not see a hammock.

"So Cheyney's working for you now," she said coldly. Paul looked up from a corner keyout.

"As a matter of fact, I've just signed him to permanent contract in the crewroom. He's bright enough. A bit green. Ought to do well."

"Then you admit that you put him up to grilling me about your puerile argument in the debate?" Garble struggled in her arms. She juggled him into a more comfortable position. "And that you staged the argument for my benefit in the first place?"

"Ah," Paul said. "I knew the training was going somewhere. You've become very wary in an extremely short time."

"Don't evade the questions."

"I needed your honest reaction," Paul said. "Not the answer you would have given me, knowing your chances of crossing Ginungagap rode on it."

Garble made an angry noise. "You tell him, Garble!" she said. "That goes double for me." She stepped out the door. "You lost the debate," she snapped.

Long after the door had irised shut, she could feel Paul's amused smile burning into her back.

Two days after she returned to kick Cheyney out of her hammock for the final time, Abigail was called to the crewroom. "Dry run," Paul said. "Attendance is mandatory." And cut off.

The crewroom was crowded with technicians, triple the number of keyouts. Small knots of them clustered before the screens, watching. Paul waved her to him.

"There," he motioned to one screen. "That's Clotho—the platform we built for the transmission device. It's a hundred kilometers off. I wanted more, but Dominguez overruled me. The device that'll unravel you and dump you down Ginungagap is that doo-hickey in the center." He tapped a keyout, and the platform zoomed up to fill the screen. It was covered by a clean transparent bubble. Inside, a spacesuited figure was placing something into a machine that looked like nothing so much as a giant armor-clad clamshell. Abigail looked, blinked, looked again.

"That's Garble," she said indignantly.

"Complain to Dominguez. I wanted a baboon."

The clamshell device closed. The spacesuited tech left in his tug, and alphanumerics flickered, indicating the device was in operation. As they watched, the spider-designed machinery immobilized Garble, transformed his molecules into one long continuous polymer chain, and spun it out an invisible opening at near-light speed. The water in his body was separated out, piped away, and preserved. The electrolyte balances were recorded and simultaneously transmitted in a parallel stream of electrons. It would reach the spider receiver along with the lead end of the cat-polymer, to be used in the reconstruction.

Thirty seconds passed. Now Garble was only partially in Clotho. The polymer chain, invisible and incredibly long, was passing into Ginungagap. On the far side the spiders were beginning to knit it up.

If all was going well.

Ninety-two seconds after they flashed on, the alphanumerics stopped twinkling on the screen. Garble was gone from Clotho. The clamshell opened, and the remote cameras showed it to be empty. A cheer arose.

Somebody boosted Dominguez atop a keyout. Intercom cameras swiveled to follow. He wavered fractionally, said "my friends," and launched into a speech. Abigail didn't even listen.

Paul's hand fell on her shoulder. It was the first time he had touched her since their initial meeting. "He's only a scientist," he said. "He had no idea how close you are to the cat."

"Look, I *asked* to go. I knew the risks. But Garble's just an animal: he wasn't given the choice."

Paul groped for words. "In a way, this is what your training has been about: the reason you're going across instead of someone like Dominguez. He projects his own reactions onto other people. If—"

Then, seeing that she wasn't listening, he said, "Anyway, you'll have a cat to play with in a few hours. They're only keeping him long enough to test out the life-support systems."

There was a festive air to the second gathering. The spiders reported that Garble had translated flawlessly. A brief visual display showed him stalking about Clotho's sister platform, irritable but apparently unharmed.

"There," somebody said. The screen indicated that the receiver net had taken in the running end of the cat's polymer chain. They waited a minute and a half, and the operation was over.

It was like a conjuring trick: the clamshell closed on emptiness. Water was piped in. Then it opened and Garble floated over its center, quietly licking one paw.

Abigail smiled at the homeliness of it. "Welcome back, Garble," she said quietly. "I'll get the guys in Bio to brew up some cream for you."

Paul's eyes flicked in her direction. They lingered for no time at all; long enough to file away another datum for future use, and then his attention was elsewhere. She waited until his back was turned and stuck out her tongue at him.

The tug docked with Clotho, and a technician floated in. She removed her helmet self-consciously, aware of her audience. One hand extended, she bobbed toward the cat, calling softly.

"Get that jerk on the line," Paul snapped. "I want her helmet back on. That's sloppy. That's real—"

And in that instant Garble sprang.

Garble was a black-and-white streak that flashed past the astonished tech, through the airlock, and into the open tug. The cat pounced on the pilot panel. Its forelegs hit the controls. The hatch slammed shut, and the tug's motors burst into life.

Crewroom techs grabbed wildly at their keyouts. The tech on Clotho frantically tried to fit her helmet back on. And the tug took off, blasting away half the protective dome and all the platform's air.

The screens showed a dozen different scenes, lenses shifting from close to distant and back. "Cheyney," Paul said quietly. Dominguez was frozen looking bewildered. "Take it out."

"It's coming right at us!" somebody shouted.

Cheyney's fingers flickered: rap-tap-rap.

A bright nuclear flower blossomed.

There was silence, dead and complete, in the crewroom. *I'm missing something*, Abigail thought. *We just blew up five percent of our tug fleet to kill a cat.*

"*Pull* that transmitter!" Paul strode through the crewroom, scattering orders. "Nothing goes out! You, you, and you"—he yanked techs away from their keyouts—"*off* those things. I want the whole goddamned net shut down."

"Paul . . ." an operator said.

"Keep on receiving." He didn't bother to look. "Whatever they want to send. Dump it all in storage and don't merge any of it with our data until we've gone over it."

Alone and useless in the center of the room, Dominguez stuttered, "What—what happened?"

"You blind idiot!" Paul turned on him viciously. "Your precious aliens have just made their first hostile move. The cat that came back was nothing like the one we sent. They made changes. They retransmitted it with instructions wetwired into its brain."

"But why would they want to steal a tug?"

"*We don't know!*" Paul roared. "Get that through your head. We don't know their motives, and we don't know how they think. But we would have known a lot more about their intentions than we wanted if I hadn't rigged that tug with an abort device."

"You didn't—" Dominguez began. He thought better of the statement.

"—have the authority to rig that device," Paul finished for him. "That's right. I didn't." His voice was heavy with sarcasm.

Dominguez seemed to shrivel. He stared bleakly, blankly, about him, then turned and left, slightly hunched over. Thoroughly discredited in front of people who worked for him.

*That was cold*, Abigail thought. She marveled at Paul's cruelty. Not for an instant did she believe that the anger in his voice was real, that he was capable of losing control.

Which meant that in the midst of confusion and stress, Paul had found time to make a swift play for more power. To Abigail's newly suspicious eye, it looked like a successful one, too.

For five days, Paul held the net shut by sheer willpower and force of personality. Information came in but did not go out. Bell-Sandia administration was not behind him—too much time and money had been sunk into Clotho to abandon the project. But Paul had the support of the tech crew, and he knew how to use it.

"Nothing as big as Bell-Sandia runs on popularity," Paul explained. "But I've got enough sympathy from above, and enough hesitation and official cowardice, to keep this place shut down long enough to get a message across."

The incoming information flow fluctuated wildly, shifting from subject to subject. Data sequences were dropped halfway through and incomplete.

Nonsense came in. The spiders were shifting through strategies in search of the key that would reopen the net.

"When they start repeating themselves." Paul said. "We can assume they understand the threat."

"But we *wouldn't* shut the net down permanently." Abigail pointed out.

Paul shrugged. "So it's a bluff."

They were sharing an aftershift drink in a fifth-level bar. Small red lizards scuttled about the rock wall behind the bartender. "And if your bluff doesn't work?" Abigail asked. "If it's all for nothing—what then?"

Paul's shoulders sagged, a minute shifting of tensions. "Then we trust in the good will of the spiders." He said. "We let them call the shots. And they will treat us benevolently or not, depending. In either case," his voice became dark. "I'll have played a lot of games and manipulated a lot of people for no reason at all." He took her hand. "If that happens, I'd like to apologize." His grip was tight; his knuckles pale.

That night Abigail dreamt she was falling.

Light rainbowed all about her, in a violent splintering of bone and tearing of flesh. She flung out an arm, and it bounced on something warm and yielding.

"Abigail."

She twisted and tumbled, and something smashed into her ribs. Bright spikes of yellow darted up.

"Abigail!" Someone was shaking her, speaking loudly into her face. The rocks and sky went grey, were overlaid by unresolved images. Her eyelids struggled apart, fell together, opened.

"Oh," she said.

Paul rocked back on his heels. Fish darted about in the water beneath him. "There now." He said. Blue-green lights shifted gently underwater, moving in long, slow arcs. "Dream over?"

Abigail shivered, clutched his arm, let go of it almost immediately. She nodded.

"Good. Tell me about it."

"I—" Abigail began. "Are you asking me as a human being or in your official capacity?"

"I don't make that distinction."

She stretched out a leg and scratched her big toe, to gain time to think. She really didn't have any appropriate thoughts. "Okay," she said, and told him the entire dream.

Paul listened intently, rubbed a thumb across his chin thoughtfully when she was done. "We hired you on the basis of that incident, you know," he said. "Coolness under stress. Weak body image. There were a lot of gravity bums to choose from. But I figured you were just a hair tougher, a little bit grittier."

"What are you trying to tell me? That I'm replaceable?"

Paul shrugged. "Everybody's replaceable. I just wanted to be sure you knew that you could back out if you want. It wouldn't wreck our project."

"I don't want to back out." Abigail chose her words carefully, spoke them slowly, to avoid giving vent to the anger she felt building up inside. "Look, I've been on the gravity circuit for ten years. I've been everywhere in the system there is to go. Did you know that there are less than two thousand people alive who've set foot on Mercury and Pluto? We've got a little club; we get together once a year." Seaweed shifted about her; reflections of the floor lights formed nebulous swimming shapes on the walls. "I've spent my entire life going around and around and around the sun, and never really getting anywhere. I want to travel, and there's nowhere left for me to go. So you offer me a way out and then ask if I want to back down. Like hell I do!"

"Why don't you believe that going through Ginungagap is death?" Paul asked quietly. She looked into his eyes, saw cool calculations going on behind them. It frightened her, almost. He was measuring her, passing judgment, warping events into long logical chains that did not take human factors into account. He was an alien presence.

"It's—common sense, is all. I'll be the same when I exit as when I go in. There'll be no difference, not an atom's worth, not a scintilla."

"The *substance* will be different. Every atom will be different. Not a single electron in your body will be the same one you have now."

"Well, how does that differ so much from normal life?" Abigail demanded. "All our bodies are in constant flux. Molecules come and go. Bit by bit, we're replaced. Does that make us different people from moment to moment? All that is body is as coursing vapors, right?"

Paul's eyes narrowed. "Marcus Aurelius. Your quotation isn't complete, though; it goes on: all that is of the soul is dreams and vapors."

"What's that supposed to mean?"

"It means that the quotation doesn't say what you claimed it did. If you care to read it literally, it argues the opposite of what you're saying."

"Still, you can't have it both ways. Either the me that comes out of the spider black hole is the same as the one who went in, or I'm not the same person as I was an instant ago."

"I'd argue differently," Paul said. "But no matter, let's go back to sleep."

He held out a hand, but Abigail felt no inclination to accept it. "Does this mean I've passed your test?"

Paul closed his eyes, stretched a little. "You're still reasonably afraid of dying, and you don't believe that you will," he said. "Yeah. You pass."

"Thanks a heap," Abigail said. They slept, not touching, for the rest of the night.

Three days later Abigail woke up, and Paul was gone. She touched the wall and spoke his name. A recording appeared. "Dominguez has been called up to Administration," it said. Paul appeared slightly distracted: he had not looked directly into the recorder, and his image avoided Abigail's eyes. "I'm going to reopen the net before he returns. It's best we beat him to the punch." The recording clicked off.

Abigail routed an intercom call through to the crewroom. A small chime notified him of her call, and he waved a hand in combined greeting and direction to remain silent. He was hunched over a keyout. The screen above it came to life.

"Ritual greetings, spider," he said.

"Hello, human. We wish to pursue our previous inquiry: the meaning of the term 'art' which was used by the human Dominguez six-sixteenths of the way through his major presentation."

"This is a difficult question. To understand a definition of art, you must first know the philosophy of aesthetics. This is a comprehensive field of knowledge comparable to the study of perception. In many ways it is related."

"What is the trade value of this field of knowledge?"

Dominguez appeared, looking upset. He opened his mouth and Paul touched a finger to his own lips, nodding his head toward the screen.

"Significant. Our society considers art and science as being of roughly equal value."

"We will consider what to offer in exchange."

"Good. We also have a question for you. Please wait while we select the phrasing." He cut the translation lines, turned to Dominguez. "Looks like your raft gambit paid off. Though I'm surprised they bit at that particular piece of bait."

Dominguez looked weary. "Did they mention the incident with the cat?"

"No, nor the communications blackout."

The old man sighed. "I always felt close to the aliens," he said. "Now they seem—cold, inhuman." He attempted a chuckle. "That was almost a pun, wasn't it?"

"In a human, we'd call it a professional attitude. Don't let it spoil your accomplishment." Paul said. "This could be as big as optics." He opened the communications line again. "Our question is now phrased." Abigail noted he had not told Dominguez of her presence.

"Please go ahead."

"Why did you alter our test animal?"

Much leg waving. "We improved the ratios garble centers of perception garble wetware garble making the animal twelve-sixteenths as intelligent as a human. We thought you would be pleased."

"We were not. Why did the test animal behave in a hostile manner toward us?"

The spider's legs jerked quickly, and it disappeared from the screen. Like an echo, the machine said, "Please wait."

Abigail watched Dominguez throw Paul a puzzled look. In the background, a man with a leather sack looped over one shoulder was walking slowly along the twisty access path. His hand dipped into the sack, came out, sprinkled fireflies among the greenery. Dipped in, came out again. Even in the midst of crisis, the trivia of day-to-day existence went on.

The spider reappeared, accompanied by two of its own kind. Their legs interlaced and retreated rapidly, a visual pantomime of an excited conversation. Finally, one of their number addressed the screen.

"We have discussed the matter."

"So I see."

"It is our conclusion that the experience of translation through Ginungagap had a negative effect on the test animal. This was not anticipated. It is new knowledge. We know little of the psychology of carbon-based life."

"You're saying the test animal was driven mad?"

"Key word did not translate. We assume understanding. Steps must be taken to prevent a recurrence of this damage. Can you do this?"

Paul said nothing.

"Is this the reason why communications were interrupted?"

No reply.

"There is a cultural gap. Can you clarify?"

"Thank you for your cooperation," Paul said, and switched the screen off. "You can set your people to work," he told Dominguez. "No reason why they should answer the last few questions, though."

"Were they telling the truth?" Dominguez asked wonderingly.

"Probably not. But at least now they'll think twice before trying to jerk us around again." He winked at Abigail, and she switched off the intercom.

They reran the test using a baboon shipped out from the Belt Zoological Gardens. Abigail watched it arrive from the lip station, crated and snarling.

"They're a lot stronger than we are," Paul said. "Very agile. If the spiders want to try any more tricks, we couldn't offer them better bait."

The test went smooth as silk. The baboon was shot through Ginungagap, held by the spiders for several hours, and returned. Exhaustive testing showed no tampering with the animal.

Abigail asked how accurate the tests were. Paul hooked his hands behind his back. "We're returning the baboon to the Belt. We wouldn't do that if we had any doubts. But—" He raised an eyebrow, asking Abigail to finish the thought.

"But if they're really hostile, they won't underestimate us twice. They'll wait for a human to tamper with."

Paul nodded.

The night before Abigail's send off they made love. It was a frenzied and desperate act, performed wordlessly and without tenderness. Afterward they lay together. Abigail idly playing with Paul's curls.

"Gail . . ." His head was hidden in her shoulder; she couldn't see his face. His voice was muffled.

"Mmmm?"

"Don't go."

She wanted to cry. Because as soon as he said it, she knew it was another test, the final one. And she also knew that Paul wanted her to fail it. That he honestly believed that traversing Ginungagap would kill her, and that the woman who emerged from the spiders' black hole would not be her.

His eyes were shut; she could tell by the creases in his forehead. He knew what her answer was. There was no way he could avoid knowing.

Abigail sensed that this was as close to a declaration of emotion as Paul was capable of. She felt how he despised himself for using his real emotions as yet another test, and how he could not even pretend to himself that there were circumstances under which he would not so test her. *This must be how it feels to think as he does,* she thought. *To constantly scrabble after every last implication, like eternally picking at a scab.*

"Oh, Paul," she said.

He wrenched about, turning his back to her. "Sometimes I wish"—his hands rose in front of his face like claws; they moved toward his eyes, closed into fists—"that for just ten goddamned minutes I could turn my mind *off.*" His voice was bitter.

Abigail huddled against him, looped a hand over his side and onto his chest. "Hush," she said.

The tug backed away from Clotho, dwindling until it was one of a ring of bright sparks packing the platform. Mother was a point source lost in the starfield. Abigail shivered, pulled off her armbands, and shoved them into a storage sack. She reached for her cache-sexe, hesitated.

*The hell with it,* she thought. *It's nothing they haven't seen before.* She shucked it off, stood naked. Gooseflesh rose on the backs of her legs. She swam to the transmittal device, feeling awkward under the distant watching eyes.

Abigail groped into the clamshell. "Go," she said.

The metal closed about her seamlessly, encasing her in darkness. She floated in a lotus position, bobbing slightly.

A light gripping field touched her, stilling her motion. On cue, hypnotic commands took hold in her brain. Her breathing became shallow; her heart slowed. She felt her body ease into stasis. The final command took hold.

Abigail weighed fifty keys. Even though the water in her body would not be transmitted, the polymer chain she was to be transformed into would be two hundred seventy-five kilometers long. It would take fifteen minutes and seventeen seconds to unravel at light speed, negligibly longer at translation speed. She would still be sitting in Clotho when the spiders began knitting her up.

It was possible that Garble had gone mad from a relatively swift transit. Paul doubted it, but he wasn't talking any chances. To protect Abigail's sanity, the meds had wetwired a travel fantasy into her brain. It would blind her to external reality while she traveled.

She was an eagle. Great feathered wings extended out from her shoulders. Clotho was gone, leaving her alone in space. Her skin was red and leathery, her breasts hard and unyielding. Feathers covered her thighs, giving way at the knees to talons.

She moved her wings, bouncing lightly against the thin solar wind swirling down into Ginungagap. The vacuum felt like absolute freedom. She screamed a predator's exultant shrill. Nothing enclosed her; she was free of restriction forever.

Below her lay Ginungagap, the primal chasm, an invisible challenge marked by a red smudge of glowing gases. It was inchoate madness, a gibbering impersonal force that wanted to draw her in, to crush her in its embrace. Its hunger was fierce and insatiable.

Abigail held her place briefly, effortlessly. Then she folded her wings and dove.

A rain of x-rays stung through her, the scattering of Ginungagap's accretion disk. They were molten iron passing through a ghost. Shrieking defiance, she attacked, scattering sparks in her wake.

Ginungagap grew, swelled, until it swallowed up her vision. It was purest black, unseeable, unknowable, a thing of madness. It was Enemy.

A distant objective part of her knew that she was still in Clotho, the polymer chain being unraveled from her body, accelerated by a translator, passing through two black holes, and simultaneously being knit up by the spiders. It didn't matter.

She plunged into Ginungagap as effortlessly as if it were the film of a soap bubble.

In—

—and out.

It was like big reversed in a mirror, or watching an entertainment run backward. She was instantly flying out the way she came. The sky was a mottled mass of violet light.

The stars before her brightened, from violet to blue. She craned her neck, looked back at Ginungagap, saw its disk-shaped nothingness recede, and screamed in frustration because it had escaped her. She spread her wings to slow her flight and—

—was sitting in a dark place. Her hand reached out, touched metal, recognized the inside of a clamshell device.

A hairlike crack of light looped over her, widened. The clamshell opened.

Oceans of color bathed her face. Abigail straightened, and the act of doing so lifted her up gently. She stared through the transparent bubble at a phosphorescent foreverness of light.

*My God*, she thought. *The stars.*

The stars were thicker, more numerous that she was used to, large and bright and glitter-rich. She was probably someplace significant, a star cluster or the center of the galaxy: she couldn't guess. She felt irrationally happy to simply be; she took a deep breath, then laughed.

"Abigail Vanderhoek."

She turned to face the voice, and found that it came from a machine. Spiders crouched beside it, legs moving silently. Outside, in the hard vacuum, were more spiders.

"We regret any pain this may cause," the machine said.

Then the spiders rushed forward. She had no time to react. Sharp mandibles loomed before her, then dipped to her neck. Impossibly swift, they sliced through her throat, severed her spine. A sudden jerk, and her head was separated from her body.

It happened in an instant. She felt brief pain, and the dissociation of actually seeing her decapitated body just beginning to react. And then she died.

A spark. A light. *I'm alive*, she thought. Consciousness returned like an ancient cathode tube warming up. Abigail stretched slowly, bobbing gently in the air, collecting her thoughts. She was in the sister-Clotho again, not in pain, her head and neck firmly on her shoulders. There were spiders on the platform, and a few floating outside.

"Abigail Vanderhoek," the machine said. "We are ready to begin negotiations."

Abigail said nothing.

After a moment, the machine said, "Are you damaged? Are your thoughts impaired?" A pause, then, "Was your mind not protected during transit?"

"Is that you waving the legs out there? Outside the platform?"

"Yes. It is important that you talk with the other humans. You must convey our questions. They will not communicate with us."

"I have a few questions of my own," Abigail said. "I won't cooperate until you answer them."

"We will answer any questions provided you neither garble nor garble."

"What do you take me for?" Abigail asked. "Of course I won't."

Long hours later she spoke to Paul and Dominguez. At her request, the spiders had withdrawn, leaving her alone. Dominguez looked drawn and haggered. "I swear we had no idea the spiders would attack you," Dominguez said. "We saw it on the screens. I was certain you'd been killed . . ." His voice trailed off.

"Well, I'm alive, no thanks to you guys. Just what is this crap about an explosive substance in my bones, anyway?"

"An explosive—I swear we know nothing of anything of the kind."

"A close relative to plastique," Paul said. "I had a small editing device attached to Clotho's translator. It altered roughly half the bone marrow in your sternum, pelvis, and femurs in transmission. I'd hoped the spiders wouldn't pick up on it so quickly."

"You actually did," Abigail marveled. "The spiders weren't lying: they decapitated me in self-defense. What the holy hell did you think you were *doing?*"

"Just a precaution," Paul said. "We wetwired you to trigger the stuff on command. That way, we could have taken out the spider installation if they'd tried something funny.

"Um," Dominguez said, "this is being recorded. What I'd like to know, Ms. Vanderhoek, is how you escaped being destroyed."

"I didn't," Abigail said. "The spiders killed me. Fortunately, they anticipated the situation, and recorded the transmission. It was easy for them to re-create me—after they edited out the plastique."

Dominguez gave her an odd look. "You don't—feel anything particular about this?"

"Like what?"

"Well—" He turned to Paul helplessly.

"Like the real Abigail Vanderhoek died and you're simply a very realistic copy," Paul said.

"Look, we've been through this garbage before," Abigail began angrily.

Paul smiled formally at Dominguez. It was hard to adjust to seeing the two in flat black-and-white. "She doesn't believe a word of it."

"If you guys can pull yourselves up out of your navels for a minute," Abigail said. "I've got a line on something the spiders have that you want. They claim they've sent probes through their black hole."

"Probes?" Paul stiffened. Abigail could sense the thoughts coursing through his skull, of defenses and military applications.

"Carbon-hydrogen chain probes. Organic probes. Self-constructing transmitters. They've got a carbon-based secondary technology."

"Nonsense," Dominguez said. "How could they convert back to coherent matter without a receiver?"

Abigail shrugged. "They claim to have found a loophole."

"How does it work?" Paul snapped.

"They wouldn't say. They seem to think you'd pay well for it."

"That's very true," Paul said slowly. "Oh, yes."

The conference took almost as long as her session with the spiders had. Abigail was bone weary when Dominguez finally said, "That ties up the official minutes. We now stop recording." A line tracked across the screen, was gone. "If you want to speak to anyone off the record, now's your chance. Perhaps there is someone close to you . . ."

"Close? No." Abigail almost laughed. "I'll speak to Paul alone, though."

A spider floated by outside Clotho II. It was a golden crablike being, its body slightly opalescent. It skittered along unseen threads strung between the open platforms of the spider starcity. "I'm listening, "Paul said.

"You turned me into a bomb, you freak."

"So?"

"I could have been killed."

"Am I supposed to care?"

"You damn well ought to, considering the liberties you've taken with my fair white body."

"Let's get one thing understood," Paul said. "The woman I slept with, the woman I cared for, is dead. I have no feelings toward or obligations to you whatsoever."

"Paul," Abigail said. "*I'm not dead*. Believe me, I'd know if I were."

"How could I possibly trust what you think or feel? It could all be attitudes the spiders wetwired into you. We know they have the technology."

"How do you know that *your* attitudes aren't wetwired in? For that matter, how do you know anything is real? I mean, these are the most sophomoric philosophic ideas there are. But I'm the same woman I was a few hours ago. My memories, opinions, feelings—they're all the same as they were. There's absolutely no difference between me and the woman you slept with on the *Clarke*."

"I know," Paul's eyes were cold. "That's the horror of it." He snapped off the screen.

Abigail found herself staring at the lifeless machinery. God, that hurt, she thought. It shouldn't, but it hurt. She went to her quarters.

The spiders had done a respectable job of preparing for her. There were no green plants, but otherwise the room was the same as the one she'd had on the *Clarke*. They'd even been able to spin the platform, giving her an adequate down-orientation. She sat in her hammock, determined to think pleasanter thoughts. About the offer the spiders had made, for example. The one she hadn't told Paul and Dominguez about.

Banned by their chemistry from using black holes to travel, the spiders needed a representative to see to their interests among the stars. They had offered her the job.

Or perhaps the plural would be more appropriate—they had offered her the jobs. Because there were too many places to go for one woman to handle them all. They needed a dozen, in time perhaps a hundred Abigail Vanderhoeks.

In exchange for licensing rights to her personality, the right to make as many duplicates of her as were needed, they were willing to give her the rights to the self-reconstructing black-hole platforms.

It would make her a rich woman—a hundred rich women—back in human space. And it would open the universe. She hadn't committed herself yet, but there was no way she was going to turn down the offer. The chance to see a thousand stars. No, she would not pass it by.

When she got old, too, they could create another Abigail from their recording, burn her new memories into it, and destroy her old body.

*I'm going to see the stars*, she thought. *I'm going to live forever*. She couldn't understand why she didn't feel elated, wondered at the sudden rush of melancholy that ran through her like the precursor of tears.

Garble jumped into her lap, offered his belly to be scratched. The spiders had recorded him, too. They had been glad to restore him to his unaltered state when she made the first request. She stroked his stomach and buried her face in his fur.

"Pretty little cat," she told him. "I thought you were dead."

# Michael Swanwick

A master of the short story form, Michael Swanwick is an oddity in the novel-driven world of modern science-fiction and fantasy, with his numerous short story collections rivaling his novels for shelf space and proving that there's still an audience hungry for such things—at least, if you're as good as Michael Swanwick. With four Hugo Awards, a World Fantasy Award, and the Theodore Sturgeon Memorial Award for his short stories, plus a Nebula for his 1991 novel *Stations of the Tide*, Swanwick has made his mark and gathered all the pedigrees he needs to keep his legions of fans following his every word.

And let it never be said that he doesn't take them for a ride. From the twisted fantasy of *The Iron Dragon's Daughter* and *The Dragons of Babel*, in which dragons act as fighter jets and business-suited elves bet on dwarven knife-fights in their highrise towers, to the time travel and dinosaurs of *Bones of the Earth*, Swanwick spins out world after unique world with the boundless energy and innovation only he can provide. In "Ginungagap," Swanwick blends all of his characteristic charms—big-ticket scientific ideas, strange races, morally dubious characters, and a healthy dose of absurdity—into one of the most impressive debut stories in the genre.

**Looking back, what do you think still works well in this story? Why?**

The theme and ending still work, because they address a philosophical question that can probably never be resolved. Also, there's a youthful energy in "Ginungagap" which came from my throwing in every idea and inventive detail I could make fit.

This latter is a technique that still suits me well. New writers are sometimes stingy with their ideas, in the belief that they're a non-renewable resource. Not so. The more ideas you use, the more that rise up to fill the vacancy they leave behind. Plus, it's pointless to hoard ideas—as they age, they grow stale. Best to use them while they're fresh.

**If you were writing this today, what would you do differently? What are the story's weaknesses, and how would you change them?**

I'd ditch those damned "keyouts." Personal computers were brand new at the time and all of us who were working in the extrapolative end of SF could see they were going to be ubiquitous, so for a season they were everywhere in our fiction. Worse, there was no agreed-upon name for them, so I had to make one up. And worst of all, the name I came up with was lame. Having failed to come up with something cool, I should have sidestepped the issue altogether.

Nowadays, I think I'd just have the characters ask questions and let voices out of thin air answer them. I wouldn't explain a thing.

**What inspired this story? How did it take shape? Where was it initially published?**

The story was triggered by a long conversation with a physics Ph.D. candidate about his mentor's speculations on the nature of black holes and by—this is embarrassing—a *Star Trek* novelization in which Dr. McCoy has a running argument that the transporter beam actually kills the person who goes into it and creates a new person with the original's memories. I was fascinated by the fact that the truth or untruth of the proposition was not only impervious to proof but passionately held by whomever I discussed it with. So I put the two together in order to create a thought experiment which I hoped would clarify my thinking on the matter.

Originally the protagonist was male. But then I realized that this was why the story wasn't moving forward—I was identifying too strongly with him. Why did he behave as he did? He was a space hero! Where did he come from? Schenectady, New York. Which didn't make for a very convincing character. So I switched genders and, because all the women I've known always had good and sufficient reasons for their actions, Abigail came to life.

"Ginungagap" appeared in a special science fiction issue of the literary journal *TriQuarterly*, guest-edited by David Hartwell. I hadn't known it was a potential market, but my agent, Virginia Kidd, sent the story in. How I happened to have an agent and why she was handling short fiction are stories for another time.

**Where were you in your life when you published this piece, and what kind of impact did it have?**

I had just turned thirty and lost my job and gotten married and I was in the middle of a nine-month-long writer's block. So seeing my first story in print was a greatly needed encouragement that I wasn't entirely mad to think I could be a writer. Later, it and my second story, "The Feast of Saint Janis" both made it onto the Nebula ballot, which brought me a lot of attention, and that helped too.

Probably the best thing that happened, though, was that neither story won. I've known people who won major awards right off the bat, and it made every time they didn't win one feel like another failure. I had the good fortune of getting on the ballot often, so that by the time I did actually win a Nebula many years later, I felt that I deserved it.

**How has your writing changed over the years, both stylistically and in terms of your writing process?**

The process is still the same—I write as far into the story as I can and then go back to word one and rewrite from there. Eventually, the first page or so is as good as it's going to get, so I start from the first iffy sentence. By the time I reach the end of a novel, every page has been rewritten at least ten and probably twenty times, but there's no need to go back and do revisions because they've already been made. It's a slow and laborious way to create fiction and I recommend it to no one. The only advantage it has is that it works for me, while methods that work for other writers do not.

Stylistically . . . well, I don't have a single style. Some stories are written very plainly and others are written as ornately as possible, depending on what they're about. I simply write as best as I can. That hasn't changed a bit.

**What advice do you have for aspiring authors?**

Write what you love to read rather than what you think you should write. Charles Stross introduced me to Martin Hauer, who's writing an Edgar Rice Burroughs-esque novel about tanks versus magic swords, simply because that's the sort of thing he likes. He's got the right idea. He's far more likely to be a success with that than if he wrote in slavish imitation of, say, Thomas Pynchon.

Also, keep your day job. Even if you're lucky enough to be reliably productive, money you're owed can be routinely delayed for a year or more.

**Any anecdotes regarding the story or your experiences as a fledgling writer?**

I showed the opening section of the story to Gardner Dozois (this was before he became editor of *Asimov's*) to get his advice. Later I saw him again and he asked how the story was going. "Great," I said. "I just wrote a scene in which a cat hijacks a spaceship."

"Oh, you did not!" he exclaimed.

But of course I had.

That was the only time I've ever been able to flat-out boggle Gardner with something I wrote. I've often tried to since, but never succeeded. It was a once-in-a-lifetime thing, like having your first story published.

# Acknowledgments

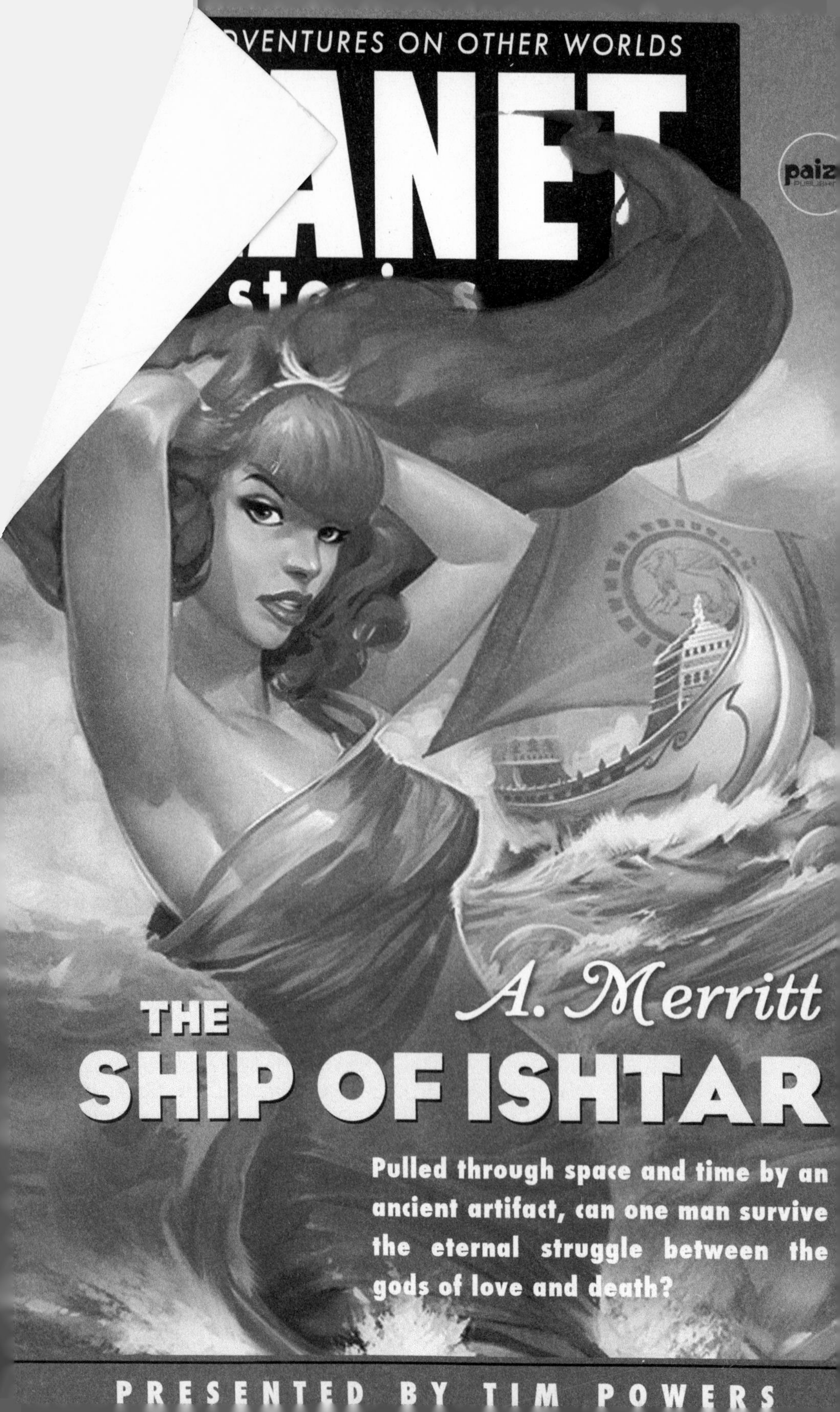
ON OTHER WORLDS
A. Merritt
THE SHIP OF ISHTAR
Pulled through space and time by an ancient artifact, can one man survive the eternal struggle between the gods of love and death?
PRESENTED BY TIM POWERS

# Sword & Sorcery Lives

## A. Merritt's
## *The Ship of Ishtar*

"This is pure adventure . . . one of the great fantasy novels. This novel, like the Ship of Ishtar itself, is timeless."

### Tim Powers

"The most remarkable presentation of the utterly alien and non-human that I have ever seen . . . [a] unique type of strangeness which no one else has been able to parallel."

### H. P. Lovecraft

Amateur archaeologist John Kenton didn't know what he expected when he broke open the stone block from Babylon, but it wasn't to be hurled through time and space into an ageless conflict. On a golden ship in a strange dimension of endless sea, the goddess of love and vengeance lies locked in an eternal stalemate with the god of the underworld—and the coming of an outsider might just tip the balance once and for all. With the beautiful priestesses of Ishtar and the pale warriors of the Black God both seeking to bend him to their own ends, will Kenton become a slave of alien powers, or take up his sword and prove himself the true master of the Ship of Ishtar?

A major inspiration for H. P. Lovecraft and Clark Ashton Smith, A. Merritt remains one of the most celebrated fantasists of all time. This complete edition, introduced by Tim Powers (*The Anubis Gates*), presents *The Ship of Ishtar* as it was meant to be read, with original illustrations by pulp legend Virgil Finlay—a classic not to be missed.

**Available now at quality bookstores and paizo.com/planetstories**

...D THE **WARWOLF**
...OK
...TION BY **CHINA MIÉVILLE**

...year-old Drake Duoay loves ...g more than wine, women, and ...ng into trouble. But when he's ...oducted by pirates and pursued by a new religion bent solely on his destruction, only the love of a red-skinned priestess will see him through the insectile terror of the Swarms.

ISBN: 978-1-60125-214-2

### WHO FEARS THE DEVIL?
### BY MANLY WADE WELLMAN
INTRODUCTION BY MIKE RESNICK

In the back woods of Appalachia, folksinger and monster-hunter Silver John comes face to face with the ghosts and demons of rural Americana in this classic collection of eerie stories from Pulitzer Prize-nominee Manly Wade Wellman.

ISBN: 978-1-60125-188-6

### THE SECRET OF SINHARAT
### BY LEIGH BRACKETT
INTRODUCTION BY MICHAEL MOORCOCK

In the Martian Drylands, a criminal conspiracy leads wild man Eric John Stark to a secret that could shake the Red Planet to its core. In a bonus novel, *People of the Talisman*, Stark ventures to the polar ice cap of Mars to return a stolen talisman to an oppressed people.

ISBN: 978-1-60125-047-6

### THE GINGER STAR
### BY LEIGH BRACKETT
INTRODUCTION BY BEN BOVA

Eric John Stark journeys to the dying world of Skaith in search of his kidnapped foster father, only to find himself the subject of a revolutionary prophecy. In completing his mission, will he be forced to fulfill the prophecy as well?

ISBN: 978-1-60125-084-1

### THE HOUNDS OF SKAITH
### BY LEIGH BRACKETT
INTRODUCTION BY F. PAUL WILSON

Eric John Stark has destroyed the Citadel of the Lords Protector, but the war for Skaith's freedom is just beginning. Together with his foster father Simon Ashton, Stark will have to unite some of the strangest and most bloodthirsty peoples the galaxy has ever seen if he ever wants to return home.

ISBN: 978-1-60125-135-0

### THE REAVERS OF SKAITH
### BY LEIGH BRACKETT
INTRODUCTION BY GEORGE LUCAS

Betrayed and left to die on a savage planet, Eric John Stark and his foster-father Simon Ashton must ally with cannibals and feral warriors to topple an empire and bring an enslaved civilization to the stars. But in fulfilling the prophecy, will Stark sacrifice that which he values most?

ISBN: 978-1-60125-084-1

## CITY OF THE BEAST
### BY MICHAEL MOORCOCK
#### INTRODUCTION BY KIM MOHAN

Moorcock's Eternal Champion returns as Michael Kane, an American physicist and expert duelist whose strange experiments catapult him through space and time to a Mars of the distant past—and into the arms of the gorgeous princess Shizala. But can he defeat the Blue Giants of the Argzoon in time to win her hand?

ISBN: 978-1-60125-044-5

## LORD OF THE SPIDERS
### BY MICHAEL MOORCOCK
#### INTRODUCTION BY ROY THOMAS

Michael Kane returns to the Red Planet, only to find himself far from his destination and caught in the midst of a civil war between giants! Will his wits and sword keep him alive long enough to find his true love once more?

ISBN: 978-1-60125-082-7

## MASTERS OF THE PIT
### BY MICHAEL MOORCOCK
#### INTRODUCTION BY SAMUEL R. DELANY

A new peril threatens physicist Michael Kane's adopted Martian homeland—a plague spread by zealots more machine than human. Now Kane will need to cross oceans, battle hideous mutants and barbarians, and perhaps even sacrifice his adopted kingdom in his attempt to prevail against an enemy that cannot be killed!

ISBN: 978-1-60125-104-6

## NORTHWEST OF EARTH
### BY C. L. MOORE
#### INTRODUCTION BY C. J. CHERRYH

Ray gun blasting, Earth-born mercenary and adventurer Northwest Smith dodges and weaves his way through the solar system, cutting shady deals with aliens and magicians alike, always one step ahead of the law.

ISBN: 978-1-60125-081-0

## BLACK GOD'S KISS
### BY C. L. MOORE
#### INTRODUCTION BY SUZY MCKEE CHARNAS

The first female sword and sorcery protagonist takes up her greatsword and challenges gods and monsters in the groundbreaking stories that inspired a generation of female authors. Of particular interest to fans of Robert E. Howard and H. P. Lovecraft.

ISBN: 978-1-60125-045-2

## THE ANUBIS MURDERS
### BY GARY GYGAX
#### INTRODUCTION BY ERIK MONA

Someone is murdering the world's most powerful sorcerers, and the trail of blood leads straight to Anubis, the solemn god known as the Master of Jackals. Can Magister Setne Inhetep, personal philosopher-wizard to the Pharaoh, reach the distant kingdom of Avillonia and put an end to the Anubis Murders, or will he be claimed as the latest victim?

ISBN: 978-1-60125-042-1

## THE SWORD OF RHIANNON
### BY LEIGH BRACKETT
#### INTRODUCTION BY NICOLA GRIFFITH

Captured by the cruel and beautiful princess of a degenerate empire, Martian archaeologist-turned-looter Matthew Carse must ally with the Red Planet's rebellious Sea Kings and their strange psychic allies to defeat the tyrannical people of the Serpent.

ISBN: 978-1-60125-152-7

## INFERNAL SORCERESS
### BY GARY GYGAX
#### INTRODUCTION BY ERIK MONA

When the shadowy Ferret and the broad-shouldered mercenary Raker are framed for the one crime they didn't commit, the scoundrels are faced with a choice: bring the true culprits to justice, or dance a gallows jig. Can even this canny, ruthless duo prevail against the beautiful witch that plots their downfall?

ISBN: 978-1-60125-117-6

## STEPPE
### BY PIERS ANTHONY
#### INTRODUCTION BY CHRIS ROBERSON

After facing a brutal death at the hands of enemy tribesmen upon the Eurasian steppe, the 9th-century warrior-chieftain Alp awakes fifteen hundred years in the future only to find himself a pawn in a ruthless game that spans the stars.

ISBN: 978-1-60125-182-4

## WORLDS OF THEIR OWN
### EDITED BY JAMES LOWDER

From R. A. Salvatore and Ed Greenwood to Michael A. Stackpole and Elaine Cunningham, shared world books have launched the careers of some of science fiction and fantasy's biggest names. Yet what happens when these authors break out and write tales in worlds entirely of their own devising, in which they have absolute control over every word? Contains 18 creator-owned stories by the genre's most prominent authors.

ISBN: 978-1-60125-118-3

## ALMURIC
### BY ROBERT E. HOWARD
#### INTRODUCTION BY JOE R. LANSDALE

From the creator of Conan, Almuric is a savage planet of crumbling stone ruins and debased, near-human inhabitants. Into this world comes Esau Cairn—Earthman, swordsman, murderer. Can one man overthrow the terrible devils that enslave Almuric?

ISBN: 978-1-60125-043-8

## SOS THE ROPE
### BY PIERS ANTHONY
#### INTRODUCTION BY ROBERT E. VARDEMAN

In a post apocalyptic future where duels to the death are everyday occurrences, the exiled warrior Sos sets out to rebuild civilization—or destroy it.

ISBN: 978-1-60125-194-7